PRAISE FOR *THE CORRECTION*

"Very good AU. I loved this book.
this was one of the most entertainin
there." ~ Mary Jo, Amazon US reviev

"An absorbing read. This was an exce ... variation! There is so little Sense and Sensibility fanfiction out there, so it was nice to stumble upon this one. I am looking forward to the next in the series!" ~ JAFF Lover, Amazon US reviewer

"One of the best fan fiction books I have ever read! I love this book! The entwined story of Sense and Sensibility and Pride and Prejudice is amazingly well done. The characters are spot on and the nuances, the details, the richness of characters add to the wonderful story." ~ Rufus, Amazon US reviewer

"A Faithful and Intriguing What If? Story … Combe provides a sound argument for why Elinor and the Colonel would be an ideal couple, and expanding upon it, even including guest appearances from other characters in Austen's universe." ~ Mr. D.P. Obrien, Amazon UK reviewer

"Really enjoyable! I thoroughly enjoyed reading this well-written JAFF book. It was a different take on S+S with some extra cameos from P+P, who the author fitted into this story well without any jarring." ~ Helen M, Amazon UK reviewer

"Absolutely loved this book!!!! I first read Sense and Sensibility a month ago. And while reading I had thought Colonel Brandon and Elinor Dashwood would have been good together. So I was so happy to stumble upon this book!" ~ Dani Blandford, Amazon CA reviewer

"Good story. I enjoyed this au. Brandon and Elinor are two of my favorite characters and I have always felt they were better suited to each other. So I was very thrilled to find a story that explores this pairing. This is not only an engaging story but it is also very well written." ~ Anne, Goodreads reviewer

"Unbeatable! I will read this again and again! What a beautifully written novel! It is very difficult to find variations of Sense and Sensibility but this encompasses everything I'd hoped for. The characters stayed true and the plot ever changing!" ~ Tommi, Goodreads reviewer

"I absolutely loved this it was different from the other jaff novels I have read. I have often wondered why the colonel never fell for Elinor and finally he does." ~ Tracey, Goodreads reviewer

CHOICE *and* CONSEQUENCE

WHAT MIGHT HAVE BEEN, BOOK TWO

CHRISTINE COMBE

PUBLISHED BY BLACK ROOM PRESS

ISBN-13: 9798743528141

Foreword

Two years, nine months, twenty-four days.

That's how long it has been since I published the first book in the What Might Have Been series. Never in my life could I have imagined it would take so very long to bring the second book to you.

I am more sorry than I can properly articulate that so much time has passed, but there is a very good reason for it. You see, I suffer from anxiety and depression, the latter of which holds the greater part of the blame for the lengthy delay. The way my brain works is that writing goes on in my head all the time—I'm always thinking of new ideas, writing and re-writing scenes, etc. However, when I'm caught in a low mood period, I cannot drum up the motivation to actually work on getting the story out of my head and into words, no matter how much I want to or feel it needs to be done. So my writing suffers along with the rest of my life (the lows affect non-writing tasks as well), and though I have worked on the book intermittently over all this time, there were too many periods where I did not.

Good news is, I finally found the spark I needed, and so *Choice and Consequence* is here at last!

I have also been, I freely admit, rather intimidated by the Austenesque/JAFF community. *Pride and Prejudice* is the prevailing favorite of Jane Austen's novels among readers, and it is the favorite book for authors to rewrite. I know from the publication of *The Correction of Folly* and through my relationships with other writers in the genre that readers can be very protective of 'their' darlings Darcy and Elizabeth. So of course I was afraid of taking on their part in the series and writing a story the readers wouldn't like.

But Darcy and Elizabeth demanded their story be told—and we

all know that only one woman has ever said no to Fitzwilliam Darcy! And although it has taken me far longer than I expected, I have at last written a tale that I hope very much will delight and entertain.

Thank you so very much for choosing *Choice and Consequence,* and happy reading to you!

~ Christine Combe, May 2021

Acknowledgements

My deepest and most heartfelt thanks to everyone who has been supportive of me throughout the last three years, who have encouraged me to keep at it in light of the difficulties.

Special thanks to fellow JAFF author Jayne Bamber and my good friend Derek O'Brien, my most vocal cheerleaders and sounding boards, for listening to my crazy ideas and letting me vent when I needed. You guys are awesome.

Dedication

For Colin, Matthew M., Martin, Matthew R., David, Elliot, Sam, and Laurence—every Mr. Darcy I have ever seen on screen.

Thank you for bringing one of the most incredible gentlemen in literature to life, each of you adding something of your own uniqueness to a character that has been admired for over 200 years.

Cast of Characters

ELIZABETH BENNET. Second of five daughters. Known for her wit and impertinence and love of long walks in the country.

FITZWILLIAM DARCY. Master of Pemberley, a grand estate in Derbyshire. He is in Hertfordshire to take a break from hunting for the villainous scoundrel who assaulted his sister.

JANE, MARY, CATHERINE (KITTY/CATE), AND LYDIA BENNET. Eldest and three younger sisters of Elizabeth. All with their own personalities, hopes, dreams…and ideas about marriage.

THOMAS AND JANE BENNET. Parents of the five Bennet sisters, one is idle and the other silly and frivolous. Mr. Bennet is master of the estate of Longbourn.

MR. AND MRS. PHILLIPS. Mr. Phillips is an attorney in Meryton, and his wife—sister to Mrs. Bennet—is an idle gossip.

THEODORE FITZWILLIAM. A colonel in the army and second son of the Earl of Disley. He is Darcy's cousin and has joined him in the hunt for Georgiana Darcy's attacker.

CHARLES BINGLEY. Longtime friend of Darcy. He has leased Netherfield Park, an estate three miles from Longbourn, and excited all the local matchmaking mammas by being single.

CAROLINE BINGLEY. Sister of Charles Bingley. Single, and very desirous of being mistress of Pemberley.

LOUISA AND REGINALD HURST. Sister and brother-in-law to Charles and Caroline Bingley. Mrs. Hurst is too much like her sister, and Mr. Hurst too fond of his drink.

CHARLOTTE LUCAS. Best friend of Elizabeth Bennet, and often the voice of reason when Elizabeth is vexed.

SIR WILLIAM AND LADY LUCAS. Parents of Charlotte Lucas and her five siblings. Sir William received a knighthood and serves as mayor of Meryton.

ALAN AND ELINOR NORTHAM. The Earl and Countess of Sotheby. Formerly known as Colonel Brandon and Miss Dashwood, before learning—after their marriage—that he was, in fact, born a nobleman. Lord Sotheby is heir to the Duke of Mildenhall.

MARIANNE DASHWOOD, LADY AMELIA NORTHAM. Marianne is Lady Sotheby's sister and Lady Amelia, daughter of the Duke of Mildenhall, is Lord Sotheby's cousin.

WILLIAM COLLINS. A cousin of the Bennet family, he is the parson of Hunsford parish in Kent and heir to the Longbourn estate, due to an entail.

GEORGE WICKHAM. Former childhood friend of Darcy, they had a falling out years ago. He is believed to be the libertine who assaulted Darcy's sister.

EDWARD AND MADELENE GARDINER. Mr. Gardiner is the younger brother of Mrs. Bennet and Mrs. Phillips. He owns a lucrative import business in London, and he and his sensible wife are favorites of the Bennet girls.

JOANNA JENNINGS. A good friend to the Dashwood family, Mrs. Jennings has a tie to Mrs. Bennet, Mrs. Phillips, and Mr. Gardiner.

RICHARD AND FRANCES FITZWILLIAM. The Earl and Countess of Disley. They are parents to Theodore and Philip.

PHILIP AND MARIANNE FITZWILLIAM. The Viscount and Viscountess Rowarth. Eldest son and heir of the Earl of Disley, and his wife. They have a young daughter named Josephine.

ANNE DE BOURGH. Cousin to the Darcy and Fitzwilliam siblings. Like her mother, Lord Disley's sister Lady Catherine, she mistakenly believes that she and Mr. Darcy will marry one day.

EDWARD FERRARS. Parson of Lambton Parish in Derbyshire, he is accidentally caught in an untenable position while staying at Darcy House in London.

HENRY TILNEY, ELEANOR TILNEY. A brother and sister who take up residence in the London townhome next to Darcy's. Henry is an old schoolmate of Darcy and Wickham's.

ANSEL TILNEY, FREDERICK TILNEY. Father and brother, respectively, to Henry and Eleanor. Both men serve in the army, and neither is very well liked.

GEORGE KNIGHTLEY. Master of Donwell Abbey in Surrey, older brother of John Knightley. He is host to the Fairleys and Georgiana Darcy.

FITZROY AND ROBERTA LESLIE. The Laird and Lady of Glenfairley in Scotland. Fitzroy is a cousin to Lady Disley and Roberta a cousin to George, John, and Arthur Knightley.

GEORGIANA DARCY. Younger sister of Fitzwilliam Darcy. She is under the care and protection of Laird and Lady Fairley.

EDINA ANNESLEY. A resident of Donwell Parish who is hired as a companion for Georgiana.

LADY DIANA MARKHAM. A cousin of Lady Disley, who is wife to a baronet.

JOHN AND ISABELLA KNIGHTLEY, ARTHUR AND CASSANDRA KNIGHTLEY. John Knightley is Darcy's solicitor, Isabella is his wife. Arthur is a cousin to John and George, and Cassandra, Arthur's wife, is sister to Lord Sotheby.

Chapter One

Wednesday, 12 September 1798

"It is a truth universally acknowledged that any single young woman of beauty and good breeding must be in want of a husband possessed of a large fortune."

Elizabeth Bennet's sister Jane did not look up from her stitching. "I believe you quote *First Impressions* incorrectly, Lizzy," said she.

"It is not incorrect, it is a vagary," challenged Elizabeth as she sat down beside her on the garden bench. "And either way, it is no less true."

She tilted her head then. "That is a very pretty peacock, Jane."

Jane smiled. "Thank you," she said. "It is coming along rather well—I think I shall buy another of these patterns when I am able, that I may have a matched pair of pillows for my bed."

"Indeed, they will go well with your cover," murmured Elizabeth.

"What have you to say, Lizzy?"

"What do you mean?"

"You may be the most romantic of our family, dear sister, but you are not one given to spout random quotations," said Jane. "So your vagary must have some purpose."

Elizabeth grinned. "You know me too well, Jane. Mamma was told by Mrs. Long just today that Netherfield Park is let at last."

"That is wonderful news. I think it very sad such a lovely home has sat empty for so long."

Elizabeth bumped her shoulder. "And do you not want to know

who has taken it?"

"A single young man in possession of a great fortune who is in want of a wife?" asked Jane in a disinterested tone. "I shall not spoil your fun and ask you, Lizzy. It seems you possess a great desire to tell me, and so I shall not object to hearing it."

Elizabeth groaned. "Sometimes, Jane, you really are no fun at all. As it is, the gentleman hails from the north and he does have a large fortune, but he is sadly not single."

The both of them looked up when a particularly loud wail issued from the house. "Our mother must be quite vexed by such news," observed Jane.

"Indeed, which is why I have come to warn you that it has aggravated her nerves," said Elizabeth. "We shall hear of nothing else for days, even though I cannot imagine what his being married or single should have to do with us."

Jane paused in her work again. "Can you truly not, Lizzy? From Mamma's perspective, his being single would mean he could marry one of us."

Jane and Elizabeth were the first and second, respectively, of five daughters; Mary, Catherine—who was called Kitty by the family—and Lydia were the others. For some years, since it was accepted by their parents that no son would be issued, Mrs. Bennet had made it her sole purpose in life to see her daughters well situated...and preferably with *very* wealthy husbands of which she could boast every day to her own sister, Mrs. Philips, and all her friends.

"Remember, dearest sister," said Jane, "that we have none of us enough dowry to be attractive to a gentleman of means—there are only our pretty faces and our charms to recommend us. If we wish to avoid becoming dependent on our friends and family once our father is gone, or forced to take a position as a governess or lady's maid, the unfortunate reality is that one of us must marry well."

"Only the deepest abiding love shall entice me into matrimony—which is why I will die an old maid," bemoaned Elizabeth.

"I know, and with all three of our younger sisters bearing little to no sense, the saving of the family will fall to me."

This observation sobered Elizabeth. "Surely you do not intend to marry only for security, Jane. Your angelic nature would wither living in such circumstances."

Jane put her embroidery aside. "Be sensible for a moment, Lizzy. You know very well that our home is entailed, and will be given over to a cousin we have none of us even met on the occasion of our father's death, and *he* may turn us out of the house before Papa is even in his grave. Who will take care of a silly, simpering widow and her five unmarried daughters then? Who would have the means?'"

A sigh escaped her before Jane continued, "I am only being practical about the matter of our future—*someone* in this family must think on it sensibly."

Elizabeth's expression fell and Jane reached over to take her hand. "I do not mean to give offense. But I know you are as aware as I that our mother is very silly and not too intelligent, and our father—while he *is* intelligent—is essentially absent. He does not take the trouble to check our younger sisters, nor has he been wise enough to manage the family finances that his daughters might have a more substantial dowry."

When a tear suddenly fell down Elizabeth's cheek, Jane put an arm about her shoulders. "Come now, Lizzy. There is no cause for tears."

Elizabeth wiped the offending droplet away with some vexation, as she was usually not so easily overcome with melancholy. "Perhaps not, but… I had no idea you felt our situation so deeply. I am aware of our precarious circumstances, of course… I suppose I always thought there would be more time."

"Unfortunately there is not, at least not for me," said Jane. "I am two and twenty now. Soon society will judge me as being on the shelf, in spite of my pretty face and 'angelic' nature."

With a sigh, she gathered her sewing things. "Do not mistake me, Lizzy—I dream of finding true love as much as you do. I've just accepted that I may not be *in* love with my husband when I take my vows. The love will, I desperately hope, come in time."

She stood then and so did Elizabeth; Jane reached over and took her arm. "Forgive me. I know you came out here to tease and I have spoiled your fun. It's just… The matter of marriage, of securing not only my future but that of my sisters and my mother, has oft been on my mind of late. I have given the matter a great deal of thought, weighing my hopes against my duty. It has not been an easy task."

Elizabeth drew a breath. "I understand you, Jane, truly. Just promise me one thing—that you will not marry simply for security's sake, yours or ours. At least make sure you *like* the man before you accept him."

Jane smiled. "Of that, Lizzy, you need have no doubt. Not even I could bind myself to someone I could not say I like or respect. Now, let us go inside and do our duty of listening to Mamma's lamentations about this stranger from the north having the audacity to already be married."

Elizabeth laughed, and the two of them entered the house to find their mother and younger sisters in the drawing room. Mrs. Bennet was waving her handkerchief about, raving about how it would have been far better for her girls had the new tenant of Netherfield been a single man. After a time, the repetitiousness of her mother's complaints grew tiresome, and Elizabeth quietly rose with the intention of hiding away in her father's study with him and a good book.

She had just reached the entry hall when there was an insistent knock at the door. Elizabeth went to open it and smiled to find Mrs. Phillips, who was her mother's sister, on the other side. "Good afternoon, Aunt Phillips," she greeted the older lady as she opened the door wider to invite her in.

"Lizzy, dearest, where is your mother? I have such news to tell her!" Mrs. Phillips said excitedly.

At once curious but not wishing to show it, Elizabeth said only, "Why, she is in the drawing room—though I warn you she is not in high spirits and has complained of her nerves all morning."

Mrs. Phillips bounced in her slippers and smiled with giddiness. "She will feel much better once she hears what I have to tell her!"

Her aunt then hurried toward the drawing room, leaving Elizabeth to follow. She stopped in the doorway to lean against the frame as Mrs. Phillips shooed Kitty from the chair nearest her mother and sat down, then leaned close to whisper in her ear. Whatever she told her indeed lifted Mrs. Bennet's spirits, for her mother emitted a high-pitched squeal of delight such as Elizabeth had never heard before. Even Lydia, the one of her sisters whose character was most like their mother's, cringed at the sound.

Mrs. Bennet immediately launched out of her chair and bustled past Elizabeth into the hall. Mrs. Phillips was right behind her, as were Kitty and Lydia, who talked over each other to try and get their mother to reveal the "juicy gossip" their aunt had come to reveal. Mary shook her head and returned her attention to her book, and Jane glanced at Elizabeth with an expression of curiosity. The latter shrugged and moved to follow her mother and sisters, and caught up to them just before Mrs. Bennet launched herself unceremoniously through the door of Mr. Bennet's study.

"Oh, Mr. Bennet!" said his wife. "My dear sister Phillips has brought the most glorious news!"

"Pray, Mamma, what news?" asked Lydia.

"Yes, tell us!" cried Kitty.

Mrs. Bennet turned a sharp gaze upon her second-youngest daughter. "Hush child, and allow me to speak to your father!" she said, then turned back to Mr. Bennet with a wide smile. "Mrs. Long was apparently misinformed, or she got mixed up, it is hard to say which. In any case, it turns out that it is Mr. Bingley's *sister* who is married, not he!"

Kitty and Lydia both squealed with delight and began to jump up and down in their excitement.

"How Mrs. Long could have gotten the truth mixed up, I cannot say, brother," added Mrs. Phillips. "But my husband has told me that he spoke to Mr. Prentiss, the solicitor who handled the lease for Mr. Morris. He said Mr. Prentiss told him that Mr. Bingley came down in a chaise-and-four to see Netherfield on Monday, and that he means to be in residence by Michaelmas. Further, he is to bring a party of ladies and gentlemen with him when he comes."

She turned to Mrs. Bennet. "Perhaps that is how Mrs. Long became confused. I believe Mr. Bingley mentioned his sister and her husband would be coming to Netherfield with him, to stay for a time in the country."

Mrs. Bennet waved her handkerchief in a huff. "What a twitter-pate, to confuse Mr. Bingley and his brother-by-marriage!" she said. "But then, I have just thought that she might have misspoke on purpose, for she does have two nieces she hopes to see married well. I am sure of it now, for she would know how such news as Mr. Bingley's being married would set off my nerves! Oh, how very vexed I am, sister!"

She then stepped further into the room to stand before her husband, who had yet to speak. "Mr. Bennet, you simply *must* be the first to go and call on him when he comes, otherwise we may not!"

"My dear lady," said Mr. Bennet at last, as he slowly removed his spectacles. "I cannot imagine what Mr. Bingley's being single after all should have to do with any of us."

Elizabeth found herself hard-pressed not to laugh—had she not said almost the same thing to Jane only that morning?

"Mr. Bennet, how can you be so tiresome?" cried Mrs. Bennet. "Surely you know precisely what it means! I am determined that Mr. Bingley should marry one of our girls and *not* one of Mrs. Long's nieces. I *insist* you go and visit him when he comes!"

Sitting back in his chair, Mr. Bennet looked up at his wife and said, "Mrs. Bennet, you may rest assured that I will call upon Mr.

Bingley as soon as propriety allows—but *not* to parade our daughters before him as though they were brood mares being sold at market. I will go only to welcome a new neighbor to our quaint little neighborhood and nothing more."

Mrs. Bennet ignored his last remarks and leaned forward to kiss her husband on the cheek. "Oh, Mr. Bennet, what a good father you are to our girls! I should very much like it indeed if a daughter of mine were to become mistress of such a fine house as Netherfield! We must be sure to introduce him to the girls, Jane especially and maybe Lydia as well."

"Lydia?" spoke up Kitty. "Why should she be specially introduced to Mr. Bingley, when I am two years older?"

"Elizabeth is older than both of you, Kitty," said Mr. Bennet. "Perhaps I will make a point to introduce Mr. Bingley to her."

Elizabeth smiled and shook her head, and turned away from the scene and her mother's effusions of happiness to return to Jane.

Saturday, 6 October 1798

They had not been long in Hertfordshire before Fitzwilliam Darcy knew he would find little comfort here. Almost as soon as they had all settled into Netherfield, the local gentlemen came calling. Caroline Bingley, sister to his good friend Charles, who had let the estate, had posited in private conversation her suspicion that each had unmarried daughters they hoped to foist off on their rich new neighbor. Indeed, there was a Mr. Long who expressed great delight in learning that not only was Mr. Bingley unmarried, but that Darcy and his cousin, Theodore Fitzwilliam, were also.

After the first few days, Darcy had made it a point to be out of the house early in the morning. He was supposed to be relaxing, not fending off the unwanted advances of fathers seeking to marry off their daughters.

The search for George Wickham had not gone as well as he'd hoped, nor as quickly. Darcy had imagined they'd be at it a few weeks, perhaps a month, but no—*seven months* had passed, and little had he and his cousin found other than gambling debts, unpaid shop accounts, and the ruined virtues of more than one young lady or maid. Part and parcel with Wickham, he knew, who yet remained one step ahead of them. On Lord Disley's advice, Darcy and Fitzwilliam had kept meticulous record of every person to whom their quarry owed money and then bought up the receipts, that if nothing else he could be turned over to a debtor's prison when at last he was caught.

Darcy had no intention of him getting off so easily. Not after what his sister had endured at the hands of that fiend.

Frustrated that the months of searching had not turned up their quarry, it was determined that a break was in order—Darcy had reluctantly acquiesced to Theodore's suggestion they take Bingley up on his invitation to accompany him to Hertfordshire and assess the estate of Netherfield Park. Though a part of Darcy had agreed that time away from the hunt would help clear his head, there remained a part of him desperate to continue. The need to capture Wickham so that he could not harm another young woman as he had harmed Georgiana burned within him so brightly that he could not escape the quest even in his sleep. There he was also frustrated, always waking just before he caught up to the man.

Today Darcy had chosen to ride out to a place called Oakham Mount, a site reputedly blessed with a pastoral view of the country-side. Though he had little faith in the boasts of the Meryton populace, as surely there were no panoramas which could compare to those in Derbyshire, he hoped to find at least *some* pleasure in the sights that awaited him there. Surely there would be something in this part of England which held true beauty, or at least enough of a pretty view to help him get his head back on straight.

Upon arrival at the spot where one of the locally employed servants had directed him, Darcy was forced to admit that the maid had not been wrong. While the scenery before him was still nothing compared to the beauty of Derbyshire's hills and dales, the valley below was indeed lovely to look upon. As far as his eyes could see, there were plains divided by hedges, dabbed with groves, sprinkled with manors and villages, and bisected by lanes and streams.

"It is quite beautiful, is it not?"

Surprised to hear a voice when he had not even heard the speaker approach, Darcy turned his head and was startled to find himself gazing upon something far more beautiful than the view. A pair of fine, brown eyes and a soft smile greeted him on the face of a young woman in a sky blue walking dress and a black Spencer, with a matching bonnet and gloves. The toes of black boots peeked out from under her hem and wisps of sable hair had escaped the confines of her hat.

Her smile began to fade and she took a step back. "Forgive me, sir, if I have disturbed you. I shall go and leave you to your solitude."

"Wait," he called after her as she turned away. The young lady turned back. "Pray forgive me, madam. I was merely surprised by your sudden appearance."

She surprised him again by grinning. "Then you must surely have been bewitched by the spectacular view, sir. Or perhaps it is because you are very new to the area, as many in Meryton are aware of this spot being quite a favorite destination of mine. I do very much enjoy a good walk."

Ah, no wonder her eyes were so bright, her cheeks slightly flushed. She must have come quite far for the exercise to give her countenance such radiance.

"Perhaps it is a little of both," he granted, then bowed his head. "Fitzwilliam Darcy."

She curtsied. "Elizabeth Bennet."

Bennet. The name was familiar to him. Did not Netherfield have a neighboring family by that name?

"Do you live in Meryton, Miss Bennet?" he asked.

"Very near, Mr. Darcy. My family lives on the estate of Longbourn, which is but a mile from Meryton. And you, sir? Am I right in supposing that you are not familiar with Hertfordshire?"

Darcy nodded. "Indeed I am not," said he. "I am come with my good friend, Mr. Charles Bingley, who has leased an estate not far from your own, I believe."

Miss Bennet's eyes widened a fraction. "You are one of the party at Netherfield? I do hope you are enjoying our part of the country, Mr. Darcy."

"More now than I was before, that much is certain," he said, delighted when his words caused her to blush.

Heavens, Darcy, what are *you doing?* he thought to himself, turning toward the view as casually as he was able. *You are usually not so amiable with strangers.*

But then, Miss Bennet was only one person; he was far less comfortable in a room full of people that he did not know than he was on making a singular acquaintance. Though he was still somewhat surprised he was able to converse with her so easily.

Miss Bennet moved forward again and stood next to him near the edge of the hilltop—though far enough away as to adhere to propriety. "If I may make a presumption, Mr. Darcy… You came to

Oakham Mount to escape, I imagine."

Darcy bit back a chuckle. "And what evidence have you to prove your belief, Miss Bennet?"

"Only that Netherfield, though I have not been inside it, is said to be a very fine house," she began. "You told me just now that Mr. Bingley is your 'good friend', thus why would you be here instead of at his new home with him—unless your intent was to escape?"

"But what need would I have to escape?" Darcy countered. "Perhaps I merely sought to go for a pleasurable ride."

"That is certainly possible, sir, but I remain firm." Miss Bennet then turned to him, her smile playful as she added, "I suspect your reasoning to be the near-endless parade of gentlemen that have come to welcome Mr. Bingley to the neighborhood. No doubt you think they all call to make out his character and determine his likelihood of choosing one of their daughters for a wife."

That she could read him so well was disconcerting, but then it was just as likely she had merely guessed. Still, he could no longer hold back his smile as he shook his head and replied, "I concede, Miss Bennet, you have caught me out. Indeed, the parade grew tiresome, not only because they seek to judge Bingley's probability of being in the marriage mart, but that of myself and my cousin, Colonel Fitzwilliam, who are as unmarried as he."

"Really? And the colonel does not share your desire to escape the possible matchmaking plots of the local fathers?"

Darcy laughed. "Indeed not. Fitzwilliam takes too much pleasure in it all, besides believing he will not soon become acquainted with a young lady for whom he will develop any particular attachment."

He did not say that neither he nor his cousin had been expecting to meet such a person in this part of the country, as what few of the local residents they had encountered were too vulgar and unrefined for men of their station. Aside from that, Fitzwilliam had long ago admitted he would need a lady with a sizable dowry in order to live a comfortable life independent of his father's generous allowance and meager military pay.

The young woman beside him defied his expectations. Not only was she quite handsome, but he suspected a sharp wit lay within her mildly impertinent attitude. In truth she was refreshing, and a welcome change from society girls like Caroline Bingley who fawned all over him and pretended interest in his every word simply because of who he was. It was likely Miss Bennet had no idea who he was, who his connections were, or the value of his yearly income.

He almost frowned at how that all would be likely to change once she became fully acquainted with him.

Miss Bennet turned to him then, her movement drawing him from his suddenly maudlin thoughts. "And what about you, Mr. Darcy? Are you of the same mind as your cousin?"

"I was at first, I admit," he heard himself say, "but I am now of the belief that one should only expect the unexpected."

"Quite so. Here in the country, society may not be as refined as a gentleman of your station may wish it to be, but you are also less likely to be censured if you let loose a little," said his companion.

Darcy frowned. Was she really that astute, as to have made so close a judgment as his own earlier thoughts? "A gentleman of my station? Pray, what is your meaning?"

Miss Bennet, who just reached his shoulder in her boots, looked up and replied, "I mean no offense, Mr. Darcy, and refer only to your being a close friend of Mr. Bingley. I imagine that like him, you are a very wealthy gentleman. In my experience, though I admit it is limited, gentlemen and ladies of means prefer to spend their time with others of their ilk. Very few—if any—cultivate relationships of any kind with persons they consider beneath their social sphere. And while here in Hertfordshire we do observe all the general rules of propriety, our manners are not so rigid as I have heard those in Town to be. Therefore, I surmise that you and your friend, his family, and your cousin are likely to find our society lacking in the social graces you value so highly. You will think us all greatly inferior and hardly worth your notice for it."

"Are you really so prejudiced against those of means, because we have a preference for manners and good breeding?" he challenged.

"Certainly not, sir," Miss Bennet returned. "In fact, I own that there are some of my close acquaintance that I wish were more restrained in their behavior than they are. I suppose I mean only to warn you of what you may experience when you move about Meryton, if ever you do; that folk here are more…open…than you may be used to. I pray you would not look down upon my friends and neighbors simply because they have not your strict standards of behavior, is all."

He studied her countenance for a moment, before he inclined his head. "For you, Miss Bennet, I shall endeavor to keep an open mind regarding the citizens of Meryton."

A blush came to her cheeks and she looked away. A moment passed, and then, "I should probably be heading back."

"I suppose I ought as well," Darcy said. "Might we walk together part of the way, Miss Bennet? I believe we are going in the same direction, after all."

Miss Bennet raised a hand to her chin and tilted her head as though she were giving the idea very serious contemplation. "Well, Mr. Darcy, given that you are correct and for a time we shall be going in the same direction, we may as well walk together as not."

Darcy laughed again as they turned away from the view of the valley. Though he knew he should keep some distance between them and walk on the opposite side of his horse, he felt inexplicably drawn to this virtual stranger and chose instead to maneuver himself around his mount so that he and Miss Bennet were side by side. Certainly the distance would be wiser, for he knew not her situation and had no wish to give rise to any expectations of more than polite regard. But then, her conduct thus far had given no indication she was so fickle a creature as to believe him desiring her after but one conversation.

Truly, he was of no mind to be desiring anyone. He had a criminal to catch.

Chapter Two

When Elizabeth returned to Longbourn, so lost in thought was she over her conversation with Mr. Darcy that she near did not see Kitty and Lydia running toward her up the lane.

"Lizzy! Lizzy, you will never guess who was just here!" cried her youngest sister.

"Oh, do let her try, it will be so much fun!" declared Kitty.

Elizabeth fought a smile and attempted a serious expression as each one of the girls took her by the arm. "Let me see… Was it Father Christmas?"

Lydia rolled her eyes. "Oh, don't be so stupid! You know very well it was not. 'Tis only October after all!"

"Well then, you will just have to tell me as I can think of no one else who would excite the two of you so much."

"It was Mr. Bingley!" chimed her sisters in unison.

"I'm surprised you did not encounter him on the road," said Lydia immediately after.

"You know Mamma has been in such a state since Father told her he had called upon him," said Kitty.

"Are you sure you did not see him, Lizzy?" demanded Lydia as they entered the house. "Surely you must have. We did not, except from the window in Jane's room. He looked like he *might* be handsome, but Papa kept him in his bookroom the whole time. And he would not let us come down to be introduced so we cannot know for sure!"

"I assure you, Lydia, I did not see Mr. Bingley on the road," Elizabeth told her. "Perhaps he decided to go into the village before returning to Netherfield, or he may have called at Lucas Lodge."

"Oh, don't say that where Mamma can hear," warned Kitty with a smirk. "She is already determined that Mr. Bingley will suit Jane very well, and you know how she gets when she thinks someone will get in the way of what she wants."

Elizabeth knew only too well. Her mother, bless her, could be trying on the best of days. When some scheme of hers to promote her eldest and most beautiful daughter was threatened, Mrs. Bennet could be truly unbearable.

"And what does Jane think?" she asked then.

Lydia scoffed. "She would like to meet Mr. Bingley and hopes he is amiable. But she will say nothing beyond that—not even whether she hopes he is handsome! Oh, I do hope he is, for who knows? Perhaps *I* will be the one to catch his eye and then I will be married before all my sisters. What a joke that would be—the youngest married before the eldest!"

Lydia and Kitty laughed together before disappearing into the house. Elizabeth sighed as she removed her spencer, hat, and gloves and passed them to a waiting maid, and then went in search of Jane. Her elder sister she found with her first younger in the dining room; Jane and Mary were both working on some embroidery.

"Good morning, my sisters," said Elizabeth brightly as she dropped into a chair beside Jane, who asked,

"Have you heard the news?"

"If by news you mean that Mr. Bingley returned Father's visit to him, I have."

Jane smiled. "Kitty and Lydia were quite disappointed to not be allowed to meet him."

Mary scoffed. "Kitty and Lydia were more disappointed that he did not wear a red coat, I imagine," she said without looking up from her work.

Elizabeth shared a look with Jane and the two giggled. Kitty, Lydia, and even their mother had been all aflutter over the red coats of the militia that was now quartered in Meryton for the winter. Mary was usually not so witty, but occasionally she did surprise them—her lighthearted barb was especially on point.

"Well, Jane," said Elizabeth, "having caught a glimpse of the infamous Mr. Bingley, which of us do you think is most likely to make a match with him? Do you still consider it your duty to be the one who marries well?"

Jane's responding gaze was reproachful. "Now Lizzy… If this Mr. Bingley is an amiable gentleman, and if I find his manner agreeable, should he pay me any special attention, then yes, I would welcome it. I would also be just as pleased, if not more so, should he pay his attentions to you, or to Mary, or any of my sisters that he chooses."

At this, Mary did pause and look up at them. "Thank you, Jane, for including me."

"Of course, Mary. Why would I not?"

Their sister looked down at the material in her hands. "Because I am so often left out," she said softly.

Elizabeth glanced at Jane again, and saw in her elder sister's countenance the same emotion she was suddenly feeling: shame. It came upon her unexpectedly and with great force. And they should feel it, she mused, because Mary was right. She was close with Jane, and Kitty was close with Lydia—their number being uneven, Mary didn't have a sister to be the best of friends with. She had only her passion for music and for the church; she could not sing but played the pianoforte fairly well, and she pored over books such as Fordyce's *Sermons to Young Women*, often attempting to preach the books' lessons to her family simply in an effort to be noticed.

They were both of them guilty of ignoring Mary in favor of each other, or being too distracted by the antics of Kitty and Lydia to take notice of her need to be included. It was so easy—too easy, really—to forget their middle sister, or to ignore her in light of their own concerns, or simply to dismiss her altogether. When she wasn't on her instrument or preaching at them, she was quiet, preferring to remain at home rather than go out in society. Mary was often talked over whenever she made any attempt to join in a conversation. She rarely made an effort with her appearance other than to be fastidious, and Elizabeth recalled then her having once said that there was little point to doing more when she was so plain. And why should she not think that when her younger sisters and even her mother constantly told her it was so?

Mary had never before spoken up about being ignored or left out—or maybe they just had not been listening. Now that the words had been uttered, and heard, her elder sisters could do naught but feel as badly as they knew they should for their part in it. Elizabeth, a little overwhelmed at being made aware of so painful a truth, felt compelled to move and sit beside Mary on her side of the table. Taking one of her sister's hands she said, "Do forgive us, Mary. I have just now seen what I have been wrong in refusing to see before—that we have done you so very great a disservice."

Mary withdrew her hand and waved it in a dismissive gesture. "It's all right, Lizzy. I'm used to it. You and Jane are not the only ones who ignore me."

"It does not make it any less wrong, dearest," said Jane. "We should include you more in our outings, in our concerns—in everything!"

"Jane is right," said Elizabeth. "I propose to ignore all this foolishness about Mr. Bingley and his five thousand a year, as I've no real desire to marry anytime soon anyway, and shall focus my energies on being a better sister to you."

At this, the corners of Mary's lips turned up ever so slightly. "To be perfectly honest, I've not much desire to be married as yet either. I would rather focus on my music—though not singing. I know I am horrible at it, however much I wish I was not."

The three of them laughed together, quite possibly for the first time in years. Elizabeth felt both bad and good about it, and swore to herself there would be more such moments so that the bad feeling would eventually disappear. "Perhaps, then, you and I should focus our efforts entirely on Jane—*she* seems to be amenable to being married."

Mary smiled more fully then. "Jane will require little assistance from us to secure Mr. Bingley if he is handsome and amiable… though she could possibly use some in curtailing Mamma's efforts to force them together should she end up disliking him."

Elizabeth feigned shock. "Our Jane, dislike someone? Is it even possible?"

Mary tried to keep her expression serious but failed, and the two of them dissolved into laughter again—this time ignoring Jane, who protested that there were plenty of people she did not like…though she could not name a single one.

Later that night, as Elizabeth readied for bed, her mind drifted as it often had throughout the day toward a certain gentleman. She had not spent enough time conversing with Mr. Darcy to paint a full picture of his character, and that vexed her greatly—for she had long prided herself on her ability to sketch a person's character on first making their acquaintance.

Mr. Darcy, however, was a conundrum. He had seemed an odd mix of amiable and proud, with a hint of haughtiness. She was sure he would not find the society of Hertfordshire to his liking, yet he had been agreeable enough to say he would keep an open mind. He had not denied being rich like Mr. Bingley and seemed to hold his status in high regard, but he had not once censured her for her impertinence or forwardness.

She tried very hard not to think about what else she had noticed about him—that he had a fine figure and a handsome mien, one made even more attractive when he smiled. Elizabeth liked the sound of his laugh, a deep-timbred rumble that seemed to rise from deep in his chest much like his voice. She wondered what it would be like to have a philosophical debate with him, or any sort of meaningful conversation.

A soft knock at her door drew Elizabeth from her musings. She turned away from the mirror over her dressing table as she called out for her visitor to enter, and was little surprised to see that it was Jane. After closing the door, her sister moved to sit on the end of Elizabeth's bed, favoring her with a quizzical expression.

"Is something the matter, Jane?"

Jane's brow rose. "I could ask you the same question, Lizzy."

Elizabeth laughed. "I do not know what could possibly give you reason to think anything was the matter with me," she said.

"Come now, dearest. I know you best of all your family, and I was not remiss in taking notice of a persistent distraction today. Will you not share with me what is on your mind?" Jane pressed.

Elizabeth sighed. Of course Jane had noticed—even their father had directed a quizzical expression her way over dinner, though he was not one to pry. Neither was her sister truly doing so; Jane was merely expressing concern and offering to listen should she desire to open up. And really, there was no reason to keep her unexpected meeting concealed for she had done nothing inappropriate. Elizabeth supposed she had kept it to herself because she had so few secrets and had wanted to cherish the event on her own for a while—not to mention that had her mother heard tell of it, she'd have pressed her about Mr. Darcy's eligibility and fortune, the latter of which she had not asked after because that would have been grievously indecorous, not to mention none of her concern.

Besides, what did it matter what Mr. Darcy's fortune was? Once he set eyes on Jane, Elizabeth knew she would cease to exist for him, as she and her younger sisters always did whenever a gentleman gazed upon her elder sister's beauty.

"I met someone today," she said at last. "When I reached Oakham Mount on my walk this morning, there was already a gentleman there—a Mr. Darcy, who happens to be a friend and guest of our new neighbor, Mr. Bingley."

Jane's eyes widened in surprise. "Really?" she cried softly. "What was he like?"

"Agreeable, I suppose," said Elizabeth, "though I suspect him to be somewhat proud. I mentioned that our local society is likely to be quite different than that he is used to, and he asked if I was prejudiced against those of means for having a preference for manners and good breeding."

"Do you think him to be very rich?"

She nodded. "At least as much as Mr. Bingley, if not more so, though I could not say for sure as he did not speak of his fortune nor did I ask."

"I should think not," said Jane with a shake of her head. "For all your willful impertinence, Lizzy, even you know better than to ask so rude a question."

Elizabeth grinned. "Thank you so much for that resounding endorsement, Jane."

Her sister's expression became apologetic. "I do not mean to give offense, of course. It's just that I know how you like to make sport of our neighbors and laugh at their foolishness."

"Now Jane, even I know better than to ply my trade on someone with whom I have so little an acquaintance," Elizabeth countered. "In truth, Mr. Darcy and I spent no more than ten minutes together, if even that. We spoke for a few moments at the outlook, then upon mutually deciding to return to our respective residences, walked together to the road and there we parted. And that was the end of it."

Jane grinned as she drew her knees up and wrapped her arms around them. "And yet the mysterious Mr. Darcy has been on your mind all day. I begin to suspect, dear Lizzy, that you found him to be much more than 'agreeable'."

Elizabeth rolled her eyes and turned away from Jane, refusing to acknowledge that her sister just might be right.

Friday, 19 October 1798

Darcy, much to his own surprise—let alone that of his companions—found himself looking forward to the assembly they were to attend. He was anticipating the possibility of meeting Elizabeth Bennet again and actually being able to converse with her.

Perhaps she would honor him with a dance.

The day after their meeting at Oakham Mount, he had seen her across the church in Meryton, had wanted to acknowledge her and perhaps speak to her after, but they had not been formally introduced so it would not have been proper. It didn't help that every mother with a single daughter—including Elizabeth's own, no doubt, for he had been made aware by Bingley that there were *five* girls in the family—had conspicuously eyed the trio of single gentlemen from Netherfield from the moment they had alighted from Bingley's carriage. It had made Darcy decidedly uncomfortable, and while Charles had been delighted to take a few moments to converse with some of the men he had already met at the end of the service, he had made haste to the carriage with his cousin in tow. Fitzwilliam had shaken his head and chided him for his reticence to mingle, and Darcy had chided himself for missing a chance to look into a certain pair of fine eyes again.

Tonight, however, he was sure he would get the chance.

The ride to the assembly hall was filled with Charles' excited musings and Theodore's eager responses; they were both hoping to dance for most of the evening. Bingley said that there were sure to be enough pretty girls that they need not dance with the same young lady more than once, if the number of gentlemen he'd of late become acquainted with was any indication.

"Their being plentiful does not mean they will be beautiful, Charles," Darcy heard himself point out.

"Is a beautiful woman all you care about Darce?" asked Fitzwilliam. "If that is so, I know of a young lady in the carriage directly behind ours that would certainly meet your standard."

Darcy refused to rise to the bait, though his cousin and even Bingley chuckled. The latter's still unwed sister had made no secret of her desire to become mistress of Pemberley. Caroline wasted no moment in his presence attempting to capture his attentions, though he always rebuffed her as politely as propriety allowed and he made sure never to do anything that would encourage her pursuit. It was his hope that she would eventually come to understand she did not appeal to him, though as she had been fawning over him for much of the last three years, Darcy was beginning to think only the announcement of his marriage would put an end to her scheming.

That would, of course, require him to find a suitable woman to whom he would actually want to make an offer. High society was bursting with young women of good family and large dowries—not that he was in need of such an inducement—and it was true that many of them were very pleasing to look upon. But he wanted *more* than just a pretty face and fine figure to stand beside him at balls and assemblies. Darcy desired an accomplished young lady—no, more than that. He desired for his wife a woman possessed not only of skill in singing, dancing, drawing, and the modern languages; he hoped deep in his heart to meet someone who had a great love of reading with whom he could converse about books. Someone with a cheerful mien that would bring life back to Pemberley's halls, whose easy smile and wit would challenge him to step out of his self-imposed boundaries.

Someone like Elizabeth Bennet, perhaps? said his inner voice.

Perhaps. Miss Bennet had certainly had a ready smile, and a laugh that had haunted him. In the few moments of their conversation she had been playful and witty and she had stirred in him a desire to know more about her. But even with her fine eyes and her smile and her wit, would she truly be a good match? Her father was but a country squire with a small estate, and he had five daughters to endow. How much would he be able to give each of them when they married, if anything at all? And what were her mother's connections? Had she any family in society?

There was but one way to find out the answers to all of his questions: he would have to ask her. That meant a proper introduction was required, and then a dance, and *then* he would have to somehow manage to wrestle his usual reticence into submission and begin the conversation with something simple. Like the weather.

Oh, for goodness' sake, Darcy! The weather? Yes, that was certainly a *fabulous* way to begin an acquaintance. He was going to make a fool of himself if he tried to start a conversation by talking about the bloody weather.

"At last!" cried Bingley suddenly, snapping Darcy out of his maudlin thoughts.

He looked out the thin pane of glass in the carriage door as the vehicle came to a stop. The assembly hall looked respectable enough, though it would certainly not pass the muster of the *ton*. Probably wouldn't pass the inspection of Bingley's sisters, either; Louisa Bingley Hurst was also at Netherfield with her husband Reginald, and she and Caroline shared their opinions more often than not. Ever since their family had come into money, they had believed themselves far above the very circle into which they'd been born. A country hall like this the two would consider beneath them.

In fact, he could hear Caroline disparaging the place already as he alighted from the carriage. Darcy drew a breath and shook his head, and started forward as Miss Bingley was handed out by Mr. Hurst before she could force her company upon him.

The interior of the hall was just as filled with people as one might expect at a hall in Town, but was a great deal louder. Boisterous laughter and shouted conversation assailed him almost from the moment he stepped through the doors, and it was all he could do not to turn around and flee. How could he have allowed himself to be talked into attending such an event? Had he gone mad? The place was too crowded, too noisy, the manners of the people too unchecked. He would never be comfortable enough to begin a conversation with anyone, let alone the only person besides his own party that he knew. For that matter, how would he even find Miss Bennet in such a crush?

"Say Darce, think we might all get in?"

Blinking, he turned his head to find Fitzwilliam grinning at him. Resisting the urge to scowl, he forced himself to move further into the room, allowing the others to come inside.

"We are a great distance from true society, are we not, Mr. Darcy?" said Caroline on his left.

He almost agreed with her on reflex, until he recalled Elizabeth Bennet's admonition: *I pray you would not look down upon my friends and neighbors simply because they have not your strict standards of behavior…*

"Meryton is not London, that is true," he conceded. "But I once heard someone say that in such a place as this, a person of our stature is less likely to be censured if we were to let loose a little."

Darcy could see that he had shocked her, and was grateful for the clap on his shoulder that came from Fitzwilliam. "I say, old boy, whoever told you that is an absolute genius! Really, who here besides our lot is going to care if we loosen our starched cravats a little, eh?"

"Wonderful!" cried Bingley before Darcy could reply to his cousin. "I see Sir William Lucas over there—he is the mayor here, you see, and likely the master of ceremonies. He can take us 'round and introduce us to everyone we've not met."

A nod was his only reply, and so Bingley took the lead, walking in a straight line to the thick-middled gentleman that stood across the hall. Darcy dutifully followed, and was formally introduced not only to Sir William but also his wife, Lady Lucas, and their two daughters, Charlotte and Maria. The elder girl, who was thin and plain, looked to be about the same age as himself, while the younger appeared close in age to his own sister. She was pretty, he supposed, but her looks were nothing compared to Georgiana's.

"I've four sons also; the two eldest are away at present, and the younger two are at home for they are not old enough to attend assemblies," said the aging knight. "William, my eldest boy, is at university, and my son John serves in His Majesty's Navy."

A son at university was certainly a good thing, mused Darcy, and he surprised himself as much as Bingley and Fitzwilliam by asking which school the Lucas boy attended.

"I say, being knighted with a presentation at St. James has done such a wonder for my family, Mr. Darcy. We were able to get William into Cambridge," was the reply.

"It is an exceptional school. I attended there myself," Darcy said.

"Indeed," spoke up his cousin. "It is a Fitzwilliam family tradition!"

Sir William seemed pleased to have a connection to such noble families as theirs, however tenuous it was. The man's chest puffed out just a little bit more and his smile widened, and when Bingley asked him if he would be so kind, said he would be more than happy to take them 'round and make the introductions.

Darcy stood silent and grave through the meeting of the Long family. Mr. and Mrs. Long had borne no children of their own but were raising the lady's two nieces from her sister, who had passed from the grippe along with her husband. He could not help but think it a bit classless for such personal history to be spoken of in an introductory conversation, but given the way Mrs. Long was none-too-subtly pushing her wards forward, she no doubt hoped that having volunteered their sad story would garner sympathy with the unmarried gentlemen of their party. In fact, the lady made more than one attempt to facilitate a conversation between him and her eldest niece, but Darcy was able to avoid it by doing what he always did—remaining silent and adopting a countenance that proclaimed he was bored to tears.

As Bingley was, per usual, happy to engage in a few moments of conversation, Darcy grasped the opportunity to have a look around the assembly hall. He tried to tell himself it was so he could make note of all the exits, but he could not fool his own conscience. He was hoping very much to capture a glimpse of the elusive Miss Bennet. Would she even remember him? he wondered. Had she departed his company with a favorable opinion of him? He genuinely hoped so, as it would be refreshing to have an acquaintance beyond his party for however long Bingley needed him to stay.

Netherfield, so far as he could tell, *did* look to be a promising estate. Though it had been neglected in recent years, he could see the property's potential for growth and increased income. However, as Caroline was to be mistress of her brother's house until such time as he married, Charles was likely to be heavily influenced by her opinion, and she had already indicated in subtle and not-so-subtle ways that she found country life tasteless and the society in Meryton severely lacking.

His attention was drawn by the sound of laughter—a particular laugh, in fact—and it was but a moment before he found the source of those bright and happy notes. There, not twenty feet away, was the girl from the Mount: Elizabeth Bennet. She stood with an older woman and four other young ladies, all of whom bore features similar enough to tell any who looked upon them that the party were all related. The woman, likely to be the girls' mother, was casting furtive glances their way and waving her fan almost frantically. Darcy suspected she was desperate for an introduction so that she, like Lady Lucas and Mrs. Long, could attempt to entice Bingley, Fitzwilliam, or himself with one of her daughters.

I am already enticed, he thought, and a moment later his breath caught as Miss Elizabeth turned her gaze in his direction. Recognition alighted in her eyes and she smiled, though gave no other indication that she knew him.

Relief flooded through him when at last Bingley was extricated from his intercourse with the Longs by Sir William; he led them over to the Bennet ladies next. After his party's names were given and Mrs. Bennet was introduced, she took over from Sir William and presented her daughters herself. Elizabeth, he discovered, was the second of the five, after Jane. The younger three were Mary, Catherine, and Lydia, and Darcy could tell straight away by their fidgeting and giggling that Catherine and Lydia had not the discipline displayed by their elder sisters.

"La! I see that the musicians are at last setting up for the dancing," observed Mrs. Bennet. Indeed, a number of men were tuning fiddles and violas and even an upright pianoforte at the far end of the hall. "Do you dance, Mr. Bingley?"

"Oh indeed, ma'am! I love a good country dance!" Bingley replied cheerfully. "There is nothing I like better."

"Mrs. Bennet," said Fitzwilliam, "I can assure you that my friend came here with no other intention than to dance the night away, as did I."

This announcement, no doubt intended to tease the lady given the tone with which it had been delivered, greatly delighted Mrs. Bennet, who squealed and clapped her hands together. "How marvelous, Colonel Fitzwilliam! And what excellent timing—for the music is about to start and before you are four of the finest dancers in all of Hertfordshire!"

"Only four of the finest?" drawled Caroline. Her words, while in appearance merely inquisitive, fairly dripped with disdain. For the first time since finding her, Darcy's eyes were drawn from Miss Elizabeth's and he glanced at Bingley's sister with a frown. She might not find the society to her liking, but it was no excuse to be rude.

"I regret that I do not find much pleasure in dancing," said Mary Bennet. "Indeed, I prefer to play the pianoforte or read a good book. I also enjoy discussing music and the subjects of the books I have read, as I believe that conversation—rather than dancing—to be a more appropriate means of becoming acquainted with someone."

"Oh, my Mary is such a delight on the pianoforte," said Mrs. Bennet then. "You'll not find a more accomplished young lady in all the county, I assure you."

"Mamma, please. Your opinion is biased," Mary countered, as an embarrassed blush filled her cheeks.

"Come now Mary," spoke up Elizabeth, her voice once more capturing Darcy's attention. "Mamma's opinion may be biased, but it is true that you are fairly well accomplished. Your playing has much improved of late."

Mary nodded her head. "Thank you, Elizabeth. That is kind of you to say."

"And why should she not praise a sister's accomplishments?" Darcy said then, seizing the first opportunity he had noticed to join in the conversation. "My own younger sister is also fond of the pianoforte, and when occasion presents itself, I speak of her talents to anyone who will listen."

"He's not jesting, I can assure you," piped up Fitzwilliam. "I declare, it's often that once he gets started singing the praises of my dear young cousin, he never stops!"

"On that, *he* jests," said Darcy, his eyes yet again flicking to Elizabeth. The soft smile on her lips and the sparkle in her eyes told him she found the byplay amusing.

"Do you dance, Mr. Darcy?"

Mrs. Bennet did not give up, he thought. "Not if I can help it," he replied automatically, as usually he didn't. Crowds of people he didn't know, even if he *had* been introduced, simply made him too nervous; though he was an accomplished dancer, he feared making a fool of himself. Not to mention how tiresome it was to have all the society mothers pushing their daughters at him with the hope of his choosing one to be the next Mrs. Darcy.

A look of disappointment came into Elizabeth's eyes, which she immediately attempted to conceal by dropping her gaze. Darcy was strangely bothered to have upset her, and as he *had* meant to take advantage of whatever opportunities were presented to become better acquainted with Elizabeth, he quickly amended his statement. "That is, I do not dance with young ladies with whom I am unfamiliar. But as we are now introduced, I would be delighted if Miss Elizabeth would do me the honor."

Mrs. Bennet had been subtly pushing Jane toward him; her entire face lit up with surprise when he spoke his desired partner's name. Bingley quickly offered for Jane himself, and Fitzwilliam begged of Mary to dance just this once, as he was rather intrigued with the idea of having at least one partner with more than fripperies on her mind.

Darcy paid little attention to his cousin or his friend, or his friend's sister who voiced her displeasure that *she* was not his first partner with a none too subtle, sharply indrawn breath. It pleased him more than it should that Elizabeth was looking at him again, gracing him with her fine, bright eyes and a brilliant smile.

"Mr. Darcy, I would be delighted to further make your acquaintance," said she. "After all, I was just about to suggest that perhaps the best means of encouraging acquaintance and affection was to dance."

"But what if Miss Mary is correct, and conversation is the best means?" he asked.

Elizabeth laughed. "Allow me to put it this way, then: I will know if I desire to become better acquainted with someone by how willing he is to dance."

Darcy returned her smile before bowing slightly and then offering his arm. "Then it is fortunate, I daresay, that I find myself uncharacteristically willing."

"Fortunate indeed, sir," she replied as they moved toward the center of the hall, where other dancers were already starting to line up. "I suppose I ought consider it a great honor to be chosen."

"I do not know about that," he countered. "As I said, I usually do not dance if I can help it, when I know no one outside my own party. I… do not possess the ability to recommend myself to strangers."

"Oh my—are you saying you are *shy*, Mr. Darcy? Is it terrible of me that I find such a revelation amusing?"

"More than terrible, Miss Elizabeth, it is *appalling* that you would think so, let alone admit to it," Darcy replied.

She laughed again, as he had hoped she would. It was not like him to tease any young lady other than Georgiana, but Miss Elizabeth Bennet seemed not to be just any young lady. From the first moment of their acquaintance she had intrigued him; her smile and her unabashed delight in laughing filled him with an emotion he could not quite define. It was not like him, at all, to behave so—to actively seek out a young lady's acquaintance. Darcy knew that he should check himself, that he did not appear too interested, so as not to mislead her as to his own intentions. He still did not know anything about her family or connections or her fortune.

By the time the night was over, Darcy determined, he would find out.

Chapter Three

Although she had done her best to conceal her distraction from her mother and younger sisters—as if they could even be bothered to notice anyone other than themselves or the militia—Elizabeth had been forced to admit after only a day or two that she was hoping to meet Mr. Darcy again.

Only with Jane did she share her growing anticipation for the monthly assembly, and then only at night when all the rest of the family had gone to bed. Never before had a man possessed such a power over her mind—that Mr. Darcy had managed to do so was most vexing. She hoped to meet with him again in order to discover what about him it was that had so captured her attention.

Jane, of course, attributed her infatuation with Mr. Darcy's appearance. All of Meryton had been blessed with a glimpse of the man, as well as his cousin the colonel and Mr. Bingley and his family, at church the Sunday after Mr. Bingley had paid his visit to Longbourn. Mrs. Bennet had insisted on going to services in Meryton rather than Longbourn village, for, Elizabeth was certain, the sole purpose of seeing the single gentlemen. Much was said between the mothers of unwed daughters of how handsome they were and what fine matches would be made if one—or all—could be persuaded to make an offer to their daughters.

Much to the chagrin of her elder three daughters, Mrs. Bennet was among the most effusive of the ladies, for she was very much in competition with the other mothers—and Mrs. Long especially—as to who would get one of their girls married first.

A proper introduction was not to be had that day, however, for the veritable deluge of ladies pushing their husbands to make introductions with the Netherfield party had led to Mr. Darcy fleeing Meryton Church as soon as the service had ended. Elizabeth was disappointed but could hardly blame the poor soul, who likely had to fend off matchmaking mothers on a regular basis. Well, he'd not have to be concerned with *her* in that regard—she had just found him inexplicably fascinating and wanted to know why. Marriage to a man she barely knew was the furthest thing from her mind.

Besides, he was undoubtedly *very* rich. Indeed, if what Mrs. Long told her mother the following Monday was true, Mr. Darcy's fortune was twice that of Mr. Bingley. Elizabeth had been hard-pressed to imagine what she could do with Bingley's five thousand a year—to have *ten* thousand at her disposal was unfathomable! A man with such an income as Darcy's would never be interested in a simple country girl, even if they were technically equals, he being a gentleman and she a gentleman's daughter. With no fortune of her own to add to his and no important family connections, the chances of attracting such a man as he were utterly impossible for one such as she. Mr. Bingley, perhaps—he seemed amiable enough not to care if his lady had a large dowry or not. Mr. Darcy and his cousin the colonel, however, were out of reach.

So it was a good thing she desired only to be friends with them, for however long they might be staying at Netherfield.

Of course, this assertion did little to stop Elizabeth from walking to Oakham Mount three times since meeting Mr. Darcy there. She had wondered if she might meet him again, but she did not. Perhaps it was for the best, as they had not been properly introduced. She should not even have spoken to him at all that day—society's rules said the proper thing to do would have been to leave, since he had arrived at the outlook first. But she had stayed, had spoken, because she had always thought such a rule rather silly and terribly unfair. Why should she have been denied the pleasure of the view just because a man she had never met before got there before she did?

After thirteen days of speculation, of listening to the gossip relayed by Mrs. Long or her Aunt Phillips, she was to hopefully have her curiosity satisfied at last, as Lady Lucas had assured her mother that the party from Netherfield was to attend the ball. Mr. Bingley himself had accepted the invitation from Sir William, and surely he would bring his friend with him. Mrs. Bennet had been in high spirits at hearing the news, and when the day came she behaved as though she were an instructor in the regiments—or so Mr. Bennet joked—ordering the maids and even her daughters about, impressing upon them all the importance of making a good impression upon Mr. Bingley, Mr. Darcy, and Colonel Fitzwilliam.

She was certain that Jane's beauty would attract at least one of them—preferably Mr. Darcy and his ten thousand a year—and save them all from being thrown into the hedgerows after Mr. Bennet's demise, as was sure to happen since Longbourn was entailed. And with Lydia's fondness for officers, she might just catch the colonel's eye! These were the hopes of Mrs. Bennet, oft followed by a dramatic sigh, and musings about how fine their gowns and carriages would be should her girls make such spectacular matches.

Though Jane was somewhat hopeful of Mr. Bingley and Colonel Fitzwilliam being amiable enough to dance with, she had promised Elizabeth in secret that Mr. Darcy was safe from her charms; despite her sister's protestations to the contrary, she considered the gentleman to be spoken for. "Until you meet him again, Lizzy, and tell me once and for all whether you like him, I shall not consider him."

Jane was too sweet and kind for her own good. Elizabeth still believed the consideration to be unnecessary, but it did not stop her being disappointed when their family arrived at the assembly hall to find that the Netherfield party had not yet done so. Quite all right, she assured herself. After all, was it not a habit of the rich to arrive "fashionably late"?

Elizabeth had been talking with Jane when she noticed Mr. Darcy had arrived at last. He stood off to the side of his party and truthfully looked quite bored as Sir William was introducing them to the Long family, much to her mother's vexation.

"Why should he introduce them to the Longs first? Mrs. Long only wants to get her hooks into the rich men before anyone else can. Well, I won't allow it! Mr. Darcy or even Mr. Bingley will do quite well for Jane, and oh, that colonel does look fine, even if he is not wearing his red coat this evening. Perhaps Kitty for him—why Jane, if you can get Mr. Darcy, then Lydia will do for Mr. Bingley and then the colonel would be free for Kitty. Oh, how vexed Mrs. Long would surely be if my girls got them all!"

"Mamma, please do keep your voice down, they will hear you," Jane admonished her softly.

Though she heard this exchange, Elizabeth was paying little attention—Mr. Darcy was looking at her now. She smiled softly to let him know she remembered him. He smiled subtly in return, and even seemed relieved when finally Mr. Bingley acceded to Sir William's prompting and came away with him.

Meryton's mayor brought him straight over to her family, and after presenting Mr. Bingley, Mr. Darcy, and Colonel Fitzwilliam, along with Miss Bingley and Mr. and Mrs. Hurst, he began to introduce her family. Here Elizabeth felt some embarrassment, as once her mother's name had been given, Mrs. Bennet decided to speak over him and introduce her daughters herself. She hoped Mr. Darcy did not note the flush of her cheeks as she curtseyed. It was then that the musicians began to settle on the raised platform at the end of the hall; her mother noticed, and asked Mr. Bingley if he danced.

Elizabeth felt Mr. Darcy's eyes upon her again, and she looked up with a smile. Her attention was then caught momentarily by her mother's praise of Mary, something she hardly ever did when there were eligible gentlemen around. Seeing her sister's flush of embarrassment, she had gently concurred with their mother's assessment, and was delighted when Mr. Darcy responded with an anecdote regarding his own sister. That Colonel Fitzwilliam joked with him about his boasting she found delightfully amusing, though his reply to her mother's query about dancing was a sharp disappointment.

Though she had no interest beyond friendship, in secret Elizabeth had been wondering what it would be like to dance with him.

Her head lifted in surprise and tempered excitement when Mr. Darcy immediately followed his statement by saying, "That is, I do not dance with young ladies with whom I am unfamiliar. But as we are now introduced, I would be delighted if Miss Elizabeth would do me the honor."

Her responding smile felt as though it would split her face. She could not help but feel flattered that the admittedly handsome gentleman had singled her out over Jane, who was often hailed—by her mother most of all—as the beauty of the county. In fact, she had not been entirely deaf to her mother's hopes for Jane and Mr. Darcy to make a match, nor was she remiss to the stunned expression on her mother's face when he asked *her* to dance and not Jane.

Elizabeth expressed her desire to make his acquaintance, and quipped that she had just been about to suggest dancing as the best means of doing so. Much to her delight, Mr. Darcy teased her back, and the repartee continued as they made their way over to where the first set of dancers were lining up. Her sisters followed with their partners, and she shared a look with both Jane and Mary, knowing they were as aware as she of the envious looks being cast their way by the mothers whose daughters who had *not* been favored by one of the new arrivals.

The first dance of the evening was a lively reel as per usual, intended to get the blood pumping and the dancing off to a merry start. Elizabeth had not the opportunity to speak with Mr. Darcy again until near five minutes had passed.

"So, Mr. Darcy, you have a sister?" she asked across the line.

"I do, yes. Her name is Georgiana—she's about Miss Lydia's age, I believe."

"And is she truly so very accomplished that once you begin boasting of her you never cease?"

Darcy smiled, and conversation was halted again as their places changed and they moved further away from one another. When they came back together again in another few minutes, he said, "My sister is indeed very talented, as I am sure any young woman would be if she applied herself as diligently to her studies as Georgiana does."

Elizabeth nodded. "Quite so. Mary has recently given up singing, which she came to admit she could not do very well, and has chosen to focus on the pianoforte. Since redirecting her efforts I believe she has come to enjoy practicing all the more, and her playing is not so stiff and forced as it once was."

Once more they moved apart and could not speak, and when they were rejoined, Elizabeth asked, "If I may, Mr. Darcy, are you truly uncomfortable amongst strangers? You need not answer, of course, if my query is too personal."

"Not at all, Miss Elizabeth," Darcy replied. "After all, I opened the proverbial door to such a line of questioning. And the unfortunate truth is that yes, I am. Something about being in a large crowd or a room full of strangers just…unnerves me."

"And so you are content in such circumstances to walk the room or to sit in a dark corner and be unsociable and taciturn?"

Again he was prevented answering by the moves of the dance, each of them skipping down the line in turn. When the pair were across from each other at the end and the dance had at last finished, they curtsied and bowed before turning together and applauding the musicians along with the rest of the attendees. Elizabeth took note of Jane smiling at something Mr. Bingley said to her, and even Mary beamed a little under the attention of Colonel Fitzwilliam. She would have to make a point of thanking him for his kindness, as Mary did not do well at balls and had more than once sat through an entire event without dancing at all.

Mr. Darcy offered his arm to Elizabeth to lead her back to her mother; he walked slowly in order to match her shorter stride. "In regard to your last question, Miss Elizabeth, I am afraid I must concur in the positive yet again. In such a place as this, or the Upper Rooms in Town—even at a private ball hosted by family or friends—I am more likely to offend with my manner than recommend myself. I believe I must extend to you my gratitude, for you have somehow managed to bewitch me into behaving in a more gentlemanlike manner."

Although she softly laughed at his words, Elizabeth felt a great warmth beneath her breast—to be praised so was a great compliment.

"Do keep that to yourself, sir," she whispered conspiratorially. "It is my intention to bewitch every single gentleman in attendance tonight, that at least one unmarried young lady might find herself the object of affection for one of you."

Darcy paused mid-stride. "You seek a husband?" he asked.

Elizabeth scoffed and waved a hand at his words. "Good heavens, no! Please, be not alarmed, sir, for I've no intention of marrying anytime soon. I only meant to jest, though it *would* please me if one of my sisters were to catch a gentleman's eye this evening. I *do* have quite a number of them to see happily situated, if you'll recall."

"And what of you, Miss Elizabeth? Do you not also wish to be happily settled?"

"Someday, perhaps," she replied. "But for now I am content with my life, and if all my sisters should find their happiness before I do, I shan't be the least upset about it."

It was then that Mr. Darcy delivered her back to her mother, who immediately tried to talk him into dancing with Jane, whom she was certain "would not mind dancing again with such a fine partner" as he. Miss Bingley sidled up to their party and placed her hand at Darcy's elbow; he started at the touch, and politely declined a dance with Jane in favor of his friend's sister.

"I regret that I cannot partner with Miss Bennet, ma'am, for I have promised the next to Miss Bingley," he said, wishing Caroline's possessive clutch of his arm had not forced him to lie.

"Already Mr. Darcy has danced with one of your daughters, Mrs. Bennet. Surely you cannot expect to monopolize his time the whole of the evening?" said Miss Bingley.

Elizabeth felt her hackles rise. How rude she was to speak as though she owned Mr. Darcy. It was in that moment that Elizabeth determined she would probably never like the other woman.

"A dance with each of my girls would not take up the whole of Mr. Darcy's evening," snapped Mrs. Bennet softly.

Clearly her mother did not much like Caroline Bingley either. Whilst Elizabeth was usually the first to try and curb her mother's often crass behavior, one of the few things that brought them together was a fierce protectiveness of the other girls. Miss Bingley's words had been spoken in a polite tone, but their underlying meaning was not lost on anyone with half a mind to listen. On this, at least, Elizabeth would side with her mother—if Mr. Darcy chose to dance with each one of her sisters that was his choice.

"Take care, Mrs. Bennet!" spoke up Colonel Fitzwilliam brightly. "Darcy rarely dances more than once at a ball—I should not get Miss Bennet's hopes up if I were you, for when the next set is done, he is like to find a chair in the darkest corner and sit there until the festivities are ended!"

Where Miss Bingley had instantly put her off, Colonel Fitzwilliam had just won Elizabeth's admiration. He was obviously an astute fellow, as a man in His Majesty's Army must surely be to achieve his rank, and had deduced as she had that Miss Bingley's words had riled up her mother and put her on the defensive. Smart move to play on the reticence Darcy himself had spoken of to calm the situation before it could get worse—though it was entirely possible that having said this of him, his cousin might just do as he'd described.

It would be unfortunate if he did, as she had enjoyed their dance and conversation, and before it had even finished had found herself hoping he might ask her to dance a second time later in the evening. It would set the tongues of the gossips to wagging, certainly, but she could easily ignore them. The only person who might be more delighted than she to be asked again was her mother, for if she could not interest Mr. Darcy in Jane, she would push Elizabeth to pursue him.

On second thought, perhaps it is best we don't share a second dance, she thought. It would not do at all for her mother to assume she had formed an attachment to the man when she merely found his company pleasing. Of course, to Mrs. Bennet, she knew, finding a gentleman's company pleasing was a sure sign that a lady was halfway to being in love.

It was all she could do not to roll her eyes at the thought.

"Elizabeth Bennet, do not be so rude—I raised you much better than that!"

Elizabeth blinked, snapped from her reverie by her mother's sharp tone. She noticed then that Miss Bingley had managed to lead Mr. Darcy away, Mr. Bingley was now across the room apparently asking Charlotte Lucas to dance, and Jane, Lydia, and Kitty were partnering with three local young men. Only her mother, Mary, and Colonel Fitzwilliam remained of the party from moments before, and all three were looking at her rather expectantly.

"Forgive me," she stuttered. "I did not mean to be rude, I was simply distracted. Might I ask a repeat of what was said?"

Colonel Fitzwilliam smiled, as did Mary, and her mother looked as if she were about to have a fit. "Young lady, Colonel Fitzwilliam has done you the honor of asking you to dance! How could you become distracted when there were three fine gentlemen speaking with us—you could have driven the colonel to ask another girl!"

"Not at all, Mrs. Bennet," Colonel Fitzwilliam. "I am as patient as a saint. Besides, in my experience, a lady that is distracted in a room full of people is a lady that thinks."

"Oh, my dear sir, pray do not encourage her!" Mrs. Bennet retorted with a laugh and a tap of her fan on his shoulder. "Lizzy already spends far too much time with books when she should be engaged in more ladylike pursuits."

"Mamma, please," Elizabeth admonished. "Continue on that vein and the colonel may ask another yet!"

She then turned her focus to Colonel Fitzwilliam and said, "Forgive my wandering thoughts, sir. I would very much be delighted to dance."

"Excellent!" said the colonel as he moved to stand beside her and offer his arm. "I must say, I do hope for a waltz or a quadrille, that I may keep you as my partner throughout the dance and learn your secret."

Elizabeth raised an eyebrow as they started toward the other dancers. "My secret, Colonel?"

Fitzwilliam laughed. "Indeed, Miss Elizabeth. I should like to know how you got my cousin to dance the first dance!"

The two joined the line—much to the colonel's delight, a quadrille was called. A moment after the dance began, Elizabeth said, "I cannot answer your query, Colonel, as I do not know myself what possessed him to ask me. Jane is, after all, the prettier of us."

He grinned. "I will grant that Miss Bennet is a lovely creature, but do not dismiss yourself so easily, Miss Elizabeth. If I may be so bold, I would venture to say that you are an uncommonly pretty girl yourself. In fact, I believe that every young lady, even the plain ones, have their own particular beauty."

She rewarded his kind remark with a bright smile. "That is very gentlemanly of you to say, sir."

"Actually, Miss Elizabeth, I must confess something," the colonel said after a moment of silence. "Darcy told me about meeting you when he went for that ride a fortnight past, and frankly he has been rather distracted himself ever since. Certainly he pays attention when assisting Bingley with going over Netherfield or when we've gone shooting, but oftentimes in the evenings I have glimpsed him gazing rather pensively into the fire or out of a window."

Elizabeth fought the flush that threatened to turn her cheeks a rosy red. She cleared her throat delicately, then said, "I am greatly flattered, Colonel, that you would consider so brief a meeting as cause for Mr. Darcy's thoughtful reposes. However, I think it would be arrogant of me to presume you are correct, and therefore must point out that there are likely a great many reasons he would present himself so, with myself the very least among them."

"Your modesty does you credit, Miss Elizabeth," countered Fitzwilliam. "I shall thus believe it for both of us until proven wrong. We are cousins after all, Darcy and I, and never have I seen him so eager to attend a ball as he was tonight. And once we arrived, he said nothing to anyone until we were introduced to you charming Bennet ladies."

Here she laughed. "My mother will be quite flattered to hear that you called her charming," she said.

"Why should I not?"

They moved through the dance in silence again as Elizabeth considered how to respond. She had no wish to belittle her mother, but she had long been aware that the elder lady's "charm" had dissipated years ago, and left in its place an excitable, loud, and often vulgar woman who believed herself riddled with nerves.

"I believe I understand your reticence, Miss Elizabeth," Colonel Fitzwilliam said then. "I have observed your mother a number of times since our arrival, and her manners are…"

"Sorely lacking?" she interrupted with a short laugh. "I did caution Mr. Darcy as to what he might expect here in Meryton. I would imagine that if he spoke to you of our chance encounter, then he also relayed my warning."

"He did," Fitzwilliam conceded with a nod. "And you are right—the people here are, while observant of the basic rules of propriety, a great deal less restrained than our usual circle. And while Miss Bingley, her sister, Mr. Hurst, and even Darcy may find themselves affronted by the comportment of local society, I frankly find you all incredibly refreshing. No doubt it is due in large part to my having been on the battlefield a time or two, where the rules of society are all but cast out and surviving to see the next day takes precedence."

"Indeed," said she. "You are used to the rules being bent, if not broken. My mother knows the rules, understands them, but more often than not ignores them, as she seems not to care whether she is being rude, or loud, or utterly foolish."

Embarrassment that she had spoken so candidly suddenly filled Elizabeth, and she fell quiet again. A few turns later the dance ended, and after curtseying and acknowledging the musicians, she turned to go, hoping that she could avoid further entrenching herself in the shame of disparaging her own mother—exactly what she had *not* wanted to do.

Colonel Fitzwilliam touched her elbow and she stopped. Without looking at him she said, "Colonel, I humbly beg your pardon. It was not my intention to be so forward or to speak so ill of my mother—"

Fitzwilliam took her hand and laid it in the crook of his arm, then began to lead her away from the dance floor. "Miss Elizabeth, do not trouble yourself to feel as though you spoke out of turn. Truthfully, I welcome your candor, as it helps me to decipher just what kind of lady you are."

"One who insults her own mother to a stranger?"

"On the contrary. I see you now, based on your words, as a young lady who is oftentimes frustrated that someone she loves dearly is not more genteel in her manner," he told her. "I imagine you feel the same way about your youngest sisters."

Here she looked up, and was relieved to find no censure in his gaze. "Thank you for the kind words, Colonel. Truly, I do not know what possessed me to say such things."

The colonel winked and smiled. "What can I say but that it is my own natural charm—young ladies just seem to tell me nothing but the truth."

Elizabeth was compelled to laugh. "Now you are being cheeky, I daresay. Surely not all of them are so honest."

Colonel Fitzwilliam sighed. "Indeed, no. I've met far too many for my taste who simper and smile and tell me sweet little lies because they are attracted to my father's title and my family's money—of which, I am forced to point out, my brother will have the lion's share, given he is the elder and I the younger of my father's sons. I shall be doomed to bachelorhood, I'm afraid, as unfortunately there are some—even the son of an earl—who must think of money and seek a lady of fortune to marry."

Elizabeth understood all too well. What the colonel did *not* say was that he could not consider *her* as a potential bride because she did not have a dowry which would support his style of living. How he knew that was likely due to the local gossips, who possessed no qualms about revealing the extent of their neighbors' fortunes.

"I appreciate *your* candor," she said, mimicking his earlier words to her. "Though I warn you, Mamma will be vastly disappointed to hear it."

Her companion grinned. "And I am sorry to disappoint her, for she has some very fine daughters."

She ignored his last words. "No doubt your cousin and your friend are equally as restrained in their choice of bride," Elizabeth went on. "Not because they have need of a lady's fortune, clearly, but because it is expected by their families and society that they should marry very well. The eligible ladies of Meryton are likely far beneath them then, which will be a great disappointment to more mothers than my own."

At this Colonel Fitzwilliam started, his eyes widening a fraction in surprise. His lips parted in preparation for response to her statement, but Elizabeth felt very suddenly that she had had enough of rich society. She knew she would only find relief by seeking solace with someone familiar and comforting.

She needed Charlotte, whose intelligence and sense had often helped her find reason.

"If you will excuse me, Colonel, I have just come to realize that I have been neglecting a dear friend of mine, and I had promised to visit with her," she said.

The colonel set his lips in a thin line, then nodded. "Of course, Miss Elizabeth—though I do hope we shall get to speak again soon."

Elizabeth made a noncommittal sound and curtsied, and she broke away from him before he had even straightened from his bow. Charlotte was not difficult to find, as after her dance with Mr.

Bingley, she had returned to her mother's side.

"Elizabeth, I'm so happy you've come to see me!" Charlotte exclaimed as she reached for her hands. One eyebrow rose as she took a moment to observe the countenance of her friend, and then the older girl said, "Come, you look like you could use some refreshment. Do excuse us, Mamma."

Lady Lucas waved them off with a flick of her hand, too distracted was she to even take notice of them. Elizabeth knew that while she and Sir William had all but lost hope of their eldest daughter finding a husband, Maria was yet still young, and very pretty. Charlotte's mother had as much hope of her youngest catching the eye of one of the eligible gentlemen as the other mothers of young, unwed daughters.

Elizabeth allowed Charlotte to lead her by the hand toward the refreshment table, where she soon pushed a cup of punch into her hand. After filling a cup for herself, she took a sip and then said, "Now tell me, dearest, whatever has you so vexed?"

She just prevented herself from groaning, and settled instead for a heavy sigh; Elizabeth took a large gulp of her punch before she replied with, "Honestly, Charlotte, I am not sure at all what has come over me."

"Well, I know you were hopeful of meeting a certain gentleman again," said Charlotte softly, her voice low so that others would not overhear. "I noticed you talking to him as you danced."

"Charlotte, you know I talk as a rule while dancing," Elizabeth replied.

"Then did you not find him amiable? You seemed to get on well enough."

"I did—we did. Mr. Darcy was perfectly agreeable."

Her friend shook her head. "Then I do not understand what has you so out of sorts. You got on with Mr. Darcy, and it seemed to me that Colonel Fitzwilliam recommended himself to you as well."

"It is probably nothing, Charlotte," said Elizabeth, before taking another drink of her punch. "And yet… it is everything."

For a long, silent moment, Charlotte stared at her in confusion, and then suddenly she smiled and laughed. "Upon my word… I get it now—you *like* him!"

Chapter Four

Elizabeth stared wide-eyed at Charlotte, utterly disbelieving what she had heard.

"What rubbish!" she protested firmly.

"Oh no, I'm sure of it!" Charlotte declared with a wide smile. "Not entirely certain which one you're besotted with, though if I were a betting lady I'd say it was Mr. Darcy. But you, my dear Elizabeth, are most definitely at sixes and sevens over a man! I declare, I never thought I would see the day!"

Elizabeth set her cup down, stood with her hands at her hips, and faced Charlotte with a stern glare. "I may be out of sorts, Charlotte, but that by no means has *anything* to do with either Mr. Darcy or Colonel Fitzwilliam. You'd best put that thought straight out of your mind."

Charlotte chuckled. "Methinks the lady doth protest too much," she parried.

"Don't be ridiculous! I am somewhat confused, yes, but only as to why I have behaved in a manner so much out of character for me. Even I am not normally so open with strangers, and yet this night I have been very frank with two gentlemen with whom I am little acquainted, about topics which normally I only speak of with you, Jane, and Mary."

"And why do you think that is?" Charlotte challenged her. "I know you, Lizzy—sharp-tongued and quick-witted you always are, and frankness is your stock-in-trade, but I have never known you to twist yourself up in knots like this. Both Mr. Darcy and the colonel must have made you instinctively at ease when, as you said, even you are typically more guarded."

Her eyes narrowed. "What did you say to them, anyway?"

Elizabeth drew a breath and then relayed both conversations to her friend. Charlotte remained silent and thoughtful throughout, but before she could make any sort of reply, the two noted the approach of the very subjects of their conversation, along with Mr. Bingley.

Taking hold of Charlotte's hand, Elizabeth quickly pulled her away from the refreshment tables to hide behind a nearby wooden pillar. "I do not think they saw us," she mused aloud.

"Why should you desire to avoid them? It would be terribly rude, Elizabeth, to ignore them now you've danced with two of them," Charlotte pointed out.

Elizabeth hushed her as Colonel Fitzwilliam's voice carried over to their hearing. "I say, Darcy, something must be in the air in Meryton. In a place like this, amongst such company, you normally find it a punishment to stand up with anyone other than Miss Bingley or Mrs. Hurst."

"Agreed, Theo!" cried Mr. Bingley; Elizabeth peeked around the pillar to find that the three were fetching drinks. "On such occasions I would not be as fastidious as Darcy for a kingdom, but tonight he is almost a different man. Why, he *willingly* spoke to a group of ladies he had only just met, and even asked one of them to dance!"

"Now Charles," began Mr. Darcy. "You know perfectly well that I had, technically, met Miss Elizabeth already."

"I recall the mention of your sharing a few words with a local young lady some time ago," his friend continued. "Miss Elizabeth is very pretty, is she not? I daresay you found her very agreeable."

"You know my taste, Bingley. She is tolerable, but not handsome enough to tempt me," came the reply, and Elizabeth found she could bear no more. Through her recital of her conversations with the two gentlemen, she had begun to see why Charlotte believed her to have formed an attachment to Mr. Darcy. Indeed, she *had* liked him from the very first moment, had looked forward to his attending the ball to perhaps further their acquaintance. That she had never felt that way about any man before made her wonder if perhaps her friend was right after all—that if she didn't already, she was certainly on the way to liking him.

His harsh words, however, had proven she was entirely wrong about him, and it was with an uncharacteristic burning sensation behind her eyes that she moved around the column and pushed through the crowd to get away—as far away from Mr. Darcy of Pemberley as she could possibly get!

A sharp cry of the last name he would want to hear in that moment startled Darcy, and he whipped his head around just in time to see its bearer, Elizabeth, pushing her way through the throng of people nearest to where he stood. Dread roiled in his chest as her friend Miss Lucas, who'd called her name, quickly moved to follow her.

"Miss Lucas, wait!" he heard himself call out, taking a step toward the woman.

She turned to him sharply, her eyes like daggers as she snapped, "Mr. Darcy, I think you've said quite enough, sir! Good evening!"

Miss Lucas dropped into a perfunctory curtsey and turned away again in pursuit of the retreating Elizabeth.

"Blast and botheration!" Darcy muttered at her disappearing form. Fitzwilliam and Bingley came up on either side of him then.

"Tough luck, old chap," said Bingley. "Bloody bad timing, that was."

"Indeed, Bingley," put in Fitzwilliam. "Don't twist yourself up too much, Darce. We know you were only jesting—"

"Aye, but she doesn't," he said. "Blast it, I had no idea she was even nearby! Had I known she could hear us, I would never have employed such crude sarcasm."

His companions shared a look, then both turned their eyes to him. Fitzwilliam spoke first, saying, "You really are upset over this, aren't you, Darcy? Do I take it to mean that you like this girl?"

Darcy stifled a groan and settled for running a hand through his hair in frustration. "Not particularly," he lied. "I found her interesting at our first meeting, yes, and admittedly I had hoped I would meet her again—properly, this time. My only wish was to understand the uncharacteristic ease with which I found myself able to speak with her…"

He forced himself to turn away from where he had seen her go. "I should consider myself fortunate. I have driven away a girl who likely has no fortune and no connections—a match between us would be inadvisable. Not to mention I have far more important things to occupy my mind, such as catching that scoundrel Wickham."

Fitzwilliam lifted an eyebrow. "Yet how often have you thought of him since meeting Miss Elizabeth, Darcy? I'm certainly not saying he should not be caught, and he'll be lucky to live long enough to see the gallows when he has been."

"Then what *are* you saying, Theodore?" Darcy snapped.

"I'm saying that perhaps there are other things that are equally as important as justice," his cousin replied. "Like happiness."

"I could not pursue her even if I wanted to!" Darcy protested. "Her father is a gentleman, yes, but who is her mother? What are her family connections?"

"Um…" Bingley uttered, then cleared his throat when the two turned their eyes to him. "I, er, I asked Miss Jane Bennet about her family, and she was surprisingly candid. Her father's fortune is about two thousand a year, and they've a cousin who is a clergyman. On her mother's side, one uncle by marriage—a Mr. Phillips—is an attorney here in Meryton. There was another uncle, a Mr. Jennings, who was quite well off indeed, but he died several years ago. Her mother's own brother, a Mr. Gardiner—he is the favorite of Miss Bennet and her sisters—is in trade. He and his family live in London, in Gracechurch Street near Cheapside."

Fitzwilliam's brows rose again. "Did you say Gardiner—as in Mr. Edward Gardiner?"

"Miss Bennet did not give his Christian name, I'm afraid."

"What difference does it make, Theodore? Her family is not of our class—her uncles are an attorney and a tradesman!" said Darcy in exasperation.

"My father was a tradesman, as was his father," Bingley said, and his sharp tone was enough to bring Darcy up short. "Does that mean I and my sisters are beneath your class?"

"Charles, I didn't mean—"

"Didn't mean what, Darcy?" Bingley interrupted. "That my family is better than the Bennets because we have more money? Our fortune was made in trade. We are the *nouveau riche*—barely even considered respectable by your 'circle', and my personal respectability will not be firmly established until I have purchased a profitable estate and begun a family. If you judge a person by their roots, then perhaps I should be standing with the Bennets instead of you."

"Come now, Bingley," said Fitzwilliam. "Let us all take a moment to collect ourselves, eh? I am quite sure Darcy meant no offense."

Bingley scoffed. "Perhaps he did not, but to look down upon the likes of the Bennet family because they have no fortune and a connection to trade would be to look down upon all with such connections, including me. Their having little money does not make them inferior to us. In fact, if I read Miss Bennet's unspoken words correctly, it makes them more appreciative of what they *do* have."

Darcy drew a breath. "When you put it in those terms, Bingley, I see that I must admit you are correct. Miss Bennet and Miss Elizabeth, and Miss Mary as well, all seem to be perfectly respectable young ladies. But even were I able to disregard their lack of connections, not to mention my own obligations to family and station, I could not simply disregard their immediate relations. Surely you have not been blind to the almost wild behavior of the two youngest girls in the mere hour or so we have been here, or the obvious regard Mrs. Bennet has for our pocketbooks."

"Darcy, every mother of single daughters in this room has an obvious regard for your pocketbooks," Fitzwilliam pointed out. "Mrs. Bennet is hardly an exception. And it is not as if we three do not have relations of our own by whom we are embarrassed on a regular basis. Do you not recall our conversation about this very subject with the Brandons back in March?"

Darcy did recall. He sighed heavily and drew a hand down his face, then looked at his cousin then and asked, "Why did you wish to know about Mr. Gardiner?"

"Well, the Mr. Gardiner I was thinking of owns a number of warehouses in London, as well as a small fleet of ships, as he owns an import business—one that does *very* well, apparently. Textiles are a large part of Mr. Gardiner's stock and he recently got in several bolts of a fabric called sarsnet. It changes color as it moves, as I was told, and both Mother and Marianne are over the moon for it."

"Where did you hear all this?" Bingley asked.

Fitzwilliam looked to him. "Philip mentioned it in the last letter I received from him," he said. "He also said that for a tradesman, Mr. Gardiner is extraordinarily learned and genteel, and that Mrs. Gardiner—whom they met when they visited the warehouse on recommendation of Lady Markham—was as fine a lady as he'd ever met. In fact, he went so far as to say she was a better *lady* than some of the *ton*, her manners much more kind and welcoming. Oh! And apparently Mrs. Gardiner is not altogether unfamiliar with your family, Darcy—she was reared in Lambton. Philip said she spoke of it to Mother and Marianne, and that she had only kind things to say of your father's generosity to the people of the village."

Darcy was rather stunned by the revelation. His cousin the viscount and his wife—as well as his aunt, the Countess of Disley—had visited a warehouse in Cheapside! More than that, they had got on quite well, it would seem, with the owner of the warehouse and his wife, the latter of whom had heard of his own family. If this Mr. Gardiner was indeed a relation of Elizabeth's, and his aunt found him amiable, could it mean that she would approve of Elizabeth?

His sudden hope was quickly dashed when he considered that just because his aunt and cousins had found the Gardiners to be agreeable people, did not mean they would approve of their becoming family through marriage to the gentleman's niece.

"Oh, this is hopeless," he said with a soft moan and dropped his chin to his chest.

Fitzwilliam clapped him on the shoulder. "I wouldn't say hopeless, Darce. Mucked up a bit, I'll grant you that, but not hopeless. First order of business is to find your lady and make things right by offering an apology."

Darcy looked to him with a frown. "She's not 'my' lady, Theo. You really should not say such things in our present company. If Miss Elizabeth overheard me making a sarcastic comment, any one of these people could hear you call her that, and then what a mess I'll be in!"

His cousin grinned. "There's already been an improvement in circumstances—you didn't call me Theodore. 'Tis usually how I know you're cross."

"Don't make me call you something worse," Darcy warned.

"What could be worse than addressing him by his full name?" asked Bingley.

Darcy quirked an eyebrow. "Just ask him what Lady Disley calls him when *she* gets cross because he still hasn't found a wife."

At this Fitzwilliam groaned. "Which is every bloody time I'm at the Court," he mumbled.

Ignoring his cousin's grousing, Darcy drew another deep breath and squared his shoulders. Turning back around to face the ballroom, he said, "I must go and find Miss Elizabeth. If nothing else, I do owe the lady an apology."

Strolling around a room full of strangers and appearing casual whilst doing so did not come easily to Darcy, especially as he was attempting to conceal his desire to locate one particular person amongst them—and avoid another; he'd narrowly missed being blindsided by Caroline Bingley. Elizabeth was proving an elusive creature, as was her friend Miss Lucas. In fact, he could not seem to find the eldest Miss Bennet either, or Miss Mary—though Miss Catherine and Miss Lydia could hardly be missed, the way they carried on. Oh, what joy he would take in suggesting the two of them be sent away to a proper finishing school, seeing as it was clear that neither of the Bennet parents could be bothered to take them in hand.

That is, if he could ever locate their sister, make his apologies, and then determine whether or not courting her was worth the risk of…well, everything.

He'd been about his search going on half an hour and was on the verge of giving up when the sound of Mrs. Bennet's voice carried to him over the din of music, dancing, and conversation. He knew he was going to have to choke on his pride and speak to the woman directly if he had any hope of speaking to Elizabeth before the ball was over.

"…an absolutely insufferable man!" he heard Mrs. Bennet say to her companions as he slowly approached her from behind. "I still cannot believe what he said about my Lizzy! Oh, how I wish Mr. Bennet were here to give him one of his set-downs—I daresay the proud and conceited *Mr. Darcy* would not feel he is so high above us then!"

"If what Lizzy said is true, he is indeed much less handsome now than he was before," said the lady to Mrs. Bennet's left.

"Oh, my sister Phillips… Such hopes I had, for he has ten thousand a year! But I would not marry Jane to such a disagreeable man for all his wealth—not even a shilling of it! Lizzy is not usually so easily wounded, as you know, but one can hardly blame her the headache caused by such an insult. So kind of my dear brother to allow the use of his carriage, that she could go home early and lie down."

Darcy froze at hearing such remarks about himself; for a moment he was very much affronted by the audacity of her words—until he realized that he had behaved no better by joking that Elizabeth was not handsome enough for him, and therefore deserved the lady's censure. Normally, he would have brushed it off and not cared that a country nobody such as Mrs. Bennet thought him insufferable, as he had never given credence to what anyone below his station thought of him.

But he did, it seemed, care what Elizabeth thought, and she as just as below him as her mother.

Feeling doubly disgusted with himself, he turned away so quickly that he nearly knocked his cousin to the ground.

"Forgive me, Theo," he said with a stiff nod.

"'Tis nothing," said Fitzwilliam, and then, "Darce, I've just come to tell you that I managed to get Miss Lucas to hear me out. I explained what happened; that it was but a joke you said and that you only did so knowing that Bingley and I would understand you meant nothing by it—as we are familiar with your particular brand of sarcasm—*and* that obviously Miss Elizabeth was never meant to hear you say those words."

"And what was her reply?" Darcy asked.

Fitzwilliam sighed. "She is both pleased and cross with you; pleased that you do not, in fact, find her friend merely tolerable, but cross because—and I quote—'No gentleman should say such things about a lady, even in jest'."

Darcy inclined his head. "Miss Lucas is right, I should never have spoke those words."

"She also imparted that she is pleased you mean to offer an apology and says she will forgive you fully when Miss Elizabeth does," Fitzwilliam went on. "However, you won't be able to do it tonight, as she has parted with her sister Miss Mary, having complained of a sudden headache."

"Yes, I know—I've just overheard Mrs. Bennet speaking of it, after thoroughly disparaging me to another lady." He allowed himself to groan. "No doubt by evening tomorrow it will be all over the village that I insulted Elizabeth."

Fitzwilliam's eyebrow winged up in that annoying way he had when he'd picked up on something to tease him about. "Elizabeth, is it now? Are you sure you've not formed an attachment?"

"Theodore, I barely know her," Darcy pressed.

"And we're back to Theodore…" Fitzwilliam groused. "Listen, Will—please, just listen to your older and wiser and clearly far more observant cousin… You *like* her. You'd not have been so preoccupied with thoughts of the girl these last two weeks if you did not, nor would you be in such a state as you are now over a misunderstood jest. You want to apologize to Miss Elizabeth not only because it is the gentlemanly thing to do, but because you truly desire her forgiveness. You want her to like you back and I daresay she does, or she'd have brushed off your words and laughed about the whole affair with her friends instead of being hurt by them."

"Well, there's nothing to be done about it now," said Darcy then. "Frankly, I'm no longer in a mood to remain, and I believe there's still yet two more hours to this event."

"Should I go and pry Bingley from the dance floor then, tell him we're leaving?" Fitzwilliam asked, turning toward where their friend was again happily engaged in a dance, this time with a girl Darcy did not recognize. He sometimes envied the younger man's cheerful mien and ability to brush off melancholy.

"Wait until this dance is finished, then tell him I require the use of his carriage," he replied. "He can either return to Netherfield with us, or remain and depart with his sisters and Hurst."

Minutes later, when the dancing had ended for the fourth round, Fitzwilliam quickly moved to Bingley's side and spoke close to his ear. Bingley glanced up in Darcy's direction, looked back to Fitzwilliam and nodded, and then his cousin returned.

"We are sprung, Darcy," he said. "Bingley says he will remain and take Hurst's carriage—he's having too much fun getting to know the local girls, either to stay mad at you or to leave."

"Why does that not surprise me?" countered Darcy as he and Fitzwilliam made for the exit.

"Because you know Bingley too well—were he not so quick to forgive or have a good time, he wouldn't be himself, and then we'd have *him* to worry about as well as you."

Darcy fought the urge to roll his eyes, and he breathed only marginally deeper as he and Fitzwilliam made their way out onto the street. The Bingley carriage was quickly brought around and in moments they were at last away from the scene of misfortune.

The start of the ride was blessedly silent, but after a time Fitzwilliam interrupted the quiet by giving his opinion that the conversation he'd had with Elizabeth and the one Bingley'd had with her elder sister had each had the same purpose. When Darcy asked him to clarify, he explained that as both had been rather more forthcoming than each was like to normally be, he'd come to the realization that *they* were being tested.

"Tested? For what purpose?" Darcy asked.

"Why else, Will, but to gauge mine, or yours, or Bingley's likelihood of being put off by their frankness or circumstances, should any of us be inclined to courtship?" Fitzwilliam replied. "I think, perhaps, they were in their own delicate way letting us know exactly what we'd be getting into."

Darcy made no reply, but could feel his cousin's eyes boring into him from across the carriage. "What?" he asked tersely.

"Does it truly matter to you, Miss Elizabeth's circumstances?" Fitzwilliam queried. "I mean, so what if one uncle is a country solicitor and the other a tradesman?"

"How can you ask me such a question, Theo?" Darcy parried. "You know well the circles we move in— "

"Which I believe your Miss Elizabeth could handle remarkably well."

"They would not accept her! For goodness' sake, they barely tolerate the Bingleys, and then only because of their association with me!" he cried. "Can you imagine what the harpies of the *ton* would do to someone like Elizabeth, whose birth as a gentleman's daughter ranks her higher than Bingley by society's standards, but whose lack of fortune makes her inferior even to the son of a tradesman?"

Fitzwilliam laughed. "Will, they wouldn't dare speak against her if she were your wife," he said, "as they wouldn't want to incur *your* wrath. If they did, I daresay she would take it all with a stiff upper lip and a spine of steel."

Darcy snorted. "If she were that unshakeable, then why did she flee the assembly?"

"Because the man she was beginning to like said she wasn't handsome enough to tempt him," his cousin pointed out. "Even a saucy lady like her has feelings that can be hurt, Darcy—would you want to remain in the same room as someone who'd just insulted you?"

For a moment neither spoke, then Darcy said, "All right, suppose that I *did* find Miss Elizabeth agreeable enough to pursue regardless of what the *ton* would have to say about her situation. I cannot do the same in regard to our family and you know it."

"Darcy, you *do* recall my saying Mother got on with her uncle in Cheapside, do you not?"

"Just because the countess liked the man does not mean she would accept him as family," Darcy retorted.

"You won't know until you ask her, though given I know my mother far better than you do, I think I can safely say she'd accept the Gardiners, and she would adore Elizabeth," Fitzwilliam countered. "Marianne would also—and if Mother and Marianne find her agreeable, surely Father and Philip will as well; I know I already do. She's not afraid to be completely honest, which I like very much."

"I admire her wit," Darcy confessed softly. "She made me laugh, and you well know why I've not had much reason to do that of late."

"Speaking of that reason," his cousin continued, "I think someone like Elizabeth would do wonders for Georgiana. Her manner might shock your sister at first, but someone not afraid to openly tease you might help your sister climb out of the shell she's been hiding in since she was hurt."

Anything that helped Georgiana could be nothing but agreeable.

Sometimes he despised Fitzwilliam's being so often right, Darcy thought, and told him so.

"Sometimes *I* hate being right all the time," Fitzwilliam rejoined with a laugh.

"I believe the words I used were 'so often'," said Darcy then. "Besides, even if your parents, brother, and sister were to find Elizabeth and her family agreeable, you are forgetting one very *dis*agreeable factor in our own familial equation: Aunt Catherine."

Fitzwilliam snorted. "If you refer to that preposterous fantasy of hers that you will marry Anne… I declare, Darcy, I don't know why Father never sought guardianship of our cousin after Uncle Lewis passed—Aunt Catherine's so changed since she lost him. I truly believe Anne's constitution would be vastly improved if her mother didn't keep her locked up at Rosings all the time."

"In that, if nothing else, we are in agreement," Darcy conceded.

Moments later the carriage pulled up to the steps of Netherfield. Darcy quickly stepped out onto the gravel drive and Fitzwilliam followed, and no other words were spoken until they were inside the great house and standing outside Darcy's chambers.

"Listen, Will…" Fitzwilliam began, "I by no means desire to pressure you into a courtship you truly do not want. If Miss Elizabeth's situation in life really is such that you cannot overcome your feelings about it, then by all means, make your apologies and be done with her. I'll see to the arrangements for us to leave Netherfield in a day or two so you won't have to see the lady—you've given Bingley enough education about operating an estate, I think, for him to have a handle on it by now, and if not he can write with any questions.

"If, on the other hand, you decide that every mark against her means nothing—that the fact you enjoy each other's company is all that truly matters—then you will have my full support of your suit. I was not blind to the way she smiled at you, Darce, nor the way you smiled at her. I truly believe there could be something between you, as you've lit up like that for no lady since your own dear mother left us. But you'll never know unless you give it a try."

Fitzwilliam fell silent and heaved a sigh. He then dipped his head and turned toward his own rooms, and when he had opened his door, he said, "Just think about it, cousin. Sleep on it tonight and we'll talk again in the morning, if you like. Good night, Will."

Darcy nodded. "Good night, Theo."

Chapter Five

Mary was blissfully silent the whole of the ride to Longbourn, and broke the quiet only to thank their uncle's coachmen when they had been handed out of the carriage.

Elizabeth was quick to make her way into the house. She hoped fervently that their arrival would go unnoticed by their father, who had chosen not to attend tonight's assembly for the opportunity to have a few hours' peace and quiet in a house that near never was. She wished now that she had stayed home with him, curled up in the corner of his study in what had long been designated her chair, enjoying her own book as well as the silence.

Her wish was not to be granted. She was halfway up the stairs and Mary had just shut the front door when Elizabeth heard her father call out from his study, "Home early, Mrs. Bennet? It is unlike you to leave an assembly before it is ended."

"It is only Lizzy and I, Papa," Mary answered. A look over her shoulder showed Elizabeth that her sister had moved over to the study door. She opened it a fraction and ducked her head inside, then said, "My sister has developed a headache, and Uncle Phillips was kind enough to lend his carriage that she could come home to rest, so Mamma and our sisters might remain to enjoy the rest of the ball. Not wishing her to travel alone, I elected to return with her."

"Need I send for Mr. Jones?" her father asked. Elizabeth was touched to hear a note of concern in his voice.

"Oh no, Papa," her sister replied. "It is only a headache, I am sure. Lizzy just needs a good night's rest, I think."

"Very well, then. You'll come to me if her condition becomes more than a headache, won't you Mary?"

"Of course, Father. Good night, sir."

As soon as her sister had closed the door to their father's study, Elizabeth resumed her climb and was soon in her bedchamber. She hastily removed her slippers and stockings, then her Spencer, and placed her shoes by the door and piled the garments in the chair at her dressing table. She sat then at the end of her bed and reached back as well as she was able to begin undoing the ties of her dress.

A soft knock sounded at the door, and then Mary poked her head in. "Lizzy, would you like some help?" she asked softly.

Elizabeth stared for a moment, contemplating whether she wished for company, and then nodded mutely—her dress would be easier to remove if someone else undid the strings. Mary slipped inside and crossed the room, and Elizabeth turned her back to her sister.

She was thankful that a fire already burned in the hearth, low but still crackling. It covered up the sniffle that escaped her unbidden. If Mary heard it she did not say, but when Elizabeth reached up to wipe the tear that followed, a hand came to rest gently on her shoulder.

"I don't know why I am so upset," Elizabeth muttered. "He is a thoroughly disagreeable man."

"He was not so disagreeable when you danced with him," Mary observed.

Elizabeth loosed an unladylike snort. "I have come to believe that he only asked me to dance because he was pressed into it by his cousin or his friend. His conversation was only given so as to maintain the politeness that is required when one is out in society, even society that is beneath one's standards."

"I cannot speak of Mr. Darcy because I did not engage with him, but I do not think it beyond my scope to say that what you say is certainly true of Mr. Bingley's sisters, of that I am certain," said Mary.

A look over her shoulder showed an expression of disgust on Mary's countenance. "You noticed their manner as well, did you?"

Mary nodded. "Indeed. Though their gowns were fine and fashionable, their manners most certainly were not. Oh, they were all politeness, to be sure, but there was something in their posture and their tone when speaking that said to me they found their present company a punishment to endure."

"I sensed the same—I say, Mary, you are becoming a finer judge of character by the day," said Elizabeth. "Your observational skills are vastly improved."

Mary shook her head and went back to loosening the dress ties. "Do not think I am not *observant*, sister, of what you are attempting to do."

"And what is that, pray tell?"

"Divert me from the main subject, which is Mr. Darcy."

Elizabeth snorted again. "If so, it is only because I no longer wish to think of him. Odious man! To be so kind and genteel one moment, and so vile the next... Whatever was I thinking?"

Mary pulled at her shoulder until they were facing one another. "Elizabeth, I daresay you were thinking that you liked him—or were beginning to. Mr. Darcy was every moment from our first meeting a gentleman. You found his conversation during your dance diverting enough to laugh with him. In truth, he is the only man I have ever seen you interact with in so open a manner as you did with him. It is no wonder, then, that the insult you overheard shocked and injured you so."

Elizabeth shifted her gaze to the fire. "I suppose you are right, especially since..."

"Since what?" Mary asked.

"Since the assembly tonight is not the first time I met Mr. Darcy," she replied with a sigh, and then described her first meeting with him.

"Perhaps you and Charlotte are right and I was beginning to find him very agreeable, but it is no matter. He has made his true feelings abundantly clear. And as neither Colonel Fitzwilliam nor Mr. Bingley showed any particular interest in any of us, I think it likely we shall see very little of the whole party."

Looking to Mary again, Elizabeth forced a smile. "Do not worry for me, sister, I shall be fine. By tomorrow morning, I will be over the whole affair and back to my usual good-natured impertinence. There is naught that any man can say which would bother me for long."

Mary did not seem entirely convinced, but she nodded acquiescence and rose to depart. At the door she paused and bid her good night, and after returning the words, Elizabeth found herself alone at last. She stood and finished dressing for bed in a deliberate manner, as her thoughts tumbled over each other in rapid succession.

She had been forced to admit that she *had* begun to like Mr. Darcy, but what of it? It explained not one jot why his gibe had so wounded her. Usually she had a much thicker skin, and insults—whether said in jest or meant to harm—were easily dismissed as meaningless to her. She just did not understand the power that Mr.

Darcy, whom she knew so little, inexplicably wielded over her feelings.

Frustrated with not understanding her own heart, Elizabeth climbed into her bed and pulled the coverlet over herself with an angry jerk. *Blast that insufferable Mr. Darcy!* she thought, as annoyance crept into her mind and blessedly began to smother the hurt. Her whole evening had been ruined because of him! Elizabeth rather enjoyed the monthly assemblies in Meryton, more for the chance to visit with her neighbors and friends than the dancing—though she certainly enjoyed taking a few turns around the dance floor if there were enough partners to be had.

Thus, taking her leave early—even for the very logical reason of a headache—led to her now feeling quite put out. Even in the absence of a gentleman to dance with, she could have spent the last of the hours in enjoyable conversation with Charlotte or any other of her friends in the village.

In such a state as she was, Elizabeth knew with dreaded certainty that sleep would be a long time in coming.

Although she fell asleep late, it was still fairly early when Elizabeth woke the next morning. A peek out her window showed that the sun had not long crested the horizon, for there were wisps of fog still low to the ground here and there. It had also rained in the night, and she contemplated whether she ought to take her morning walk. A dirty petticoat would mean little to her, but it would give the maids extra work and her mother something to complain about—and she could do without being forced to endure a lecture on how hard it was to clean the linen.

It then occurred to her that she knew not precisely when her mother and sisters had returned home, and it was not uncommon at all for Mrs. Bennet to keep to her rooms the whole of the day after a ball with complaints of exhaustion.

So it was that Elizabeth dressed quickly in a simple walking gown after combing through her hair and pinning it at her nape, then donned her half boots and headed for the stairs. She pulled a bonnet and pelisse out of the cupboard and was outside in moments, and glad she was for choosing to go out as the crisp, clean air suffused her being with delight on every breath she drew.

It was some time before she took note of the direction of her rambling, and she paused when it occurred to her she was going towards Oakham Mount. That then brought to mind the man she had met there, whom she had liked so well that day and could now only think of with loathing. As she had not seen him there in the times she had gone since that first meeting, Elizabeth reasoned that in all likelihood she would not find him there again—truly, what were the chances?

Still, she turned herself away from the overlook and in the direction of Meryton. Few shops would open so early of a morning, save perhaps the butcher and baker, but it was just as well as she'd brought no money with her. That did not mean she could not stop in and greet the shopkeepers.

By the time she reached the village, the sky had begun to darken again. Elizabeth saw that there were few signs of life on the main street, which she supposed was to be expected when half or more of the town had been at the assembly last night.

As she walked, the view from Oakham Mount came to mind once more, and as it was one of her favorite things to see in the whole of the country, she determined to go there in spite of the miniscule risk that Mr. Darcy might go there again. It would please her a great deal to look upon the valley below even with rain threatening to fall again. A glance up at the clouds gave rise to the hope that she would be able to reach the mount and enjoy the view from the outlook for more than a few minutes, as well as be on her way home again before the rain came down upon her.

When at last Elizabeth reached her destination, she was pleased to find nobody else there. She stepped as close to the edge as she dared and drew as deep a breath as her lungs could hold, and released it slowly as she gazed upon the fields and woods so far beneath her feet. As tended to happen when she went there, she paid little heed to the passing of time, and it was only when thunder rumbled over her head that she gave a thought to making her way back home once more.

Elizabeth turned around and gasped in surprise, as coming toward her from the direction of Netherfield was none other than Mr. Darcy! Ignoring the flutter in her heart at the sight of his handsome face and admirable riding form, she swallowed hard and fought to regain her composure. Thunder rolled again, reminding her that time was growing rapidly short before the weather turned.

What was the fool man thinking anyway, going out for a ride in such conditions? she wondered. Surely one such as he knew how to gauge the weather!

The moment he took notice of her, he urged his horse into a

canter. Not wishing to speak to the him, she bobbed a curtsey and started away.

"Miss Elizabeth, please wait!" he called out.

"I think not, Mr. Darcy!" she yelled back without turning to face him. "The weather will turn at any moment, and if I've any hope of reaching Longbourn before the clouds burst, I must go at once—or are you deaf to the thunder rolling over our heads?"

"Indeed, I have heard it," said Darcy as horse and rider drew up on her left. "And as the rain is sure to come in but moments, from what I have observed, I beg you would allow me to offer the services of my horse."

"No thank you, I shall walk."

The horse stopped and she heard him climb down; Elizabeth kept on, determined to put distance between them. Of course, Mr. Darcy was by her side again shortly.

"Madam, I understand that you are angry with me and rightly so, but do not let that anger make you too stubborn to listen to reason," said he. "You are as sure to get caught in the rain as I. Allow me to set you in Diamond's saddle—"

Elizabeth scoffed. "You named a horse whose hide is black as night Diamond? Whatever possessed you to do such a thing?"

"He is called Diamond because he is as beautiful as that gem; diamonds are found in coal mines, and coal is black," he replied. "Naming him thus was my sister's idea, and that was her reasoning."

She could not argue with Miss Darcy's logic. Perturbed by this, Elizabeth pursed her lips and chose not to respond, and hoped that he would take the hint and leave her alone.

Mr. Darcy did not. Instead he stepped in front of her with his horse and blocked the path just as the rain began to drizzle on their heads. "Miss Elizabeth, please be reasonable—you shall be wet through in minutes. Allow me to take you to Netherfield, which is less than a mile away."

"And in the exact opposite direction than that which I wish to go," she argued.

He drew a breath to counter her logic, but they were both of them startled by a deafening crack. Diamond neighed and Elizabeth cried out fearfully, nearly jumping out of her skin as she looked to see that a tree not thirty feet from where they stood had split; lightning had struck it and the wood was now smoking. Small flames licked at the tinder from inside the crack.

"Elizabeth, let me take you back to Netherfield, I beg you," she heard Mr. Darcy say, and it was only in that moment that she realized he had drawn her to him in a protective embrace.

"I'm not a very good rider," she muttered. In fact, she did not ride at all—had not since childhood due to lingering fear caused by a bad fall.

He patted her shoulders and took a step back; Elizabeth took a breath, not liking that she felt both relieved and bereft to no longer have his arms around her.

"Do not worry yourself over that—you need only sit and relax, for I will guide Diamond from the ground," Darcy told her.

Elizabeth realized then that she had lost the desire to fight and wanted only to be safely inside somewhere—anywhere—and away from the lightning. With a resigned sigh she nodded her head, and Darcy turned the horse so that his left side was facing them. She stepped over and took a firm hold of the pommel and seat, but because of the cut of her dress she could not lift her foot into the stirrup.

"Allow me," Darcy said, his voice and breath so close to her ear that she knew the shiver snaking its way down her spine was not from the chill of the rain. He placed his hands about her waist and lifted her as though she weighed only a trifle, and in a moment she was seated as comfortably as could be on a saddle not meant to be sat on sideways. Oh, this was too high! Why had she let him lift her to the saddle? She must get down!

Instead of slipping off again, her hands wrapped around the pommel tightly and she squeezed her eyes shut, worrying her bottom lip between her teeth as Darcy pulled the reins over Diamond's head and started off.

The light drizzle became a downpour within a few minutes of their departure, soon proving that upon them was only the beginning of a nasty storm. Elizabeth tried not to jump or cry out whenever the thunder was loud or lightning flashed overhead but it was difficult to remain still and quiet as the horrible weather grew in intensity (though at least it kept her from dwelling on the fact that she was on horseback for the first time in many years). Earlier she had disparaged Mr. Darcy in her mind for going out, and was chagrined by the truth that she'd been just as foolish as he.

"Are you well, Miss Bennet?" Darcy said, looking back over his shoulder.

By now her teeth were on the verge of chattering, so Elizabeth gave only a nod in reply. The gentleman must have noticed that she wasn't being entirely truthful, for he urged the horse into a faster walk. It seemed her very bones could feel the chill by the time the party of three reached the park.

A groom came immediately out from under a small shelter at the side of the drive to take the horse as Darcy was helping Elizabeth down. He kept an arm about her shoulders as he guided her up the steps and through the front door.

Mr. Bingley stepped into the large foyer at that very moment and rushed over to them, calling out the name of a lady whom Elizabeth assumed was the housekeeper.

"Darcy! Good heavens, man—what happened?" he said next.

"As you can see, Bingley, Miss Elizabeth and I were caught in the rain," Darcy replied in a droll tone.

"I… I beg your… your p-pardon, sir, t-to call up-pon you unannounced," Elizabeth managed.

A woman who appeared close in age to her mother came into the entryway then, and she cried out softly as soon as she saw Elizabeth. "Oh, my dear child! We must get you out of those garments before you catch your death!"

"Right so, Mrs. Hubbard," said Bingley. "Do see to it that a warm bath is prepared in our finest guest suite for the lady, and locate her something dry and comfortable to wear."

"M-Mr. Bingley, I beg you, do n-not trouble your staff so," Elizabeth stuttered with a shake of her head.

Mrs. Hubbard *tsked* as she wrapped an arm around her shoulders in much the same manner as Mr. Darcy had. "Nonsense, my dear, 'tis no trouble at all! Come now, let us get you dry."

Elizabeth only nodded, and allowed herself to be led away.

Darcy gave a brief explanation to Bingley regarding the exact circumstances of Elizabeth's being there at Netherfield as he divested himself of his soaked hat and coat.

"So you didn't even get a chance to speak with her about last night?" Bingley asked as the two started up the stairs to the first floor.

"Only insofar as to tell her she had a right to be angry with me," Darcy replied. "The storm came upon us quite suddenly."

"A bit foolish of you—both of you, really—was it not, to go out knowing that rain was coming?"

"Perhaps," Darcy conceded as he tugged on the knot of his cravat. "But I could not resist the urge to go out. I had hoped I might meet her again at the outlook."

"At least the effort was not entirely wasted, though poor Miss Elizabeth looked quite frightful," Bingley mused. "I do hope she does not become unwell."

Fitzwilliam was exiting his bedchamber at that moment, and with a raised eyebrow said, "Darcy, why do you look as if you stepped into a pond with all your clothes on—you've not been out in this ghastly weather, have you?"

Darcy sighed as he stopped before his own door. "Charles, will you explain? I'd like to get out of these wet clothes. And see to it that a note is delivered to Longbourn—inform Mr. Bennet that his daughter is safe and being tended to. The family will worry if they wake to find her gone from the house, if they have not done so already."

"Capital idea, Darcy, I'll do that straight away," Bingley agreed, then gestured to Fitzwilliam. "Come to my room, Theo, so I can write the note. I'll explain what I know."

A mixture of curiosity and bewilderment crossed Fitzwilliam's face as he turned and followed Bingley down the hall. Darcy turned into his own room, where his waiting valet expressed his own feelings as to the state of his master's dress with only a raised eyebrow. He then helped him out of his drenched garments and asked if he wished a bath to warm up. Darcy told him no, just to build up the fire; Vincent nodded and saw him into dry clothing and his flannel banyan before stoking the fire and departing with the wet clothes to have them laundered.

Once his hair had been combed through, Darcy sat in the armchair nearest the fire to draw some of its warmth into himself. He could not stay still for long and soon rose to pace. Elizabeth was at the fore of his thoughts; he wondered how she was getting on.

Obstinate, headstrong girl, he thought. Whatever possessed her to go out with the promise of rain in the sky?

Not likely to be the same reason as his own sojourn, he supposed. She liked a good walk, she had told him, and had probably hoped to be back home again long before the rain started. Indeed, so had he—in truth, he had not expected the deluge so soon as it had fallen. They were neither of them infallible in that regard.

A knock sounded at the door and he turned to Bingley and Fitzwilliam coming in. "Have you had word from Mrs. Hubbard?"

he asked.

"No, but in the hall we met one of the maids—I shall send her to Mrs. Hubbard to get word on Miss Elizabeth," Bingley said, and stepped back out.

For a moment Fitzwilliam only looked at him, then his cousin laughed. Darcy frowned. "Don't look at me like that, old boy," said Theodore. "'Tis not my fault you have the absolute worst timing."

Darcy shook his head and gave a mirthless laugh. He moved back to his chair by the fire and sat in it heavily, and as Fitzwilliam took the other chair, Bingley returned and said that Letitia had been sent to Elizabeth's room for an update on her condition. He then sat on the end of the bed and asked, "I must ask, Darcy... Why did you bring her here instead of taking her home?"

"Because Netherfield was closer than Longbourn; Oakham Mount is just under a mile's distance from here," he replied. "At first she refused to let me escort her anywhere, her upset from last night surely clouding her judgment. The weather was already turning, and I pleaded with her to let me aid her to safe shelter. 'Twas not until lightning struck a tree near us that she accepted my offer."

He looked over at his friend then. "Did you send a note to her father?"

"Of course. I sent it off with a footman before we came to see you," Bingley replied.

"What are you going to do about clothing for her? She obviously cannot be left in her own morning dress, and a maid's gown would be inappropriate for her station."

Bingley shrugged. "What else can I do but ask one of my sisters to lend her a gown? Only I shall have to wait until they are awake, as you know Caroline and Louisa—they'll not leave their rooms until breakfast is ready to be served."

"Speaking of, Bingley," put in Fitzwilliam, "could you have the cook send up some pastries or fruit and coffee for us? Will could use the sustenance, I'm sure, and the coffee will help warm him."

There was a second knock at the door then. Darcy bid the visitor enter; it was a young maid who bobbed immediately into a deep curtsey.

"Begging your pardon, sirs. Mrs. Hubbard bid me inform you that Miss Bennet is wrapped up tight in some warm blankets while water is being heated that she may have a bath. She has also bid me ask you, with pardon begged, if I may fetch a proper gown from the wardrobe of either Miss Bingley or Mrs. Hurst for the lady."

Bingley grimaced, obviously disturbed at the thought of looting one of his sisters' closets without their consent. "Bingley, I do not think it would hurt, if the girl can be quiet about it," said Fitzwilliam. "Miss Bennet is sure to be finished with her hot bath before either of your sisters rise, given what you've just told us. Let us preserve the poor girl's dignity as best we can. If you're truly worried about taking anything that would upset them, just have the maid fetch a night dress—I daresay all she'll want after this morning's outing and a hot bath is a decent rest."

"And have the kitchen prepare something gentle for her stomach, some broth and bread, in case she feels up to eating," added Darcy.

Bingley pondered their suggestions for a moment and then nodded. "Very well. Letitia, you've my permission to enter Caroline's room for a night dress—do your best to be as quiet as a church mouse, please, as there's none here who will want to hear her should you be discovered rifling through her wardrobe. When she wakes I'll tell her myself about the borrowed item. And please, do as Mr. Darcy suggests once you've taken the garment to Mrs. Hubbard. We would also like a pot of coffee and a platter of light refreshments prepared for the three of us. Have that delivered to my study, we shall be down there in a few moments."

"Yes, Mr. Bingley," the girl acknowledged, then dipped into a curtsey and departed.

"I'd rather stay here," Darcy said when she had gone.

"Darce, there's nothing you can do for Miss Bennet at the moment that you have not already done," Fitzwilliam pointed out. "Mrs. Hubbard has her well in hand, and the best you can do now is tend to yourself. It would not do for *you* to become ill."

Darcy groaned and drew a hand down his face. "I so hate when you are right, Theodore," he groused.

Fitzwilliam grinned. "I know. It happens *so often*, does it not?"

Shooting a scowl in his cousin's direction, Darcy said nothing as he stood and doffed the banyan. Fetching a waistcoat and jacket, he followed the other two men down into the study, where Fitzwilliam directed him to sit himself by the fire. "I would never hear the end of it from Mother if I allowed you to neglect yourself, Darcy," he said as he lowered himself once more to sit in an opposing chair.

Bingley brought the chair from behind his desk and sat it between them, then settled himself in it before asking, "What is your next move, Darcy? In regard to Miss Elizabeth, I mean."

"When she is settled and willing to receive a visitor, I shall go to her and tell her why I rode to Oakham Mount today. I will explain about last night's poor attempt at humor, and then offer my sincerest apologies for wounding her feelings."

"And after that?" Fitzwilliam pressed. "Do you intend to pursue the lady?"

He sighed and glanced toward the fire. "On that matter, I must admit, I still am not certain. I considered all that you said last night, Theo, and have measured it against my own feelings."

"You could not reach any conclusion, then?"

Darcy looked to the cousin that was in many ways to him an older brother. "Not entirely. I cannot help but find it still very difficult to even consider her. Besides her family relations being so beneath my own, there's the fact that we are not well acquainted—"

"Well, that's easily remedied, Darcy—you just have to get to know her!" said Bingley cheerfully.

"I've also my responsibilities to my station and my family to consider, Charles," Darcy returned.

Fitzwilliam snorted derisively. "Oh please, not that rubbish again," he said. "Really, Will, your 'station'? Who bloody cares if society disapproves of your choice—you're always saying you'd be content to stay at Pemberley the whole year 'round if you could."

"You are forgetting that who I marry may affect my sister's prospects," countered Darcy. "I must think of her as well as myself."

Fitzwilliam rolled his eyes. "And I've already told you what I think of the *ton* accepting whomever you choose. If society cannot accept your choice of bride, then perhaps society are the ones whose choices should be questioned. It is not necessary that you marry to improve your standing, or even Georgiana's. Do not let the snobs of London's so-called higher circles dictate who you marry—choose a wife who makes *you* happy, not *them*."

"I wholeheartedly agree, Will," said Bingley. "Though certainly marrying a lady of fortune would improve my own—especially given my family's tenuous standing in society—I would much rather take to wife a woman who truly loves me, and whom I love equally in return."

"And," Fitzwilliam pressed, "if the eligible bachelors in the *ton* choose not to consider your sister because of your wife, then the pigs do not deserve her."

"And what of Aunt Catherine? You know she will brook my marrying none other than Anne," Darcy reminded him.

"Good God, is she still on about that?" said Bingley. "I thought you said it was only a wish of hers and not anything formal, that you'd no desire at all to marry your cousin?"

"I did, it is not, and no, I haven't the faintest wish to be married to Anne," Darcy agreed. "I know it is commonly done, but I cannot reconcile myself with taking to my bed a woman to whom I am so closely related. The thought unnerves me."

He drew a breath then, and conversation was paused as a knock sounded and then a maid came in with a serving cart. Bingley dismissed her saying that they would serve themselves, and only when he'd had a mouthful of strong black coffee did Darcy say, "I am no closer to making a decision about whether to court El—Miss Bennet or not. I think, ultimately, it will depend first and foremost upon her capacity for forgiveness."

"And if she does forgive you?" asked Fitzwilliam over his own coffee cup.

"If she does… I will choose my direction thence."

Chapter Six

It was a little uncomfortable to be tended by a maid not her own, for the housekeeper to not be Hill, but Elizabeth endured it, and prayed each moment that the chill that had crept into her would soon go away.

And really, Mrs. Hubbard had been nothing but kind to her. Her gentle, motherly manner actually reminded Elizabeth a lot of Mrs. Hill, who had been with her family as long as she could remember. Thus, she was able to bear the woman's attentions with relative ease. After helping her undress, Mrs. Hubbard had wrapped the blankets from the bed around her as though she were a caterpillar in a cocoon and directed her to lie down until she could get the bath ready. Having done exactly as she was told, Elizabeth drifted off under a fog of inexplicable exhaustion, and felt as though she'd only just closed her eyes when she was gently shaken awake by a maid.

The girl, Letitia, aided Mrs. Hubbard with getting Elizabeth into the bathtub, and then the housekeeper left them after instructing the maid to help her wash and then don the night dress that had been retrieved for her, and then Miss Bennet was to be put straight back into bed. Elizabeth tried to protest, but she was too weary—that ride through the rain had truly knocked all the fight out of her. *Lord, I pray I'm not catching cold,* she thought as Letitia was helping her with her hair.

When she was settled once more in the large four-poster bed, Elizabeth began to wonder what would happen next. She was a partly-unwilling guest in the same house as the man who had gravely insulted her just the night before. She was at the mercy of her host, who was a friend of Mr. Darcy's—at least until her gown and undergarments were dry—and then she would have to hope that the rain had stopped so that she could make her way home. She did *not* want to have to beg the use of Mr. Bingley's carriage.

Unfortunately, from the sound of things outside the house, she would either have to make use of his carriage, or she would have to impose on Bingley's hospitality and spend the whole day at Netherfield, and possibly the night as well.

Elizabeth dropped her face into her hands and moaned her misery.

A soft knocked sounded at the door, and she drew a breath as she lifted her head to acknowledge the visitor. Letitia came in carrying a serving tray, and when it had been set on the bedside table, she noted a cup of tea, a rye bread roll, and a covered bowl.

"What is this?" she asked.

"Mr. Darcy requested Cook prepare you something light in case you were feeling ill but wanted to eat, miss," said the maid. "'Tis a bone broth with bits o' ham in it."

"That is…most considerate of Mr. Darcy," Elizabeth mumbled as Letitia handed her the soup. And it was, strangely so, though she supposed that while he may not think her handsome, he must feel some responsibility to see she was cared for while she was with them.

She studied the maid as she uncovered the bowl of broth and slipped a spoon into it, and judged her to be near to her own age. More than that, her features brought to mind a sense of familiarity, as though she had met her before.

"Are you from the north as is Mr. Bingley, Letitia?" Elizabeth asked. "For you seem familiar to me, though I cannot place from where I might have known you."

Letitia smiled. "I were wondering if you would remember me, miss. I'm actually from here in Hertfordshire—born in Meryton I was, as were me younger brothers. My papa worked in the butcher shop, and we met a number of times, you and me. When Papa died we had no way to keep paying our rent, so Mamma took us to live with her sister—that's Mrs. Hubbard, that is. We went north when I were about nine, I think."

"La! I thought we had met before—and you were called Letty back then, were you not?"

The girl smiled. "I was, yes. Aunt Hubbard thought I should be called Letitia when she talked of asking old Mr. Bingley 'bout taking me on, said my full name sounded more respectable like, but to be honest I do miss being called Letty."

Elizabeth offered her a smile. "I rather like Letty myself, so I shall call you that when we are alone, though I do not know how long I shall be here."

Letty glanced toward the window, where rivulets of water cascaded down the pane and thunder still rumbled every few minutes. "I think it may be a while, miss, with how that rain be coming down."

She then said she would come back for the tray in an hour, before dipping into a curtsey and leaving Elizabeth alone.

The broth was very good, but she found she could only take about half of it before she could stand no more. She again hoped she would not develop a cold, and was thankful that the tea was a mint blend—it was kind of the cook to consider other ways to care for a sour stomach besides the broth, and she made a mental note as she sipped to remark on the thoughtfulness of the gesture to Mr. Bingley when she saw him again.

That she would have to speak to Mr. Bingley and thank him for his hospitality did not concern her so much as the likelihood she would also have to see Mr. Darcy again—and thank him as well. Netherfield was indeed closer to Oakham Mount than Longbourn, and his escorting her there instead of seeing her home or allowing her to go on her own was, she reluctantly admitted, a wiser course of action. Though falling ill was only a chance with how quickly she had been tended by Bingley's staff, had she traveled the longer distance to Longbourn, it would surely have been a certainty.

Heavens, how could she do it? How could she express her gratitude to a man she had only that morning sworn to loathe for all eternity for his contemptuous, insulting manner? Elizabeth groaned inwardly as she accepted the truth that she *must* do so whether she wanted to or not, for his discourtesy to her would not excuse any that she shewed to him.

With a sigh, she set her teacup on the tray and slid under the coverlet, pulling it up to her chin as she next considered that her family would be waking about then, if none had already, and that Jane or Mary, possibly both, would have been to her room and found her absent. With how the weather had turned they would become frantic with worry, and feeling suddenly fearful that her relations were needlessly concerned for her, she threw back the cover and moved over to the bell pull to summon a maid. By the time Letty turned up, Elizabeth was pacing in agitation before the fireplace.

"Are you well, miss?" the maid asked.

"I must have writing paper and a pen at once, and I must speak to Mr. Bingley post haste," said Elizabeth. "I must get some note to my family, they will worry for me!"

Letty's eyes widened and she nodded. "Yes, miss. I shall speak to Mrs. Hubbard about getting you those writing things, and I'm sure she will speak to Mr. Bingley for you."

"Please do, Letty. I have been so foolish as to think only of myself."

When the maid had gone again, Elizabeth returned to pacing. The activity stirred her body's natural processes and she stifled a groan as she searched under the bed for the chamber pot. When she finished, she took herself to the wash stand to clean her hands, and she jumped when a knock rattled on the door. It sounded almost hesitant, suggesting to Elizabeth that Mr. Bingley had come straight away.

She was grateful if it was him, but given her state of dress she now had to hurry across the room to dive under the coverlet that she would be respectably able to receive him.

"Come in," she called out she had settled herself with the blanket up under her arms.

It was not Mr. Bingley who entered behind Letty, but Mr. Darcy. Elizabeth flushed and fixed her eyes on the fireplace, and fought to hold an expression of indifference.

"Mr. Darcy," she said simply.

"Miss Bennet," he replied. "I am come to inform you that you need not trouble yourself to write a note to your family. I put that task to Bingley near as soon as Mrs. Hubbard took you away. The footman has not yet returned, but we expect him any moment."

"Oh," she said, her eyes falling to her hands. She'd not considered that the task would already have been seen to. "I... I thank you, Mr. Darcy, for your forethought."

"You need not thank me, madam. As I had taken charge of your welfare, it was therefore my responsibility to ensure your relations did not worry," he replied.

Elizabeth nodded. "Regardless, it is a relief to know that they shall not be concerned."

An awkward silence fell, and she could not help but wish he would just go away.

"Miss Bennet," said Darcy suddenly. "I must speak with you regarding my conduct at last night's assembly, but I would much rather our conversation be private. May I send the maid into the hall?

Certainly the door shall remain open and she will be right outside."

She was not sure she desired to be alone with him even if Letty would still be in shouting distance, but it occurred to her that he might not leave her be until he'd said his piece, and that he would not do unless he was assured of greater privacy. Thus, it was with a reluctant nod that Elizabeth agreed to his request, though she still did not look at him.

Her heart beat twice after Letty had gone through the door before he spoke again. "Miss Bennet, I rode to Oakham Mount this morning in spite of the promise of inclement weather for the express purpose—that is, with the hope—of seeing you there."

A mirthless laugh escaped her. "You went out knowing it would rain hoping I would be just as foolish?"

Beside her Darcy chuckled. "I know, it was not one of my brighter ideas."

"Neither was last night."

"That is precisely that matter I wished to discuss with you. May I sit?"

Elizabeth waved her hand. "I certainly cannot stop you."

A moment later Mr. Darcy stepped into her line of vision, taking one of the two armchairs from before the fire and bringing it nearer to the bed. He set it a few feet from the left side in full view of the partly open door, and when he was seated he drew a breath and sighed.

"I am come to offer my sincerest apologies for my ill-considered words last evening," Darcy said. "I spoke in jest to my friend, and I hope I can assure you that I did not mean them. Bingley and Fitzwilliam were teasing me about you and I wanted them to stop—I knew they would note the sarcasm in my voice and know that I didn't actually mean what I said. I'd not considered that anyone nearby would hear, least of all you."

He pushed to his feet and paced away from her. "The truth is, Miss Bennet, that I can be horrid unpleasant when forced to be among strangers. More often than not, what conversation I do make is construed as proud and conceited, or as snobbish and cruel. As I said to you when we danced, I am ill-qualified to recommend myself to those I don't know. Unfortunately, I have long been bereft of the talent which some possess of conversing easily with persons I have never met before."

Darcy turned back then, and in his countenance Elizabeth was certain that—for the first time since he had entered—she saw only sincerity.

"Normally I dread such gatherings as last evening's assembly. That I was able to so easily converse with you the first time we met was so much a surprise that I found myself looking forward to it with hope that I would see you there," he went on. "I felt some measure of relief that I would know *someone* outside our party, despite the fact I could not claim to know you well."

Elizabeth drew a breath. "I cannot say that I quite understand you, sir," she began. "I am near always at ease in company—even amongst strangers, for my courage always rises at any attempt to intimidate me. Perhaps it is from this refusal to show weakness that I developed the natural impertinence for which I am so often scolded by my mother or cautioned against employing by my sisters and my friend."

"I beg you, do not," said Darcy, his words drawing her eyes to his. Their gazes held and a smile formed on his lips. "What I mean is, in my presence you need never censure yourself—I find your frankness refreshing."

Elizabeth drew a steadying breath—this visit had not at all gone as she had supposed it would. She found herself beginning to feel a little like her old self, and so replied with, "Quite weary are you, Mr. Darcy, of all you meet telling you only what they think you wish to hear?"

He chuckled. "It can be tiresome, yes."

She arched an eyebrow. "Well, I can assure you that will never happen with me. Disguise of every sort is my abhorrence."

Mr. Darcy acknowledged her words with a bow of his head. "As it is mine, Miss Bennet."

"The truth may hurt on occasion," Elizabeth went on, "but I would far rather endure a temporary wounding than the lasting injury of discovering that I had been lied to."

"And…will my unintentional wounding of your feelings be temporary or lasting?"

On seeing a flicker of vulnerability in his countenance, Elizabeth could only imagine what it had taken for a man in his position to ask for forgiveness. Men like him did not seek absolution from those who were below their circle nor did they ever require it, for their positions in society deemed it should be so. That Mr. Darcy had behaved in a more gentlemanlike manner today, had apologized for his inconsiderate words, told her that perhaps he was not so much like the high elite as she had come to assume he was. And if he could bring himself to admit his error and beg her pardon, she could be no less a lady than to bestow it.

"I should very much like it to have been temporary," she at last replied with a smile.

Darcy smiled again in return. "Thank you, Miss Bennet. Something tells me that to have you as a friend is a far better prospect than to make you my enemy."

"Oh, absolutely, Mr. Darcy!" Elizabeth conceded with a saucy air. "Did you never hear that an impertinent woman is the last person you should ever cross?"

He laughed as he moved back to the chair beside the bed. "No, but now I have, and I know it would do well to keep that in mind."

Darcy then returned the chair back to its original place and moved to the door. On turning back to her, he said, "Thank you, Miss Bennet, for your willingness to hear me, and your forgiveness of my error in judgment. I shall endeavor not to repeat it."

"And I shall endeavor not to think the worst of you before hearing an explanation for your behavior," she returned.

With another smile and a bow, Darcy quit the room. Elizabeth dropped her head back, wondering how their relationship had altered so quickly. She was not even sure how to define it now—were they now friends, or had they just mutually decided they did not despise each other?

She then recalled that her family now knew she was at Netherfield, a house in which three potential husbands resided. No doubt her mother, upon learning of her whereabouts, had begun to pray she didn't do anything stupid. Elizabeth was well aware that of Mrs. Bennet's five daughters, she was the one who was least liked. Perhaps she should be bothered by the knowledge, but she never had been, not once realizing that their personalities were too impossibly different to one another. She did not doubt that her mother loved her, and she certainly loved her mother, but loving someone did not mean you had to like them all the time.

And there were definitely times when Elizabeth didn't like her mother very much at all, so she held no grudge for her mother feeling the same about her.

Still, she knew that Mrs. Bennet would want her to take full advantage of her circumstances and do everything within her power to secure one of the single gentlemen, because then she could promote her sisters to the other two. How she would go about doing so, even if she wanted to, would matter not a jot to Mrs. Bennet so long as she returned to Longbourn with an offer of marriage, or at the very least an understanding of courtship. Of course, such a thing could hardly be likely to happen in less than a day of being in each other's company, so some remarkable event would have to take place for a proposal to happen in so short a time. Knowing that Elizabeth would never purposely orchestrate a compromise of her own reputation, it was probable that her mother was also praying she'd fall ill and be required to remain Mr. Bingley's guest for a few days.

She sighed then and wondered what to do with herself. She was wearing a borrowed night dress, had no dressing gown, no slippers… Elizabeth wondered if it would be too much to hope for that either the clothes she'd been wearing would quickly dry or that Mr. Bingley's footman would be sent back with something for her to wear. As soon as she was properly attired, she could beg the use of the Bingley carriage to go home.

The soft clearing of a throat brought Elizabeth sharply back to the present. Letty stood by the table expectantly. "Begging your pardon, miss, but did you want me to take the tray? I see you've not finished, so I thought I would ask."

Elizabeth glanced at the bowl of half-eaten soup. "You may take it. I'm hungry, but I'd rather have a real breakfast," she said, then looked down at herself. "Of course, that's not likely to happen in my present state."

"If I may, miss, Mrs. Hubbard had me ask Mr. Bingley 'bout borrowing a gown from either Mrs. Hurst or Miss Bingley when they come down to breakfast. That be one of Miss Bingley's night dresses you're wearing now."

Elizabeth frowned. She did not much care for the idea of being beholden to the likes of Caroline Bingley. "What about you, or one of the other maids? Have any of you an extra gown I could borrow?"

Letty's eyes widened. "A gentlewoman can't wear no maid's frock, miss."

"Poppycock, I say! Yes, I am a gentleman's daughter, but I am not above borrowing a gown from a maid so long as it is in good condition and fits me well."

"You…you don't care if it's plain? Wouldn't you prefer something finer than plain cotton?"

With a smile, Elizabeth told the girl, "I am sure that Miss Bingley or Mrs. Hurst would have something quite pretty for me to wear for a few hours, but truly, I would not mind at all if it were a simple dress—I have plenty of my own at home. Besides, I suspect it will be another hour or more before either of the ladies rise from their beds, and my own things ought to be dry by then."

She studied the maid, gauging her waist and bust and height, then said. "Actually, Letty, I think you and I are about the same size, though you're a little taller. If you have another gown you'd not mind lending me for a time, I'd be most appreciative. I could at least visit the library instead of being cooped up in here the whole of the morning."

Letty nodded. "I've not many, but I've got more than one—Mr. Bingley pays us more than fair wages. One I even made up a little—nothing fancy, just added a bit of ribbon to it."

"That will do just fine," said Elizabeth. "Now I've a dress sorted, I have only to worry about a pair of stockings and some slippers."

"Well, your own stockings be there by the fire, miss, and your boots. The shoes aren't like to be dry yet, but the stockings should be, so at least you'll have those."

Elizabeth began to nod. "Yes, it will be nice to have something that is my own... With the length of your dress, I may possibly get away with having no slippers to wear. Thank you very much, Letty, for your kindness, though I am sorry to put you to the trouble."

Letty smiled. "Oh, it ain't no trouble at all, miss. I'll go and fetch that dress for you, and see if I can't scare up a few stray hair pins as well."

After she had picked up the tray with the soup and gone, Elizabeth let out a relieved sigh. She understood why the gentlemen hadn't considered asking one of the maids for a gown, but really, it wasn't worth the trouble of asking one of Mr. Bingley's sisters for a dress—it was bad enough she'd been wearing one of Miss Bingley's night dresses for the last hour. While the fabric of the sisters' gowns from the assembly had been fine indeed, they'd also been rather garish. What could have possessed Miss Bingley's *modiste* to think she would look good in orange, of all colors? *Nobody* looked good in orange, one of the few things Elizabeth had agreed with her mother on, which is why Mrs. Bennet had only allowed her and her sisters to use orange in their hat trimmings, and then only sparely. A light shade of orange might do well for a ribbon about the waist for a white dress, or perhaps a pale yellow one, but Elizabeth could think of no other garment for which the color was suitable.

While Letty was gone, she untied the string at the end of the long braid over her shoulder and combed through her hair with her fingers. Leaving it free for the moment, she went over to the fireplace and noted that her stockings had been hung from the mantel and her boots beside the screen, close to the heat of the low blaze—she simply hadn't noticed before with how agitated she had been. The stockings were indeed dry and she had just finished with putting them on when Letty returned.

"I did get a few pins from the girls for your hair, miss, and I've got a chemise and petticoat too," she said as she laid the garments on the bed.

"Thank you, Letty," said Elizabeth as she approached to take a look at the dress. It was, as the maid had informed her, a plain one—the light blue fabric had no embroidery or pattern to it, but there was a white satin ribbon at the waist, and at the cuff of each sleeve Letty had attached a small white bow.

She looked to the maid and smiled. "Did you sew it yourself?"

Letty nodded. "Yes, miss. Took me some days, on account of I had to do it in me off hours, but I think it turned out all right."

Elizabeth took the gown by the shoulders and held it up. "I think you did very well indeed. Will you help me?"

"Oh, of course, miss!" Letty replied, and in just a few minutes, though she was wearing borrowed clothing, Elizabeth began to feel much more like herself—less vulnerable and more confident. Her waist was a fraction smaller than Letty's and she'd brought no stays, so the strings had to be tightened a bit, but it otherwise fit perfectly well. The sleeves were three-quarter length and the hem met the floor, so she would have to take care not to catch it when walking.

When her hair was once more braided and then pinned, she drew a breath and said, "Now that I am properly dressed, I think it time you return this nightdress to Miss Bingley's room, and I should locate Mr. Bingley and thank him for his hospitality."

"The gentlemen were in the study, miss, last I saw of 'em. I can take you there," said Letty.

Again Elizabeth favored the girl with a smile. "Once again I must thank you. You've been incredibly helpful to me, Letty, and I shall be sure to tell Mr. Bingley so."

Letty blushed and looked at her feet. "Oh, you don't have to do anything like that, miss. I'm just doing me job and all."

"Yes, and you are doing it very well," Elizabeth countered. "As such, I think your master should be made aware of your exemplary service. Now, I should like to go and see Mr. Bingley, if you please."

"Of course, miss," the maid replied, dipping into a curtsey and then whirling to lead her out of the bedchamber.

Chapter Seven

Darcy rubbed the back of his neck, feeling uncommonly weary.

"Are you all right, Darce?" asked Fitzwilliam.

"Quite all right, Theo," he lied.

The truth was, in addition to feeling tired he'd begun to ache. His head felt full and his throat had developed a mild burning sensation that he felt every time he swallowed. More than once since he had first noticed he was beginning to feel unwell, he had remonstrated himself for not taking Vincent's suggestion to have a hot bath.

A knock at the door drew his attention and that of the others. Darcy momentarily forgot his discomforts the moment Elizabeth Bennet gingerly stepped into the room, the soft smile she wore somehow making her fine eyes all the brighter.

The three men stood and bowed to her, and she dipped into a curtsey. "I do hope I am not intruding," she said.

"Not at all, Miss Bennet!" cried Bingley as he stepped toward her. "Do come in, won't you?"

"Wherever did you get that dress, Miss Bennet, if I may ask?" queried Fitzwilliam. "Its cut is simple, but it looks rather fetching."

"Thank you, Colonel. It was generously loaned to me by Letty—that is, Letitia, the maid who has been tending me," she replied. "She did tell me that it had been suggested Mr. Bingley would ask one of his sisters to lend me a gown, but if they are anything like my two youngest or my mother after a ball, they'll not even rise from their beds until breakfast is due to be served."

Darcy laughed with the others, and then Bingley said, "How right you are, Miss Bennet."

"Just don't let either one of them hear you say so," Fitzwilliam added.

Elizabeth grinned. "Do not concern yourself, Colonel, that I shall allow myself to speak such blasphemous words within the hearing of Miss Bingley or Mrs. Hurst, for I believe I well discerned their natures at the ball last night."

She then turned her gaze to Bingley. "Forgive me, sir—I mean no offense to your relations."

Bingley laughed again. "Do not concern *your*self, Miss Bennet, that any offense is taken on their behalf. I am sadly all too aware of my sisters' particular proclivities, and their behavior does no credit at all to their upbringing. Still, I'd have ensured one or the other lent you a gown more befitting a gentlewoman."

She glanced at the dress she wore. Darcy thought that fetching, as Fitzwilliam had described her, came nowhere near how lovely a creature Elizabeth was in the simple dress. Were she ever able to wear a gown of high fashion, she would surely be stunning.

"I think it fits me rather well, Mr. Bingley," Elizabeth replied then. "A little long, perhaps, but otherwise it is perfectly serviceable. Unlike some of your friends in London, I don't need to be dressed in silk at half-nine in the morning. A simple morning dress like this one, be it of cotton, linen, or muslin, will always be acceptable to me—I prefer comfort over fashion."

Bingley nodded to her, a grin on his face. "Very well, Miss Bennet, if you are comfortable."

"I am indeed. Besides, I found the prospect of waiting an indeterminate number of hours in my room far less desirable than borrowing a dress from one of the maids," she said nonchalantly. "I wished to speak to you, to offer you my sincerest gratitude for your kindness to a virtual stranger such as myself, and I could hardly do so in such a state as I was."

Darcy's chest filled with unexpected warmth when at last her eyes turned to his, and her smile now seemed to be for him alone. "I must also thank you, Mr. Darcy, if I neglected to do so before. It was rather foolish of me to go out at all, let alone so far from home that I was sure to be caught in the rain."

"Think nothing of it," he replied with a nod. "It was my pleasure to see you safe and well."

"I second that, Miss Bennet," added Bingley. "I'm not sure what's keeping my footman, though. He's been gone going on an hour and a half."

Elizabeth laughed. "I daresay the fault is not his. I am certain my mother has made him wait so that one of our maids or perhaps one of my sisters can pack a trunk for me, because *surely* I shall not be able to come away home before the rain is done. Also, I've no doubt I shall receive a letter with instructions to make the most of my visit here."

Fitzwilliam said to her, "If you are now thinking, Miss Bennet, that we believed you had any sort of ulterior motive, you can just do away with such thoughts. Though I know you very little, I believe after the frankness of our conversation last evening that you are perhaps the most guileless person I have ever met."

"I do thank you for that, Colonel, it's just… I feel I must explain what is like to have delayed your man."

Fitzwilliam scoffed lightly. "What's to explain? Your mother has five unmarried daughters, and like many a society mother, her sole purpose in life is to see you all married well."

Elizabeth looked down at her hands. "Unfortunately, my mother does not seem to understand that her methods materially lessen the chances we have of making a good match. Which is fine, it's fine… I've no problem at all remaining unmarried if it should come to that," she mumbled, then suddenly lifted her head and wore a bright smile that Darcy could tell was more than a little forced.

"Do forgive me for going on so," she said. "I'm sure you've no desire at all to listen to the ramblings of a silly little girl. I only wished to assure each of you that while my dear mother may have hopes of an attachment arising from this unfortunate incident, you need not fear any scheming from me. I seek only amiable companionship, if you are agreeable to it."

"Certainly, Miss Bennet," said Fitzwilliam, whose eyes then turned sideways to look at Darcy.

Should he speak up? he wondered. He still had not come to a firm decision on whether he would court her, but somehow seeing her in a dress that though plain still flattered, and listening to her acknowledge her chances of a good match had just endeared her to him more. Though she had grown embarrassed as she spoke, she had fought her way through the speech and found her strength again.

It stirred in him something akin to pride. Darcy gave no reply, however, other than a nod of acknowledgement. He turned slowly away and moved toward the window as she was asking Bingley for permission to browse his library and perhaps lose herself in a book until breakfast. His friend offered to direct her there himself, and a moment later they were gone from the room.

Fitzwilliam was immediately at his side. "Bloody hell, Darcy!" he cried. "You had a perfect opportunity there and you blew it!"

Darcy raised an eyebrow at him. "An opportunity to do what, Theodore?"

"Well, I don't know, Fitzwilliam—to tell her you like her, perhaps?" cried his cousin in a frustrated tone.

"For goodness' sake, *Teddy*, I've not even decided whether I truly do or not. Can I not have a moment to think?"

Fitzwilliam blinked, either in shock at his tone or the use of the dreaded nickname. He took a step back as he said, "Forgive me, Darcy. I'll not say another word about it."

Darcy sighed. "I know you mean well. But with so many obstacles as would lie before me on such a path, I need far more than one evening to determine whether the lady is worth it."

"You're right this time, instead of me," his cousin quipped. "I am well aware that you don't make important decisions lightly. And really, who *could* say they know someone well enough to determine their compatibility as a life partner after only knowing them an hour or so?"

"Thank you, Theo."

"Oh, thank goodness—we're back to Theo. I swear, Darcy, when you pulled out that blasted nickname of my mother's I thought for a moment I'd gone one too far."

Darcy shook his head. "You annoy me more often than not, but I've never been *that* cross with you. I just wanted you to be silent for a moment."

He pinched the bridge of his nose, feeling the pressure of a headache beginning. How wonderful, some other ailment to plague him, he thought morosely.

"I made my apologies to her earlier, as you know," he said as Bingley was returning to the study. "I have been granted forgiveness for my blunder, so there is at least peace between us. But even were I to choose to disregard every reason there is *not* to pursue her, that peace is no guarantee she would be receptive to my attentions."

"I don't know about that, Darcy," said Bingley. "I've noticed since moving in the higher circles that young ladies, when they speak to a gentleman, do so in one of three ways: Either they say all the practiced, pretty things they think we want to hear so as to win our favor, or they are so nervous that they say whatever comes to mind, things that aren't always appropriate—and *that* is if they are not so nervous as to not speak at all!"

"Elizabeth Bennet does not get nervous," Darcy countered. "Her courage always rises at any attempt to intimidate her—she told me so herself."

"Aye, but we weren't *trying* to intimidate her," Fitzwilliam pointed out. "And from what I've heard of her—I danced with one of her sisters as well, if you'll recall—Miss Elizabeth has been rather a little out of sorts of late. More specifically over the last two weeks. Now why do you think that is?"

"Aye," Bingley chimed in. "The eldest Miss Bennet spoke of her as well, when she talked of their family. I think it safe now to say that nobody makes her nervous except for you."

"But she has no reason to be nervous," Darcy protested. "I would never do her harm."

"I daresay she's not afraid of you, Will, but of herself," Fitzwilliam said then. "Each time she has spoken of the subject of marriage, she has protested she has no intention of marrying or has attempted to assure us she is no adventuress."

Bingley's countenance lit up. "I get what you're saying, Theo: you think the lady doth protest too much."

Fitzwilliam nodded. "Precisely. A girl who has declared she is perfectly content to remain single has suddenly found herself smitten—and very much so, if the strength of her protestations are any indication. The reason you make her nervous, Will, is because you're the only man who's ever made her feel this way."

Darcy looked between his two companions for a moment, then to his cousin and said, "Theo, how the devil would you know anything about how a woman thinks? It's not as if you've any sisters on which to base your opinion."

"True enough, but I've been forced by my mother to dance with enough society girls to form the same hypothesis about women that Bingley did, as well as my own theories. Now, you'll never know if a suit would be accepted if you do not indicate to the lady that you are interested, and you'll never be able to decide whether you *are* or not without spending time with her—so get yourself to the library and…spend time with her."

Darcy suppressed the urge to express his annoyance with a growl—he really did despise it when Bingley and Fitzwilliam made so much sense, his cousin especially so. Theodore had the unnerving capability of making him feel ignorant, though he knew he would eventually have come to the same conclusions.

He would *not* confess that Elizabeth made him just as nervous as he allegedly made her. No point in giving his cousin fodder with which to torment him.

With a sigh, he moved to do as the two suggested and left Bingley's study—there were certainly less agreeable ways to spend a rainy morning than in the company of a pretty woman. He found the library door open and froze on the threshold: curled up on the end of the sofa in front of the fireplace was Elizabeth, her head propped up by one hand, a book in the other. A soft smile adorned her lips, and out from under the hem of the borrowed dress peeked two stocking-covered toes. For a fraction of a moment he wondered why she wasn't wearing any shoes, then surmised that the half-boots she'd been wearing on her walk were probably still wet.

The vision seared itself onto his memory, and he knew with unwavering certainty that he would enjoy such a moment often at Pemberley, should he choose to court her.

He cleared his throat softly, not wishing to startle her. Elizabeth looked up and moved to stand. "Please, do not trouble yourself to rise," he said. "I only came to ask if you would mind some company? Bingley would normally break his fast before ten, but after a night out his sisters rise late, so it is not served until half past."

A smile was his reward as she drew her knees back up, quickly covering her feet with the skirt of her dress. "I recall that from our conversation earlier. And I do not mind at all, Mr. Darcy, though I warn you: when I am captivated by a novel, I make a poor conversationalist."

He returned her smile as he stepped further into the room. "A trait we have in common," he replied. "May I ask what you are reading?"

Elizabeth gestured with the book. "You will think me a hypocrite, given my words in the study, if you are familiar with this novel. It is *Evelina*."

His brows rose. "It so happens I am familiar, to some extent. I know only that it is a romantic novel and a favorite of Georgiana's."

"Now your sister and I have something in common, Mr. Darcy. And while romance is certainly a part of the story, it also depicts the main character's misadventures as she enters into society," said Elizabeth. "Evelina and I have much in common, for we both have relatives that embarrass us."

A blush colored her cheeks and she looked back to her book. "My sister has read the story near half a dozen times since I gave it to her at thirteen. Have you read it often?" he asked.

Elizabeth looked up again. "Perhaps once a year. It takes some time to get through it—Mr. Perkins has to keep a waiting list for many books, most especially novels that are popular of which he has but one copy. The author of this one has two other novels I am fond of as well. I should very much like to add them to my collection of books someday in future as my father will not add them to his library, for he will only allow 'serious' novels in his book room."

Silence fell between them as she once more turned her attention to the book she held. Darcy found himself pleased that she did not press him for further conversation; if she was content to share the room as she read, he would be as well. He browsed the books on the shelves as though he had not been in this room before, musing not for the first time that while it was a fine collection of novels and educational tomes, the Netherfield library was nothing to that of Pemberley. Darcy soon found himself as delighted as Elizabeth must have been to have located a favorite story, as he discovered one of his own and wondered how he had missed it previously. Moving to the armchair adjacent to Elizabeth's left, *The Adventures of Roderick Random* was opened and he settled in to read.

About an hour passed in contented silence before they were summoned to breakfast when Fitzwilliam came to the open door. Darcy snapped his book shut and set it on the side table before standing and offering to serve as escort for Elizabeth.

She smiled as she set her own book aside and stood, her gaze lifting to his. "I should like a guide to the breakfast room, seeing as I've no idea of its location."

He decided he would play along, and countered with, "How good it is, then, that I am here to rescue you from the possibility of getting lost."

Elizabeth laughed and placed her hand at his elbow. "Pray, let me not suffer the humiliation! It is well enough that I am at the mercy of Mr. Bingley's kindness for the duration of this awful weather."

They had started for the door, outside of which Fitzwilliam remained standing. "Has my cousin been so very boring that you are eager to escape his company, Miss Bennet?" he asked.

"Not at all! Mr. Darcy and I had a brief discussion of books before we settled to reading our individual selections," she replied. "I found it quite pleasing to spend time in his company doing something we both enjoy."

A blush colored her cheeks and she looked away. Darcy caught a grin and a wink from Fitzwilliam before he turned on his heel and led the way. Utensils clattered when they entered the breakfast room, Caroline Bingley having been startled—or vexed, he did not particularly care which—at the sight of Elizabeth on his arm.

"What is she—" Caroline began, then seemed to recall that she was, for all intents and purposes, mistress of the house, and therefore required to be polite. "Do forgive me, Miss Eliza, I was merely astonished at seeing you here. I did not expect the pleasure of your company this morning."

"Nor did I expect to bestow it, Miss Bingley," Elizabeth replied. "And pray excuse me, but no one calls me Eliza, not even my family."

Darcy watched Caroline blink, then draw a breath. "I beg your every pardon, Miss Elizabeth," she said with cold politeness.

"It's quite all right," said Elizabeth brightly as she released his arm and reached for a plate. "I only wished to make you aware; though I know Eliza is a common nickname for Elizabeth, I've simply never gone by it. My family has always called me by the short name my father chose, which is Lizzy. My friends, when I have deemed our acquaintance intimate enough, are also granted that privilege."

"And how long before you deem an acquaintance intimate enough?" Darcy asked her as he began to fill his own plate.

Elizabeth looked up at him with a coy smile. "Well that depends, Mr. Darcy, on just how intimate I desire the acquaintance to be."

Darcy lifted his brow at her, uncertain if her words indicated that she desired further acquaintance with him—or that she did not.

Their plates filled with all the delights prepared by Bingley's cook, Darcy and Elizabeth headed toward the dining table, already occupied by Bingley and the Hursts. He pulled out the chair at Bingley's left for Elizabeth—his friend, naturally, claimed the head of the table—and took the chair to her left for himself. Fitzwilliam saved him from having to endure Caroline's "accidental" touches by setting his plate at the chair beside Darcy before gallantly pulling out the chair at the end opposite her brother for Caroline. Her disappointment was obvious in the frown that creased her brow.

"My, my, Miss Bennet," said Louisa Hurst. "That's quite a breakfast you have. Are you not concerned with maintaining your figure, dear?"

"Not one jot, Mrs. Hurst," said Elizabeth. "I enjoy food too much to deny myself anything."

"You also enjoy a good walk, as I recall, Miss Bennet," Darcy put in. "I would imagine all those rambles about the country do their part in maintaining your figure."

"Indeed they do, Mr. Darcy. I am as fond of a country walk as our host is of a country dance," she replied with a smile.

Bingley grinned. "And dancing is certainly a fine way to maintain one's figure, be they a lady or a gentleman," he said.

"Was it one of your country walks that brought you here this morning?" Caroline asked.

Elizabeth shook her head, careful of the cup of hot tea at her lips. "Actually, it was a black horse named Diamond."

Darcy felt Caroline's eyes on him, but he ignored her in favor of turning a smile in Elizabeth's direction. Unexpected pleasure raced through him to find her smiling as well.

"Charles, why didn't you call for the carriage?" pressed Caroline. "Did you not think Miss Bennet would want to go home?"

"Indeed, brother!" said Louisa, doing her part to add weight to her sister's argument. She had long supported Caroline's misguided pursuit and too often shared in her snobbery.

"Actually, I rather thought that what Miss Bennet desired most when Darcy brought her to Netherfield was to be warm and dry," Bingley said simply.

"Quite right, Mr. Bingley—have I thanked you too much for your kindness yet?" said Elizabeth. "Mrs. Hubbard and Letty have been most attentive to your unexpected and unwanted visitor."

"Unexpected, perhaps, Miss Bennet," said Bingley, with a pointed look in Darcy's direction.

"But hardly unwanted," Darcy finished with a smile. "We are most delighted to have you as our guest, for however long the rain holds."

"Here, here!" cried Fitzwilliam. "I always say, don't I Darce, that every place can always do with a fresh face and lively conversation."

"Blasted rain! We were supposed to go shooting today," muttered Mr. Hurst.

A door opened at the far end of the room then, followed by the entrance of Foster, the Bingleys' butler. He came to a stop in between his master and Elizabeth and bowed.

"Eddie has returned, Mr. Bingley," he said, then held up an envelope. "He says this letter is to be given directly to Miss Elizabeth Bennet, per instructions from Mrs. Bennet."

Bingley gestured to Elizabeth. "She's right here, Foster."

Foster turned smartly and offered the letter to Elizabeth, bowing when she took it from him. He turned to Bingley once more and said,

"Eddie also brought back with him a small trunk, sir, and said it was to ensure Miss Bennet's comfort during her stay with us. Mrs. Hubbard had it taken to the lady's room."

"Very good, Foster. Thank you."

The butler bowed again and departed through the nearer door.

"Oh honestly, Charles!" whined Caroline. "Whatever possessed Mrs. Bennet to send clothes for the girl—it's only a rainstorm, for goodness' sake. She's not spending the weekend."

Darcy frowned at the rudeness of her query, and would surely have spoken if Bingley had not.

After setting his coffee cup down with a definite thump, Bingley told her, "Caroline, Miss Elizabeth is a guest in *my* house—do be more polite."

"Miss Bingley, both Miss Bennet and I were quite wet through by the time we arrived at Netherfield," Darcy pointed out tersely. "I should think it quite obvious why Mrs. Bennet would send a change of clothes for her daughter."

"Whilst I *am* thankful to have been leant something comfortable to wear while my own things are dried," added Elizabeth, "it will be nice to put on something I actually own and return this lovely day gown to its rightful owner. Mr. Darcy, do remind me to thank my mother for her thoughtfulness when you escort me home—I can only imagine what my family would have thought if I were to return in a dress that wasn't mine."

Caroline scoffed. "Miss Eliza, it is awfully presumptuous of you, do not you think, to be volunteering Mr. Darcy to see you home again?"

"No more presumptuous than your addressing the lady by a short name she has already told you she is not called," snapped her brother. "Stop behaving like a petulant child who's had her plans ruined—I'm sure they taught manners at that ridiculously expensive school Father sent you to. Miss Bennet's presence is no inconvenience to you."

Elizabeth cleared her throat softly; Darcy looked and noted that her cheek of a moment ago had fled and she now looked embarrassed. "Mr. Bingley, I've no wish to be the cause of conflict with your sister. If it would not be a terrible inconvenience to have your carriage made ready, I would be happy to take my leave."

"Nonsense, Miss Elizabeth," said Darcy before Bingley could speak. "I will not hear of you being sent away in such conditions, not even in a carriage. The storm has not grown worse, but nor has it eased. A tree was struck by lightning not fifty feet from us, if you'll recall, and a carriage with metal parts would make for an even more likely target. No, you will stay here until the weather is abated. Bingley, as I am the one who brought her here I am responsible for her welfare, and I won't stand for it."

"Do not concern yourself, Darcy," said Bingley evenly. "I would not dream of sending Miss Bennet out in the storm, anymore than I would one of my own sisters."

He then reached over and laid a hand atop of Elizabeth's. "Please, do not feel you are in any way unwelcome or a burden."

"Now Charles," spoke up Caroline, her tone placating, "you know I meant nothing at all by what I said. Of course Miss Bennet is welcome to wait out the storm here at Netherfield. I only meant to suggest that she might prefer to be with her family; I know I would want to be with mine."

A sidelong glance in her direction showed Darcy that, in appearance at least, she meant what she said. Her posture was straight, her expression full of the appearance of contrition. But he knew her better than that, as did Bingley, and save perhaps for Hurst—whose only interest in joining them in Hertfordshire had been for the sport—there was not one person at the table unaware that Caroline most certainly did not welcome Elizabeth's presence.

What young woman interested in bettering her position in society would welcome the competition?

Not that Elizabeth *was* competition, for Caroline had not a chance of securing his affections and he'd yet to determine whether or not Miss Bennet did. Though if she continued to flirt with him as she had been, and was forced to remain for more than a day at Netherfield, he reasoned he might well find himself very much in danger of being smitten.

For her part, Elizabeth appeared mostly unaffected. Though it had seemed for a moment that she had wished to be anywhere else but there, she now sat with her back straight and a determined set to her shoulders. To Bingley she looked with a soft smile and said, "You are a most gracious host, Mr. Bingley."

To Darcy she next bestowed her gaze, and much to his relief, there was a familiar sparkle in her eye. "I am grateful for your diligence to duty, Mr. Darcy. I am sure my family will also be as grateful for your concern for my well-being as am I."

From there, the tension around the table eased as conversation was turned to other topics. Darcy found himself distracted, however, by a persistent throbbing in his head. Caroline's thinly veiled nastiness had only made it worse.

He focused all his attention on Elizabeth as best he could. "Aren't going to read your letter, Miss Bennet?"

"I would not dream of being so rude as to ignore my tablemates for a letter, Mr. Darcy," she quipped lightly. "Though the hand of the address is Jane's, I've little doubt that much of the words are my mother's. I told you earlier what she was likely to say, and as such it can surely wait."

Elizabeth looked to him then and said in a low voice, "Speaking of what I said this morning in Mr. Bingley's study, I pray you and the other gentlemen did not think me improper to be speaking of such things. Though I freely admit to being rather blunt by nature, it is not my practice to discuss such delicate matters as I did with persons with whom I am so little acquainted. To be sure, I cannot rightly say what possessed me to do so."

"If I may offer an opinion on the subject…"

She chuckled as she picked up a berry tart from her plate. "You might as well, I've already heard the thoughts of the colonel and Mr. Bingley," she said, before biting into the pastry.

Because her tone was light, he felt safe in venturing his honest thoughts. "I imagine that you spoke so freely due in part to nervousness at being in something of an untenable situation. As I am the one that forced it upon you, allow me to offer my apologies. Again," he added. Elizabeth smiled at the last, and so he continued. "Now, I know from your own declaration to me that you are not easily intimidated, but even the best of us may suffer from nervousness on occasion."

"I cannot imagine you being nervous, Mr. Darcy," she said. "Shyness does not equate nervousness."

"It *is* a condition with which I am little familiar," he conceded. "Only recently have I been forced to acclimate myself to it. But as I was saying, I suspect you felt at least a little nervous—and, knowing what your mother would want you to do, desired to assure us that you were not the sort of young woman who would seek to take advantage of the circumstances in which you had found yourself. You could very easily compromise one of the three of us who are not married and thereby make your life much more comfortable.

"But that is not who you are, Miss Elizabeth. Though I do not know you well at present, I believe it safe for me to say that artful entrapment is not in your nature."

Elizabeth smiled, and in her countenance he noted relief. "Indeed it is not, Mr. Darcy. I cannot fathom why any person would want to bind themselves in lasting marriage in such a fashion, even to better their circumstances in life. In my opinion, a marriage should be an equal partnership where both persons can honestly say that they trust and respect the other one. To wed without either is only courting disaster and a lifetime of unhappiness."

"And what of love?" Darcy queried.

"To marry for love would be the greatest of blessings, sir."

The two of them shared a smile, and in that moment Darcy felt ever more in danger. But it was a pleasant feeling, one he could not say he was sorry for.

Although he continued to feel very strange and did not eat as much as he often did at breakfast, Darcy was pleased that the rest of the meal passed without incident. When Elizabeth indicated she was finished, he asked if she intended to return to her book. She said that she did; as she had no notion of when she might get to enjoy the story again, in this, at least, she intended to take advantage of Mr. Bingley's hospitality. After she had risen and picked up her letter, he stood as well—and prayed that no one noticed how unsteady he suddenly felt.

"Allow me to escort you then," he said, offering his arm. "I think I should like to return to my book as well."

Elizabeth turned a smile up at him and once again placed her hand in his elbow. Darcy ignored the clatter of utensils that came from the direction of Caroline Bingley's chair as he and Elizabeth made their way to the door of the breakfast room. The two of them were companionably silent as they walked back to the library, where they found the books they had been reading just where they'd left them.

"Actually," said Elizabeth as she released his arm, "I might just read Jane's letter first—best to get my mother's foolishness out of the way so that I can enjoy Evelina's adventures, and the rest of my morning."

Darcy nodded and moved toward the chair he'd sat in. His head swam as he bent to reach for his book, and without warning he fell to the floor.

Chapter Eight

"Mr. Darcy!"

Elizabeth cried out his name as he unexpectedly crumpled to the floor before her. Throwing aside the letter she had just opened, she rushed to kneel at his shoulder. When she touched his cheek with her fingertips, she felt heat.

"Help!" she yelled in the direction of the open door. "Mr. Bingley, Colonel Fitzwilliam! Somebody help!"

Looking back to Darcy, she laid a hand to his shoulder and gave a light shake. He moaned and blinked his eyes languidly as she heard the sound of running footsteps.

"Thunder and turf!" cried Fitzwilliam when he entered the library, Bingley on his heels. "What happened?"

The two men came to kneel by Darcy; Elizabeth stood and moved out of the way. "I don't know—he just collapsed. He's caught a fever, I think."

Fitzwilliam laid a hand to his cousin's brow. "He's burning up. Blast and botheration, why didn't he tell anyone he wasn't feeling well?"

"You know Darcy, Theo," said Bingley. "He's not one to reveal his weaknesses if he can help it."

The colonel snorted. "All too well I know it. All right, let's get him up."

The two worked to pick Mr. Darcy up off the floor. Getting him upright was easy enough, but keeping him on his feet was not; he required the support of both to remain standing.

"Miss Elizabeth, would you be so kind as to ring for a servant?" Fitzwilliam asked. "I would have them begin preparing remedies."

"Of course, Colonel," said Elizabeth. She hurried to do as he asked as he and Bingley slowly made their way toward the door. Her fingers were just wrapping around the bell pull when both the butler and housekeeper came into the library, likely having also heard the cry for help, each exclaiming shock. Bingley fired off instructions, telling Mrs. Hubbard to see what remedies they had in store and for Foster to hurry ahead to Darcy's room and work with the man's valet to prepare it for his return.

Elizabeth wrung her hands, not sure what to do. She wished to be sure that Mr. Darcy would be well, and reminded herself as his cousin and his friend slowly guided him away that he was in the best of hands. Taking a breath to calm herself, she forced her feet to carry her back to the sofa. There was nothing she could do for Mr. Darcy beyond what she had, though she knew she would continue to worry. He'd seemed just fine one moment, and then the next he had fallen.

She closed her eyes and offered up a prayer, asking that he would soon be healed of his illness. Elizabeth felt better after speaking to God, and took it as a sign that He would show His mercy. She took up her sister's letter then, and with a lighter heart began to read.

My dearest Lizzy,

Thank Providence you are safe and well! I'm sure you can imagine our worry when it was discovered you were not in the house with such thunder shaking the rafters. Mary and Papa were particularly concerned since you had left the assembly early last night with a headache.

Of course, we all know it was not really a headache—yes, Mamma has made it well known "what a disagreeable man" Mr. Darcy was to say what he did. How great was our surprise, then, when the footman from Netherfield arrived with a letter that said the very same man who had abused you so had rescued you from the storm! Lizzy, I hope it was not his fault you were caught in it, and I still cannot believe what he said about you. Mary believes that you might have easily forgiven Mr. Darcy's vanity had he not wounded yours. She thinks you were beginning to form an attachment, but surely that cannot be true.

But what do I know of matters of the heart? Perhaps you will fall harder and faster than any of us, in spite of—or because of—your determination that only the deepest love will secure you.

Now, as I am sure you had guessed long before this letter was in your hands, Mamma made the poor footman wait—Papa was kind enough to allow him to sit in the entry hall by the fire, and Hill gave him a coffee to help warm him – whilst Mary was sent to pack a trunk for you. Our mother is determined that you should make the most of your being at Netherfield and do what you can to secure an offer from either Mr. Bingley or Colonel Fitzwilliam. She says if you come home early or without an offer, she will never see you again. Of course, we all know she would never be able to keep from speaking to you for long, but as it is, you have three days' worth of gowns, including evening dresses. Mamma insisted – Mary had packed only a couple day dresses and under-things for you – that you should have everything you would need for a lengthy stay, as in her mind the rain is sure to be pouring for days and days.

As you are surely laughing by now, Lizzy, I will close. I do hope that you will not be made to suffer much time in Mr. Darcy's company, if he is truly so disagreeable. I pray also that you find the colonel, Mr. Bingley, and the latter's sisters as engaging and friendly as I did, that at least our acquaintance with them is furthered. Oh, how I wish you were here to talk of the fun we had at last night's ball before you went away, and of our new neighbors; however, Mary and I have been getting on well speaking of it. Truly, Lizzy, I am so happy that you and I have made a point of knowing her better, for I have found comfort with her in your absence.

Do come home soon, my dearest sister. All my love,

Jane

On the back of the page with Jane's neat, curly script were – to little surprise – several lines in Mrs. Bennet's always hasty scrawl:

Elizabeth Bennet, do not listen to your sister. You will do as I say and take advantage of your time at Netherfield to secure an offer from one of the gentlemen! Not Mr. Darcy, of course – such an odious man, to speak of you so. You may not be as handsome as our Jane, but you are still a very pretty girl when you try. No, I believe you should set your cap at Mr. Bingley, for though he is not as rich as his friend, he does have five thousand a year! Mind your tongue, though, that you do not offend him. And when he is yours, be sure to put forward that Lydia is very fond of officers to Colonel Fitzwilliam. I think they will do well together.

Oh! To have one daughter as mistress of such a fine house as Netherfield, and one wed to the son of an earl… Oh, my Lizzy, do not fail us! Remember that we shall all be sleeping in the hedgerows when your father is dead if one of you does not marry well. I see Jane told you I said you were not to come home without an offer and I mean it! I shall never see you again if you do!

With a shake of her head and a soft laugh, Elizabeth placed the cover page behind her letter and folded them back together. As she did so, her eyes fell on the book Mr. Darcy had been reading, and she instantly began to wonder how he fared. She wondered if she should go up and see if she could be of help, as she was at least partly responsible for his having been out in the rain so long.

So determined, she rose and left the library. Minutes later she found her way toward the family wing, sure his rooms would be near Bingley's, with the help of a passing maid. She arrived as Bingley himself was coming out of Darcy's room. Once they had greeted each other, she inquired as to his friend's welfare.

Bingley grimaced. "I'm afraid he's not well," he said. "According to Vincent, his valet, he decided to forego a hot bath after you arrived. Seems to his detriment, as he's rapidly developed quite the fever and is a little delirious. We've given him a dose of laudanum to help settle him down."

"Good gracious!" she exclaimed. "I'm so sorry—is there anything I can do?"

"A couple of things, actually," said Bingley as he took a step closer. "First, we need the name of the local apothecary, as Fitzwilliam is insisting Darcy be seen by him. Second, would you mind terribly sitting with him whilst Vincent rides into town to fetch the apothecary and bring him here?"

"I would not mind at all—I've tended all four of my sisters when they've been ill—but would not Colonel Fitzwilliam or yourself be a better choice? I'd not want to be accused of impropriety."

"Of course, I understand," replied Bingley. "And you are right, it should be one of us, but I've some business to see my steward about and Fitzwilliam has his own correspondence he meant to see to today. I'm sure it can wait, but it would be a great help to us both. I can have a maid sit in with you if you'd feel more comfortable that way."

Elizabeth smiled and nodded. "I think that will be best. I will be happy to look after Mr. Darcy until Mr. Vincent returns from town. If you would, please ask the maid to fetch two books from the library—one is on the sofa and the other on the side table. I should like to have them to pass the time, as I'll retire to my room once I am no longer needed."

"Certainly, Miss Bennet," Bingley agreed, and he turned about to show her into the bedchamber of Mr. Darcy.

It was a larger room than her own, though set up in a similar fashion. However, instead of the bed being directly in front of the door, it was on the far side of the room. Fitzwilliam looked up when they entered.

"Ah, Miss Bennet," said he as he stood from sitting on the side of the bed. He bowed his head, and then, "I'm pleased to see you. Did Bingley speak to you of our request?"

Elizabeth inclined her head. "He did, Colonel. I am happy to help, as some fault for Mr. Darcy's condition is my own doing."

"Hardly so, Miss Bennet—he did, after all, act the fool by going out in the first place," Fitzwilliam replied. "I do not wish to put you in an uncomfortable position, but I can assure you it will not be for long. A few of my letters can certainly wait for a response, but the one I received from my father yesterday cannot. At least, not any longer than it already has."

"I'm going to have a maid come and sit with them, so no one's reputation is compromised," said Bingley then.

"Ah, capital idea, Charles," said Fitzwilliam. Bingley went to the bell pull as a door in the wall to the left of the bed opened to admit an older man with gray in his hair. Elizabeth assumed him to be Mr. Darcy's valet, as he was as dressed for the inclement weather as he could be.

"I am ready to be off, sir," he said to the colonel.

"Mr. Jones is the apothecary in Meryton," spoke up Elizabeth. "His shop is on the main street and he has a sign over the door. You cannot miss it."

Vincent bowed. "Thank you, miss," he said, and then hurried out.

Moments later, as Fitzwilliam was setting a chair by the bed for Elizabeth, Mrs. Hubbard entered with a tray. On it was a bowl and a number of folded towels; this she placed on the bedside table. Elizabeth looked and noted there was water in it that smelled of vinegar.

Mr. Bingley explained to the elderly lady that Elizabeth would be tending to Darcy for a short period. Mrs. Hubbard acknowledged with a nod and bobbed a curtsey, then turned to depart. As the housekeeper quit the room Letty entered, and she was quickly told by Bingley what they wished for her to do. The girl was not long in returning after she had been dismissed, and she carried with her the two books in one hand and a basket in the other.

"All right, as you're well situated for the moment, Fitzwilliam and I will dash off," said Bingley. "I'm sure it won't be long before one of us relieves you."

Elizabeth smiled. "I will be fine, Mr. Bingley. And so will Mr. Darcy, I am sure."

Fitzwilliam stepped up to her and unexpectedly took her hands in his. "With such capable, caring hands as these, I have not the slightest doubt. Though I am sorry to employ you so, when we had thought your time here—however brief it may be—would be enjoyable."

She gave his hands a squeeze before pulling her own from his grasp. "Even tending to Mr. Darcy will be a welcome reprieve from the chaos of Longbourn," she told him with a laugh. "With so many sisters running about, there are few moments of actual peace until everyone is abed at night."

The two gentlemen laughed, and then they went away to take care of their business. Elizabeth set her sister's letter on the tray beside the bowl of water and then picked up a towel and soaked it; after squeezing out the excess, she patted the thin sheen of sweat from Darcy's face and neck, they being all that were left exposed by the dark coverlet pulled over him. She soaked and squeezed it again before folding and laying it across his brow.

After directing Letty to bring a few more candles over so that she could see better, she then settled in to read. The maid moved to sit by the window and pulled out what looked to be stockings from her basket and began to work. Silence settled over the room, punctuated intermittently by light moans from the patient. The third time he did so, Elizabeth rose, patted him dry again, and re-soaked the towel. After she had replaced the folded cloth on Mr. Darcy's warm face, she recalled why she had asked for his book as well as hers.

"Letty, do you mind at all if I read aloud?" she asked.

The maid looked up. "Not at all, miss. My mamma used to read to us when we were ill as little ones. I remember I liked the steady sound of her voice."

"Does your mother still live?" Elizabeth asked.

Letty nodded. "She does—and married herself another butcher, she did, a few years after we went north. I've got sisters now meself, two of 'em, though they're fair young yet."

Elizabeth grinned. "Be glad then that you have steady employment away from home. Young girls can be quite boisterous and loud, and unless properly educated on decorum, they will not get better as they grow up."

"Oh, I know all about that, miss, from when I've visited home," said Letty with a laugh. "They get riled up some, sure, but my mother don't let them run wild. She never let me or the boys do it either."

"Now you mention it, I seem to recollect that. If memory serves, she once boxed the ears of one of her boys right out in the street because he told her no."

Letty laughed again. "I remember that too! Billy was so stunned she cuffed him in front of all those people that he did what she told him without sayin' another word."

With a smile to her lips, Elizabeth took Darcy's book in hand and opened it. The first few pages consisted of a preface and an apologue, which normally she would read, but figured her patient to be well familiar with those particulars already.

"You will forgive me, I hope, Mr. Darcy," she said, "for reading that which you already have, but I have not had the pleasure of reading *The Adventures of Roderick Random* before, and as such, I must start at the very beginning."

Clearing her throat in a dramatic fashion, which earned her a giggle from the maid, Elizabeth began to read. "Chapter One. Of my birth and education…"

After a time, Letty remarked softly that Mr. Darcy seemed less restless than he had when she had first entered. Elizabeth paused only long enough to observe that she was correct; after asking the maid to come and tend him as she had done, she smoothly went back to reading. Privately, she found herself more than a little pleased that the sound of her voice apparently soothed Darcy and enabled him to rest.

She had just begun chapter three when to her right she heard the sound of a throat clearing. The tone was feminine, and her head turned to find Caroline Bingley in the doorway.

"Has the apothecary arrived yet, Miss Bingley?" she asked.

"No. I wanted to talk to you," said Caroline sharply.

Elizabeth closed the book, holding her place with one finger, and turned in her chair. "By all means."

Miss Bingley came further in. "I know what you are about, and I will not allow it. Not in my house."

A brow lifted. "Your house? Forgive me if I am mistaken, but I thought that Netherfield had been leased to Mr. Bingley?"

"Do not trifle with me, Eliza Bennet— "

"My name is Elizabeth," said she, her voice firm as her ire began to rise. "Though as you and I are not personally acquainted, I request that you use the proper address and refer to me as Miss Bennet, unless my elder sister is present, at which time I am to be called Miss *Elizabeth*."

She emphasized the enunciation of her name, then turned resolutely to face Mr. Darcy's still form. Caroline marched closer, saying, "I don't really give two figs what your name is or what you want to be called! You are a witless country nobody without a penny to your name. Do you really think that he will want *you*—a classless, ill-bred chit of inferior birth with no fortune and no connections?"

"And do you really think he will want *you*, a woman who attacks a guest in her brother's house, one she has known herself for not even a day, in a fit of misplaced jealousy?" Elizabeth asked casually.

Caroline scoffed, the sound as though she choked on her own breath. "I am *not* jealous, certainly not of you!"

Elizabeth lifted her head slowly to look at her. "Then why, I might ask, have you come into Mr. Darcy's sick room to rage at me as though there were a competition for his affections?"

"I came to warn you," Caroline sneered. "Your tricks, your arts and allurements, will not work on Mr. Darcy. He holds the highest respect for his place in society and is far too intelligent to be taken in by an impertinent *croqueuse de diamants* like yourself!"

A diamond cruncher, am I? Elizabeth thought, translating the French literally in her mind though she knew the term was used to characterize someone—typically a young lady—as a gold digger. "How interesting, Miss Bingley, that you mistake my not having a respectable dowry as my not having an education. I am no fortune hunter, a fact that I have already assured Mr. Darcy of, as well as your brother and Colonel Fitzwilliam. Now, I cannot speak as to all of Mr. Darcy's thoughts as regards myself, but he did tell me this morning that he found my *bon mot comme il faut*."

Miss Bingley's back straightened and she stepped back as though she had been struck. Her hands moved to her hips and a scowl marred her countenance as she stared open-mouthed for several seconds.

"Why, you little… How *dare* you speak to one of your betters in such a wretched manner?! I've half a mind to throw you out into the hedgerows myself!"

Laughter bubbled up from Elizabeth's diaphragm at that remark, knowing as Caroline did not her mother's rantings about hedgerows.

"Miss Bingley, I daresay you have not the courage to even try," she said as she carefully set *Roderick Random* on the edge of the bed, laying it open so that she could easily find her place again. She then stood and turned to face Caroline, lacing her hands together before her.

"Allow me to make something clear to you, madam," she began deliberately. "I am not one of the poor and broken that the likes of you are happy to trample beneath your expensive leather boots because you think you are so far above them. If you malign my character or that of my family, I *will* stand up to you, be assured of that. And although I owe you no explanation of any kind, allow me to set your mind at ease regarding Mr. Darcy: I did not come to Netherfield in order to use my 'arts and allurements' on him, or any other unattached gentleman in this house. I am here simply as a victim of circumstance.

"However, if I *were* of a mind to pursue Mr. Darcy, I believe that would be my business and no one else's, save Mr. Darcy. And I'm quite sure that his willingness to receive my attentions would be for him to decide, as it would be mine as to whether I am open to receiving his should he have any to bestow. Who either of us chooses to court as a romantic partner is, in essence, none of your concern."

Miss Bingley began to turn an unattractive shade of puce in her outrage, though all color soon drained from her face as slow applause sounded from behind her.

"Well said, Miss Bennet," said Colonel Fitzwilliam. Elizabeth looked to find him propped against the door jamb, though on meeting her gaze, he stood straight and moved into the room.

Caroline turned to him, her expression shifting as she did so. "Colonel Fitzwilliam, allow me to ex—"

Fitzwilliam's hand snapped up and she fell instantly silent. His own expression hardened as he regarded her, then said, "You are not to enter my cousin's bedchamber again, nor are you to accost Miss Bennet again while she is with us. You only embarrass yourself and your brother with such behavior, Miss Bingley, and do not think I will not mention this incident to him. Challenge me, and I will see to it that Bingley locks you in your rooms or has you sent back to London."

With a haughty sniff, Caroline lifted her nose into the air and marched around him to depart. When she was gone, Elizabeth blew out a sigh of relief.

"Thank you, Colonel. I regret that I may have provoked her attack with my behavior at breakfast," she said.

"Even had you not flirted with Darcy, Miss Bennet, she would be aggrieved at your being here," said the colonel. "She set her cap at him years ago, though how she is still blind to his indifference is beyond my comprehension."

He narrowed his gaze then. "You *were* flirting, were you not?"

She would not do herself the indignity of denying it. "Will you think less of me if I confess that I only did so because of her attitude?" Elizabeth asked him. "I regret that her manner struck a nerve in me and I retaliated in such a way as I knew would anger her. It was foolish and unladylike, and I am sorry if it leads to any sort of trouble."

Colonel Fitzwilliam waved off her words with a laugh. "Think nothing of it. I rather enjoyed watching her squirm."

He moved closer to the bed then. "How does my cousin fare?" he asked softly.

"I think his fever is a little improved, but not much," she replied. "There is an old country remedy I would suggest we try—our housekeeper, Mrs. Hill, often uses it when tending to our colds—but it was improper for me to do it on my own."

The colonel crossed his arms, one hand raised to his chin in thought. "What is your suggestion?"

"Well, whenever my sisters and I, or our parents, have caught a fever, she will soak towels in apple cider vinegar and wrap one around each foot. It somehow helps to draw the fever down," Elizabeth explained. "Mrs. Hubbard must have also heard this, or at least that the vinegar aids in reducing fevers, because there is vinegar in the water she brought to keep him cool."

"Since I am here now to observe the proprieties, would you care to do it? I will help you."

Elizabeth nodded and looked to the maid, who had sat in silence during the engagement with Caroline Bingley—probably too frightened to even leave, let alone speak. "Letty, go and fetch some more towels. We'll need them to go under his feet so that the wet ones do not soak the mattress."

"Right away, miss," the girl said, before darting through the door Vincent had used.

Probably a servant's hall, Elizabeth mused, then moved to help Colonel Fitzwilliam uncover Mr. Darcy's stocking-clad lower legs. She next went to the bowl of vinegar-infused water and put the two remaining towels in to soak. When Letty returned she pulled them out again, wringing each only a little before she wrapped it around a foot and calf as she had seen Hill do; Letty placed a folded towel down on the bed before Fitzwilliam set each to rest again.

As they were covering his feet once more, Mr. Bingley led in a somewhat bedraggled-looking Mr. Jones. "Miss Elizabeth!" said the apothecary with a smile. "I did not expect to see you here."

"I did not expect to be here, Mr. Jones," she replied. "However, poor Mr. Darcy and I were both caught in the rain, and as we were much closer to Netherfield than Longbourn, he escorted me here to freshen up and wait out the storm."

The portly fellow's scrutinizing gaze passed from her to the man in the bed and back again. "Did you have a hot bath, Miss Elizabeth?"

She nodded. "I did, sir. Mr. Bingley's housekeeper and a maid were most attentive."

Mr. Jones turned to the other men. "Did he have a bath?" he asked, pointing to Darcy.

"No, fool that he is," replied Fitzwilliam.

The apothecary *tsked* as he stepped closer to the head of the bed, muttering under his breath. Elizabeth moved out of the way so that he could do his work. She, Bingley, and Fitzwilliam watched in silence as he checked Mr. Darcy's temperature, the reaction of his pupils, and listened to his heart with a scope.

"I smell vinegar," he said when he straightened and returned the instrument to his bag.

"Mrs. Hubbard, my housekeeper, always adds apple cider vinegar to water for fevers, sir," said Bingley.

"Good woman," Mr. Jones said. "Towels around the feet?"

Elizabeth and Fitzwilliam nodded. "Just before you arrived," she said. "We've wiped his face and neck as well, a few times."

"Good. Keep doing that. And re-soak the towels around his feet in an hour or so if his fever does not come down." He looked to Bingley. "How well stocked is your remedy chest?"

Mr. Bingley rubbed the back of his neck. "We, uh, do not have one at present. I looked, but we apparently did not bring it with us from Town."

Mr. Jones *tsked* again and shook his head as he reached into his bag once more, pulled out a small packet, and handed it to Elizabeth. "Fever powder. See that Mr. Darcy takes some now, and again every four to six hours if the fever remains. Tomorrow morning, if he is still not better, summon me again. And Mr. Bingley? If your intention is to remain in the neighborhood, might I strongly suggest that you either fetch your remedy chest from London or come to my shop on Monday to purchase another?"

Bingley nodded enthusiastically. "I will be in the village to see you Monday, sir. Thank you, again, for coming out in this dreadful weather. I'm sorry to have made you do it."

Here Mr. Jones offered a small smile and a chuckle. "The weather is something awful, I grant, but coming out here was a break in the monotony of checking and rechecking my stock. Now I have a mission when I get back as well, to prepare a home remedy chest for you. I'll actually have something to do for a time—this kind of day, I don't usually get many customers."

"I'll see you out so you can get back to your shop and dry yourself out quickly," said Bingley.

Fitzwilliam stepped toward them as they started for the door. "Thank you, sir, for your attendance to my cousin. I know it is only a trifling cold, but he gets ill so rarely and it came upon him so quickly that I could not help but be concerned."

"It's quite all right, young man. Miss Elizabeth here has things well in hand, I can assure you," said Mr. Jones, then he leaned closer to the colonel and added in a low voice that Elizabeth could still hear, "She might have a sharp tongue, that one, but she's a dear girl. You single gents ought to keep that in mind, if'n you happen to be in the market for a missus."

Biting her lip to keep from smiling and showing she'd heard every word, Elizabeth remained silent as Mr. Bingley and Mr. Jones made their way out again. When they had gone, Colonel Fitzwilliam turned to her with a smile and a wink, and she had to laugh.

"Don't mind Mr. Jones, Colonel. He's a kind man and means well, but because they never had the daughter he and Mrs. Jones longed for—only a son—they both tend to dote on the young ladies in town," she told him.

"I can't say as I disagree with his assessment," said Fitzwilliam. "After what happened last night, you've been most surprisingly attentive to Darcy."

She felt a blush blooming in her cheeks and looked away. "He, ah, spoke to me this morning and offered his apologies. It would have been unchristian not to forgive him."

"That may be, madam, but I can assure you he meant that apology. His words last night were a jest—admittedly a very poor one—that he knew Bingley and I would understand because of the tone with which he spoke. Quite unfortunate that the only jokes my cousin *can* tell are bad ones, as he hasn't the faintest idea how to tell a good one, nor is he quite aware when such sarcasm as he employed last evening is fit to be used."

Elizabeth bit her lip again in an effort not to laugh. Colonel Fitzwilliam then stepped closer and lightly touched her shoulder, and when she lifted her eyes to his, he wore a serious, almost imploring expression.

"Miss Elizabeth, he's a good man, with a good heart," he said slowly. "He may seem cold at times, or arrogant, or even downright conceited, but that is only because he is rather shy, if you can believe it, and is often unsure how to promote himself favorably to strangers. I can assure you that his servants and tenants have the highest respect for Darcy, and his sister adores him."

"Are you campaigning for Mr. Darcy, Colonel?" she could not help asking.

He grinned. "I don't know—is it working?"

She looked down again at the sleeping man in the bed and sighed softly. "In our conversations before his…bad joke…and those we've had since he begged my pardon, I will admit that I have found Mr. Darcy to be very agreeable. But even were I inclined toward marriage, I know that a match with him would be impossible."

Fitzwilliam scoffed. "What makes you say such a thing?"

Elizabeth looked at him. "Mr. Darcy is a very rich man, and I have no dowry to make him richer. I am well aware, Colonel, that such connections as I have would make a marriage between us insupportable, both in society and within his family."

"Present company excluded," Fitzwilliam asserted. "As to the rest of the family, I can say with assurance that my parents and my brother—once they got to know you—would accept you so long as you truly made Darcy happy. My sister by marriage and Darcy's own sister would adore you. I already think you're incredibly charming. The only person who might challenge a match between you would be our Aunt Catherine, and then only because she's wanted him to marry her daughter since they were born. Claims it to be the dearest wish of both her sister and herself, though I know for a fact that Aunt Anne never made any mention of it, as she surely would have if it were true—my Aunt Anne being Darcy's late mother."

"And what of my family?" Elizabeth challenged. "It's already been established that my mother can be impolitely loud and vulgar and my two youngest sisters behave improperly with the soldiers, as too few corrections to their behavior have been made."

"A finishing school or governess would set them to rights. Darcy could see to that."

"I'm sure he could," she said. "But I also have an uncle who is an attorney and one who works in trade. He lives in London, but his house is in Cheapside. Would not the earl and countess be humiliated by such relations?"

"So he *is* your uncle! This is capital!" When she frowned in confusion, Fitzwilliam laughed and said, "I got a letter from my brother Philip yesterday. His wife and our mother were directed to the warehouses of a Mr. Edward Gardiner in Cheapside, as he allegedly had the most delightful selections of fabric. They found this stuff called sarsnet there that my brother says they went mad for. And apparently, Mr. and Mrs. Gardiner were very well regarded by my mother and sister."

Elizabeth could not but feel stunned by his revelation. But before she could formulate words with which to respond, Colonel Fitzwilliam took her gently by the shoulders and dipped his head until their gazes met. "Be not alarmed, madam, by what I have told you, nor should you feel any obligation to act in any way that does not constitute your own happiness. It is just that I wish wholeheartedly to see my cousin happy—he's suffered enough tragedy in his life by losing his parents, both before he was one and twenty. He had to become master of his estate, his fortune, and become a father-figure to Georgiana before he was of age, and that's taken a toll on him.

"What I am saying is, he's a good man and he would make a fine husband for you, *if* you were to find yourself of a mind to consider marriage."

Chapter Nine

A moment of silence followed the colonel's declaration, and then an indescribable emotion began to overwhelm Elizabeth.

Suddenly it was imperative to her that she escape the room. Thrusting the packet of fever powder at Colonel Fitzwilliam, she said in as steady a voice as she could manage, "I thank you for your insights, Colonel, and I shall consider them carefully. Now you are returned, I believe it would be best for me to turn Mr. Darcy's care over to you. Good day, sir."

She dropped into a quick curtsey and, after whirling to grab the letter from Jane and her own book, Elizabeth quickly departed.

Fitzwilliam sighed, and hoped he had not just made things more difficult for Darcy. He glanced down and noted an open book on the edge of the bed. On picking it up and scanning a few lines, he noted that it was one of Darcy's childhood favorites—one of his own favorites as well. Darcy must have been reading it in the library, but why would Elizabeth have asked for it?

"She was reading it to him."

Blinking, Fitzwilliam looked to see that the maid—Elizabeth had called her Letty—had not yet departed.

"Reading it *to* him, you say?" he asked.

Letty nodded. "Yes, Colonel. Miss Bennet asked me if I minded she read aloud, then started reading to him. After she started, I observed that Mr. Darcy fretted less when she was speaking. I… I figure he liked the sound of her voice. Sir."

Fitzwilliam smiled. "I daresay you are correct. You've been tending Miss Bennet this morning, Letty?"

The girl nodded. "Yes, Colonel. Mrs. Hubbard told me to see to any and all of her wishes, since she has no maid of her own here, and that she would clear it with Mr. Bingley and have the other girls take care of my regular duties."

"Very good. Why don't you go and see to your lady now, perhaps see if she would like some refreshment?"

"At once, Colonel," Letty replied, and took her leave.

With a sigh, Fitzwilliam set the book down again and went to the wash stand. Darcy always kept a small cup by his pitcher in case he grew thirsty in the night, and rather than waiting for a maid to bring more, he used what was left in the pitcher to mix with a bit of the fever powder. After he had managed to get a little down Darcy's throat, he then sat in the chair Elizabeth had occupied and picked up *The Adventures of Roderick Random*.

Might as well pass the time until Vincent's fit to take over, he thought as his eyes sought the beginning of the first paragraph on the even page.

"But *I* will not read to you," he said aloud to the sleeping Darcy. "I'm not *that* sentimental."

Elizabeth hurried to her room as quickly as she could. Once she was there, she dropped into one of the chairs by the fire, and tried to discern precisely *why* she had fled.

She knew instantly—it was what Colonel Fitzwilliam had said about Mr. Darcy. It wasn't much, really, but what *had* been said gave her a little more insight as to why Darcy behaved as he did. That he'd had to grow up and truly become a man before he was ready certainly explained the social awkwardness. Some might call the reluctance to engage in intercourse he had spoken of pride, such as that felt by so many of the wealthy who truly thought themselves above those who were not. She'd not seen evidence of it in him as yet, but that didn't mean it did not exist. Perhaps she could somehow arrange for him to spend more time amongst her neighbors, that he might lose some of the conceit and selfish disdain that seemed always to go hand-in-glove with the *ton*, if those were traits he possessed.

And even if he didn't, the exposure to persons less fortunate than himself could only do Mr. Darcy a world of good.

Colonel Fitzwilliam seemed to believe that his cousin was ready to marry—why else would he wax eloquent about him? It was made plain by his words that the colonel believed she and Darcy would make a good match, but social and family concerns aside, *why* would he believe that? They knew so little about her beyond her baffling willingness to recount her family's foibles to virtual strangers. Elizabeth really could not fathom any reason for her being so forthcoming—it was more her nature to attempt to conceal the flaws of her relations than to highlight them. Truly, what on Earth could she have been thinking?

"Begging your pardon, miss..."

Elizabeth started and turned to find Letty standing to her right. "Forgive me, Letty, I did not hear you come in."

"It's all right, miss. I was just come to ask if you needed or wanted anything," the maid said.

"Some tea to drink would actually be very nice—some more of that hot spearmint I had this morning, but with a cube of sugar instead of plain."

Letty nodded. "Anything else?"

She thought for a moment, then said, "I would still like some writing things, if Mr. Bingley doesn't mind. I may not *need* to send a letter now, but I think I would still like to write one. It helps me to think."

Elizabeth looked around the room, noted how neat and tidy it was, and tried to think of what else she might have need of. She realized after having surveyed the whole room that she did not see a travel trunk.

"Letty, it was my understanding that a trunk with some of my things was brought from my home, but I don't see it," she said.

"I've already unpacked it and put your things in the wardrobe in the dressing room, miss," said Letty.

"I didn't know I had a dressing room," Elizabeth replied.

The maid grinned and walked over to the bookcase that stood against the wall to the right of the fireplace. There she pulled down a book that was not really a book at all, for when she did so there was a click, and the case began to slowly swing away from her. Elizabeth rose and walked into the other room she hadn't even known was there. By her judgment it was half the size of her bedroom, but it could easily have fit the wide four-poster along with the immense wardrobe and mirror-backed dressing table. Stepping over to the wardrobe, she opened it and passed her gaze over the gowns that had been chosen for her. Mary, thankfully, had been sensible with her choice of morning gowns, though it was clear that the evening dresses were all her mother's idea, for they had the lowest necklines.

Elizabeth shook her head at the frivolity of even sending them, as they were hardly necessary. She wasn't likely to spend more than a day at Netherfield, and that only if she could school herself to withstand Caroline Bingley's snobbery.

It wasn't until she was closing the wardrobe that she noted two pair of shoes—her low-heeled black mules and a pair of cream colored slippers.

"Thank you, Mary," she said, making a mental note to express her gratitude in her writing.

"Would you like me help you change into your own things, miss?" asked Letty. "There's a chemise, stays, a petticoat, and your own nightdress in the drawer."

A look down showed a drawer beneath the wardrobe doors. Turning to the maid, she smiled and said, "While I am grateful to you for having lent me your dress, I do think I should give it back to you, now I've my own things to wear."

Letty nodded and helped her to change, folding and setting the borrowed garments aside as they were removed and helping her with the ties on her own. Elizabeth breathed a sigh of relief and contentment as she slipped a gown of pale yellow muslin embroidered with blue flowers over her head. Yes, she could have worn Letty's dress the whole day, but there was no feeling that compared to putting on a clean, comfortable garment that was wholly your own.

"That's a very pretty dress, miss," said Letty when she'd finished tying the strings.

Elizabeth smiled as the maid picked up the pile of borrowed items. "Thank you, Letty. If you would while you are out, find out what became of the things I was wearing when I arrived. I know where my boots are, I'm wearing my stockings, but where everything else went off to, I couldn't say."

"Mrs. Hubbard took 'em down to the laundry, miss," Letty told her. "I'll stop by after takin' my things to the maids' dorm, and then I'll get you that tea and see about the writing things."

After showing Elizabeth the fake book that opened the bookcase door, should she desire to go into the dressing room again, Letty went off to complete her tasks. Elizabeth went over to the wide window of her bedroom and brushed aside the curtain; she knew the rain had not eased, but had hoped a look might give her an idea of when it would. Given the disappointing visage that met her eyes, it appeared the storm would continue long into the night. A black sky hung over the estate, and clouds that were dark gray in color poured out such a steady flow of rain that she thought immediately of flooding in the fields at Longbourn, and was grateful that the planting season was long over. Bad storms such as this one early in the season always delayed planting, and if the ground had already been sown, it had the potential to ruin many crops.

Resigned to the fact that she would not be returning home anytime soon, Elizabeth returned to her chair by the fire and picked up her book. Unfortunately, *Evelina* did little to keep her occupied and her thoughts frequently returned to Colonel Fitzwilliam's speech. He had spoken almost fervently in favor of Mr. Darcy as though hopeful to win her favor. Was it merely because he thought they would do well together, or was there another reason?

Was Mr. Darcy's appreciation of her frankness an indication that he *did* think her handsome enough to tempt him? Had he said as much to his cousin, or had Fitzwilliam merely guessed—and if he had guessed, was it an educated one or only wishful thinking?

Oh, this is madness! Elizabeth groused silently as she snapped the book shut. Why did it even matter if Darcy *did* like her? She'd been saying ever since news of Mr. Bingley's coming to Meryton was made known—and her mother's determination to get one of her daughters married to him had risen to a maddening level—that she had no intention of marrying anytime soon. That she was content to be governess to Jane's ten children, if that should be her lot. For goodness' sake, why was she fretting over whether or not Mr. Darcy liked her when she had not even determined whether or not she liked *him*?

It was at that moment that there was a knock at her door, and Elizabeth was relieved for the distraction. When she had bid the visitor to enter, saw that Letty and another of the maids had come; one carried a small silver serving tray with her tea and the other a small wooden box.

"Your things have been washed and are drying down in the laundry, miss. Mr. Bingley bid me offer his apologies there's no writing desk in your room, and offered his travel secretary that you may write as many letters as you wish," said Letty. "Where would you like Henrietta to put it?"

"The vanity table in the dressing room is probably best, and if you could bring in some candles or a lamp, that would be lovely," said Elizabeth.

So it was that she was set up in the dressing room to write, with two candles and a small oil lamp from the bedroom to provide illumination for her scrawls. When she was alone again, Elizabeth sat for some minutes sipping her tea and staring thoughtfully at her reflection in the mirror, before a desire to make *any* kind of sense of her thoughts and feelings overcame her, and sat forward to take the pen in hand.

Her only conclusions by the end of the missive were an affirmation that yes, she had begun to like Mr. Darcy, and that there was at least some small possibility that he returned her regard. But was she ready to be married? She honestly could not say, and hoped that if Colonel Fitzwilliam's apparent belief was true, that Mr. Darcy would allow her time to get used to the idea before he expected her to just up and away to the north.

Some of her family were ridiculous, it was true, but they *were* her family, and she loved them. Elizabeth knew she would miss them all if she were to move to Derbyshire—or anywhere, really, that was not within walking distance of home.

Dinner that afternoon was a vastly different affair than breakfast. Claiming a headache, Caroline Bingley had elected to remain in her room. Though Mrs. Hurst was at first distant, she eventually joined in the conversation between Elizabeth, Colonel Fitzwilliam, and Mr. Bingley, and even laughed at a story Elizabeth told.

After the meal, while the men were having their brandy and cigars, Elizabeth sat in the drawing room alone with Mrs. Hurst. Not wishing the time before the men's return to be awkward, Elizabeth studied the other woman as surreptitiously as was possible, searching for something in her ensemble about which she could make a favorable remark, for any conversation was better than none.

"Are feathers quite fashionable in Town, Mrs. Hurst? I noted that you and your sister have both worn them in evening hairdressing."

Clearly surprised by the question, Mrs. Hurst replied, "Oh, quite so, Miss Bennet! All the fashionable ladies in society wear them! On turbans and wraps and hats and bonnets, mostly, though the astute society lady may add feathers to her fan or reticule—some even to her dress, though it takes an *especially* gifted *modiste* to accessorize a gown and not make both the dress and the lady wearing it look ridiculous."

Elizabeth suddenly recalled something her Aunt Gardiner had once said. "I have heard that one ought to establish something of a relationship with her dressmaker, if they are highly skilled, that she would then know the best look and colors for her clients."

Mrs. Hurst smiled. "Oh, absolutely! A lady must be able to trust her *modiste* not to let her be seen in *anything* that does not flatter her."

The comment brought to mind the orange gown Miss Bingley had worn to the assembly the night before, which made it very difficult for Elizabeth not to laugh.

"Earth tones."

Elizabeth blinked. "I beg your pardon?"

"For you, Miss Bennet," Mrs. Hurst replied. "With your skin tone and eyes and hair coloring, I quite think earth tones would best suit you—that is, if you do not mind the suggestion."

As she had been told something similar before, Elizabeth smiled and told her she did not mind. Mrs. Hurst then switched places, moving from the sofa across from her to sit beside her. For a moment she studied Elizabeth's features, then gave a nod. "I am certain of it—browns, yellows, greens…some reds as well, though nothing too bright or the color would look garish. This is not to say that blues or whites would not look good on you, but for perfection you must look to the earth tones."

Surprise flooded through her again, to be given what seemed to be entirely sincere advice from a woman she had thought haughty and snobbish only a day ago. Elizabeth began to wonder if perhaps she had misjudged Mrs. Hurst. It seemed to her that Louisa was a much different person without Caroline's presence to influence her, a thought that brought to mind Elizabeth's own youngest sisters: Kitty was often much more subdued in her manner and less inclined to call across the street to the officers she knew when Lydia wasn't around. Unfortunately for Kitty, they were not often out of each other's company.

When the gentlemen came into the drawing room, it was suggested by Bingley that his sister entertain them with some music. Mrs. Hurst exclaimed that she would be delighted to play for them, and so the party moved into the music room. She played a lovely concerto on the pianoforte with impressive skill, and so Elizabeth's applause at the end was not perfunctory.

"Do you play, Miss Bennet?" asked Fitzwilliam.

She laughed. "I do, yes, but very poorly. I'm afraid I have never been as dedicated to practicing as my sister Mary, or Mrs. Hurst."

"Oh, do play for us, Miss Bennet!" said Mrs. Hurst. She slid over on the bench seat of the instrument and patted the space beside her. "I'm sure we can find something you are comfortable with, and I'll turn the pages for you."

"Allow me to add my pleading as well," said Mr. Bingley. "I've no doubt Louisa would be happy to entertain us all evening, but surely you will not leave her to do so alone. If you will not play the pianoforte, perhaps you can sing for us. Do you sing at all?"

"Now *that* I can do, Mr. Bingley—you have discovered my secret talent," said Elizabeth with a smile. "Besides having a propensity for saying things I really ought not to, I can actually carry a tune. I warn you though, I may be a tad rusty—I'm not used to performing in front of an audience."

Thus she stood and moved to the pianoforte and sat next to Mrs. Hurst. The two perused the music sheets for a song that Elizabeth could sing and Louisa could play. After their selection had ended, Elizabeth received praise from all but Mr. Hurst for the "loveliness" of her voice (he seemed more interested in getting into his cups than actually paying attention to the entertainment). Encouraged by the reception, she gave in to the request for another, and chose a lively folk song in which she was eventually joined by the two gentlemen and Mrs. Hurst as well.

Colonel Fitzwilliam asked her to sing a third time, but Elizabeth begged off. She was now relaxed enough to be able to enjoy her book. She bid them a good evening and said she would indeed see them at supper, and on leaving made for the library. There she pulled the second and third volumes of *Evelina* from the shelf, to have them on hand when she finished the first.

Her slippers were quiet on the stairs as she ascended, though on the landing she paused. She'd not seen to Mr. Darcy in some hours, and decided it might be a good time to check on him. His valet appeared only mildly surprised to see her, and his bow was from the waist when he had invited her to come inside.

"I'll not stay long," said she. "I only came to see how Mr. Darcy fared."

"I believe my master to be a little better," said Vincent. "His fever broke about an hour ago."

"That is wonderful news!" Elizabeth exclaimed softly, and the worry that she had carried in the back of her mind went blissfully away. Despite admonitions to the contrary from her host and Colonel

Fitzwilliam, she had begun to feel she was at least partly responsible for Darcy's illness.

"If I may be so bold as to make a request, madam, would you mind terribly sitting with Mr. Darcy again for a short time?" Vincent asked. "If I have overstepped my boundaries, I do beg your pardon, but I've not eaten since this morning and— "

Elizabeth held up a hand to stop him. "Say no more, Mr. Vincent," she told the valet with a smile. "Go and see to your dinner, but I ask that you inform our host or Mr. Darcy's cousin, and ring for a maid to come and sit with us on your way out."

"Yes, madam," Vincent said, and then he bowed again and quit the room, leaving the door open.

Sitting in the chair at Darcy's right side again, Elizabeth took a moment to study him. He did appear less fevered, the flush having receded from his face, and he breathed more evenly than he had that morning. She smiled softly and sat back, saying aloud in a soft voice, "Whatever shall we talk about, Mr. Darcy? Or rather, what should I say that you will not even hear? Would it interest you to know that your cousin seems to think you and I would make a good match? Though how he has determined this when he hardly knows me I cannot say, but he spoke very strongly in your favor this morning."

Feeling suddenly very silly for her one-sided conversation, she rose and walked to the window, her arms wrapped around herself as she stared out of it. She thought of the emotions she had wrestled with, how she had poured out her heart in her letter, telling Jane and Mary how she could not understand her own confusion. How could she like Mr. Darcy if she was not even ready for marriage?

"And how…how did you respond?"

Elizabeth whirled around in shock at the sound of Mr. Darcy's raspy voice; Henrietta entered at the same moment as he spoke, but she did not acknowledge the servant as she found herself staring into Darcy's weary eyes.

"Are you all right, miss?" asked the maid.

Blinking, she shook herself mentally. "Go at once and fetch Colonel Fitzwilliam. Tell him Mr. Darcy is awake."

Henrietta curtsied and hastened out. Elizabeth walked back around the bed and sat in the chair, Darcy's eyes following her as she moved.

"How did you respond?" he asked again, and then began to cough.

Alarmed, Elizabeth searched the room for a way to alleviate his distress. Relief flooded through her when she noticed a cup on the wash stand and she hurried to it, praying that there was still water in the pitcher. It had been refilled sometime during the day, thankfully, so she poured some into the drinking cup and carried it over to the bed. Darcy pulled a hand from under the cover to take the glass but it shook, so she placed her fingers around his to steady it as he lifted his head to take a drink.

"There now, just a bit. Don't rush it, Mr. Darcy," she said.

When he nudged the cup away from his lips, she took it and placed it on the bedside table, then sat down again. "How do you feel, sir?"

Darcy's eyes held hers. "I am well," he said. "And you have not answered my question."

"That is because I have no answer," replied Elizabeth. "I did not speak to Colonel Fitzwilliam of my thoughts save to say I was unsure your family would approve of me. On my own I pondered whether or not his assumptions about you were wishful thinking or the result of years of studying your character. I wondered why he felt as he did when we've all only just met last evening and you hardly know me. And *then* I was forced to consider that even if you should find me handsome enough to tempt you, how I felt would mean very little if you found yourself unable to form any serious design on me given that my circumstances are so decidedly beneath your own."

At this she found herself no longer able to continue returning his gaze, and so lowered her eyes to her lap. A moment later his voice called to her to look at him, and it was with some trepidation that she did so.

Darcy smiled weakly. "It is true that we have not yet known one another four and twenty hours—that is, I assume a full day has not passed since our formal introduction. It is also true that your family's circumstances and your connections are not what I would wish them to be. I will admit that I have struggled with whether I ought to repress the thoughts of how pleasing I find your company. If I were to pursue you, it would be in spite of every perceived wrong and every objection that might be raised."

Elizabeth's expression fell, though she managed to keep from scowling. "I do believe I understand you perfectly, Mr. Darcy," she said, and stood to leave.

"Miss Elizabeth, I do not say these things to wound you. I say them only because I desire to always be honest with you."

She turned back slowly, and after regarding his earnest expression for a moment, Elizabeth nodded and sat down again. "What then did *you* conclude, Mr. Darcy?"

He smiled again, stronger this time. "That I should like to be friends with you, if you would accept my overtures. You are not the only one who is at present of no mind to marry—though I am certain our reasons differ—not to mention it would be highly impractical to even be thinking of marriage when we have only just met. That said, I will not discount the possibility of there one day being more between us, if we should each of us find that our feelings have changed."

His words were spoken with a sure and steady voice, and Elizabeth could find no fault in his reasoning. Being honest with herself, she would not mind at all becoming friends with so worldly a gentleman. She sensed he knew a great deal about many subjects, and it would be a refreshing change to have someone besides her father to discuss such things as politics and culture and even the running of an estate with.

"I find your overtures to be acceptable, sir," she said with a smile.

Darcy laughed, though it was followed soon by another coughing fit. Elizabeth reached for the cup of water to give it to him, and it was at that moment that Colonel Fitzwilliam strolled in, a little too casually to have just arrived. Elizabeth shared a knowing look with Darcy, who said, "Theodore, how long have you been standing outside the door?"

Fitzwilliam grinned hugely. "Long enough," he replied. "So we're all friends now, eh?"

"Do not read more into what you may have heard than there is, Theodore," said Darcy. "And no more singing my praises to the lady, your voice may frighten her away from us all."

Elizabeth laughed at Colonel Fitzwilliam's frown. "I guess you are feeling better. Looks like we'll not have to send for Mr. Jones again," he observed.

"I still feel very warm, and sour in my stomach."

Elizabeth studied Darcy's face again, and felt a blush to find him smiling at her. She turned her eyes up to Fitzwilliam after a moment and said, "Mr. Vincent said his fever had broken, but that does not mean a mild one will not linger. Perhaps we should do the vinegar towels again, unless there is any fever powder left."

Fitzwilliam moved around her and picked up the packet sitting on the bedside table. "I think there's just enough for one more dose," he said, and tipped it out into the cup his cousin still held.

"Bottoms up, Will," he instructed.

Darcy grimaced but nonetheless swirled the water and did as he was told. He made a face that Elizabeth was hard-pressed not to laugh at, and held the cup out. "Can I get some more water, and perhaps some help sitting up?"

"Don't you think you should rest some more?" Elizabeth asked as Fitzwilliam went to the washstand.

"Perhaps, but I've already slept much of the day away and would like to stay up a while, if I can," he replied.

"What do you think, Colonel?"

Fitzwilliam stopped at her side. "I probably should have warned you that Darcy is as stubborn as they come, Miss Elizabeth. Now he's decided he wants to be up a while, he'll stay up until the cold knocks him out again. Could be just a few minutes, could be a few hours—no telling with him."

This time she did laugh when Darcy shot his cousin a sour look. Fitzwilliam laughed as well, and then Elizabeth stood and moved aside so that he could help the other man into a sitting position. When she saw how far down the open neck of his shirt went, revealing a patch of dark, curly chest hair, she turned away from them.

"Should I even be here when Mr. Darcy is in such a state of undress?" she asked.

"It's only an open neck, Miss Elizabeth," Fitzwilliam observed. "With his cover in place he is otherwise decent, and I am in the room to chaperone."

"I will tie it—please, Miss Elizabeth, do not go just yet," said Darcy.

She nodded in acquiescence and turned around slowly. By the time she had, the gap at his neck had closed and he had the cup of water in his hand.

"Since you're determined to stay awake for the time being, would you like me to have the cook prepare something for you?" Fitzwilliam asked as Elizabeth returned to her chair.

"He had broth and bread sent to me this morning," said Elizabeth. "If the kitchen has any more of that, it should suffice."

"I think I can take more than that," Darcy protested.

"And I think not," she retorted. "I had not even shown signs of illness when you bid the remedy be sent to my room, and you've been abed with fever for most of the day. You'll have broth and bread, Mr. Darcy, or you'll have nothing."

Colonel Fitzwilliam burst out laughing, a full belly laugh that doubled him over and had him gripping the bedpost. "Oh, I really like her, Will," he said when he could manage to speak. "If nothing else, she's someone else to pester you into looking after yourself."

Darcy scowled. "Miss Elizabeth could very well pester *you* in the same fashion, Theo," he rejoined. Fitzwilliam lifted his hands in surrender, then went to the bell-pull to ring for a maid. The light repast Elizabeth had determined Darcy could have for his dinner was brought up by Vincent, who expressed his delight in seeing his master restored.

"Not quite, Vincent, but I am well on my way," said Darcy as the bowl of broth was handed to him.

Darcy's energy lasted only long enough for him to finish the broth, and he was soon resettled in his bed by his valet and the colonel to sleep comfortably. Elizabeth rose to leave and Fitzwilliam offered to escort her back to her room. The walk there was silent until they reached her door, at which time he said, "So how do you feel about your day at Netherfield so far, Miss Elizabeth? It must be challenging for you to be trapped here with no sister to comfort you."

"That is indeed the hardest part, Colonel," Elizabeth conceded. "I am indebted to Mr. Darcy for his service to me, as I'd no doubt be in a worse position than he had I gone home to Longbourn. I am also appreciative of Mr. Bingley's willingness to shelter me when he knows me so little, as well as see to my comfort and health."

"I've known Charles Bingley about as long as Darcy has. He's young yet, and eager to establish himself, but he's a genuine good fellow, Miss Bennet. He'd not have turned you away even if you were a complete stranger."

She smiled again. "That is good to know, as it seems our acquaintance is to be furthered. As regards what you said before, I *do* feel somewhat alone here, having no one to confide in, but I no longer feel as though I am not among friends."

Fitzwilliam returned her smile. "I am most pleased to hear it. As I see you've more books selected from the library, I'll leave you now to read in peace."

Elizabeth nodded. "Enjoy the rest of your evening, Colonel, what you can of it. I will see you at supper."

They parted ways there and Elizabeth slipped into her room.

Chapter Ten

Sunday, 21 October 1798

Darcy slept peacefully that night, enjoying perhaps the most restful slumber he had had since receiving the letter from Alan Brandon that his sister had been attacked.

He knew he owed much of that peace to Elizabeth Bennet. She had forgiven his blunder, had tended him while he was ill, and had accepted his friendship. He could ask no more of her than that, nor could he at present give her more.

In the morning of the next day, he felt marginally better. Hardly any fever, and his appetite had increased. The only lingering effects of his condition were a persistent weakness and a cough. How the cold had come upon him so suddenly he was at a loss to understand, and whether time in a hot bath would have prevented it no one could say, but it was clear that the effects of it would be felt for a few days more.

Elizabeth came to check his progress after she woke, and voiced her pleasure that he had continued to improve. Darcy surprised her by asking her to read to him again, at which she said she was not aware that he even knew she had. He confessed that Fitzwilliam had let it slip before her arrival, and that *he'd* heard of it from a maid. He smiled when she agreed, pleased by her willingness to stay with him in his sick room, and settled back against the pillows to listen.

Before she could begin, however, Bingley rapped a knuckle on the open door and stepped in. "Forgive me for disturbing you."

"There is nothing to forgive. Good morning, Mr. Bingley," said

Elizabeth in welcome.

"What is it, Bingley?" Darcy asked, having long ago learned to read the younger man's expressions. He'd come to deliver what he believed to be bad news.

"It finally stopped raining, so I've had men out to check the roads," he began. "I had thought perhaps Fitzwilliam, the Hursts, Caroline, and Miss Bennet would desire to go to church, that we might even be able to return our guest to her family there."

Elizabeth sighed. "I sense a 'however' coming," she said.

Bingley nodded. "However… When the footmen returned and described the road to me, I had to see for myself, and it really is in terrible condition. Been a long time since I've seen mud so thick—a carriage simply wouldn't make it through. I am afraid you'll be with us a while longer, Miss Bennet. At least until tomorrow."

Darcy watched her expression shift between emotions. He wondered if she was as torn as he was, both wanting her to stay and wanting to see her happily reunited with her family. She turned her face to his and he worked to maintain a neutral countenance, and after a moment of studying his expression, she turned back to Bingley and said, "I understand, sir. And it's all well, my being here among new friends, is it not?"

"Indeed it is," said Darcy and Bingley in unison, at which she laughed a little.

"Miss Bennet," Bingley went on, "pray, do not think for a moment that you are a burden, for we are happy to have you. Well, most of us."

Darcy frowned. "Most of us? Whatever do you mean, Charles?"

Elizabeth returned her gaze to his. "Miss Bingley and I had a bit of a row yesterday. She is unhappy with my presence and believes I mean to take advantage of the situation to trap you into marriage."

He snorted with derision. "Caroline Bingley has been under the mistaken impression that she would one day be mistress of Pemberley for far too long," he muttered. "Charles, you'd best do something about her behavior. I won't stand for her accosting Miss Elizabeth again."

Bingley snickered. "I don't think you've a need to come to her defense, Will. From what Fitzwilliam said, she handled my sister superbly, and without even raising her voice." He then loosed an aggravated sigh. "I swear, sometimes, I do not know what to do about her. Neither your pointed indifference nor my directly telling her you've no affection for her has got into her head."

"Marriage would certainly settle the matter for her, either her own or Mr. Darcy's," observed Elizabeth. "Unfortunately, she will apparently accept none other than Darcy, and he cannot marry me for he has not even asked me, let alone spoken to my father."

The last she said with her usual impertinence, and so he responded in kind. "If that is your wish, my lady, the first of those challenges I can remedy in moments, the other I can complete tomorrow."

Elizabeth laughed. "Do not put your carriage before your horses, Mr. Darcy. There is no point in asking when you cannot even be certain I will give you a favorable reply."

"But I am a very wealthy man! You should be honored I would even speak to you, let alone consider marriage—the very cheek of you, Miss Elizabeth," said Darcy with a shake of his head.

Bingley looked on the verge of apoplexy, his shock at the exchange was so great, but Darcy felt certain that, his brand of humor having been explained to her, Elizabeth would understand by his tone—as she had not the night of the assembly—that he spoke in jest. After all, she *had* deliberately provoked him.

Or so he thought. When her eyes narrowed his heart fluttered, and he began to consider that he had judged in error.

"Oh yes, Mr. Darcy. What *nerve* a poor country chit such as I would have to turn down the offer of a man who could save her entire family from destitution," she replied in the same saucy tone, the wink that accompanied her words filling him with relief. "I daresay you have not even considered the possibility that I would give any reply other than that which you expect."

Elizabeth then lifted her gaze up to Bingley, who stood beside her. Her eyes widened at the expression he wore. "Oh dear," said she. "Mr. Darcy, I am quite afraid we have given Mr. Bingley a heart attack."

Bingley blinked rapidly. "You… you were joking? The both of you—together?"

With a glance in his direction, Elizabeth smiled and started to laugh. Darcy laughed as well, then Elizabeth said, "My dear Mr. Bingley, please do not worry so. I promise you, I am not the indelicate creature I may have appeared when I fled the assembly with wounded pride. Once the particulars were explained to me, and given a few things that Colonel Fitzwilliam told me, I came to understand that Mr. Darcy was not truly disparaging me. He has been forgiven. In fact, now that I understand him a little better, he and I can satirize the ridiculously wealthy together—it really is so much more enjoyable to poke fun at the rich with a partner."

Bingley shook his head as though to clear it. "I can't believe this. Now there are two of you—good God, I don't think Fitzwilliam realizes how much trouble we are in."

Joint peals of laughter met his remark.

Elizabeth, when Darcy suggested he might join them all for breakfast, insisted he was not yet strong enough. His illness had hit him hard and fast, she reminded him, and though he was no longer feverish, he still had a cough and was still weak—this she knew from his own mistake in revealing that before she'd come to visit, he had tried to walk into his dressing room and had gotten dizzy, and had been forced to rely on Vincent's aid to get back into bed. Darcy pleaded his case to Fitzwilliam and Bingley and the two had sided with Elizabeth, but they did convince her to allow him to come down to dinner with assistance.

Dinner proved an enlightening affair. All of those in residence were pleased to see Darcy up and about—even Hurst had remarked that it was good to see him back on his feet. Bingley casually suggested that Caroline sit opposite him at the other end of the table as she had done the day before, saying that he thought it had seemed much more of a 'mistress of the manor' seat rather than beside him. For a moment his sister appeared to battle against her ego—not to mention her desire to be near Darcy—but she relented, and with her nose in the air she flounced to her chair. Darcy himself was seated to his friend's left with Fitzwilliam to Caroline's right, and Elizabeth sat between the two of them.

Even more surprising than the one sister's behavior was that of the other. Louisa Hurst seemed almost friendly in her civility toward Elizabeth as the two discussed music and singing, though the former often flicked her eyes toward her sister, who spent much of the meal in a moody silence unless she was directly spoken to.

After dinner, the party retired directly to the music room, the gentlemen foregoing cigars and brandy out of respect for Darcy's being ill. Caroline seemed to take exception to the change in routine and demanded to know their excuse for it. Louisa had then tried to placate her sister by saying she'd only suggested it because "Mr. Darcy missed yesterday's entertainment, and with his condition, I thought he might wish to join us for as long as he is able."

Bingley and Fitzwilliam voiced their agreement, with the former saying to his sister that if she did not wish to participate, she was welcome to do as she pleased. Caroline had huffed dramatically and announced she was retiring to her room. The rest of the party proceeded to the music room (Hurst requested that he at least be allowed his brandy there), where Darcy found himself delighted by the combined talents of Louisa and Elizabeth. The two seemed inordinately well matched to playing and singing together, and both seemed to rather enjoy it. Best of all was the blessing of listening to Elizabeth's angelic voice, which seemed even more so when she sang two hymns in honor of the Sabbath.

He realized he was quite tired when the ladies announced they'd had enough of performing, and asked that Fitzwilliam help him upstairs again.

"Can I trust you with a secret, Theo?" he asked as he was settling himself under the cover.

Fitzwilliam scoffed. "Don't be daft, Will, of course you can."

"Do you think it possible to know you will never want anyone else after knowing a person just two days? Does it not sound like foolish romantic nonsense?"

His cousin stood straight and regarded him with a serious expression. "I honestly cannot answer those questions, perhaps because I have never been in your situation. Why do you ask?"

"She has bewitched me," said Darcy sleepily. "I feel that I am… quite in danger…of being very much…attached to her."

He waited until Darcy's eyes were closed and his breathing even, and then Fitzwilliam smiled. "Good," he said softly to his cousin's sleeping form. "You fall in love, Darcy. Be happy. Leave that bugger Wickham to me."

When morning came it was determined that the roads had dried enough for Elizabeth to return to Longbourn at last. Although she would be glad to see her sisters and parents again, she found herself at the same time reluctant to leave. In spite of Caroline Bingley's thinly disguised hatred of her, she had enjoyed the unexpected visit immensely. Conversation with Mr. Bingley and Colonel Fitzwilliam was never lacking, Louisa Hurst had warmed up to her—thus altering her own opinion of the woman—and she had quite enjoyed being able to read all three volumes of a favorite novel.

And then there was Mr. Darcy.

She had woken Saturday morning determined to hate the man, but after two days in his company… her feelings for him were quite the opposite. She found herself rather pleased that they had made peace and were now to be friends, as she did enjoy his company as much as that of Fitzwilliam and Bingley. She could see how a young woman might find herself very much in love with any one of the three, though Elizabeth had been forced to admit to herself that it was indeed Mr. Darcy who had captured her special attention.

She was a romantic at heart and had hoped one day to fall deeply in love, but she had never really believed it possible to form an attachment to someone she knew so little. Yet here she was, terribly close to being smitten after only two days. She would have to be sure to guard herself against disappointment, as Mr. Darcy had been honest enough to admit that he did not know if the objections which might be raised regarding anything more could be overcome.

They were to be friends, and that might just have to be enough.

Darcy, although he had been determined well enough to come down to breakfast, was quite displeased on hearing she was soon to depart. He immediately announced he would see her home, the duty being his since it was his action of bringing her to Netherfield which had kept her from her family. But seeing that he was in no condition to travel the relatively short distance of three miles even by carriage—for any activity shewed him to still be very weak—it took some pleading on Elizabeth's part, with assistance from his friends and his cousin, to get him to agree to remain at Netherfield and allow Bingley the honor.

Caroline had, with cool civility, suggested that perhaps she need only a maid as companion, and had been no little amount surprised when Elizabeth agreed. But all of the gentlemen (save Mr. Hurst, of course, as he had no opinion either way) had overruled them both, Darcy the most forceful among them.

So her trunk had been packed, Bingley's carriage prepared, and after a surprisingly emotional goodbye for Elizabeth, they were soon on their way. "Remember, Mr. Bingley, he must rest a few more days before he begins to go out again. I would say not before Thursday should he leave the house," she said to the man across the carriage.

Bingley smiled and tipped his hat. "Knowing Darcy, it will be difficult. But I will do my best, and shall enlist the colonel's help."

Elizabeth grinned. "Perhaps you can threaten to call in reinforcements, such as that aunt that he and Colonel Fitzwilliam dread."

The gentleman laughed. "That would certainly scare him. I'll suggest it to Fitzwilliam—he might even be willing to endure her should her authority be required. In any case, I mean to consult with Mr. Jones in the village, for I am to go and purchase a home remedy chest from him today."

Letty, who had been selected to accompany them even though Elizabeth and Mr. Bingley could travel alone together long enough for him to see her home, looked over and said, "If you please, I shall miss your being at Netherfield, Miss Bennet. I rather liked the change of pace of being a lady's maid."

"I shall miss you as well, Letty," Elizabeth replied. "It was a pleasure to reconnect with an acquaintance from my childhood."

"The two of you know each other?" asked Bingley.

"Did I not mention it?" He shook his head. "Well, as it turns out, Letitia here—I knew her as Letty when we were girls, that is why I address her so—is from Meryton. When her father passed away some years back, her mother moved up north with her children to live with her sister, who happens to be Mrs. Hubbard."

Bingley chuckled. "How incredible! I knew Mrs. Hubbard's sister was from another county, but I had no idea which. Simply marvelous that I had a connection to Hertfordshire in my house all the time and did not know it!"

"Perhaps it was Providence, then, that brought you here," Elizabeth suggested.

"Perhaps it was, Miss Bennet," he returned with a smile.

Almost before she knew it, his carriage was turning up the long drive before Longbourn. Elizabeth felt more eager to be home the closer they drew near, and by the time the vehicle had pulled to a stop, all her family had spilled out the front door to greet her.

"Oh, my Lizzy, let me look at you!" cried Mrs. Bennet as Bingley was handing her down. Her mother's arms were around her before she knew to expect them, the embrace almost painfully tight.

"You clever girl, I knew you had it in you," her mother whispered in her ear.

Elizabeth stifled a groan as her mother squeezed again before stepping back to make room for her sisters. Both Jane and Mary wore expressions of relief and curiosity, and Kitty and Lydia could talk of nothing but how grand Netherfield must have been and how fine were the gowns of Miss Bingley and Mrs. Hurst.

"I will answer all your questions, I promise!" she cried. "But please, do wait until my host has had chance to speak to my father."

Purposely she turned away from her mother's excited expression and her younger sisters' barely stifled giggles. "Papa," Elizabeth began, "I believe you have met Mr. Charles Bingley of Netherfield. Mr. Darcy rescued me from the storm, but it was he who insisted I should stay until the weather had passed and the road could be safely traveled."

Mr. Bennet held out his hand. "I thank you, sir, for your generosity to my daughter, and for the note which informed us of her whereabouts. We were very much concerned when we could not find her Saturday morning."

"It was entirely my pleasure, Mr. Bennet," Bingley replied. "Miss Elizabeth has been the most welcome unexpected guest I have ever had the pleasure to host. I almost feel as though I should thank *you*, for she was kind enough to help tend poor Mr. Darcy when he fell ill, as well as entertain my family with her lovely voice."

"Serves him right catching a cold, after what he said about my Lizzy," said Mrs. Bennet with a sniff.

Elizabeth looked to her. "Mamma, that is unkind. You should know that Mr. Darcy offered his apologies for what turned out to be a misunderstanding on my part."

Her mother huffed and looked as though she would protest, but thankfully her father stayed any further disparaging of Darcy by inviting Mr. Bingley inside for tea. This brought an instant change to Mrs. Bennet, who profusely expressed her agreement that he should. Bingley disappointed her when he gave his regret and said that he had business in the village to tend to and could not stay. Her mother would not be fully dissuaded, however, and extracted from him a promise to bring his party to Longbourn for dinner on Friday.

After her trunk was unloaded by Mr. Hill and a footman, Elizabeth bid the gentleman and the maid a fond farewell, and only when they had passed through the gate did she turn to go into the house. She was immediately set upon by Mrs. Bennet, who demanded to know "absolutely everything", including whether she and Mr. Bingley had come to an understanding.

"Mamma, please!" Elizabeth cried as she handed off her bonnet and gloves to one of the maids, and then removed her pelisse. "I hardly know Mr. Bingley at all. Two days is not enough time—"

"Not enough? Not enough?!" shrieked Mrs. Bennet, who then lifted a hand to waggle a finger in her face. "I tell you, Miss Lizzy, it is *more* than enough time! Why, your father and I had not known each other even that long before I knew I would accept him as soon as he offered!"

"Which I knew straight away, Mrs. Bennet, and is precisely why I made you wait three months," said Mr. Bennet. "Sadly, my effort to instill patience in you was for naught. Now, as Lizzy is home again where she belongs, I shall be in my book room. Do not bother me there, if you please, unless another of the girls goes missing or it is time for tea."

Elizabeth could not help but smile at his back as he walked away and closed the door to his study. She gave in to her sisters' inquiries about Netherfield and the manners of her host, his sisters, Mr. Darcy ("...who was unfortunately abed with a cold almost the whole of the time"), and Colonel Fitzwilliam. "Did he wear his regimentals?" was Lydia's only question, and when Elizabeth replied in the negative, she made it clear that she held no more interest in her sister's adventures at Netherfield.

Near an hour was gone before Elizabeth could politely excuse herself to go to her room. Mary and Jane both were soon to follow, and when the door had closed them off from the house, they each embraced her again and expressed their happiness at having her home.

"It is also a pleasure to see you did not catch cold as Mr. Darcy did," observed Mary.

"Indeed, though we believed his illness due in part to not taking the advice of his valet to have a hot bath, as I did," Elizabeth replied.

"What are you not telling us, Lizzy?" asked Jane as she sat on the end of her sister's bed. "Pray forgive me if I am mistaken, but I have the sense that you are holding something back. If you do not wish to share I will not press, but you know you can confide in us if it is your wish."

Elizabeth smiled warmly at her. "There really is nothing to confide," said she. "No secret intrigues, assignations, or compromises. Mr. Darcy, Mr. Bingley, and Colonel Fitzwilliam were each of them every bit a gentleman."

"Did Mr. Darcy truly apologize?" asked Mary.

"He did."

"And you are certain, sister, that you do not forgive him too easily?" Mary pressed. "I have read tales of a lady promising herself to a man for the sake of comfort and fortune, and it did not always bring happiness."

"I have not promised myself to him, Mary," Elizabeth pointed out with a laugh. "I have agreed to be friends with him, which is entirely different. Mr. Darcy was very forthright in his offer of friendship, for he said he wished to know me but like me was of no mind to be married anytime soon. He also agreed with me that we could hardly be considering such a thing as marriage when we know each other so little."

"And what of his words at the assembly, Lizzy?" pressed Jane. "Are you truly certain he did not mean them?"

"If he did, Jane, why would he have a design of knowing me better?" Elizabeth moved to sit at last in the chair at her vanity. "I know it seems rather strange, our being friends now, but he *did* apologize, and I did spend two days in the same house as he, which afforded me the chance to know him better. I believe that his repentance is genuine, that his manner on further acquaintance makes him very agreeable, and..."

"And what?" asked Jane when her voice fell off.

Elizabeth felt a blush color her cheeks. "Mr. Darcy did say that he would not discount the possibility of there one day being more between us, if our regard for one another should change."

Jane raised a hand to her lips and glanced at Mary. "Oh my, Lizzy... I should like to hope that your regard for him—and his for you—*will* change once you are better acquainted, for I should so much like to see you *very* happy. Despite your protestations, sister, I believe you would make a wonderful wife and mother. But I do agree that guarding yourself, should nothing change, is for the best. I could not bear to see you heartbroken."

"And I would not like to know what it is to *be* heartbroken," said Elizabeth.

"There is a passage in Romans which says 'O the depth of the riches both of the wisdom and knowledge of God! how unsearchable are his judgments, and his ways past finding out!'" offered Mary. "I have come to liken the meaning of that verse to the opening of a poem by Cowper, which says 'God moves in a mysterious way / His wonders to perform'."

Jane smiled again. "I think what Mary means to say is that it is perhaps *because* you were so firm in your insistence that you are not ready to marry that God has put Mr. Darcy in your path."

Elizabeth laughed. "Do you propose that God means to teach me some sort of lesson?"

"Perhaps He does," agreed Mary. "And I would surmise the lesson is that one should not presume their plan will out over His. Just because waiting may be what *you* intended, Lizzy, does not mean it is also what He wanted *for* you. Surely *something* will come of your acquaintance with Mr. Darcy—even if the eventual marriage is not to him, but to another gentleman."

"Well said, Mary!" Jane praised her.

Well said, indeed, thought Elizabeth, and she filled the next couple of hours with more detailed stories of her time at Netherfield. When the three made to go down for tea in the afternoon, Jane offered her own wise observation as to the purpose behind Elizabeth's speaking so bluntly about their family.

"I think, Lizzy, that what made you uncharacteristically candid is that you have admired Mr. Darcy from the first moment you met him, even though you did not acknowledge it at the time," said she. "However, knowing our circumstances would, in their eyes, make us an unfavorable match for any of the single gentlemen, you were blunt to the point of improper because you sought to frighten Mr. Darcy away before he could harm you with a rejection."

"It is a natural defense for me, I suppose," agreed Elizabeth, "to wound before I can be wounded. I did try to deny that I found him to be agreeable, to my sisters and Charlotte as well as to myself, for I was very much confused. How could someone so sure she is not ready to be married be suddenly so very captivated?"

"I am afraid I cannot answer that, Lizzy," said Jane. "As Mary said, only God knows His plan. But, if I may… Do guard yourself, as you said, so you are not disappointed, but perhaps do not guard yourself so closely that your heart cannot be touched. I would not have Mr. Darcy disappointed anymore than you."

Elizabeth stayed back a moment as her sister moved on to the dining room, considering Jane's words. She had been advised that she ought not hope too much for love to grow between her and Mr. Darcy, but she also that she should not say no to it if it did.

Chapter Eleven

The days leading up to the dinner party were filled with frustration for Elizabeth.

She made all possible attempts to fill her time with practical pursuits. She would practice singing when Mary played at the pianoforte, spend hours doing needlework with Jane, read until she was exhausted, and of course took some very long walks.

It was not always easy to remain focused on a task when Mrs. Bennet frittered about wondering if Mr. Bingley would call. When he did not, she wondered why. She pestered her daughter with numerous questions about her days at Netherfield, asking again and again for Elizabeth to describe their interactions so that she could determine the meaning of his "odd" behavior.

It came to a head on Wednesday when, feeling completely exasperated with her mother's queries, she at last told her that she had actually spent most of her time in the company of Mr. Darcy or in her own room. Mrs. Bennet went into one of her fits, calling Elizabeth headstrong and foolish, saying she was surprised she had managed to catch Mr. Bingley's eye at all with her having spent so much time with his "disagreeable" friend. At this Elizabeth determined she had had quite enough, and declared she would be walking into Meryton. This idea was immediately taken up by her younger sisters, who begged to go along citing a need to purchase ribbons to make over their gowns for the dinner party. In the end all five girls went out, with none of them surprised by their mother's shouting after them to bring Mr. Bingley back should they meet him while in the village.

Elizabeth was relieved when Kitty and Lydia ran several paces ahead, that she and her other sisters could speak in private. "I declare, Mamma will drive me to madness with her constant badgering about Mr. Bingley."

"Then why do you not just tell her you have no understanding with him?" asked Jane.

"I had hoped that my avoiding speaking of Mr. Bingley—or attempts thereof—would dissuade her," Elizabeth replied sullenly. "I ought to have known better."

"Indeed, Lizzy," said Mary. "You know when Mamma gets an idea into her head there is little that can be done to dislodge it."

Elizabeth groaned. "Too right you are, Mary. If I am to have any peace at all, I must tell her that I neither sought a courtship nor was one offered, by *any* of the single gentlemen."

Mary covered up a snort with a hand to her nose. "I daresay, Lizzy, that even telling her the truth will not bring you peace."

"Do you think it possible we will meet any of the Netherfield party in Meryton?" Jane queried then.

Elizabeth shrugged. "Anything is possible, Jane, but I would not count on seeing them until dinner on Friday."

After spending more time than she cared to at the haberdasher's looking over ribbons and buttons and beads, Elizabeth was happy to move on to the bookshop with Mary and Jane while Kitty and Lydia ran off to do as they always did when in Meryton these days, which was chase after the militia. They had two favorites, named Denny and Carter, and while her sisters' behavior could make her cringe, she had to give the two young officers some credit for always acting as gentlemen.

"Miss Elizabeth! How delightful to see you again so soon!"

The sisters were greeted thus by Mr. Bingley in Benson's Books and Sundry, where one could buy not only books, but also sheet music, drawing paper and pencils, playing cards, and board games. Elizabeth noted Louisa Hurst over by the music papers browsing the selection; she looked up with a smile at her brother's bright greeting and joined them.

Elizabeth and her sisters curtsied. "Mr. Bingley, Mrs. Hurst, you may remember my sisters, Miss Jane Bennet and Miss Mary Bennet."

Greetings were exchanged, and then Mary—usually the last of the sisters to begin a conversation with anyone—spoke up first, saying, "Mrs. Hurst, my sister has told us you play the pianoforte beautifully. Would you be opposed to our perhaps playing together at the dinner party on Friday?"

"In fact, I had hoped Miss Elizabeth and I could entertain everyone together—your sister really does have such a lovely voice," replied Mrs. Hurst. "And she did say you have been working so hard on your playing, Miss Mary. I should be delighted! Ought we to look and find something new to entertain our family and friends with?"

At Mary's nod, the two went over to the music together. Elizabeth turned her gaze to Mr. Bingley and asked, "How is the patient at Netherfield? Is he any better?"

Bingley laughed. "Darcy is much improved, Miss Elizabeth, and paces like a caged tiger! I declare, the only reason he has not attempted to leave the house as yet is because you decreed he should not until tomorrow."

Elizabeth laughed then. "I am surprised he has listened. Mr. Darcy does not seem the type to take orders."

The gentleman leaned down a little, then said in a whisper, "I believe it has much to do with your suggestion about calling in his aunt, Lady Catherine, as reinforcement. I told Fitzwilliam what you said and I believe he has employed the threat to tremendous effect."

She giggled again and looked to Jane, who appeared quite bewildered. Elizabeth explained to her about Darcy and Fitzwilliam's overbearing relative, at which her sister giggled and blushed.

"By and by, though we are to see you all on Friday for dinner, my friends and I should like to call at Longbourn tomorrow," Bingley said then. "Because he detests being cooped up in the house, Mr. Darcy is eager to take his leave of it as soon as he is able. We are all of us agreed that we should like to visit with our first true friends in the area when he is able to come out with us."

Elizabeth grinned. "*All* of you?"

Bingley chuckled. "Well, no, not *all*, for certain. My brother Hurst will stay at Netherfield along with Caroline, who has declared that since we are to see you all at dinner on Friday, she will wait until then. As Louisa and Mary are to entertain us afterward, she may join Darcy, Fitzwilliam, and I so that she and your sister may practice together."

"I think that sounds like a splendid way to spend a morning, Mr. Bingley," Jane told him.

"Indeed," agreed Elizabeth. "I'm sure we should all enjoy a visit with our neighbors even if we are to see you on Friday, and as we have no other callers fixed for the morning, you may even be able to remain for longer than a quarter hour if that is your wish."

Mr. Bingley favored them with a wide smile. "Excellent! I look forward to seeing you all tomorrow, then. I expect we shall call around nine."

Shortly thereafter the two parties took their leave of the shop and each other. Jane suggested then that they might head home, as the wind had picked up and now made the chill in the air quite bitter. Elizabeth and Mary agreed, though when they looked around, they could not find Kitty and Lydia. With the hope that their officer friends would see them safely home, the three elder girls set off for Longbourn.

"I say, Lizzy," said Mary, "you were right about Mrs. Hurst. She seems almost a different person without her sister present."

"She was even civil to me with Caroline at the dining table once or twice," said Elizabeth. "I quickly came to liken their relationship to that of Kitty and Lydia. You know how forceful our youngest sister's personality can be, and how Kitty so often agrees with her just so she is not left out."

"I can understand that feeling, though it is much less felt now that the two of you include me so often," Mary confessed.

"As we said before, it is something we ought have done long ago," Jane told her. "I do hope you will forgive our neglect, Mary."

Mary smiled. "It is already forgiven. Does not the Lord tell us to forgive our trespassers?" she said. "Besides, dear Jane, in spending so much time with you and Lizzy as I have these last weeks, I have noticed a number of changes in the dynamic of our family. I am compelled to practice more and preach less, and as such I am not so often belittled by Mamma or Kitty and Lydia—even Papa has taken notice of me more than once, and it was to praise my improvement on the pianoforte. I came to realize that my own manner was a reflection of my environment, and when that environment was changed, I changed."

Elizabeth put her arm around Mary's shoulders. "When you were shewed more love, you became more lovable, though we should always have treated you as we do now."

"Truly, I beg you do not feel shame any longer for what you perceive as neglect," begged Mary. "I am quite all right, as you can see. Recall the past only to remember its pleasures."

Her sisters agreed with her wholeheartedly, and continued to huddle together against the wind until they were home at last in the warmth of Longbourn.

Thursday began with great anticipation for Darcy—he was so very relieved that he indeed felt well enough to leave the house. He paid more attention to his attire than he normally did; when looking into the mirror he noted that his hair was getting a little long, and he considered it might be time for a trim. When he was near fully dressed, he suddenly realized that the color of his waistcoat was near the same shade of brown as Elizabeth Bennet's eyes.

He didn't even know he owned articles of clothing that color—and exactly *when* had he noticed the color of her eyes? *Likely the very same moment you decided they were "fine,"* came the silent reply.

Shaking the thoughts from his head, Darcy moved to the small table by his window and sat down to the toast and coffee that had been delivered. Fitzwilliam and Bingley were at his door some minutes later, declaring they were ready to go out, and it was with a desire to feel the sun on his face again for the first time in nearly a week that he eagerly joined them.

Louisa Hurst accompanied them in the carriage, and when he inquired whether she was to go on to the village, she surprised him by refuting the idea. "I'm sure my brother has told you that Miss Mary and I are to play the pianoforte for everyone after dinner tomorrow, Mr. Darcy," she said. "We've a duet chosen that we simply *must* practice!"

His gaze traveled to her brother, who sat beside her. Bingley lifted his shoulders, though he smiled and seemed quite pleased with his sister. Darcy found he was pleased as well, to see her making an effort to be friendly with Netherfield's neighbors rather than looking down her nose at them as Caroline did. Perhaps there was hope for Louisa yet.

The time spent at Longbourn was more than pleasurable. He sat with her family and endured their stares and questions, though it seemed Mrs. Bennet was determined to despise him. He quickly understood that she believed his friend and her daughter had formed an attachment, as most of her queries were pointed at Bingley. Elizabeth explained later—they were able to take a walk together in the garden, with Fitzwilliam and Bingley entertaining Jane, Kitty, and Lydia whilst Mary and Louisa practiced their duet—confessing that she had not yet dissuaded her mother of the notion that Mr. Bingley was courting her.

"You might subtly remind her that my fortune is greater than Bingley's," said Darcy when she had spoken.

Elizabeth had laughed and pointed out that if she were to say that to her mother, Mrs. Bennet would then surely expect the two of them to make an announcement very soon. He conceded that she was probably right, and then confessed that he had written of meeting her in two letters, one to his sister and one to his aunt—though not the one she had threatened to call on him should he not take care of himself. She appeared a little nervous when asking if either had yet replied, and he said that he had received a reply from his aunt the day before.

"My sister is at present in Surrey with a distant relation; she's been ill of late, so I may not hear from her until next week. The countess, on the other hand, considers it a small miracle that I admire you enough to actually mention you, and has begged that I share a little of my good fortune with her son."

"I take it she is as eager to see the colonel settled as my mother is to see my sisters and I so," Elizabeth observed.

"Indeed. Theodore is thirty years old, which is two past the age at which his elder brother married; Philip is now three and thirty, and he and his wife have a four-year-old daughter. My aunt believes marriage will force the colonel to settle in one place for more than a few weeks."

"Something tells me she will not get her wish anytime soon."

"I imagine you are right," Darcy agreed. "In my letter, I referred to you as being the niece of a gentleman she had recently done business with, and my aunt expressed her hope that you were as amiable as Mr. Gardiner, whom she rather admired for his 'surprising gentility.'"

Elizabeth scoffed. "No doubt she expects all tradesmen and their relations to be uncouth," she said. Her cheeks immediately colored with embarrassment. "Forgive me, sir. I should not speak so about a person I have not met, let alone a noble lady."

Darcy shook his head. "Do not worry yourself, Miss Elizabeth. In the past my family has indeed held a rather dismal view of the working classes; I regret that I am as guilty as any of them. I cannot say that their view or mine will change entirely, but having met someone such as your uncle, Aunt Frances has certainly seen that it *is* possible to be both a tradesman and a gentleman. It gives me cause to think that, with the proper education, perhaps any man can be a gentleman, even if he has not a gentleman's wealth."

His companion smiled, and he felt warmth spread through him. "Then I shall consider it a step in the right direction for all of you."

The next evening came and went with surprising smoothness.

That Mrs. Bennet was now aware Bingley had no designs on Elizabeth was evident near as soon as their party entered the drawing room. She greeted Bingley, Fitzwilliam, and Mrs. Hurst warmly, was civil to himself, Hurst, and Miss Bingley, but to her own daughter she expressed thinly veiled contempt. Elizabeth bore it with a stiff spine and a bright smile, very much to her credit. Darcy was compelled to offer himself as escort when dinner was announced, and purposely held her back while the others filed ahead of them that he could inquire as to the reason for her Mrs. Bennet's ill manner.

"After your party's departure yesterday, Mamma demanded to know my reason for paying you more attention than Mr. Bingley," she said in a low voice. "As my previous efforts to dissuade her from the notion of our having an understanding had failed, I'm afraid we got into a bit of a row once I stated in no uncertain terms that no such thing existed, and that I was merely friends with all the gentlemen of Netherfield."

Darcy frowned. He could not like it if Elizabeth was being treated ill because she would not compromise herself or one of his party. "She is truly angry because you returned without having an understanding with Bingley?"

"Do not be vexed on my account, Mr. Darcy," Elizabeth replied. "My mother is merely displeased that I did not do as I was *explicitly instructed*. She has declared me a willful, disobedient child with no sense of duty to her family. She will get over it in time—she always does."

She lifted a shoulder as they fell in line behind her youngest sisters. "Truth be told, sir, I didn't *want* to form an attachment—to any of you. My sole purpose at Netherfield, once it was determined I could not come away home immediately, was to make my time there as comfortable as possible," she said. When she looked up and saw his surprised expression, her lips turned up in a coy smile. "This is not to say that I would not have welcomed any addresses, should one of the single gentlemen have been of a mind to pay me any."

Again he felt warmth spread through him, as he had the day before. Her words, her expression, the brightness in her eyes—all seemed suddenly exceptional to Darcy in that moment.

Be honest with yourself, Darcy, spoke up his inner voice. *You have felt this way every time Elizabeth Bennet has favored you with a smile.*

Darcy chose to ignore the voice for the time being. He had a dinner with the entire Bennet family to get through.

Throughout the meal, Mrs. Bennet made no attempt to conceal

her efforts to encourage Bingley to take an interest in Jane, as well as continue her campaign to foster an attachment between his cousin and her youngest daughter. Darcy mused as he observed her that the lady would only end up disappointed. Bingley had confessed that although several of the local girls—including Jane Bennet—were "uncommonly pretty" he'd not yet felt particularly attracted to any of them. Unusual, given how easily he fell in love, but it was Darcy's hope that his advice to take care in the selection of his mate was at last taking root in his friend's mind. As for Fitzwilliam, he was aware that Elizabeth's mother desired a union between him and Lydia, but he had already declared the girl still too much a child to be *any* man's wife.

Caroline behaved as well as could be expected. She was mostly polite, but spent the majority of the meal casting thinly veiled insults regarding Mrs. Bennet and her relations. No doubt she held out hope that pointing out the detriments in being connected to the family would discourage any designs her brother or even he may have had in pursuing one of the Bennet sisters, but her efforts were, in fact, having the opposite effect. The more Caroline pointed out their flaws, the more Elizabeth defended her family—and the more he found himself admiring her passionate support of them.

Somewhere amidst the conversations going on around the table, it was suggested that Bingley should hold a ball. "It would be an excellent way to establish yourself in the neighborhood, Mr. Bingley, and to make new friends!" cried Lydia.

Bingley himself was quite taken with the idea, and said that he would consult his calendar to determine the perfect day. Darcy near felt like thanking Lydia, as taking charge of the planning for a ball would occupy much of Caroline's time. She'd made no secret of her dislike of the country, but that would not stop her throwing the grandest ball she could, if only as a means of showing the local residents how much better a ball was when you had money.

Elizabeth, Louisa, and Mary delighted everyone—which included the Meryton relatives Mr. and Mrs. Phillips—with their musical talents as others played cards and games after dinner. When the party had ended at last and the guests from Netherfield were home again, Darcy, Bingley, and Fitzwilliam gathered in the study for a nightcap.

"I think the party went rather well, all things considered," said Bingley before he tipped back his whiskey. "Mrs. Bennet may be… eccentric…but she does know how to lay a table."

"One of the lady's redeeming qualities, aside from her love for her children," said Darcy. "It is not merely having five daughters and no sons that drives her—her obsession to see them all married well derives from the fact that Longbourn is entailed."

"What?" cried Bingley. "Did Miss Elizabeth tell you that?"

Darcy shook his head. "Her father, actually."

Fitzwilliam raised his eyebrows. "Oh, is that what the two of you were talking about over the chessboard? I wondered at the intensity of your conversation."

"That was part of it," Darcy returned. "Mr. Bennet was naturally concerned that, as I am essentially only a visitor here, I might be playing with the affections of his favorite daughter. I did my best to assure him I was not. He said that in all likelihood, the wealthiest of his daughters' husbands, whoever he may be, would have to take on the responsibility of their mother's care as well as that of any daughters who are unmarried when he dies, as the estate is entailed on the male line to a cousin he's not even met in the whole of his life. Do you know, I cannot be sure if he was more bitter about the entail or his not having a son."

"Perhaps it is both, as well as maybe a little shame for not seeing to the girls' welfare a long time ago," mused Fitzwilliam. "Mr. Bennet does not strike me as an ignorant man, just foolishly idle. He is now being made to see, slowly but surely, the error in being so."

"At least insofar as not putting money aside for his family to live on," said Darcy. "Mr. Bennet mentioned a hope that perhaps a relative of theirs may be able to aid the girls, but that he could not count on it."

Fitzwilliam snapped his fingers. "Speaking of, I am suddenly reminded of my cousin by marriage, Lady Sotheby—Elinor Brandon as you knew her, Darcy, as they've since taken the Northam name. I believe she once faced a similar situation when her father died. Her father's estate went to her elder half-brother and his wife, and the brother was convinced by his lady not to offer more support to his sisters than the stipend from their mother's marriage portion."

"Well, *her* mother and sisters certainly haven't to worry about money anymore, do they?" said Bingley. "I read about the Mildenhall story in the papers—astonishing thing, to find out near forty years after your birth that you're the grandson of a duke and in line to inherit. I thought Colonel Brandon was a capital fellow, though I only knew him that week they stayed at Pemberley; surely he'll see to the comfort of his wife's mother and sisters, now he's got access to greater fortune. I say, do you think they would come to a ball here at Netherfield?"

Fitzwilliam shrugged. "Wouldn't hurt to issue an invitation—I believe they're living with His Grace at Northam Park now, though Lady Sotheby is in a delicate condition, so they may pass."

"I'll do it! Worst that can happen is they decline, right?" said Bingley with a grin. "But don't say anything to my sisters, I want to surprise them if they accept."

"My lips are sealed!" cried Fitzwilliam. "I'd love to see Caroline's reaction on being introduced to actual members of the aristocracy!"

Bingley was delighted to receive a positive reply to the invitation he sent to Lord and Lady Sotheby. Fitzwilliam's cousin informed him that he and his wife were flattered that he remembered them and happy to accept the chance for one last ball, as Lady Sotheby was soon to enter confinement for their first child. They would come up from Sotheby Hall in Kent three days before the ball, and would be accompanied by the countess's sister and the earl's cousin.

About the time this welcome news was received at Netherfield, there came to Longbourn a most *un*welcome visitor. Mr. William Collins was the dreaded cousin who, if Mrs. Bennet was to be believed, would turn her and her daughters out of their home before her husband was cold in his grave. The letter received by Mr. Bennet—so Elizabeth informed Darcy during a visit to Netherfield—had been written on the advice of his patroness, that he might extend an olive branch and heal the breach in the family.

"And do you not want to know who she is, this paragon of Christian virtue?" she asked teasingly.

"Lizzy," admonished Mary, who, along with Jane and Elizabeth, had been invited to Netherfield for tea. The official invitation had been issued by Louisa for propriety's sake, and the party—minus Caroline, who had begged off citing a need to focus on preparations for the upcoming ball; and Mr. Hurst, who chose to take his tea in the billiard room—had foregone the formality of the drawing room for the comfort of the library.

"I must admit that the matter is of little concern to me, Miss Elizabeth, but as you seem eager to relay the identity of the lady, I have no objection to hearing it," was Darcy's reply.

Elizabeth flashed a wide grin at him as she stood and began to pace the room. "I am surprised, Mr. Darcy, that you do not already know, seeing as you are intimately acquainted with the lady—as are you, Colonel. If my memory doth serve me well, you are neither of you very fond of her."

Darcy and Fitzwilliam looked to one another with expressions of shock. Moments later, Bingley began to guffaw; Elizabeth laughed along with him.

"Our Aunt Catherine is your cousin's patroness?" said Fitzwilliam. "Are you serious, Miss Elizabeth?"

She came to perch on the arm of Darcy's chair. "Indeed I am, Colonel—he can hardly speak two words together without tacking on some homage to his 'noble patroness, Lady Catherine de Bourgh' and her wisdom."

"Now, sister, you are being unkind." This was said by Jane, though she clearly struggled to keep from smiling.

Elizabeth scoffed. "It is true even if it is unkind to say so." She looked over to Louisa then. "By and by, Mrs. Hurst, I really must thank you for inviting my sisters and me to tea today. It gave us the perfect excuse to be away from Mr. Collins and his fawning."

"Oh you are quite welcome, Miss Elizabeth," said Louisa. She smiled as she spoke, but there was a subtle strain in her expression. She and Caroline had been arguing near daily the last couple of weeks over her desire to actually befriend the elder Bennet girls, whom Caroline still considered to be beneath their notice. Even Jane, whom she had once said to be "a sweet girl" no longer had her favor.

"It seems Mr. Collins is convinced," Elizabeth was saying, "that the best means of bridging the divide which has led to his being the heir to Longbourn is to marry one of my father's daughters. I cannot fathom the idea of being married to such a man."

"Is he truly so disagreeable?" Darcy asked her.

A look was shared between the sisters. "I must concede that I am sure he means well, but honestly, he is perhaps the most ridiculous man I have ever met!" Elizabeth replied. "I do not think I have known anyone so full of their own misguided self-importance."

Fitzwilliam laughed. "Just wait until you meet Lady Catherine. I do not doubt he gets it from her."

"He is also the clumsiest, clingiest toad," added Elizabeth with a shiver. "Mamma has convinced him that Jane is being courted by Mr. Bingley—"

"I am so very sorry about that, sir," said Jane immediately.

"Lizzy and I have spoken to her in private about her deception, but she will not yield."

Elizabeth nodded. "Our mother may not be the most sensible woman, but even she is clever enough to discern that my angelic sister would be miserable with Mr. Collins for a husband, and is determined to save her from that fate. Unfortunately, because she still considers Mr. Darcy to be 'proud and arrogant' and is determined that the colonel will one day see our sister Lydia's worth, I became his next choice."

A sensation that could only be described as jealousy flashed through him. Darcy was suddenly very uncomfortable with the idea of Elizabeth being pursued by this cousin of hers. She deserved better than one of his aunt's sycophantic followers.

Mary set down her teacup with a click on the saucer and rose from her place on the sofa beside Jane; she paced to one wall of the library as though to peruse the books there. It was clear she was becoming discomfited by the turn of the conversation.

"At risk of offending," Louisa began slowly, "would it not be a *good* thing for Mr. Collins to marry one of your sisters? Surely he would not turn your mother and any unmarried sisters out if they were the relations of his wife."

Jane looked to her. "In principle, Mrs. Hurst, it would be a very good thing and solve many problems," she said softly.

Elizabeth interrupted her, shuddering as she said, "But I simply cannot abide it. He is an utter fool, and even Mary—who has a great love for the church and her faith—would find herself unevenly yoked."

Mary turned from the bookshelves. "Sisters, I find that I am no longer feeling very well. Might we return home?"

Elizabeth and Jane shared a look, then the former stood and crossed the room to her. "Does our conversation make you uncomfortable? I am sorry for it if it does."

"It is not that, Lizzy. I'm just suddenly feeling weary and should like to lie down."

Bingley stood. "I'll go and have your carriage brought around straight away."

Mary and Jane both thanked him for his kindness; Jane and Elizabeth wore concerned expressions, each alternately placing an arm about their sister's shoulders while they waited to depart.

When they had been handed into the carriage and set off, Darcy stood watching until it passed through the gate. When he returned to the library, Louisa declared she was feeling rather tired as well and that she would be going to lie down until dinner.

Now just the three gentlemen, the library was silent at first, then Fitzwilliam said, "It is a tough situation for them, what future the Bennet ladies are facing."

"Indeed," said Bingley. "It is clear none of those girls have a good opinion of their cousin—I cannot imagine being in such a position as to be giving up a chance at true happiness for the sake of security."

"Can you not, Charles?" Darcy countered. "You once said that your position in life is only greater than the Bennets' because of your family's fortune. Imagine your grandfather had not been successful in making it or your father not successful in improving it—would not your sisters be in such a position as are Elizabeth and her sisters?"

"They are all of them charming and agreeable—even the younger two when they are still and not fidgeting about—but their lack of fortune and connections *do* materially lessen their chances of marrying men of any consideration in the world," observed Fitzwilliam.

Darcy scowled at the expression on his cousin's face, as though he were waiting for him to say something. He turned away from him to pace over to the window.

"Elizabeth is as charming and graceful as any society girl *should* be," Fitzwilliam went on, "and would likely win over more than a few of the *ton* with her wit and her smiles alone. You know, I'm of half a mind to court her myself, now that we are much better acquainted."

It was all he could do not to turn around and lash out; Darcy instead turned slowly, a determined set to his shoulders. "You will do no such thing," he snapped.

"And why shouldn't I?" his cousin rejoined. "She is young, intelligent, witty—and certainly beautiful enough to tempt *me*."

"*No*," Darcy barked, his ire growing.

Bingley grinned. "But Darcy, Theo and Miss Elizabeth would make a wonderful couple!"

He stalked toward them. "Absolutely not—she is *mine!*"

Fitzwilliam threw back his head. "It's about bloody time!" he cried. "I swear, Darcy, I was beginning to wonder if you were ever going to admit your attachment."

Darcy's anger cooled instantly, as though he had been doused with a bucket of icy water. "You...you were baiting me?"

Fitzwilliam and Bingley laughed. "Forgive us, Darcy," said the latter. "Theo approached me the other day and suggested the ruse."

"We just needed the perfect opportunity, and you gave it right to us," added Fitzwilliam with a laugh.

As he stood there staring at the ridiculous expressions of his two closest companions, Darcy considered that, given his reaction to the mere *idea* that his cousin would court Elizabeth…

It was time to stop fooling himself—time to stop denying that his first and last thoughts each day were of her. Darcy had been fighting his attraction to Elizabeth from the very first moment of their acquaintance, telling himself it just wouldn't work—that the objections to a match with her were too great to overcome, as her immediate family was too vulgar and her connections sorely lacking.

But it was no use. Every moment spent in her company the last three and a half weeks had been the most pleasurable he had ever spent in the company of a lady not related to him. He found himself looking forward to their spirited debates as much as their quiet walks together. He relished every smile, every glance of her fine eyes, the sound of her every laugh. He had seen her be firm yet caring in her attempts to curtail her younger sisters' behavior, kind to her every neighbor, gentle with the elderly and the young, and loving even to her misguided mother. She was generous to the tenants of Longbourn to the point of giving up her extremely meager allowance if their needs were great.

How could such a woman not be already spoken for? More than that, what the devil did he plan to do about his feelings?

As the Bennet carriage trundled down the road, Elizabeth stared at her sister Mary, who had tucked herself into the squab on the rear-facing seat. Something was amiss, had to be, for Mary had been little out of sorts since she and Jane had been paying her more attention.

"Are you sure you're all right, Mary?" she asked.

Mary looked over. "I am quite well, Lizzy. In fact, I have made a decision," she said with what seemed to be forced calm. "And before you protest, Elizabeth, it is *my* decision to make. Although Mamma has been forcing his company on you, I have decided I shall put myself more forward and encourage Mr. Collins' affections so that he may, before his departure, make an offer of marriage to *me*. In this way, we shall none of us be unwelcome in the home we have known all our lives."

Elizabeth gasped. "Mary, you *cannot* be serious! You will be dreadfully unhappy!"

"Mary, are you sure you want to do this?" asked Jane in a calmer tone. "You know I dislike speaking ill of anyone, but our sister is right—Mr. Collins is quite a foolish man. If he makes an offer it will not be because he loves you. He wishes only to do as his patroness has instructed him to."

"I am not likely to make a love match anyway, Jane," Mary retorted. "I accepted long ago that I am the least handsome of my sisters—no, do not attempt to deny it; my features *are* very plain. Knowing that my chances of making a good match were far less than those of my elder sisters or even my younger sisters, I knew it would be in my best interests to take a chance when one was presented to me."

Mary heaved a deep sigh. "While I can agree that Mr. Collins is neither sensible nor always agreeable, his position in life is respectable, and the match a favorable one for a young woman like myself who would come with no fortune. I may not entirely respect the gentleman himself, but I respect his profession very much. Should he do as our mother hopes, when we are married I shall dedicate myself to serving the people who make up his congregation."

As Elizabeth regarded her, she noted the determined set of Mary's expression; her mind was made up. She felt torn, knowing that to have Mr. Collins' attentions directed elsewhere would be a blessing for herself, but that it should be one of her sisters made to suffer them... Not to mention that the Netherfield ball was in but four days, and Mr. Collins had already solicited the first two dances with Elizabeth herself. How was Mary's scheme to even work when their cousin had already set his cap?

Chapter Twelve

The arrival of the party from Kent caused quite a stir, in Meryton and at the estates of Netherfield and Longbourn.

First, Colonel Fitzwilliam got his wish in seeing Bingley's sister stunned into silence by the arrival of their visitors. When she awoke that day, she found maids scurrying up and down the stairs to the second floor, and so went in search of her brother, for he had not informed her that they were to have any overnight visitors.

"I invited some acquaintances I made in March," he replied simply to her inquiry.

"But who is it, Charles? If I am to keep house for you, brother, I should be kept informed when guests are expected, and especially when they are to stay!"

It was about two hours later that the first sounds of an approaching carriage could be heard. Bingley grinned at his sister and shared a look with his friends, then led the way out of his study to go and greet the arriving guests. Louisa met them in the entry hall.

"I take it you have seen!" she declared. "A grand chaise-and-four is coming through the gate, Charles! Whoever can it be?"

Bingley looked to her. "They are very important acquaintances of mine, and I expect you *both* to behave as the civilized ladies I know are inside you somewhere," he said, before gesturing to Foster to open the door.

When the carriage came at last to a halt before the portico, a footman climbed quickly down from the back to open the door and lower the step. A tall, finely-dressed gentleman stepped out, then immediately turned to hand out a fashionably dressed young woman with blonde hair, followed by another whose hair was red. The two stepped aside and the man turned again, and with the assistance of the footman helped a lady descend from the carriage who was very visibly with child.

"My friends," said Bingley with a bow. "I bid thee welcome to Netherfield Park."

The party were looking around them, then the man said, "And happy we are to be here, Mr. Bingley. It is good to see you again."

"And you as well, Colonel Brandon—forgive me, the address has changed, has it not? Colonel Fitzwilliam says you have taken your uncle's name and secondary title, and are called Lord Sotheby now."

Sotheby nodded as from behind him, Bingley heard Caroline mutter, "L-lord?"

Starting as though surprised, her brother moved aside and brought her and Louisa forward, then said, "Do forgive me for forgetting my manners. Sisters, it is my honor to present Alan Northam, the Earl of Sotheby, and his lovely wife Elinor, Countess of Sotheby."

As Caroline and Louisa curtsied deeply, he introduced the two of them, as well as Darcy and Fitzwilliam for the benefit of the two young ladies who had accompanied the earl and countess. Lord Sotheby introduced the ladies in turn; the blonde girl was his cousin, Lady Amelia Northam, daughter of the Duke of Mildenhall; and the red-haired girl his sister-by-marriage, Miss Marianne Dashwood. A second, smaller carriage was then pulling up; out of it stepped a man and three young ladies who, although well-dressed, were clearly the personal attendants of the Sotheby party.

"I'm sure you would all like to freshen up after your journey," Bingley said after the group had moved into the house. Mrs. Hubbard, Foster, and a couple of the maids were waiting in the entryway.

"Actually, I should like very much to lie down, Mr. Bingley," said Lady Sotheby. "I'm sure you can understand why such a relatively short journey would tire me so easily."

"Of course, my lady, and may I offer you my sincerest congratulations—that is, if it is not impolite to do so."

She smiled at him. "You may indeed, for it is not as though my condition is not obvious."

Bingley gestured toward his housekeeper. "Mrs. Hubbard, my housekeeper. She and these young ladies will show you to your rooms. My lord, if you and the other ladies should like to join us when you are refreshed, my friends and I shall be in the drawing room. The maids will be standing by to direct you."

"Mr. Bingley, if it would not be too much trouble, could you have some form of drink waiting?" asked Lady Amelia. "I know it is not yet tea-time, but I'm really quite thirsty."

Bingley nodded. "Of course, my lady. Foster, will you go and speak to the kitchen about preparing refreshments for our guests?"

"Straight away, Mr. Bingley," acknowledged the butler, and he turned smartly away to perform the task.

Mrs. Hubbard, Letitia, and Henrietta then led the guests and their attendants up the stairs to the guest wing. Bingley moved into the drawing room with Darcy and Fitzwilliam, with Caroline and Louisa following.

"Charles Bingley!" hissed Caroline. "How could you not tell me we were to host an earl and a countess and the daughter of a duke! Louisa and I could have dressed properly to greet them! How do you even know these people?!"

"At least a *little* warning would have been appreciated, brother," added Louisa in a more genial voice.

"Sisters, you look just fine—the Sothebys are two of the least pretentious people I have ever had the privilege to know," said Bingley. "I met them when I was visiting at Pemberley in March."

"And you did not think to tell Louisa and me you had met an earl and a countess?"

Fitzwilliam chuckled. "They were not technically nobility at the time, Miss Bingley," he said. "It was not until they attended my family's annual Spring Ball that Lord Sotheby's noble lineage was discovered. There, the former Colonel Brandon of Delaford and his wife were introduced to the Duke of Mildenhall, who is a friend of my father's. It was His Grace that made it known to us all, for Lord Sotheby bears an uncanny resemblance to the duke's late father. 'Twas then we learned that Sotheby and I are also related."

"And how are they related to you, if I may ask, Colonel?" queried Louisa.

"Lord Sotheby is my first cousin once removed—his father's mother and my mother's mother were sisters. Lady Amelia is Lord Sotheby's cousin on his mother's side, for his mother was the sister of His Grace," Fitzwilliam explained.

"And Lord Sotheby will inherit the duke's title?" Caroline asked.

"That is correct."

Darcy stepped into the conversation then, saying, "Though we share no blood, I am also related to Lord Sotheby—though more distantly—via the marriage of my parents; my own mother being sister to Lord Disley, who as you know is Colonel Fitzwilliam's father."

Both sisters flounced down onto the sofa. "I cannot believe this. My brother is intimately acquainted with royalty," muttered Caroline.

"Not royalty, Caroline—peers are called nobility. If His Grace was a royal duke, then 'royalty' would be an apt descriptor, and he would then be His Royal Highness, but as I understand it, he is not. And I would hardly say we are intimately acquainted—I've only met the Sothebys once, and the other two ladies I've never laid eyes on before," said Bingley.

Caroline straightened. "They were both very handsome, and so well dressed! Oh, I do hope I might be able to further our acquaintance. I presume they are come to be at the ball on Friday?"

"They are indeed, and as I told you before, *behave*," Bingley told her in a warning tone. "Be polite and courteous—be friendly, even—but do *not* force your company upon them. They are our guests, not your means to an invitation to Almack's."

His sister stood with an indignant air. "Charles, how can you even say such a thing? I would never presume any such familiarity with a member of the nobility!"

Though in appearance she was sincere in her declaration, those that knew her remained skeptical, and Bingley especially made a point to keep a close eye on his sister, whom he knew was not above a scheme.

On Thursday, Bingley and Fitzwilliam escorted their guests about Meryton while Darcy was paying a call on Elizabeth at Longbourn. The Northam carriage alone, with its ornate paneling, the gold crest on the doors, and smartly liveried coachmen drew quite a lot of attention. The stylish manner of dress of the Sothebys and their companions stirred up whispers everywhere they walked, and soon the town was abuzz with the news that Mr. Bingley had invited an earl and a countess to his ball. It made some of the mothers that much more determined that their daughters should have him, to see so young a gentleman so well connected.

Mrs. Bennet, of course, was no exception. As soon as her sister Mrs. Phillips had shared the news with her, she became more determined than ever to promote an attachment between Jane and Mr. Bingley. His knowing nobles, and being friends with the son and nephew of an earl, was sure to secure *very* favorable matches for her younger girls as soon as the gentleman could be made to see that he and Jane were perfect for one another. And seeing that Mr. Darcy appeared to have taken an interest in Elizabeth (though she could not fathom "why he should like Lizzy, with that sharp tongue of hers"), her ire at her second daughter softened, and she did what she could to support the possibility of a match between them.

Friday, 23 November 1798

The day of the Netherfield Ball had arrived, and Longbourn was in chaos. Orders were shouted by Mrs. Bennet, demands were made for special attention by Kitty and Lydia, and the servants dashed madly to and fro to do as they were instructed.

Elizabeth, Jane, and Mary had chosen to help each other dress, freeing up the maids for the other girls and their mother's demands. The close companionship they had developed since the beginning of the previous month had become subdued since Mary's revelation that she would willingly encourage Mr. Collins—that her efforts appeared to have borne fruit, as over the last few days he *had* paid her more attention than Elizabeth, did not sit well with that sister. She had expressed to Jane in private her desire to try and talk Mary out of pursuing him, but was dissuaded by Jane's admonition that although they did not approve of their sister's choice, they should nevertheless support it. Elizabeth had begrudgingly acknowledged the edict, though in secret she had prayed that God would find some way to bring her sister happiness.

Elizabeth worked on Mary's hair while Jane worked on hers. "Remember, Mary, that Mr. Collins is not the most coordinated of men. You will have to remind him of the steps as you dance," she said. Grateful as she was that Mr. Collins had asked her that morning to be kind enough to relinquish the first two dances to her sister, she still had difficulty accepting that Mary might actually receive a proposal from him.

"Of that I am aware," replied Mary. "He does trip over his own feet more often than not."

It was the first that had been said between them in regard to the blossoming courtship between Mary and their cousin, and Elizabeth was grateful her remark had not upset her sister. She resolved to make peace and accept her choice, for it grieved her deeply to be at odds.

Mrs. Bennet flew from room to room urging her girls to hurry, with poor Mrs. Hill following her mistress all the while, attempting to finish *her* preparations. Mr. Bennet, naturally, was the first among them to finish dressing, next to Mr. Collins, and as usual he took great delight in laughing at his wife's frantic rushing about.

Mary rode with Mr. Collins in his curricle, freeing up space in the already crowded Bennet carriage. The family were not the very first to arrive, but they were among the first ten, Mrs. Bennet was sure of it, and so to her they were quite on time.

Mr. Darcy was standing with the Bingleys in the receiving line, though much to Elizabeth's surprise, as soon as she had reached him he offered his arm and broke away to guide her into the ballroom. The musicians were just beginning to tune their instruments, and the continuous stream of arriving guests were milling around and visiting, among their comments many compliments about the décor.

"Miss Elizabeth," said Mr. Darcy, "if you are not already engaged, I should very much like to solicit the first two dances."

Elizabeth blushed, and when she looked up at him he smiled. "I should like that very much, sir," she replied.

"I must say," he went on, "I am most pleased with how much we have grown to know each other these last weeks. I hope that soon you might be comfortable addressing me as only Darcy—or perhaps even my Christian name."

Elizabeth felt her eyes widen with her shock. "You…you would wish so intimate an acquaintance?"

Was this really happening? she wondered. Was this perhaps Mr. Darcy's way of indicating he had developed feelings for her? To her understanding, a man and woman only granted each other the very personal privilege of using one another's Christian names if they were courting or betrothed, and sometimes not even until marriage—if ever they did. Her parents did not, at least they had never used each other's Christian names in her presence.

Darcy paused in their circuit of the ballroom perimeter and held her gaze. "Miss Elizabeth, you are too generous to trifle with me," he said. "If your feelings are still what they were three weeks ago, tell me now—one word from you will silence me on the subject forever. If, however, your sentiments have changed, I… What I mean to say is… that is, I would be honored if you were to consent to my courting you."

She was stunned—it was the only word Elizabeth could think of to describe what his declaration made her feel. Did she *want* him to court her? Was she ready to take such a step?

Elizabeth had been asking herself those questions for the last three weeks, for Mr. Darcy was very often at the center of her thoughts. She would think of him soon after waking each day, and thought of him last before she fell asleep each night. They had spent many mornings together going for walks around Meryton, or the grounds at Netherfield and Longbourn. Always they were in the company of his friends and her sisters, though always did they seem to naturally gravitate toward one another. Each week they had shared dinner together at least once, had been at one estate or the other for tea—had even spent time together at Lucas Lodge during one of Sir William's parties, and also had spent an evening together at her aunt and uncle Phillips' home.

She had to admit that she had come to like Mr. Darcy very much. He was not the proud, conceited man she had thought him to be after hearing his foolish remark at that first assembly. While he certainly had a measure of pride in his family lineage and his fortune, it was not to an excessive degree. They conversed easily, laughed together, competed good-naturedly over chess and backgammon, or were content to simply be in each other's company. He was in every way agreeable, and she knew she had begun to warm to him when she observed his interactions with the people of Meryton—especially the children; once when they had ventured into town with their relations and friends, he had surprised the party by purchasing sweets for the children who lingered outside the candy shop.

Yes, she liked him very much indeed…and in admitting that, she knew there could be no turning back.

Her delay in answering caused his expression to falter, and he took a step back. "Forgive me, Miss Elizabeth. I will not importune you—"

He fell silent in the next instant, when Elizabeth held onto his arm so he could not break contact entirely. She drew a breath and smiled, then said "Mr. Darcy, please do not mistake my hesitation for displeasure—I only needed a moment to gather my own thoughts. In truth, *you* honor *me* with your address, sir, and I cannot describe the pleasure I have in accepting."

Darcy's relief was palpable, and in apparent disregard for any eyes that might have been on them, he lifted her gloved hand to press his lips to her fingers. "Thank you, my dearest, loveliest Elizabeth. How happy you have made me. I very much look forward to hearing you call me Fitzwilliam, or William—or even Will, whichever you are most comfortable with."

Here she smiled again and gave his hand a light squeeze. "I recall that Mr. Bingley and Colonel Fitzwilliam often address you as Will. What does the rest of your family call you, if I may ask?"

He raised one eyebrow. "Lady Catherine and her daughter call me Darcy. To my sister, Philip, Marianne, and Josephine I am William or Cousin William. My Uncle Richard and Aunt Frances also call me William, save for when they are cross, and then I am Fitzwilliam Darcy."

Elizabeth giggled. "Forgive me, but I am reminded of my mother—she is much the same, using our full names with my sisters and me when she is especially vexed."

Tilting her head as she regarded him, she added, "From this moment hence, to you I am Elizabeth, unless you should like to call me Lizzy."

Darcy smiled. "So you have determined I am to have that particular privilege?" he teased.

Elizabeth laughed softly. "Given our relationship has now progressed to courtship, William, I should say our acquaintance is intimate enough for it."

She looked away from him then and her eyes fell on Charlotte. Elizabeth waved to her friend and asked that they go to visit her. Darcy obliged and they spent some minutes in conversation with the Lucases, until they were approached by four persons whom Elizabeth could only describe as fabulously attired.

"Mr. Darcy," said the gentleman. "Quite the crowd already, and the night has hardly begun."

Darcy nodded. "Indeed, my lord. May introduce you to some acquaintances?" At the gentleman's nod, he said, "Beside me is Miss Elizabeth Bennet. With us here are Sir William and Lady Lucas and their daughters, Miss Charlotte Lucas and Miss Maria Lucas. Ladies, Sir William, it is my honor to introduce to you His Lordship, the Earl of Sotheby; Her Ladyship, the Countess of Sotheby; Lady Amelia Northam, daughter of the Duke of Mildenhall; and Miss Marianne Dashwood, who is Lady Sotheby's sister. Lord Sotheby is a cousin of Colonel Fitzwilliam, whom you already know; they were gracious enough to accept Mr. Bingley's invitation to join us this evening."

Elizabeth felt stunned for a second time, and deeply honored to be introduced to the colonel's family. She knew that Mr. Bingley had invited some highly ranked guests, but she'd not been to Netherfield in the last two days, so had not met them before that moment.

"Miss Elizabeth, I am so delighted to make your acquaintance at last," said Lady Amelia. "Colonel Fitzwilliam has explained the reason for Mr. Darcy's long absences since our arrival on Tuesday, and he did not exaggerate your loveliness! I should very much like to know you better, I think, if you have power enough to distract this fellow."

Elizabeth felt a flush creep up her neck. "You are most kind to say so, my lady, though I would not put it past Colonel Fitzwilliam to exaggerate just a little."

"Who, me? I never exaggerate when I am telling the truth," said Fitzwilliam, who had heard her words as he approached.

"If it is to your advantage, you will say anything," added Darcy.

Fitzwilliam laughed and conversation flowed for a few more moments. Elizabeth could not help but notice how utterly silent Lady Lucas had fallen; Charlotte's mother stared wide-eyed at Lord and Lady Sotheby as though she could hardly believe her good fortune. In truth, Elizabeth could hardly believe her own, and it occurred to her then that if hers and Darcy's courtship should one day progress to marriage, meeting such well-to-to people would be a somewhat regular occurrence in her future.

It was not very long before the first dance was called. Darcy led her to a place in the line with a smile, and Elizabeth looked to see who her sisters were to dance with. Mary, of course, stood with Mr. Collins. Mr. Bingley had solicited Lady Amelia's hand for the first dance, and—to little surprise—both Kitty and Lydia had paired with one of the militia. Lord and Lady Sotheby had chosen to dance as well, and Colonel Fitzwilliam had taken Miss Dashwood for a partner. Jane stood with a nervous-looking William Lucas, who had come down from Cambridge for the weekend.

As soon as the music started and the dance began, Elizabeth found her focus was solely on Darcy. She was reminded yet again of how magnificent a dancer he was, how graceful and sure. It was her belief that even had she not known the steps, she would never falter, for he was a proficient lead. When he took her hand in his or held her waist, his touch was warm and made her feel more alive than ever.

Elizabeth felt a surge of emotion beneath her breast, and smiled what was surely the biggest smile she had ever worn.

"May I ask what has made you so happy?" Darcy asked.

She waited for a position switch, when she could look into his eyes as she replied, "God has made me happy, William, for He gave me you."

A smile lit upon his countenance. "I feel the same, Elizabeth."

They finished the first dance and moved through the second completely focused on each other. For a short time it was as though there was no one else in the world.

When the first set was ended, Elizabeth elected to sit the next out. She was approached by Lady Sotheby, who admired her gown and her dancing, and asked if she might consent to sit with her for a while. "As you can see, Miss Elizabeth," said the lady with a hand on her protruding middle, "I shall not dance much tonight, but I could not decline Mr. Bingley's invitation. I was forced to sit through the Reunion Ball with a broken leg, and I had so wished to dance with my husband then, for it was all in his honor that we were gathered."

The ladies were escorted to empty chairs by Sotheby and Darcy, who with their blessing went away—Lord Sotheby to dance with Lady Amelia and Darcy to dance with Louisa Hurst. As Charlotte was passing by, Elizabeth invited her to join them, then asked Lady Sotheby to tell them about the Reunion Ball. She told her and Charlotte about the discovery that her husband was the Duke of Mildenhall's long lost nephew, and how His Grace had arranged a ball in his honor to both welcome him back into the family and publicly recognize him as his heir. She'd had an accident at their home in Delaford which had led to her leg being broken, making it so she could not dance.

"I have been walking without a cast for going on a month, so Mr. Bingley's invitation was well timed. I can dance now, at least a little, for soon I shall have to give it up again," she said.

"Is this your first child, my lady?" asked Charlotte.

Lady Sotheby nodded. "It is. God blessed my husband and I fairly quickly, for we have not even been married a twelvemonth. But it is as well that I shall go into confinement in the next month, for we may then spend the entire winter at Sotheby Hall and shall not have to go into Town."

"Do you not like London?" asked Elizabeth.

"I like it well enough, but there are some people there I should like to avoid as much as I am able," she said. "Let me just say that joining the ranks of the peerage has its downs as well as its ups."

Elizabeth smiled. "I think I can guess your meaning: those you know who wished little or nothing to do with you now suddenly find they cannot see enough of you. I surmise that they speak of their relationship to you more frequently now that you are nobility, where before they would all but deny you were acquainted."

Lady Sotheby smiled. "Indeed, Miss Elizabeth. It is very much like that."

Charlotte smiled. "My good friend prides herself on her judgment of character, my lady. Most of the time she is even correct."

"Only most of the time?"

"There was something of a misunderstanding between her and Mr. Darcy soon after they met," said Charlotte.

Elizabeth laughed softly. "It is true, and for several hours I had it in my mind to loathe him for all eternity. But when opportunity presented itself, Mr. Darcy apologized and explained his behavior, and I believed his remorse to be genuine."

"I am glad to hear of it," said the young countess, whom Elizabeth guessed to be no more than a year older than she, "for the two of you truly make a very handsome couple. I have little doubt, Miss Elizabeth, that you will very soon be engaged."

"Who will soon be engaged?" asked a red-haired girl who stepped up to Lady Sotheby's left side. Elizabeth recalled her being introduced as Miss Dashwood.

"Miss Elizabeth, Marianne," Lady Sotheby replied. "I was just telling her how handsome a couple she and Mr. Darcy make."

"Oh yes, sister! I noticed as soon as she stepped into Netherfield that he had eyes for no other lady," Miss Dashwood observed with enthusiasm. "I was very much reminded of you and Alan. Truly, Miss Elizabeth, I do not think it can be mistaken by anyone that he is very much in love with you."

Her third—or was it her fourth?—blush of the evening filled Elizabeth's cheeks. "I do not think I can say with any degree of certainty that you are correct, for no such declaration has been made," she told them. "However, Mr. Darcy *has* asked if he may court me."

Charlotte gasped. "Has he?! Oh, what did you say? Pray tell me you accepted, for I must agree that the two of you look so very handsome together!"

Elizabeth laughed. "I did indeed, but please, do not speak of it to anyone. I must think of some way to break it to my parents first."

"You know, Elinor," said Miss Dashwood then, "it has suddenly struck me that Mrs. Jennings would like our new friend very much. Though she clearly has no need to try and match up Miss Elizabeth, she would certainly have a grand time parading her sisters about to try and find them husbands."

"Mrs. Jennings is a dear friend of ours," Lady Sotheby explained. "She and her son-in-law, our mother's cousin, take great delight in attempting to match up all the young people around them."

Elizabeth took a moment to glance around, to assure herself that her mother was not close by, then leaned toward Lady Sotheby and her sister. "Your Mrs. Jennings sounds very much like my Aunt Jennings," she said in a low voice.

"Why do you whisper in a crowded room?" asked Miss Dashwood.

"Because I should not like my mother to hear me speaking of my aunt; they are sisters, but there was a great falling out between them many years ago, before my parents married. My mother has since refused to acknowledge her."

"You never told me any of this, Lizzy," said Charlotte.

Elizabeth glanced at her friend. "It is something of a family secret, I'm afraid. Neither my Aunt and Uncle Phillips nor my parents will speak of her, though my father more so out of habit than a desire to ignore her existence. Only Jane and I even know about her, and then only because my Uncle Gardiner said he refused to disavow his own sister just because his other sisters choose to, and that *my* sisters and I have a right to know our family. We may introduce Mary before too long, but not Kitty and Lydia because, as you know, they are both of them terrible at keeping secrets. I actually have two cousins by my Aunt Jennings, though I have only met them a few times."

She paused when she noticed that Lady Sotheby and her sister were looking at her with incredulous expressions. "Tell me, Miss Elizabeth, does your aunt have a house in London? What are the names of her children?" asked the countess.

Elizabeth's brow furrowed. "She does indeed, it is in Berkeley Street. Her daughters are named Mary and Charlotte."

Miss Dashwood grasped Lady Sotheby's hand and squealed. "I cannot believe it, Elinor! Our Mrs. Jennings is Elizabeth's aunt—oh, this is too fabulous!"

"Miss Dashwood, please—I must ask you to lower your voice," Elizabeth begged. "Believe me when I say that my mother has the hearing of a hawk, and I dread the scene she would make on hearing I had knowledge of my aunt."

"Of course, forgive me," said Miss Dashwood. "And please, call me Marianne. I expect we shall be friends, especially when we have so intimate an acquaintance in common!"

At this Elizabeth grinned. "I should like that very much. And you are most welcome to call me Elizabeth."

The four shared a few more minutes of quiet conversation, exchanging stories of her aunt. Elizabeth was much pleased to learn that her Aunt Jennings had been kind enough to host the sisters in Town earlier that year; though Marianne claimed she had been greatly disappointed by the visit, she declared that at least *some* good had come of it, for it was during those six weeks that Lord Sotheby came to realize he loved her sister and offered for her.

"My aunt has longed to have my sister and I stay with her in Town, though it could not be done given the sad circumstances between her and my mother," Elizabeth told them. "But we have seen her there when we have stayed with my uncle, and shared many dinners and shopping trips."

Marianne laughed. "Mrs. Jennings does love her shopping. You know, I think sometimes that she misses being a mother. After all, she is widowed and her daughters are grown with husbands of their own; they both have children now, and though she is often staying with one or the other of them, she takes great pleasure in matchmaking all the young friends she makes."

"Indeed, Marianne," agreed Lady Sotheby. "Mrs. Jennings meddles because she now has no husband or children to manage. I admit that I once wondered how she could possibly spend all the wealth her husband left her when he passed, until Alan and I were so suddenly elevated in circumstances and learned we had some right to so much more than she—I could not even spend one year of the duke's income in my lifetime!"

"No doubt it is a very good thing you married him before he discovered his birthright, Elinor," said Marianne. "Otherwise, every single woman in London would be throwing themselves at his feet for the chance to be a future duchess and have your pin money."

Elizabeth exchanged a look with Charlotte, and the both of them laughed. "It is a very good thing indeed that Lord Sotheby is already married, for every mother of single daughters here would do the same!"

As the evening progressed, Elizabeth found she could not recall a night she had enjoyed more in all her life. There was dancing with William, conversation with her new acquaintances, and all around contentment in spending an evening among so many of her neighbors where everyone was in such high spirits. She did not think anything could darken the cheerful ambiance around them.

Just as the supper set was about to begin—further whetting everyone's appetite for the feast Caroline Bingley had planned—she and Darcy, along with Fitzwilliam and Lady Amelia, and Bingley and his sister Louisa, were approached by Lady Sotheby. The set of her expression was such that Elizabeth immediately felt concern.

"Mr. Darcy," began the lady. "I beg your pardon for interrupting your evening, but my husband requests your immediate presence in Mr. Bingley's study. He asks that Colonel Fitzwilliam and Mr. Bingley join you—ladies, I beg your pardon also for taking your partners from you, but His Lordship has declared it is a matter of some urgency."

Lady Amelia stepped up to her. "Is everything all right, Elinor? Should I fetch Marianne?"

Instinctively Elizabeth searched the room for Lady Sotheby's sister, and spied her across the ballroom in animated conversation with Charlotte.

"Oh no, Amelia, that is not necessary," Lady Sotheby assured her. "I just need the gentlemen to come with me to the study."

Beside Elizabeth, Darcy glanced at his cousin and his friend, then he looked down at her. "I regret that I must leave the dance, but I will return to you as soon as I am able."

"Of course. Do not worry for me, Mr. Darcy, I think I shall survive sitting out for a while," Elizabeth replied. "Go and see to what business Lord Sotheby has need of you."

"You are a gem for understanding, my dear," he replied, then drew her gloved hand to his lips and kissed the back of it.

She tried not to sigh as Lady Sotheby and the gentlemen made their way through the crowd. Lady Amelia stepped up beside her. "I am sure all is well. Come, Miss Elizabeth, Mrs. Hurst. Let us go and get some punch, and we can see what Miss Dashwood is talking of with Miss Lucas."

Elizabeth followed along, but all throughout the conversation—in which Charlotte informed her with excitement that Marianne had agreed to recommend her as a governess to her elder brother—her thoughts lay mostly with Darcy and whatever dire event had drawn him away.

Darcy was admittedly curious when Lady Sotheby had whisked him away from his second set with Elizabeth. He was also on edge, for his natural instinct told him that the matter was truly serious. What could possibly require them *all* to be called away from the ball? he wondered, unable to imagine what Lord Sotheby required his attendance for.

Bingley knocked on the door before he opened it, allowing Lady Sotheby to enter first. He fell in behind her, then Darcy stepped inside with Fitzwilliam taking the rear. Lord Sotheby was not alone in the room—another man stood behind the desk with his back to them. The build of the fellow, who wore a dark blue jacket, was vaguely familiar to Darcy, though he could not immediately think of who he might be.

"Thank you all for coming. I am sorry to have torn you away from your beguiling partners," said Sotheby to the new arrivals from where he stood to the side of Bingley's desk. He turned his head to the stranger then, and ordered him to turn around.

The man's shoulders visibly tensed, and when he turned to face them Darcy vaguely registered shouting. Perhaps it was Fitzwilliam, perhaps himself—he could not say. He only knew that the moment he looked upon the bearded face before him, he felt a rage the likes of which he had felt only once before, on the night Lord Sotheby himself had described the attack on Georgiana.

"*You bastard!*" This, Darcy knew, he cried as he flew across the room and launched himself over the desk. His fist met the face of a man he had grown to hate with such a passion that even he had feared losing control of himself should he meet Wickham again in public.

Fitzwilliam, Bingley, and Lord Sotheby struggled to separate he and Wickham, and though at last they succeeded, Darcy made sure to get several solid punches to land before they did.

"Come on, Will, settle down!" said Fitzwilliam as he and Bingley pulled him off to one side. "I want the bugger dead as much as you do, but you can't just kill him. Not until we get some answers."

Wickham winced when he touched the split in his lip. "For goodness' sake, Darcy, I know we didn't part on the best of terms, but why would you want to kill me?"

"As if you don't know!" Darcy seethed. "How *dare* you show up here after what you have done—to Georgiana, of all the innocent souls, Wickham! For God's sake, how could you force yourself upon your own sister?!"

Chapter Thirteen

A moment of utter silence filled the study after Darcy spoke.

"Sister?" asked Fitzwilliam. "Darcy, what the devil are you talking about?"

Wickham's gaze when he looked to Darcy was one of incredulity. "Force myself…? Georgiana? Do you mean to tell me some vile pig—oh God, you think it was *me?!*"

He turned away a moment and ran his hands over his head. When he turned back to face Darcy, who was still being held tight by Fitzwilliam and Bingley, he said, "I don't know who told you I did such a disgusting thing, Darcy, but I swear to you it wasn't me! For God's sake, she is my sister!"

"Now you have the audacity to call Georgiana a liar?!" Darcy cried, and he struggled to free himself.

"I'm not calling her a liar, I'm saying it wasn't me!" Wickham returned. "I would never force myself on any woman, especially not my own sister. There must be some mistake, because it couldn't possibly have been me. I haven't even set foot in England for six years!"

"A convenient lie—"

"Look at me."

Their heads turned to Lady Sotheby when she spoke; Darcy had all but forgotten she was even in the room. She had stayed by the door but now moved across the expensive rug that spanned much of the width of Bingley's study, her eyes searching Wickham's face intently. She stopped before him, her brow furrowed, and then suddenly her eyes widened and she gasped.

"It's not him." She looked to her husband. "Alan, look at his face. What is different about it?"

"Forgive me, my lady, but he could have grown a beard since March," said Fitzwilliam.

"I'm quite well aware of that, thank you, Colonel," Lady Sotheby retorted. "I do not refer to the presence of facial hair. Besides Miss Darcy and our two coachmen, only my husband and I saw the man she said attacked her, the man who had so brutalized and terrified that poor girl that she was willing to throw herself on the mercy of strangers in order to escape him."

She turned her gaze from Fitzwilliam to Darcy. "This is not that man."

Lord Sotheby suddenly cursed softly. "She's right, it's not him."

"You told me she identified George Wickham as her attacker," said Darcy.

"That is correct, Mr. Darcy," Sotheby replied. "But either that man was not George Wickham, or this one isn't."

"How can you be sure this is not the man you met?" asked Bingley.

Lord Sotheby pointed towards Wickham's face. "The man we met that day had a scar that bisected his left eyebrow. This gentleman does not."

"I *am* George Wickham," said the man who stood beside him. "I spent the whole of my first eighteen years on the Pemberley estate in Derbyshire. I attended Cambridge with Will, though I was a year behind him. Wasn't the best student—wasn't a decent man, either. I'm sure he's told you all about that. I became an angry little boy after my parents died and left me alone, and though George Darcy treated me as a second son that anger festered, because I knew I was not. I did not sleep in the family wing, I remained in servant's quarters. My peers at Cambridge certainly never allowed me to forget that I was a charity case. My anger festered and—forgive me, ma'am—I engaged in gambling, drink, and debauchery in a vain attempt to drown my pain. It didn't help matters one jot to be told that I was, in fact, a second son after all."

Fitzwilliam released Darcy and crossed his arms. "I would like to know what that nonsense is all about. You both called Georgiana your sister—surely that is in reference to your having grown up in the same house. She's not *really* your sister."

Darcy tugged his other arm free of Bingley's grasp. "She is, Theo. Wickham is my father's natural son."

His cousin blinked. "I'm sorry, could you say that *again*?"

Wickham nodded. "On his deathbed near eight years ago now, old Mr. Darcy called us both in to confess it—to apologize to me for not having the fortitude to acknowledge me until he was to meet his maker. He...he wanted Will and I to make amends, to become the brothers we always should have been, as he put it."

"But how is this possible?" Fitzwilliam demanded.

"Mrs. Wickham was an upstairs maid, Theo, until her marriage," Darcy replied. "My father told us that my mother entered a deep depression after my birth. She wanted nothing to do with him or even me for many months. Father loved her deeply, but in his frustration at not knowing how to help her, he gave in to a moment of weakness and took a maid to his bed."

"When it became known several weeks later that the maid had conceived," said Wickham, picking up the narrative, "he arranged a marriage for her. He was man enough to acknowledge that he was responsible for her condition, but as he was already married, he did the only thing he could for her in order that her reputation would not be ruined. Albert Wickham, the Pemberley steward, was good and kind enough to take her to wife in spite of knowing her child was not his. I was born 'premature' near eight months later, and named for my true father."

He looked to Darcy then. "Will, whatever you may think of me, I swear I would *never* do such a thing to Georgiana. I have always loved that girl as a sister, before I even knew that she *was* my sister. I haven't even been in England for six years, I've been in India!"

"I suppose that would explain the tan and the beard," muttered Fitzwilliam.

"Well then, if not you who was it?!" Darcy exploded. "She gave your name to these people."

"I don't know. The last time I saw Georgie, she was not yet ten years old," Wickham replied. "It can't have been too hard for her to mistake another bloke for me."

"But how would the scoundrel have known to use your name?" asked Bingley.

"Clearly the person who did this is familiar with either Mr. Darcy or Mr. Wickham—or both of them," proposed Lord Sotheby.

A knock sounded at the door, and without waiting to be acknowledged, Lady Amelia slipped inside. "Forgive the interruption, as I am sure this is very important, but there are more than a hundred guests out there who have been looking for their host. I thought perhaps you'd prefer I come into the middle of this rather than Miss Bingley or Mrs. Hurst."

Bingley cursed under his breath. "She's right, I should go. Darcy, are you going to be all right?"

Darcy nodded. "Please tell Elizabeth I will return to her as soon as I am able. She should not see me in such a state."

His friend nodded and left with Lady Amelia. Lord Sotheby then quietly said to his wife that they should also return to the ballroom, but Darcy stopped him.

"Pray, what made you call us in here?"

Sotheby looked to Wickham. "I saw him near the ballroom door, recognized him—or thought I did. Brought him here and away from the party because I knew if you were to see him it would create a scene unpleasant to more than ourselves. It was not until Elinor pointed out that he has no scar that I even remembered seeing one."

"And the two of you are certain of that?"

"I am certain, Mr. Darcy," said Lady Sotheby. "Not only does this man not have the scar I remember, but I think he may even be taller than the man we saw. *That* I could be mistaken on as I was sitting in our carriage at the time, but I very clearly remember the scar above his eye."

Lord Sotheby studied Wickham again. "No, I believe you are right, Elinor. This fellow is definitely a few centimeters taller than Miss Darcy's attacker. But whoever he is, he resembles Mr. Wickham enough that I believed this man to be the other."

When they had gone as well, there were several moments of silence, until Wickham asked, "Who were those people, anyway?"

"The Earl and Countess of Sotheby," said Fitzwilliam. "Cousins of mine on my mother's side."

"And the girl that came to the door?"

"Lady Amelia Northam, daughter of the Duke of Mildenhall—she is Lord Sotheby's cousin on *his* mother's side."

"And the other fellow that was just here?"

"Charles Bingley," supplied Darcy. "You may not remember him from our younger years. Netherfield is his house."

Wickham's eyes grew rounder. "*That* was little Charlie Bingley—the tradesman's son who used to follow after us like a puppy? And you say this is his house? Guess someone moved up in the world…"

"Wickham, what are you even doing here?" asked Fitzwilliam as Darcy paced away from them, trying to rein in his temper. "How did you know to come here?"

Wickham braced himself against the desk. "As I said, I've been in India—served two years in the East India Company, even. After Father Darcy died—that's how I think of him now—I was in even worse shape than I'd been for years. But when about a twelvemonth had gone by, I woke up one morning hung over, nearly broke, and with a woman in my bed whose name I could not even recall. I remember thinking, 'Is this *really* the life I want to live? To just wile away the hours until my next score?' I thought back on the last years of my life after my parents died, what a rotten sod I was, and I honestly felt ashamed. It was no wonder George Darcy had never wanted to admit I was his son, for who could be proud of the wastrel I'd become?"

He sighed heavily. "I felt sorry for myself, but I also wanted to *make* something of myself. I suddenly wanted very much to become worthy of the Darcy name even if I'd never bear it."

"And you thought the East India Company was the way to go about it?" asked Fitzwilliam.

Wickham shrugged. "Seemed like a good idea at the time. I'd signed a contract for two years, and though when my term was up they tried to talk me into staying, I took the out. Found work on a cotton plantation owned by this decent English fellow, and after another year I helped him get into the silk industry as well by acquiring a few hundred silkworms. It was a gamble, to be sure, but it paid off, and Mr. Franklin got real plump in the pocket. I had been his steward for almost two years when he caught malaria and died about the first week of January. I sent a letter to his solicitor here in England, as he'd once told me to do should anything happen to him, and four months ago I got a reply saying he'd named me as his heir and I needed to come to England to sign some legal documents to square it all away."

A glance at Fitzwilliam showed Darcy the same disbelief that he felt. "You expect us to believe that some old nabob made you his heir?" scoffed Fitzwilliam. "Why would he do that?"

Wickham threw his hands up. "I don't know, Fitz, perhaps because it's the truth? And according to Mr. Smith, the solicitor, Franklin left everything to me because he thought I'd earned a break. He'd written a long letter about changing his will, and that was the reason he gave. Smith actually showed me the letter, said he'd kept it in Franklin's file in case the old man changed his mind. Franklin also wrote that he saw a little of himself in me, when he was my age. That like him, I was a lad down on his luck just trying to make an honest living, even if it never got me anywhere. He wrote that he owed his success to me, so I deserved to reap the rewards."

"And how do we know you didn't swindle the old man?" Darcy asked.

"Because I didn't. You can either believe me or not, Darcy," Wickham said, his exasperation clear. Standing off from the desk he said, "Look, I'm not the angry, profligate fool I once was. I've changed. I finally grew up, I suppose you might say."

"And you're certain this Franklin fellow hasn't any family that can lay claim to his fortune?" Fitzwilliam asked.

"According to Mr. Smith, no. I asked, because I didn't want the inheritance if there was another with a greater claim to it. I told him to look into it to be sure, as I had no desire to keep what was not rightfully mine."

Darcy laughed without mirth and shook his head. "You sound so unlike the Wickham I remember. So unlike the one who raped my sister and has been leaving debts and ruined virtues in his wake the entire seven months I spent trying to chase him down."

Wickham shrugged. "That's because I'm *not* the Wickham you remember, nor am I the blackguard who assaulted Georgiana, or done any of those things. To answer Fitz's original questions, I came here because I had heard in London this is where you were. I was hoping to do what Father Darcy—our father—wanted from us the day he died: To put the past where it belongs, and be brothers again."

He shook his head. "I suppose I ought to have known it was a fool's errand. Your memory of me is too colored by the misdeeds of my past and now the despicable actions that have been done in my name."

Wickham dabbed at the split in his lip with a kerchief, and after returning it to his pocket he straightened his jacket and said, "Don't worry, I can see myself out without creating another fuss."

Darcy watched him walk with spine stiffened toward the door. *He was as a brother to you once, Fitzwilliam. Be brothers again—be the brothers you always should have been.* George Darcy's dying words passed across his consciousness, and so great was the love he still had for his excellent father that he could not simply let Wickham walk away. Not if he was truly changed.

"Wickham, wait."

Wickham stopped with his hand on the doorknob. His turn to face him again was slow and deliberate.

Darcy took a step toward him. "I remember my—our—father's words to us. If what you have told us tonight is true, and you are a changed man… For his sake if no other, I want to believe you are genuine, but it is difficult for me."

"I understand that, Will," Wickham replied. "I wish there was some way by which I could prove my fidelity to you. Might I suggest we start with conquering a mutual enemy? We are both of us now invested in discovering the true identity of Georgiana's attacker. He has violated our sister and is ruining my reputation—allow me to join you in the search for him, that this monster is brought to justice."

"Sounds like a fair start to me, Darcy," said Fitzwilliam.

Darcy nodded. "Aye, we can start with that. But I will not speak of this to Georgiana, not yet. She's still much too fragile."

Wickham's expression became pained. "How bad is she, Will? What did that beast do to her?"

Darcy explained about hiring a companion for Georgiana who had admitted to arranging for the man they'd believed to be Wickham to seduce and elope with the young heiress. Their goal had been to get their hands on her dowry, at which time they would have disappeared.

"Mrs. Younge swore to Philip that she had no idea he would force himself on her, that he'd convinced her he only meant to compromise her," said Fitzwilliam. "I'm not sure how much I believe it, but she claimed not to know where he took off to after it became clear Georgiana had somehow left Bath."

"Did this imposter approach Mrs. Younge with the scheme, or did she approach him?" asked Wickham.

"He proposed it to her," answered Darcy. "Her story is that they met shortly before I employed her services and that she fell very much in love with him, that it was he who brought her attention to my advertisement for a companion. Allegedly, he convinced her to take part in the scheme by saying that once he had control of my sister's money, they would leave England together—but Georgiana proved more of a challenge than either had anticipated."

"He must have been quite frustrated if Georgie's lack of cooperation set him to forcing himself on her," Wickham observed.

"She fought back, from what Lord Sotheby told us," said Fitzwilliam. "That probably angered the bastard more."

"Good for her. Lord, how I wish I could see her, to convince her it wasn't me who hurt her."

"Perhaps once he's caught, and we can prove it to her," said Darcy then. "I won't put her through the trauma of seeing you until then."

Wickham waved a hand. "It's all right, I understand. I'd rather wait than to hurt her further."

He sighed then. "I'll head out now, find the closest inn—Meryton's not far from here. You can find me there in the morning. I should go so that you can get back to your party and whoever Elizabeth is."

For the first time in many minutes, Darcy smiled. "Elizabeth is an angel," he said. "When I had begun to despair of finding you—of finding *him*—suddenly she was there. Of late I have begun to hope that she is God's way of telling me all will be well in the end."

"You sound like you're considering marriage to this girl. Has she a fortune and important connections? I know those have always been of consideration to you," said Wickham.

"She has neither, and frankly I do not care," Darcy replied. "For a time I fought my attachment due to her circumstances, but I found myself completely unable to deny the very great pleasure which a pair of fine eyes in the face of a pretty woman can bestow. Also, Bingley said something to me that really made me think about how I viewed those who are not as fortunate as I."

"And what was that?"

"That her family not having money did not make them inferior to me. Society would not agree with that, I know, but as soon as he said the words, I knew that he was right. In some ways, in fact, I feel as though Elizabeth is far superior. She has long known her lack of fortune and connections would not afford her many opportunities, and she accepted it with grace. She was determined to be happy no matter her future, and such a determined outlook served to humble me."

Wickham smiled. "Fitzwilliam Darcy humbled… Never thought I would see the day. As I said, you can find me in Meryton."

He had opened the door when Darcy stopped him again. "Let me speak to Bingley. Netherfield is a big house, he has plenty of room. If you're hungry, I'm sure we can have a servant bring you a tray, either here or in your room."

"That's…very gracious of you, Darcy. Thank you," Wickham replied.

Darcy nodded, then moved past him to quit the room. Fitzwilliam followed, and in the hall as they walked toward the ballroom he asked, "Are you sure about him, Will?"

"To be perfectly honest, I'm not really sure of anything right now, Theo. I only know that I want to see and hold Elizabeth again."

Fitzwilliam nodded. "Can't say as I blame you there."

Elizabeth had feigned cheerfulness throughout the time that Darcy was gone, even the interrogation her mother subjected her to; she tried a number of times to change the subject, to little avail. It helped only marginally that both Mr. Bingley and Colonel Fitzwilliam had also been called away, and when the other guests began to murmur their curiosity, Mrs. Bennet took her leave from Elizabeth at last to go and gossip with Mrs. Long and Lady Lucas.

If she could give credit to Caroline Bingley for anything, it was that she was a very attentive and gracious hostess. When her brother had been led from the ballroom by Lady Sotheby, she began a circuit of the spacious room, spending a few moments visiting with guests here and there. When Mr. Bingley returned at last with Lady Amelia by his side, Caroline's face lit with delight and she welcomed him back as though he had been gone for days. Lord and Lady Sotheby were not long behind them.

After a few moments with her host and her cousins, Lady Amelia broke away and came to where Elizabeth stood with Marianne and Charlotte. "Miss Elizabeth, I cannot tell you what detains Mr. Darcy, as I truly do not know the particulars, but I have seen him briefly and I am sure he will return to you very soon."

Elizabeth forced a smile. "I do hope so. I have the strangest feeling in my heart and wish only to be sure he is well."

Charlotte reached over and placed an arm about her shoulders. "My dear Lizzy… If that is not a sure sign that you are falling in love, I do not know what is."

She felt a blush color her cheeks. "Charlotte, please. Let us not be hasty—Mr. Darcy has just tonight declared his desire for courtship; I do not think love has yet entered the equation. It certainly has not for me."

"I think you are very fortunate in your choice of suitors, Elizabeth," said Marianne. "I am sure you will do very well with Mr. Darcy."

Elizabeth smiled. "I do like him very much, Marianne, but we have known each other only a month. I will not risk injury to myself by engaging in speculation as to when he might make an offer. For now I shall be content with courtship."

The next several minutes were spent watching the last dancing of the supper set—Kitty and Lydia, of course, were having a grand time, and even Mary seemed to be getting on well with Mr. Bingley for a partner (though Mr. Collins stood near at hand to take her back again when they were done). Elizabeth had just begun to wonder if Darcy and Colonel Fitzwilliam would return before the party broke for the meal when they suddenly appeared in the crowd. A smile formed on her face and she gave a small wave when it became clear Darcy was heading in her direction.

"Elizabeth," said he when he stopped before her. "Might we go somewhere away from the crowd? I believe there are still a few minutes before supper will be called."

She felt a sudden, strong urge to offer him comfort, so she inclined her head. He placed her hand in the crook of his arm and led her out of the ballroom; in a few moments they came to a hall she vaguely recognized, and he opened the door to what turned out to be another study, smaller than the one Mr. Bingley had claimed. There was no fire, were no candles lit—the only light was the yellow-blue of the moon coming through the sheer drapes at the window.

Elizabeth had just parted her lips to ask what they were doing there when Darcy wrapped his arms around her. "I want to hold you, Elizabeth. I just want to hold you for a few moments," he whispered in her ear.

She nodded against his shoulder and brought her arms up to wrap them about his waist. A sigh escaped her as the warmth of his embrace registered, and she hoped that this moment brought him the peace he so clearly needed. She did not count the heartbeats that passed while they held one another, but knew it was many before Darcy drew back.

He took her hands in his and brought them up between them. "Thank you. I just needed a moment with only the two of us."

"Are you all right, William? Is there anything I can do?" Elizabeth asked.

"Just be yourself, my dear. Just be you and I shall be well again," he replied. "I would share with you what has happened but I have no desire to ruin your evening with the sordid tale."

Elizabeth drew a breath. "Very well, then. I would have you put it from your mind for the next few hours also—or at least through supper. Let us go and join our family and friends and eat lots of incredible food, drink maybe a little too much wine, and be happy that we are in each other's company."

Darcy smiled and brought her hands to his lips. "That sounds like a marvelous idea, Elizabeth. Thank you for being such a calming influence on me. I don't know how you do it, but I am grateful."

Elizabeth returned his smile. "In that we are equal sir, as I've no idea how I do it, either. But I am pleased to have been a help to you."

They returned to the ballroom just as the guests were being led into supper. Though her mother did not sit near her—Mrs. Bennet was across the room at another table—Elizabeth was aware of her winks and coy smiles, and she did her best to ignore them. There was little doubt as to what her mother thought, and even less that she would be interrogated again as soon as an opportunity presented itself.

Chapter Fourteen

Only keeping Elizabeth close to his side—save for when each was obligated to dance with another—prevented Darcy from losing his mind.

How could it be that he had been so very wrong? Was the man he had met in Bingley's study truly so changed from the man he remembered? How could he even be sure, beyond a shadow of doubt, that Wickham was telling the truth? And if he was telling the truth, where was Georgiana's attacker? *Who* was he, and how on Earth were they ever to find him?

There were now, eight months after his beloved sister had been so brutally harmed, more questions than answers.

It was not without some difficulty to put the mess from his mind and participate in the remainder of the festivities, though he found that whenever he looked at Elizabeth, whenever she favored him with a smile…he felt calmer. Less angry and volatile. That her mere presence could affect him so when he was in such a state told Darcy that following his heart could not possibly be a mistake. Would there be objections? Of that he had no doubt—nor that most of them would come from Lady Catherine. But Fitzwilliam had been right about Elizabeth when he said that her grace, her wit, her determination would be a refreshing change in society. There could be no doubt of her eventually winning over every person who might think their match a mistake.

Did he love Elizabeth? That declaration he was not yet ready to make, but as he sat beside her at table, took a turn about the ballroom after and later danced the last dance of the ball with her, he felt certain that now he'd acknowledged his attachment there would be no living without her. He simply could not imagine her *not* being a part of his life.

It was well into the next morning before the ball was ended. Darcy had to give credit where it was due—Caroline had planned and executed an exceptional event. The Sothebys had retired early due to Lady Sotheby's condition, though Miss Dashwood and Lady Amelia had remained until the end; only when the first guests began to depart did they, too, retire to their rooms, happy and exhausted. Bingley, being the gracious host he was, personally saw each of his guests to the door, with Caroline and Louisa at his side. Fitzwilliam went to assure himself that Wickham had not fled the premises, and Darcy remained conversing with the Lucases and Bennets, who were the last to take their leave.

Darcy was consumed with a very strong desire to kiss Elizabeth, but knew he dared not. Not when there were so many eyes upon them. He would wait, and save the first kiss for a private moment. When at last her family was beginning to make their way out to the waiting carriage, he settled for a smile, and lifted her hands to brush his lips across her knuckles.

"I will call tomorrow, likely in the afternoon," he told her.

Elizabeth gave a nod and a smile of her own. "I look forward to it, Mr. Darcy, as I imagine we have much to discuss."

He quirked an eyebrow. "Mr. Darcy? Do you no longer wish to use my Christian name?"

She looked around; Bingley had neatly herded the other Bennets toward the door to give them a moment together. He would have to thank him for it.

"I very much want to. I just did not wish for certain others to overhear, until I've had chance to explain that we are more than acquaintances."

Darcy nodded. "I understand. Until tomorrow, Elizabeth."

He then put her hand into the crook of his arm and walked her out to her family, then reluctantly handed her into the Bennet carriage with a last smile. With Bingley standing beside him, he watched until the carriage pulled out of the gate before turning to go inside.

Caroline met them in the entryway, her arms crossed beneath her bosom. "Really, Darcy, you must put a stop to it."

He frowned. "I beg your pardon?"

"Don't think I've not noticed, sir, what has happened—that nobody Elizabeth Bennet has got her tenterhooks into you!" cried

Caroline, drawing a gasp of surprise from her sister.

"Caro, stop—please, just don't say anything further," Louisa pleaded.

Her sister whirled on her. "You would dare to censure me, sister? How dare *you*—you who have also fallen for her tricks! We used to have so much fun together picking out the faults of the less fortunate, and now look what's become of you! That bloody girl has robbed you of one of your most agreeable characteristics. She is a fashionless, penniless, *worthless* country chit who has somehow turned you against me!"

Darcy took a step toward her. "That is *quite* enough, Miss Bingley," he said through clenched teeth. "I would advise you to speak of Miss Elizabeth with a more civilized tongue if I were you."

Caroline's eyes widened. A moment later, she turned to her brother. "Are you really going to let him speak to me that way, Charles?"

Bingley crossed his arms. "Oh, I'm going to do that and more. You're going to apologize to my friend, right this moment, for insulting the lady he is courting."

"Courting? *Courting?!*" Caroline stumbled back as though she'd been struck, and lifted a hand over her heart. "Dear God, it's worse than I thought! Darcy, darling, you *cannot* be serious!"

"Do *not* address me so informal, madam," Darcy seethed. "If you refuse to offer an apology for your insults towards Elizabeth, you will leave me no recourse but to sever all acquaintance with you."

Again her eyes grew wide. "You don't mean that. Oh, can you not see what she's done? She's used her arts and allurements on you, Darcy, and it's ruining everything! She has seen how happy we are together and seeks to supplant me as mistress of Pemberley!"

Darcy took a step toward Caroline, then stopped. He was not in a frame of mind to engage with her without losing his temper. Turning to her brother, he said, "Deal with this," then turned on his heel and stalked away.

He felt Caroline's fingers on his arm as she reached for him, but he kept going, and surmised that Bingley had taken hold of her, for he could now hear them arguing. He didn't care. Caroline Bingley had just proven to them all that she was far more delusional than they had believed; Bingley might just have to put her in Bedlam for a time, though Darcy was not entirely certain even the famed asylum would do her any good.

He paused on the landing, wondering if he ought to speak to

Wickham before he retired, then decided against it. Mental exhaustion had already taken him in its grip, and he simply no longer had it in him to deal with anyone or anything that might aggravate him further. Darcy undressed himself after dismissing his clearly tired valet and took to his own bed, and with a sigh he brought Elizabeth's lovely countenance to mind. Yes, that was just what he needed, to see her again, and it was not long before sleep claimed him.

Despite taking his rest so late, Darcy awoke very early; the sun was just full on the horizon. He dressed quickly in riding breeches and boots and headed for the stables, hoping that an hour or so on Diamond might clear the last of the fog from his brain and enable him to address the matter of Wickham and Georgiana's attacker with reason.

And if Bingley hadn't found some method of securing an apology from his sister, he would carry out his threat to her. After last night's foolishness, he would no longer regard Caroline with polite indifference, nor would he treat her with any amount of respect if she refused to show any.

He stopped short when he stepped into the stable, forced to take a moment to curb his natural instinct to lash out on seeing that Wickham was already there, saddling a brown and white paint horse.

Wickham looked over his shoulder; Darcy blinked at the reminder of his violent outburst, as deep bruising marred the left side of his face. "Don't worry, I'm not planning a run for it," he said. "I'm just used to getting up early to work the farm. Actually, I'm surprised I slept as long as I did, as its past midday in India right now."

Darcy said nothing as he moved past Wickham to Diamond's stall. A groom approached and asked if he wanted his horse saddled; he declined in favor of doing it himself.

"That's a fine horse you have there," Wickham observed. "I've not seen one with a coal-black hide in some time."

Darcy fought the smile that teased the corners of his mouth. "It is fitting you should think of coal," he said after a moment. "It was Georgiana's idea to name him Diamond, after the gemstones found in coal mines."

Wickham chuckled. "Because diamonds are beautiful and so is the horse, I assume?"

"That's it exactly."

When they had finished readying their mounts, the two walked the horses out of the stable together, and once in the saddle, started off at a leisurely walk in silence. It was some time before the quiet of morning was broken, once again by Wickham.

"If I may ask, where is Georgiana now?" he asked.

Darcy contemplated whether he should tell him the truth, and then how much of it to reveal if he did. He still was not quite sure he could trust Wickham, or that he should, but since his arrival last night he'd done nothing to warrant the mistrust he'd so readily earned in the past. Again he thought of his—their—father, and knew that George Darcy would encourage him to give his brother a chance.

He suppressed a shudder on thinking the word 'brother'. Eight years he had known the truth and it still felt strange to him.

Darcy drew a breath to respond but was prevented by Wickham's next words. "You don't want to tell me, I see. I suppose I can't blame you, as you've only the past on which to base your judgment of me and have not been witness to the growth of my character. I imagine there's a part of you that isn't quite sure whether to believe Lord and Lady Sotheby have not made a mistake."

"She's in Surrey."

Wickham looked to him with surprise, then looked ahead again. "Staying at some Darcy family estate there, I imagine, while she works to overcome the trauma of her experience."

"A family estate, yes, I suppose you could say," Darcy countered. "But not anything I own. She is in the care of a relation by marriage to my Aunt Frances."

Wickham nodded, then asked, "Why Surrey? I'd have thought you might send her somewhere like Scotland to get her as far away from me as possible."

Darcy glanced at him. "Fitting, again, that you should mention Scotland, as my aunt's cousin actually hails from Glenfairley, where he is laird. And yes, I wanted her safely hidden away while Theo and I hunted you. But that is not the only reason she is there instead of Pemberley."

"But why else…? Oh… Damn. As if that scoundrel forcing himself on her was not torture enough," Wickham spat.

"Indeed," Darcy acknowledged with a nod. "When first I heard of the attack, I prayed harder than I had ever done in my life that she would not beget a child. Georgiana prayed the same. God chose to ignore us."

Silence fell again for some minutes, and then, "This relation Georgiana is with… He is a married gentleman, I presume?"

Darcy nodded. "Aye. They are all guests of a relation to the lady."

"And they are childless?"

He nodded again. "They tried for years, but the lady has not been able to carry to term."

"And this couple will accept the natural child of a rapist as heir?"

Darcy looked over again. "Yes, Wickham. Laird and Lady Fairley see Georgiana's child as their last hope for a family."

Wickham looked thoughtful for a moment, then said, "Perhaps it will one day comfort you, and our sister, to accept that God told the both of you 'no' so that He could at last tell the Fairleys 'yes'."

Again Darcy could only stare. "I did not take you for a spiritual man."

Wickham scoffed. "You did not take the *old* me for a spiritual man—you were right to deny me the Lambton living, Will. Besides your having already paid me generously for my own refusal of it, back then I was in no way suited to being a clergyman. I'm still not, but I've made my peace with God. A near-death experience tends to have such an effect on a man."

"When did you almost die?"

Wickham cocked his head. "Just over four years ago now—got shot twice in a skirmish with Bengali insurgents on the Indian subcontinent. I'd actually been considering remaining with the East India Company until that happened; I'd been injured before but never so severely, and as my contract was soon to expire, I decided I'd much rather escape with my life—quite literally, in this case."

They rode on for a time without conversation, each man captured by his own thoughts. After a time, the intermittent trill of birdsong was broken by Wickham, who made observations about the land around Netherfield and suggested how it could be improved to increase the value of the estate. His thoughtful insight baffled Darcy, and shewed him even more that the man at his side was not the man he remembered.

As they were returning to the stables an hour or so after they'd set out, Darcy observed Caroline's maid going out in a curricle. He had but a moment to ponder that he hadn't even known the girl could drive the vehicle when he took notice of Fitzwilliam approaching from the house. There was a determined set to his cousin's shoulders indicative of his having made a decision about something he would be forced to go along with. It did not signify that he more often than not agreed freely.

"Ah, there you are. I wondered if you'd run off, Wickham, and poor Darcy had been forced to chase after you," said Fitzwilliam as the two on horseback approached the stable.

"Why does that not in the least surprise me?" Wickham rejoined as he and Darcy dismounted. "What reason have I to run? Do you disbelieve your own cousins, Fitz?"

"Oh, no. I believe my cousin and his wife," Fitzwilliam countered. "This means I must, regrettably, accept that you are not the man who assaulted Georgie. It does not, however, mean that I must accept every word you say as truth. There's simply too much bad blood between us for me to do that."

Wickham regarded him for a moment before he inclined his head. "I understand. What would you have me do to prove myself?"

Fitzwilliam flicked his eyes in Darcy's direction; he gave an almost imperceptible nod, indicating his agreement with whatever scheme his cousin had cooked up to determine Wickham's trustworthiness. Their ride about the estate had been amiable, if not more than a bit awkward, but that didn't mean he trusted the younger man anymore than he had before.

"I want to go into Town and see that solicitor of yours," Fitzwilliam replied. "I should like to see if he can provide any more evidence to support your claim about inheriting a fortune. If he can answer my questions to satisfaction, then I shall consider granting you some measure of trust."

"Do you agree with him, Will?" Wickham asked.

Darcy nodded. "I'm afraid I must. As you said yourself last evening, my opinion of you is too colored by the evils of your past for me to simply take you at your word. If the attorney you spoke of is a man of character, and his word genuine, then we shall see if trust can be granted."

Fitzwilliam clapped his hands together. "It's settled then. We'll leave as soon as we can make ready."

At this declaration, Darcy paused. "You want to leave now?" he asked.

"Why not? Best to get it done and over with, I say."

With a shake of his head, Darcy turned and climbed back up on his horse. "If we are to depart for Town, I must first pay visit to Longbourn. I gave my word to Elizabeth that I would call on her today."

Fitzwilliam cursed under his breath. "Of course you should," he said. "Wouldn't do at all for you to ask the lady to consent to courtship and then not pay a promised visit to her. I'll speak to Vincent about packing a bag for you, Darcy."

"Do you think we'll not return tonight?" asked Wickham.

"London is some hours away by horseback," Fitzwilliam replied. "Even were we to conclude our business there in a short time, we'd not return until very late this evening, making an overnight stay the more acceptable option. And as nobody travels on Sunday, we shall have to remain in Town until Monday at least."

Wickham nodded. "Good point. Would taking a carriage be faster, do you think?"

"I haven't my own carriage here and neither does Theo," Darcy told him. "Bingley and the Hursts each have their own, but I cannot ask them on account of the ladies."

"No, but I can," his cousin put in with a grin. "Go on and see *your* lady. I'll speak to Bingley about borrowing his carriage. We'll only be until Monday, I'm sure, unless you really feel the need to return tonight."

Darcy gave another nod of his head, then a tug on Diamond's reins, and headed for the road at a canter.

"Charlotte! I am glad you are come, for there is a matter I wish to discuss with you."

Elizabeth hooked her arm around her friend's and turned her away from the house. She had already walked the garden path around Longbourn twice, but would not be bothered by a third turn.

"Does his name begin with D, Lizzy?" Charlotte teased.

"As a matter of fact, yes—though it is not the name I am sure you are thinking of," Elizabeth replied, fully aware of the blush that colored her cheeks. "No, I speak of Mr. Dashwood, Miss Dashwood's brother. In the midst of everything that happened with Mr. Darcy, I regret that I near paid no attention to anything else, including you. I mean to remedy my negligence by being a better friend to you today than I was last evening. So I must ask you, my dearest, longest friend... Are you certain you wish to give up your chance to be married to become a governess?"

Charlotte sighed and patted her arm. "I am certain," said she. "There comes a time, dearest Elizabeth, when one must accept the truth of their circumstances. My truth is that I am seven and twenty.

Society considers me as being on the shelf, so the chances of my marrying at all have already gone. I've no fortune to support myself and I'm a burden on my parents the longer I remain in their home."

"But to become a governess, Charlotte," said Elizabeth. "If you are determined to go out into the world and make your way by working, could you not seek position as a lady's maid, perhaps? Surely that would be more respectable a position."

"Oh hush, Lizzy," Charlotte admonished softly. "The position of governess is in every way respectable. By Marianne's account, Norland is a magnificent estate with many grand rooms, an extensive library, and grounds which are conducive to taking long walks in the fresh country air."

"And what of Norland's mistress? Did not Marianne say her sister by marriage wasn't the most pleasant of people?"

Charlotte laughed. "So you *were* paying attention after all! Really, Lizzy, I am not afraid of Mrs. Dashwood. I'm sure I could handle her being an exacting mistress, though I have been assured that she is likely to be somewhat more favorable towards me than normally she would when Miss Dashwood expresses that her sister, the countess, is *particularly* pleased with me."

Elizabeth felt a sudden realization come over her. "Oh, of course! The Dashwoods must be the ones Lady Sotheby spoke of when we sat with her during the second set!"

Her friend nodded. "Indeed they are. From what Miss Dashwood told to me—you know I do not approve of gossiping, but I really must tell you for it shall help you to understand—her brother and his wife hardly paid them any attention at all before the Sothebys' sudden elevation to the nobility. Mr. Dashwood was actually allowing his own sisters to live in what amounts to genteel poverty, as dictated by his allegedly greedy and controlling wife, but they suddenly have no compunctions at all about introducing themselves as 'brother and sister to the Earl and Countess of Sotheby'. They seek to use their limited connection to better their own position in society, and while Miss Dashwood despises them for it, she has said she will put their vanity to good use on my behalf. She says they are so very eager to be pleasing to the Sothebys that they will take me on solely on Lady Sotheby's recommendation."

"They will accept you as their son's governess without references or previous work history just because the countess says you are qualified?"

Here Charlotte frowned; she paused in her stride as they came round the corner of the house and turned to face her. "I *am* qualified to be a governess, Lizzy. You know I've seen to the education of my younger sister and brothers since I was Lydia's age."

"Come now, Charlotte, you know I do not mean it that way," Elizabeth said. "I *do* know your qualifications, and I would give you a resounding endorsement as well had I any belief that it would do you good. I only refer to the fact that the Dashwoods are silly enough to take Lady Sotheby at her word just for the sake of courting her favor. They do not seem to be the right kind of people to be working for, being possessed of such vanity and questionable morals as you tell of."

"That may be true, but my future is so terribly bleak that I really haven't much choice other than to seize this opportunity. So long as they are kind and their child teachable, I am sure I should do very well," Charlotte said. "All I ask in return for my services is a comfortable apartment and a livable wage—enough that I might be able to purchase a new gown here and there, and gifts for my family at Christmas."

Elizabeth took in the determined posture of her friend, the set of her countenance, and she sighed. "Oh Charlotte… How I shall miss your good sense when you are gone away."

Charlotte smiled. "You'll not miss it too much, dear Lizzy, for I am sure I shall write to you at least once a week."

Before Elizabeth could reply, the two ladies' attention was drawn by the sound of a horse coming up the gravel drive. On seeing it was Darcy approaching on Diamond, Elizabeth suppressed the urge to run to him, though she allowed a smile to form as she carried herself over at a sedate pace.

"Good morning, Mr. Darcy," she greeted him. "I did not expect you until after breakfast, at least."

"Good morning, Miss Elizabeth. Miss Lucas," said he as he dismounted his horse. "Such was my intention, as I said to you last evening, but I am afraid a matter of some urgency has arisen that shall take me to London this very day. I could not go without keeping my word of calling on you, though my visit must regrettably be brief."

At those words, Charlotte touched her arm. "Lizzy, I will go into the house and visit with Jane," she said, and turned away.

She and Darcy should not be left alone, but Elizabeth was grateful to have a private moment. Besides, chances were one or more of her sisters—or even Charlotte—would be watching them through a window.

When she had gone far enough away, Elizabeth said, "Has this urgent matter anything to do with that incident which took you from the ballroom for a time?"

Darcy nodded, his expression grave. "Yes, that is a part of it, though in truth the matter goes much deeper. I cannot say more at this time—not because I do not wish to, nor is it because I do not trust you. It is simply a very painful matter and I would not burden you with my sorrows. I have not the right."

She reached for the hand not holding Diamond's reins and held it between both of hers. "Sir, if nothing else we are friends," Elizabeth began. "For that reason alone, I would be glad to share your burdens if it would give you any relief from them. That is what a true friend does. But we are more than friends, or were on the way to being more; if you have changed your mind—"

He lifted their joined hands to his lips and pressed a light kiss to the back of hers. "I have done no such thing."

"Then I would have you lessen your pain by sharing it with me, if you trust me enough with your secrets," she replied. "I will not be offended if you do not, though I must tell you I shall be very much concerned for you."

This teased a smile from him. "And I shall be grateful for it. I do not know that I can tell you everything just now, for this seems hardly the time or place to go about it, but perhaps a moment may be taken upon my return."

"Do you think to return soon?"

Darcy sighed. "I would like to return to Hertfordshire this night, though it may not be possible. The plan is then to return first thing Monday, but given the nature of my business, Colonel Fitzwilliam and I may be gone from the country for some time."

"Very well," said Elizabeth, doing her best to conceal her disappointment.

"I shall send word by express if indeed we will be away longer than two days," Darcy said then. "I hate that this is happening now, when I have just asked if I may court you—it seems as though I am merely using it as an excuse to go back on my word, and I promise you I am not."

Elizabeth smiled. "If I believed that about you, or even suspected it, I should likely have turned away in an indignant huff by now," she said. "However, as I believe you to be a man of honor, I will only say that I pray your business is soon concluded, that we may begin where we leave off."

"I shall pray it also, for that reason and others," Darcy replied. He then looked into her eyes with so intense an emotion in his own that she thought for a moment he might kiss her.

"How I long to kiss you now, as a symbol of my fidelity," he said in a low voice, echoing her thoughts. "But I am afraid your two youngest sisters are watching us from what I believe is the dining room."

Elizabeth looked over her shoulder. Indeed, Kitty and Lydia were blatantly staring through the dining room window, laughing and pointing as she took notice of them. She poked her tongue at them, which sent them into a laughing fit, before she turned back to Darcy and said, "Let them watch. I find that I very much want that symbol of your fidelity."

His eyes widened a fraction and his breath quickened before he raised a hand to cup her cheek, then lowered his head and touched his lips to hers. His mouth was warm, his breath almost hot, and before the pleasure of her very first kiss had fully registered, Darcy broke contact and stepped back.

"I had better go, before reason is lost and I kiss you again," he said, his voice husky.

Elizabeth nodded, then said shakily, "I wish you did not have to go."

He turned and lifted himself into Diamond's saddle. "As do I, Elizabeth. As do I," he said, before turning the horse and urging him into a canter.

Chapter Fifteen

Elizabeth watched Darcy ride away until the figure of him atop his horse had near faded from view. On her return to the house, she was met in the entry hall by Kitty and Lydia.

"Lizzy, what was it like?" Kitty asked.

"What was what like?" she asked, knowing full well to what Kitty referred but not wishing to discuss it with her silliest sisters.

Lydia slapped at her arm. "Do not be such a twitterpate, Lizzy! You know very well what—Mr. Darcy kissed you!"

"Did you like it, Lizzy? Was it romantic? I thought it looked very romantic," said Kitty.

"Did he use his tongue?" asked Lydia.

Elizabeth drew a sharp breath and dropped her brow into a stern expression. "Lydia Bennet! You ought not even know of such things, let alone speak of them! I am sure you have heard such an inappropriate thing from all those wretched militia officers. I've half a mind to speak to Papa about forbidding you to go into the village unchaperoned."

Lydia rolled her eyes. "Oh hush, Lizzy. It wasn't one of the militia I heard it from, it was Mrs. Forster."

Of course, Elizabeth thought sourly. "I might have known—she's as much a child as you are and has just as little sense of decency. Mrs. Forster should *not* be discussing such things with you. Why Colonel Forster married a girl young enough to be his daughter is beyond my comprehension."

With that, she swept past her sisters and moved into the drawing room, where she found Charlotte sitting with Jane and Mary, telling them about her upcoming future as a governess. "I do not know precisely when, for Miss Dashwood has not yet written to her brother," she was saying, "but she is certain of his accepting her recommendation due to his desire to keep their sister's favor."

"I do not doubt it," said Mary. "I have heard that even the rich will do what they must to curry favor with the nobility—your being excellently qualified for the position sadly seems almost a bonus."

Charlotte laughed. "Indeed, Mary, though I am grateful you think me excellently qualified. Truly, I am actually looking forward to going away and becoming a governess. I shall miss my family, of course, and also my friends, but I shall be facing challenges I had never thought to face. I welcome the change of pace, as well as the chance to prove myself worthy of being entrusted with the education of someone's child."

On hearing her speak so movingly, almost passionately, about her role as a governess, Elizabeth could no longer harbor any ill feeling about her friend going. Charlotte wanted this, was eager for the new chapter in her life to begin, and though Elizabeth felt she did not need to give up on marriage to do it, if Charlotte believed and accepted that marriage was not in her future, then she knew she must simply accept her choice and support her.

"I suspect it will be very shortly after Christmas," she said as she stepped further into the drawing room, drawing the attention of the three young ladies there. "Perhaps around Twelfth Night."

Charlotte smiled at her. "That sounds likely to me. I shall ask Miss Dashwood what she thinks, for I am to call on her next. In fact, I ought best to be going, for I've a few other calls to make before breakfast as well."

Mary and Jane stood when she did and Charlotte embraced them, extracting from both girls promises to write once she was settled. Elizabeth then walked her to the front door, where they embraced and bid each other farewell. As she was returning to the drawing room, Mr. Collins was coming down from the first floor.

"Good morning, Cousin Elizabeth," said he. "Might I inquire as to whether you have seen Cousin Mary today?"

"I have, sir. She is in the drawing room with Jane."

His expression lit up. "Excellent, most excellent, for I've a *very* important question to ask her."

Mr. Collins started toward the drawing room and then stopped. He turned back to Elizabeth and stepped closer to her. "My dear cousin," he began in a whisper, "I do hope it will not stress you too much to learn that I hope very soon to be engaged to your sister. I know that I shewed you some special attention when first I came to Longbourn, for you have many amiable qualities and shall certainly make an excellent wife someday."

Elizabeth was so stunned by his declaration that for a moment she could not find words with which to reply. Mary's ploy had indeed worked—their cousin intended to offer for her. It was a relief on Elizabeth's part that the toadyish man no longer desired *her*, but she could not help pitying Mary for the life she would surely share with him.

Mr. Collins took her silence as a cue to continue. "Though I was drawn to you at first, Cousin Elizabeth, almost as soon as I entered the house God drew my attention towards your dear sister. Miss Mary's pious nature and love for the church makes her eminently suited to being a parson's wife."

Elizabeth forced a smile. "Indeed it does. I do not imagine you could find a better helpmate in spreading God's word. I wish you every success, sir."

She stiffened when he darted his head toward her and kissed her cheek. "My dear cousin, your support of my suit brings me much joy."

He turned away again and started for the drawing room. Elizabeth felt a sudden compulsion to make some remark that might clue the man in to what a gift he would be receiving.

"Mr. Collins."

Her cousin turned back to her with a curious expression. Elizabeth stepped toward him. "Sir, I have little doubt of your offer being accepted by my sister," she said, though it was difficult to move the words past her lips—there was still that part of her that rebelled against the idea. "Mary has one of the kindest souls I have ever encountered. All I would ask of you is to never take her for granted. Show her kindness every day. Tell her you appreciate her every day.

"She will be a good wife, Mr. Collins. Pray be a good husband, and do not ever give her cause to regret her choice."

For a long moment, Mr. Collins could only stare, his mouth agape. And then it seemed he grasped her meaning after all; his mouth closed, he stood a little straighter, and to Elizabeth he gave a bow of his head before he turned and made for the drawing room once more.

Elizabeth sighed, and decided then to go in search of Kitty and Lydia, who had disappeared soon after she'd entered the house. It would not do at all for one or both to burst in as Mr. Collins was making his proposal to Mary, thereby embarrassing him and their sister. She'd not put it past those wretched girls to make fun and laugh, and she would not have this day ruined. Mary deserved to derive from it what happiness she could.

When she found them in the dining room, her youngest sisters had just begun to squabble over a bonnet that Kitty claimed was hers. Lydia responded by claiming it looked better on her so it should be hers. Thankfully their mother was not yet out of her chambers, for Elizabeth knew precisely how such an argument would end: as it always did, with Lydia getting her way. It was many years now that she had recognized how her mother favored the youngest of their family. She understood that both her mother and Lydia had nearly been lost as the labor to bring her sister forth had been arduous and had lasted nearly three days. Still, it was foolish to indulge her so, always giving her what she wanted and not minding the cost, either to their finances or the relationships with other members of the family.

Kitty grabbed the bonnet from Lydia's head as she looked into a mirror and started to run away. Lydia followed and snatched it back, and from her it was taken by Elizabeth, who'd had enough.

"Lizzy, give it back!" Lydia demanded.

"Did you purchase this?" Elizabeth asked as she held the straw bonnet up.

Lydia blinked. "Well, no. But what does it matter, it really does look better on me—on Kitty it looks positively dull! She is too plain to look well in it!"

"It matters a great deal, Lydia," Elizabeth rejoined. "If you did not use your own money to purchase this bonnet, then it does *not* belong to you. If you had purchased it, you'd not want Kitty or anyone else to take it and claim it as theirs."

She handed the bonnet to Kitty who preened at her sister. "Catherine Bennet, stop that! It is immature and childish to gloat."

Kitty, thankfully, looked mildly chagrined at the rebuke. She moved away from them toward the basket full of ribbons and sewing materials across the room, where she sat down and began to pull apart the stitching of the bonnet's ribbon.

Lydia stood with her hands at her hips and stomped her foot. "This isn't fair! Who do you think you are, Lizzy, to tell us what's right and what is not? I'll just go to Mamma, and she'll let me have it. She lets me have whatever I want!"

"Which is precisely the problem with you, Lydia," said Elizabeth. "Your whims and tantrums are indulged far too often by both of our parents—Mamma especially. One of these days, I am sure, you will learn a hard lesson, my dear sister—that being that you will not always get what you want. Best you learn it now, before you are beyond reproach."

Lydia rolled her eyes. "Spare me your sanctimonious sermons, you sound like Mary. I'm going to Mamma, because I want that bonnet!"

Elizabeth grabbed her arm as she turned away. "No, you will not. You know perfectly well how Mamma likes to rest after a late evening out, as well as how cross she becomes if she is disturbed too early, so you will leave her be. She'll not be up until breakfast is served, and by then Kitty will have the bonnet remade. Just accept that you won't have it. Make over another of your bonnets if you want something different to wear to church tomorrow."

In a fit of temper, Lydia stomped her foot again, this time landing it—likely on purpose—on Elizabeth's toes. Normally she would simply ignore the pain and move on, but in that instance she was overwhelmed with a sudden urge to strike back; either to slap her sister's face or to turn her over her knee and swat her on the bottom, she did not know. But the urge lash out with violence, which she had not felt the desire to do since she was younger than Lydia, brought Elizabeth up short.

"Ow! Lizzy, you're hurting me!"

Elizabeth blinked, and realized then that she had not released her sister's arm; she'd actually been squeezing it harder as her thoughts overtook her. She let go immediately, and as the younger girl reached up to rub the spot with her other hand, Elizabeth backed away.

"I'm sorry, Lydia, I did not mean to hurt you," she said, and then pushed past her into the hall, where she rushed by Jane and ran up the stairs to her room.

Jane, naturally, followed behind her. Moments after she had shut herself away, there came a knock at the door. "Lizzy? It's Jane. May I come in?"

"I suppose so," Elizabeth replied, moving to the window and crossing her arms as her sister entered.

"Is everything all right, Lizzy?" Jane asked softly.

Emotion began building beneath her breast—if Elizabeth were honest with herself, it had been there all morning, since she had seen

Mr. Darcy ride away from her.

"Oh, Jane, I do not even know what's come over me," she replied at last, a tear slipping down her cheek. "I have never been a violent person, and yet moments ago I wanted to strike Lydia for her insolence. Before that I gave what amounted to a warning to Mr. Collins, that he should not do anything to make Mary regret choosing a life with him. Then there was Charlotte's determination to become a governess, and I also had to say goodbye to Mr. Darcy."

"Goodbye to Mr. Darcy?" Jane crossed the room to stand at her side. "I do not understand—why would you have to say goodbye to him?"

Elizabeth drew a steadying breath. "Some business or other takes him to London today. He was to call this afternoon, but came earlier as he did not wish to leave without keeping his word."

"That was very gentlemanly of him, Lizzy. But why are you so upset over his going to Town? Did he give you no word of his return?"

Sighing as she turned to sit on the window bench, Elizabeth then said, "That's just it, Jane. He said he would come back, but after what nearly happened with Lydia, I feel that my sense of balance is off, and it's because of *him*. I found myself just now with the sudden fear that it was not a temporary goodbye, but a forever one. And it hurts, Jane."

She looked to her sister with tears in her eyes. "Why does it hurt so much? I've known him only about five weeks, and there is no understanding between us save that he *did* ask if I would allow him to court me properly. But even if he were to change his mind, it shouldn't bother me this much. You know me, Jane, I am the kind of person who would just laugh it off and make a joke about being jilted. Fitzwilliam Darcy should *not* affect me so. Why does he?"

Jane smiled as she turned and sat on the bench seat beside her, and then placed an arm about her shoulders as she said, "My dearest Lizzy… I daresay he affects you so because you are falling in love with him."

Immediately after his positive reception by Mary, Mr. Collins had gone to Mr. Bennet's study to officially seek his permission to wed his daughter. After an interview with Mary following, in which she assured her father she was making this choice because she wanted to—and *not* because her mother had pushed for it—he gave his consent. The news was announced to Mrs. Bennet, Kitty, and Lydia at breakfast, and was met with squeals of delight from the mother and peals of laughter from the sisters. Mary lifted her chin and ignored the younger girls' derision, and happily accepted her mother's attentions. Mrs. Bennet even hushed Kitty and Lydia, scolding them for not yet securing an offer of marriage from any of their officer friends.

"What good does it do you to run off into Meryton every day to flirt and smile and laugh when nothing comes of it?" she admonished them.

"I might also remind you that you should be kinder to our sister," added Elizabeth with a nonchalant air. "After all, she will be mistress of this house one day, and like Mr. Collins, may turn you out as soon as she pleases when our father is dead, should you be single still when that unfortunate day comes."

Kitty actually sobered at the observation, but Lydia scoffed and rolled her eyes. "La, what a joke, Lizzy! She is our sister, she can't cast us out. Besides, Mary would never have the nerve to do such a thing."

"I cannot turn you out now, it is true," said Mary. "But when our father is gone—though certainly I do not wish that God call him anytime soon—and Mr. Collins and I are in residence as the master and mistress of the estate, I may very well do as I please regarding who lives in my home and who does not."

"Now, now, Mary my dear…" began Mr. Collins.

Mary turned to him with a smile that Elizabeth knew right away was meant to disarm him; the expression had worked so very well in the last few days to get her exactly what she wanted, which was his offer of marriage. Elizabeth suspected that she would continue to use her smiles and pleading eyes to school her soon-to-be husband, the hopeful result being a person whose presence and manners were at least tolerable. If she succeeded, Elizabeth reasoned she might just alter her opinion of the match.

"Mr. Collins, surely you have noted that my younger sisters are not exactly well-mannered girls," said Mary, earning a gasp from her mother and squeaks of indignation from her sisters. Elizabeth bit her lip so as not to laugh, Jane hid her own smile behind her napkin, and Mr. Bennet lowered the newspaper he had just picked up to read in order to watch the scene unfold, no other indication of interest save for the sparkle of amusement in his eyes.

Mr. Collins' gaze roamed quickly around the table, then fell again to Mary. "Well, my dear, I had no desire to upset you by making mention of it—"

"It's quite all right, sir," she said, still wearing the smile that made Mr. Collins stutter. She put her hand on his arm as she added, "My elder sisters and I are all too well aware of the faults in our younger sisters, and they do not seem intent on mending their ways. I would not want such careless behavior to influence our children. What would Lady Catherine think?"

Elizabeth coughed to cover up the laughter that escaped her. Mary was a quick study indeed, for she already knew precisely what threads to pull in order to maneuver the foolish parson. Any praise or even mention of Lady Catherine and he was ready to agree to just about anything. Mr. Collins' eyes grew round and he began to nod his head vigorously, though he was prevented from answering immediately by Mrs. Bennet.

"Mary Bennet!" she screeched. "How can you speak so cruelly about your sisters? There is nothing at all wrong with their behavior! I've half a mind now to have Mr. Bennet tell you that you cannot marry Mr. Collins!"

Mary drew a breath. "Really, Mamma? You would have me break my word when I have only just given it? You would pass on the chance to be the first of your friends to have a daughter married? And for what? I have said nothing about Lydia and Kitty that is not true. I absolutely would not wish for their wild behavior to influence any child of mine, and as neither you nor Papa will take the trouble to check them, if they are still unmarried when we take possession of Longbourn, I may just have to insist that other accommodations be found for them."

She stood then, and turned to her betrothed. "Come, Mr. Collins. I should like very much to walk to Meryton to share the news with our neighbors."

"Of-of-of course, my dear Mary," Collins stuttered as he rose and followed her out of the dining room.

Stunned silence reigned for several seconds, until Mrs. Bennet screeched that they should wait for her and hurried after the couple. Kitty and Lydia began to disparage Mary and her criticism. Elizabeth looked to Jane, who wore a stunned expression, and then to her father, questioning him with her eyes as to whether he would do anything when her younger sisters' commentary devolved to the point of each one trying to outdo the other with the nastiest remark.

For about two heartbeats she feared that he would actually ignore them, until he made all four jump when he pounded a fist to the table. "That is enough!" he barked. "Catherine, Lydia, you will cease your impertinent behavior at once."

"But Papa!" Lydia whined. "Mary was so mean—"

"As Mary told your mother, there was not one thing she said about you that is not true," Mr. Bennet interrupted her. "You may wish to consider your attitudes towards her, as she was right about tossing you out as well—just because she is your sister does not mean she is required to house you when the day comes that she takes your mother's place as mistress of this house. Hill!"

Mrs. Hill came immediately into the dining room as Mr. Bennet stood from the table. "Yes, Mr. Bennet?"

"Put my breakfast on a tray and bring it to my study, if you would please," he instructed the housekeeper, then took up his newspaper and quit the room.

Hill followed but returned in only a moment with a serving tray and began gathering Mr. Bennet's plate and utensils. She added extra bacon and sausages and a couple bread rolls, the longtime servant knowing her master well enough to know he'd want seconds.

The four girls were silent until she had departed, then Jane said, "What just happened?" She looked to Elizabeth. "Honestly, I don't understand it. I've never heard a cross word from Mary in all my life."

Lydia snorted. "If you ask me, I think her being engaged has already gone to her head. Thinks she's just *so* important, now she's soon to be married. And honestly, look who she is getting married to—that idiot oaf Mr. Collins is nobody to us."

"Oh, hush, Lydia!" Elizabeth admonished. "Perhaps Mary was a little braver in speaking her mind, secure as she is in the knowledge that she will soon be able to leave this house. I'm quite sure our sister is only too happy to go, if only to be away from the embarrassment that is her family—but it's not as though her words were untrue. The two of you really are impossibly wild and inappropriate. Do you honestly think you will secure an amiable husband with the way you comport yourselves?"

Lydia bit into a piece of sausage, then said as she chewed, "La! What do I care if he is amiable, so long as he as rich!"

"Lydia, do not speak while you have food in your mouth," Jane snapped. "I know our mother taught you proper table manners, if she's given you no other instruction."

"You'll never get a rich husband—or any husband at all—with the way you behave, Lydia, what with your laughing and flirting and making a spectacle of yourself with the militia," Elizabeth went on. "No gentleman of real consequence wants a wife who is ignorant and idle and vain, who cares for nothing but fripperies and balls and parties, and who shows her displeasure with not getting her way by throwing a tantrum as if she were little more than a spoilt child!"

"Not only does such behavior limit your own chances of making a good match, but your lack of decorum reflects upon your family as well," added Jane. "By behaving inappropriately in public, or in front of other guests at parties and balls, you hurt *our* chances of making a good match. No gentleman will want to connect himself with a family that is mocked for the ridiculous and vulgar behavior of even one member, let alone two."

Again Lydia loosed an unladylike snort. "As if Lizzy has to worry about that—her Mr. Darcy has ten thousand a year!"

"Yes, Lydia, I have Mr. Darcy's interest now," Elizabeth returned. "But I can assure you, if I should lose it, it will not be through any failure on my part."

Lydia rolled her eyes but said nothing more as she returned her attention to her food. Kitty also finished her meal in silence, though often her gaze was lifted to look upon Jane or Elizabeth with a queer expression. To Elizabeth it appeared as though she were wondering if they'd told the truth—at least, she certainly hoped that was the case. Though as prone to excitement as the youngest of them, Kitty did possess a fair amount of sense. She simply seemed unable to make use of it whenever Lydia was near.

Late in the afternoon, as Elizabeth read a book in the garden, a rider came up the gravel drive that she immediately recognized as Mr. Bingley. She smiled as she stood and started toward him.

"Miss Elizabeth I am delighted it is you who should greet me," Bingley said as he alighted from the saddle. "I come with two missions: one, to issue an invitation to your family to dine at Netherfield tomorrow, after church."

Elizabeth grinned. "I cannot speak for my father, as he rather enjoys having the afternoon much to himself after Sunday service, but for my mother and sisters I daresay I can accept."

"Splendid! Though if I may, suggest to your good father he may hole himself away in the library at Netherfield after we dine," Mr. Bingley said. "Surely there is a book or two in there that will entertain him while the rest of your family enjoys a visit with mine, as well as my guests."

Her eyes widened. "Oh, that's right! I'd near forgotten that Lord and Lady Sotheby and their relations remained with you. I ought to have remembered, for Charlotte Lucas was here this morning and spoke of calling on Miss Dashwood."

"She did indeed, and spent a great deal of time with Miss Dashwood and Lady Sotheby—apparently discussing employment with their brother."

Elizabeth nodded, then said, "What is your second mission, sir?"

Here Mr. Bingley's expression sobered a little, and from the pocket of his waistcoat he pulled a letter he then held out to her. Taking the folded piece of paper in hand, she took note of his address before she opened it and read—it was from Mr. Darcy, asking Bingley to convey his deepest regrets to Elizabeth that he would not be able to return until Monday at the earliest. She read it a second time, fighting to school her disappointment, before folding the letter and handing it back to him.

"It came back in the hands of my driver not half an hour ago, as I'd granted Darcy the use of my carriage. I am sorry to bring you such news, Miss Elizabeth," Bingley said quietly as he returned the paper to his pocket. "He didn't want to leave here at all, but it could not be helped."

"Nor could his staying in Town, I am sure," she replied. "He did tell me when he called that it was a possibility."

She paused to draw a breath and forced a smile. "Whatever shall you do without him, Mr. Bingley, when your other guests have gone away?"

Bingley's expression became thoughtful as he looked over her shoulder toward Longbourn. "To be perfectly candid, Miss Elizabeth, I am unsure. I have long counted on my friend as a guide in many matters."

He caught her eyes again with his gaze, and held it for a long moment; Elizabeth felt suddenly as though he were taking her measure. Mr. Bingley must have determined in her favor, for he drew a breath and said in a low voice, "Miss Elizabeth, I… I would ask your opinion on a private matter, if I may."

Surprised did not quite describe the feeling his words inspired. Nonetheless, Elizabeth gave a nod and replied, "I shall endeavor to advise you well, sir, and you have my word I shall speak of this to no one."

Her promise appeared to bring him some relief. "It was my

father's great wish," he began, "that I should purchase an estate of my own. To settle down, begin a family, and become the respected gentleman he was never quite able to manage, for all his affability and fortune. Over time it has become my great wish as well, and I have come to like Netherfield and my neighbors very much indeed."

Elizabeth chanced a smile. "And we are all of us, I am sure, very pleased you find the house and country to your liking. You make a most agreeable and charming neighbor, Mr. Bingley."

Bingley flashed a grin. "I do thank you, madam, for your kind words." He sighed again. "With Netherfield, I am fairly certain I may have achieved at least part of my father's wish for me. It is a grand house and there is great potential for increased income over time from the farms. I have only to achieve the second goal and find a wife for myself."

She took an involuntary step back. *Oh no*... Surely he did not mean... Elizabeth suppressed the urge to shake her head in disbelief. *No*, she thought. *He is too much a gentleman to betray his friend so*. "As much as I would wish to be of service to you in that regard, Mr. Bingley, I do not believe I am the proper choice for such discourse."

"On the contrary, you are the *best* choice, I think," Bingley countered. "For you are the lady to whom I have grown closest since my coming to Hertfordshire, and are therefore uniquely qualified to advise me."

"H-how so?"

"Well, you know the young ladies of the neighborhood. There is one which comes to mind, a very pretty girl of seventeen, I believe is her age. She is a lively one, very amiable, but..."

Seventeen, Elizabeth thought with some relief. He wasn't about to reveal he harbored feelings for her, thank goodness. It was a weight lifted that she did not have to hurt Mr. Bingley with a refusal of his addresses, as well as knowing it was not his intention to blindside Mr. Darcy with an attempt to undermine *his* chances.

Who did she know that was but seventeen? There was Nancy Long, the younger of Mrs. Long's nieces; Mary King, who had a dowry of ten thousand pounds, making her the most likely choice; and Maria Lucas, who had turned seventeen only a week prior.

Her eyes then widened as she considered another possible candidate for Mr. Bingley's special attention: her own sister, Kitty.

"I think you begin to understand, Miss Elizabeth," said Bingley as he studied her countenance. "The young lady, whose name I shall not speak at present, is one with whom you are very...intimately acquainted. And although I have found her to be very charming and have enjoyed her company on a number of occasions, she has shown no particular attention to me. Not to mention her comportment is somewhat…"

His words fell off, and she could not help feeling a measure of pity. "Wild," she supplied. "I do believe I know of whom you speak, and very well as you have said. I also believe I am clever enough to discern that you hesitate to make your intentions known because of the objections your family and friends might have regarding how the young lady in question conducts herself, not to mention her lack of fortune."

Mr. Bingley scoffed. "Her lack of fortune is hardly of concern to me, Miss Elizabeth—my own was acquired through trade, after all. No, you are correct in guessing the reason for my hesitation is her behavior. I should like to become better acquainted, that I might determine if I ought pursue her, but as you have discerned, I could hardly court a young lady who cannot behave properly amongst company."

Elizabeth felt compelled to ask him then, "What, if anything, have you said to Mr. Darcy or Colonel Fitzwilliam of your regard?"

"Nothing," Mr. Bingley replied succinctly. "I falsely proclaimed that I had not found anyone particularly to my liking, because I have yet to reconcile my own feelings regarding the young lady. There is also the fact that Darcy would tell you I fall in and out of love far too easily, and given what prompts my hesitation, I had for a time hoped that this feeling, too, would pass. It has not. Her appearance at the ball last night confirmed that my regard shall not easily be dismissed."

Taking a chance at having her guess confirmed outright, Elizabeth said, "Kitty *was* in very fine looks last evening, to be sure. The dusty rose shade of her gown particularly highlighted the red strands in her hair."

A smile lifted the corners of Bingley's lips and he once more held her gaze. "And the blue of her eyes, Miss Elizabeth. Heaven help me, whatever shall I do? I never imagined I would ever resist pursuing a lady, but I am sure you understand—more than anyone, I think—that I must consider not only my own reputation, but that of my sisters."

Elizabeth inclined her head, then drew a breath and released it slowly. It was then her turn to hold his gaze as she said, "Do you trust me, Mr. Bingley?"

He frowned. "How can you ask me that when I have just confessed to a secret attachment to your younger sister?"

She took his hand briefly in what she hoped was a comforting gesture. "I ask you that because I wish to do both yourself and my sister a great service. I think, if you were to find yourselves truly in love, you could be very happy together—you're both so very amiable and charming, in a way that I truly believe would complement the other if Kitty could be taught to correct her unprincipled behavior. My sister is not entirely stupid; she only needs proper direction. If you agree, I will speak to her. I'll not reveal your name as yet—only that I have it on good authority there is a gentleman who would court her if she were properly demure in public. Jane, Mary, and I actually spoke to both Kitty and Lydia regarding their conduct just this morning, and there was some indication in her reaction to our discourse that Kitty, at least, might not be as disagreeable to correction as Lydia remains."

"Do you really think so? I know I risk offense, but as much as I like her…"

"I am not offended by your candor, Mr. Bingley," Elizabeth assured him. "In fact, I'd rather you were honest with me about why you have not pursued my sister than for you to raise her hopes only to disappoint her, though it would be her own fault if you should choose another because she cannot behave as a young lady ought."

Mr. Bingley sighed. "I thank you, Miss Elizabeth, for your own candor. I should like very much to learn whether or not you are right, that Miss Catherine and I could be happy together, so I give you my consent to say and do whatever you think necessary. Don't turn her into something she's not, of course—I would not wish for her natural liveliness to be repressed, as it is one of the very things that drew my attention in the first place. That and her lovely eyes, which are so bright when she is in high spirits…"

Elizabeth could not help but grin when his voice trailed off, the flush of embarrassment coloring his cheeks. "Nor would I wish to see her become but a shadow of who she is. No woman should have to change her very essence for a man, in my opinion, nor should a man change himself to please a woman. First we must please God, and then ourselves, if we are to be perceived as agreeable to others and achieve true happiness in this world."

"I could not agree with you more, Miss Elizabeth. And on that score, I think I shall take my leave. I've had enough of soul-baring for the day, if you please—I usually reserve it for Sundays, and now I shall have nothing to say to God tomorrow."

She laughed as he made ready to mount his horse again. "On the contrary—you can ask His blessings that I am successful in getting Kitty to see reason." *For see reason she must,* Elizabeth added silently, *if there is to be any hope of her being happy in her marriage, whether it be to you or another.*

When he had gone, she returned in silence to the house. Her mother, alerted by either a servant or one of her sisters, demanded to know the purpose of Mr. Bingley's visit and why she had not invited him to stay. Elizabeth said he could not stay as he had other business to conduct, but had stopped by to issue his invitation to breakfast personally. Mrs. Bennet, as she had expected, assured her that of course they would go, and what a fine thing it was to be singled out by him. "It is a sure sign, I think, that he fancies our dear Jane," she said.

'Tis not Jane he fancies, Elizabeth thought, though she made no outward reply and continued on to her room. She still felt rather overwhelmed with the revelation that Mr. Bingley harbored a *tendre* for Kitty—of all her sisters, why her?

It was not long before Jane joined her, and asked after the "true purpose" of Mr. Bingley's brief visit. "Forgive me, sister," said she, "but I did glimpse you through the window, and I believe you stood with him for much more time than it takes to issue a simple dining invitation. Not to mention you are entirely distracted—it is clear in your countenance that whatever he said preys upon your mind. Will you not share it with me?"

Elizabeth, though she had only minutes ago given her word that she would speak of the matter to no one, felt compelled to tell all to Jane. She knew that her eldest, dearest sister could be trusted, and rationalized the breaking of her word with Mr. Bingley having consented that she do what she must to help Kitty. And in truth, she felt that the insight of another would guide her on how to proceed.

"Oh Lizzy," Jane said after, sitting back against the frame of the window seat. "I am all astonishment, as he has shown no particular attachment to any young lady. Though now you have mentioned it, I *did* notice at the ball that he looked to Kitty very often. And when they danced together, he seemed quite oblivious to anyone but her. I confess that I thought nothing of it at the time, and that I share the same wonder as you as to why Kitty in particular has captured his attention. But I must also agree with Mr. Bingley—I should not like to see Kitty changed just to gain a husband."

"He did say he liked how her eyes are bright when she is gay," mused Elizabeth, "and her personality is not entirely unlike his own. Perhaps that is the basis for his attraction. In any case, I do not propose we change her, Jane—only that we help her to see she is already at risk of losing one gentleman's regard simply because she does not behave in a more appropriate manner."

Jane looked thoughtful, then said, "Do you think it possible that if Kitty can be made to see the error of her ways, Lydia might also?"

"I am inclined to say no, but I suppose anything is possible. As Mary said, the Lord moves in mysterious ways."

Chapter Sixteen

The journey to London in Bingley's carriage was interesting, if a bit awkward.

Although Fitzwilliam had declared a lingering distrust in Wickham, it was nevertheless he who engaged him conversation, asking questions about his service with the East India Company and the work he had done on his alleged benefactor's plantation in India. Wickham seemed only too happy to oblige, though Darcy felt sure he was well aware of the true reason for the interrogation.

He was mostly silent, speaking only when spoken to, his thoughts drifting between regret at having to leave Elizabeth at the dawn of their courtship to wondering how Georgiana fared in Surrey—it seemed the more time he spent in Wickham's company, having accepted that he was not her attacker, the more he thought of his sister. It seemed so very wrong that a girl so sweet and kind, with nary a cross word for anyone, should be made to suffer so. First the attack, then the carrying of her attacker's child to term—Georgiana should never have had to endure either.

He knew she could have avoided the latter by taking certain medicines, as had been assured him by their personal physician when she'd been examined to confirm her condition. Darcy, when he proposed it to her in private conversation, assured her he would not think less of her should she choose to take the doctor's advice, and of his belief that God would forgive her if she did. In the end she decided not to, with the declaration that she could not bring herself to end the life that had begun inside her, even if its conception had not been of her choosing. He had embraced Georgiana then, deeply proud of the inner strength she had drawn from to make such a difficult choice.

It was then that they had gone to their aunt and uncle in Disley, to seek advice on what they should do next. Fortune favored them at last in the form of Fitzroy and Roberta Leslie, cousins of some remove of his Aunt Frances. The Scottish laird and his wife, both around Darcy's own age, were visiting at Disley Court when he and Georgiana arrived; a childless couple desperate to be parents, they had offered immediately to adopt the baby, and to host Georgiana at Castle Fairley until she had given birth so that the family would be able to avoid a scandal.

Georgiana had not wanted to go so far away. Lady Fairley was then inspired to suggest a relation of hers in Surrey who might be contacted to ask his assistance. Upon hearing the man's name, Darcy knew him immediately to be the elder brother of his solicitor, though he'd not met George Knightley in person and insisted on a conference being arranged before giving his consent. After speaking for some time with Mr. Knightley to take his measure, and seeing the relative privacy of the man's home, he had agreed on the scheme of the Fairleys looking after his sister there.

Darcy found himself wondering if Wickham had been right, that their prayers against Georgiana conceiving had been left unanswered so that Laird and Lady Fairley could have the child they longed for. To consider it possible gave him some small measure of comfort.

The three travelers found themselves disappointed when they arrived at last at the office of Mr. Smith. His clerk informed them that while he was often in the office on Saturdays to work on organizing his files, that morning he had sent word that his daughter was laboring for her first child and his wife had insisted they both go to be with her.

"Mr. Smith loves Mrs. Smith dearly—it's plain as day to anyone what knows them," said the middle-aged woman who did filing and housekeeping for the solicitor. "No way he was going to tell his missus no."

"Do you know if this will be Mr. Smith's first grandchild, ma'am?" asked Wickham.

"It is indeed, sir. I daresay Mrs. Smith didn't need to do much convincin'," the lady said with a smile. "I'm sure he'll be back in Monday at eight in the mornin', regular as clockwork."

Wickham smiled at her; Darcy noted her reaction was the same as nearly every other woman that he had favored with that same disarming expression, and just stopped himself rolling his eyes.

Fitzwilliam thanked her for her time and they exited the office. Outside by the carriage, Wickham turned round and asked, "What would you like to do now, seeing as we must wait for the information you so desire?"

"I am sure Darcy here would prefer we return to Meryton and come again on Monday, but that seems a waste of time," Fitzwilliam replied, glancing at Darcy.

Darcy gave a resigned sigh. "Much as I detest having to admit this, Fitzwilliam is right. We are already here; we may as well remain so until we have seen Mr. Smith. However, I will send Bingley's carriage back to him, as one of my smaller carriages is always kept at Darcy House."

As they were alighting from the carriage in front of his London townhome a quarter hour later, Darcy was surprised when one of the neighbors began hallooing to them. Turning his head, he thought he recognized the man who now waved, but could not quite recall where he knew him from.

"Tilney, hello!" Wickham called back. "I see you took my advice."

Tilney… Henry Tilney, of course! Darcy actually found himself smiling, for the young gentleman walking toward them was an old schoolmate. He had been in Wickham's year, if memory served, and was an affable fellow from an old, wealthy family.

"Yes, indeed, Wickham," Tilney replied. "Father was most pleased with the place, especially given its close proximity to the home of a certain still-unmarried gentleman."

He looked to Darcy then. "Good afternoon to you, Darcy. It is a pleasure seeing you again."

Darcy nodded. "Indeed, and the feeling is mutual. Been some time, Tilney."

"Five or six years at least, since Cambridge."

Darcy turned to Fitzwilliam and introduced him. "Ah, so this is the infamous cousin I've heard tell of," said Tilney. "I am delighted to make your acquaintance, sir."

"Infamous, am I?" Fitzwilliam queried, glancing over at Darcy.

He scoffed. "Don't let anything this reprobate says fool you—I never spoke an unkind word about you."

Tilney drew an exaggerated sharp breath. "Reprobate? Mr. Darcy, I am stunned, stunned indeed! Do you not recall I was at university to study for the Church? I am a respected parson now!"

"That signifies nothing, Tilney," Wickham replied.

"Oi, you were a greater carouser than I, if memory serves," Tilney retorted. "If anybody deserves the title of reprobate, it's you!"

"Perhaps I did, once upon a time," Wickham admitted. "But as I am trying to prove to my old friends here, I am a changed man."

Tilney grinned. "I am very glad to hear of it, Wickham. The world needs more gentlemen and fewer scoundrels."

"Speaking of gentlemen, how does your father do, Tilney?" Darcy asked. "You mentioned him a moment ago—something about his being pleased with the place?"

A look he could not quite decipher passed over Henry Tilney's countenance, though it was quickly replaced with a genial smile. "He does well indeed, thank you. You see, he was looking to upgrade our residence here in town and sent me on errand to see what properties were available in the more established neighborhoods. I encountered Wickham yesterday in Bond Street, and he mentioned he'd been by Darcy House to see you. You weren't in residence, but he had seen that the house next door was available. All I had to say to my father was that it was next to Darcy House, and the general was keen to see it for himself—I don't think he looked much past the drawing room and the dining parlor before he was ready to sign the papers."

Fitzwilliam jabbed him with his elbow. "You know what that means, Darcy," he said. "I suspect there's a young lady in the general's household he wouldn't mind setting up as mistress of Pemberley."

Darcy scowled. "Hush, Theo. You know perfectly well that I've no intention of courting anyone here in Town."

"Oh, certainly not—your interests reside in Hertfordshire."

Tilney's eyebrows rose in curiosity, but it was at that moment that a very lovely young woman with a head of chestnut hair stepped out of the townhouse next to Darcy's, catching their attention.

"Henry, whatever are you doing out here?" she called out in a scolding tone, before descending the steps and approaching them. "You know Father will be very cross if you don't get a box reserved for us at the theatre."

"Yes, Elle, I am well aware," said Tilney. "I was certainly on my way to do just that, when I encountered some old schoolfellows of mine from Cambridge."

He turned slightly to draw her next to him. "Gentlemen, may I present my sister, Miss Eleanor Tilney. Elle, this gentleman is our neighbor, Mr. Fitzwilliam Darcy; his cousin, Colonel Theodore Fitzwilliam; and my old friend Mr. George Wickham. I was at university together with Mr. Darcy and Mr. Wickham."

"Are you in the regulars, Colonel, or the militia?"asked Miss Tilney.

Fitzwilliam was so slow to respond that Wickham had to elbow him as he'd done to Darcy. "Um, the regulars, Miss Tilney. I've been in service some years, have seen combat on occasion. What else is the second son of an earl to do?"

Her eyes widened. "Your father is an earl?"

"He is the Earl of Disley," Fitzwilliam replied. "My brother, his heir, is the Viscount Rowarth."

Miss Tilney smiled. "How fascinating. Henry, I had no idea you had such remarkable friends."

"That is because you think I am a clown when I'm not standing at the pulpit," Tilney replied in a droll tone. He then drew a breath, and added, "I really should be on my way, though, so as to avoid a scene upon my return. Wouldn't want our new neighbors to think badly of us, would we Elle?"

"I should think not, Henry," she said. "Will you gentlemen be visiting Drury Lane for the performance tonight? Mrs. Siddons is to portray her most famous character, Lady Macbeth—I have not seen her in the role myself, as yet, but I have heard she is magnificent."

"I would agree with that assessment—I have seen her perform the part once, though it was some years ago," Darcy told her. "I regret that we will not be attending the theatre, however, as we had not planned to be in Town more than a few hours."

"How long shall you be staying then, if I may ask?" queried Tilney.

"We shall be here until Monday at least," replied Wickham. "We've some business with my solicitor, but he was not in his office today, as he is likely to become a grandfather for the first time ere the day ends."

"Then you should join us!" declared Tilney brightly. "Join us and take some pleasure in your unexpected stay. What say you?"

Darcy wasn't particularly of a mind to attend the theatre that evening, though considering the play to be seen, it would certainly suit his frustrated and disappointed mood. He looked to Fitzwilliam and Wickham; the latter was gazing at him with a lifted brow and an almost imperceptible nod in his cousin's direction. Indeed, Theodore had hardly taken his eyes off of Miss Tilney since she had come out the door of the Tilney residence.

It was clear that he wanted to go, if only because the lady was.

In repayment of all the time his cousin had given to aid him in the pursuit of Georgiana's attacker—he had taken an extended leave of absence from his duties, though the Army was likely to recall him soon—Darcy acquiesced, and so it was quickly arranged that they would share the box Mr. Tilney was to reserve for his own family. Henry gave him a good-natured warning before parting, saying that his father was likely to see his presence as a sign he found Eleanor to his liking.

"Be sure to remind your father that Darcy is but a gentleman, while Fitzwilliam here is the son of an earl," replied Wickham, his remark earning a laugh from both Tilneys and a glare from Fitzwilliam himself.

The permanent staff at Darcy House was only mildly surprised by the sudden appearance of their master and his companions; his housekeeper was quick to order the master suite and two guest rooms prepared moments after they entered, then sent two of the maids after provisions from the market before asking Darcy if he and the others would like any refreshments. He ordered coffee and sandwiches prepared for himself, Wickham, and Fitzwilliam, as well as Bingley's coachmen, who would begin the return to Meryton as soon as the horses were sufficiently rested.

He then went into his study, where he penned a letter to Bingley regarding their extended stay, and asked him to convey his deepest regrets to Elizabeth. He considered sending it express but just as quickly decided against it, as it could just as easily be delivered by one of Bingley's men in near the same amount of time.

He was just sealing the letter when Fitzwilliam and Wickham stepped into the room. "Darcy, I've just realized we have a bit of a dilemma," said his cousin.

"Oh, how so?"

He and Wickham looked to each other, then Fitzwilliam replied, "What the devil shall we wear to the theatre tonight?"

"We none of us thought to bring formal wear," added Wickham. "Besides the simple fact that the *ton* would laugh us all out of London if we tried to attend in day wear, Fitz here absolutely *must* make a good impression on his new lady."

"Not to mention her father," added Darcy, unable to resist the opportunity to tease his cousin.

"Oi, she is not my lady!" cried Theodore. "At least… not yet. Maybe never, she may decide she doesn't like me at all."

"And you want her to like you," Darcy supplied as he sat back in his chair.

Fitzwilliam smiled. "Let's just say I'd like to become better acquainted," he said. "She *was* very beautiful, was she not?"

Darcy nodded. "Miss Tilney was very pretty," he said. "And you need not be concerned you shall embarrass the family as I've some clothing here, including formal wear."

He glanced at Wickham. "One of my jackets may be a little loose on you, as my shoulders have always been broader than yours, but should do for an evening."

"Thank you, Darcy. I'm rather pleased the both of you are including me in your outing at all, so I shall not mind a jot if the jacket doesn't fit."

"Considering you were present when the invitation was issued, we could hardly leave you out of our plan to join the Tilneys at the theatre," Darcy replied. "I did accept on behalf of all of us."

Wickham nodded. "Certainly there is that, but given our history and the fact that we are only in Town together because Fitz isn't sure I'm telling the truth about my inheritance, well…" He lifted his shoulders as his sentence died off.

Darcy sighed as he stood and took his letter to Bingley in hand, then came around the desk. "It is some small part of that history that grants you what trust you have thus far been given. I know how much you loved Georgiana and respected my father, and it is for their sakes I am endeavoring to grant you the benefit of doubt."

"If you know how much I loved—no, *love*—our sister, Will, why did you ever believe me capable of harming her in such a beastly manner?" Wickham demanded.

"She believes it was you. I believed her."

"You have to admit, Wickham, that given the very history you mentioned, we hardly had much cause to doubt her claim," Fitzwilliam added.

Wickham sighed. "I suppose you are right," he agreed, "though I swear to you, of all the wretched things I have done, I never once forced myself on a woman. I may have been a cad and broke a few hearts, but I've never been a rapist."

Darcy studied his countenance as he had done many times since his sudden appearance at Netherfield, and he found himself looking into eyes that showed naught but honesty. "I believe you," he said.

"Thank you for that. Now I've a request—I want to tell Georgie."

Darcy shook his head. "No. She's not ready to hear it," he replied.

Wickham loosed a groan of frustration. "I know that last night you said she was fragile, but surely she's not made of glass. If she is strong enough to carry her attacker's child to term that some distant relatives she's probably never met before could become parents, she is certainly strong enough to hear the truth! It isn't right to keep it from her. Georgie's mind should not be tortured with thinking I was the one that did this to her, and it isn't fair to me that she continue to believe me guilty in ignorance."

Beside them, Fitzwilliam drew a breath. "I cannot for the life of me believe I am about to utter these words, but Wickham is right, Darcy," he said quietly.

Darcy turned a sharp gaze to him. "If you and I believe him," his cousin continued, "if there is proof of his innocence in the testimony of the Sothebys, then there is no reason she should not be told."

"And what of after she knows?" Darcy countered. "Do you not think she will be traumatized anew by learning we haven't a clue who her attacker was, or where to find him?"

"I should think a betrayal by someone she loved and trusted would have greater consequence to her equanimity than the knowledge she was assaulted by someone wholly unknown to her," Wickham observed. "A stranger's attack makes more sense than to be hurt by someone who only ever adored and protected you."

Darcy ran a hand through his hair, pulling at the strands before he dropped it and reluctantly inclined his head. "All right, I'll tell her. But give me time to think on precisely how to do so."

Wickham nodded, and no more was said. Darcy took his letter to Bingley's driver and gave his instructions, then he and Wickham and Fitzwilliam took their coffee and sandwiches in the drawing room. They were just finishing the light repast when there came a knock at the door; the three lifted their heads in curiosity, each looking to the other in confusion—no one but Bingley and their neighbors even knew they were there.

Tolliver, the butler, soon entered and announced Mr. Edward Ferrars. The parson recommended to Darcy by Lady Sotheby looked just as surprised as he.

"I beg your pardon, Mr. Darcy," said Ferrars. "I had no idea you would be in residence at this time."

"It's quite all right, Ferrars," said Darcy as he stood. "I did give you leave to come to Darcy House should you have business in town, until matters were settled with your family."

Ferrars nodded, then Darcy introduced him to the others; they greeted each other cordially, then the parson looked to him again and said, "That is, in fact, why I am here. I know I have only just taken the living at Lambton, but I have had a notion to attempt reconciliation with my mother for some time—indeed, I made a countess of our mutual acquaintance a promise that I would try. Over these last months, I came to realize I did not wish the year to end with us remaining at odds."

Darcy felt Wickham's eyes on him, though he did not turn to meet them. "It is good of you to keep your promise to try," he said. "I'll have a room prepared for you."

Ferrars nodded. "Thank you, Mr. Darcy. I shan't get in your way, as I don't imagine I shall remain long. Either my mother will be forgiving—at which time she will demand I take up residence with her for a time—or she will not, in which case I shall then simply leave Town and return to Lambton."

Darcy's housekeeper entered then with a maid to remove the serving trays. He instructed Mrs. Tolliver to set up Ferrars in a guest room, and with a bow the younger man followed the servants out.

"What's his story?" asked Wickham when they were alone again.

"It's a slightly tragic tale," replied Fitzwilliam, whom Darcy now recalled having heard the story from Ferrars himself, at Pemberley. "Apparently he hails from a very wealthy family, but the mother holds the purse strings. Ferrars was young and impetuous, as so many of us are, and entered into a secret engagement with the first pretty young thing to capture his attention. Unfortunately, she was the niece of his tutor, without fortune or connections. The engagement was a secret known only to them and the girl's sister for a good four years, until the sisters were staying in the house of his brother by marriage, as company for Ferrars' own sister. The proverbial cat was soon let out of the bag, and Mrs. Ferrars demanded he give up the engagement straight away. He wanted to, from what I heard, as he'd long lost what affection he ever had for the girl, but he's an honorable chap and held to his promise."

Wickham snorted. "Let me guess—the mother cut him off?"

"She did, and settled all his fortune on his younger brother," said Darcy, who at last took his seat again. "Lady Sotheby, who is sister to his brother by marriage, was at Pemberley when the living at Lambton again became vacant—the gentleman sadly passed in an accident—and recommended Mr. Ferrars to me so that he and his betrothed might be able to marry and live in reasonable comfort."

"Except while he was at Oxford studying to take orders, the little hoyden transferred her affection to the brother, and they eloped!" cried Fitzwilliam.

"More like she transferred her affection for his money," Wickham mused. "And I suppose Mr. Ferrars' fortune cannot be returned to him?"

Fitzwilliam shook his head. "No. It is all irrevocably settled on the brother and the adventuress now. Though certainly Mrs. Ferrars could grant him another; my own mother tells me the family certainly has enough that she could still make Edward a very desirable catch."

He then fell silent, his expression darkening slightly. Darcy could imagine what had come into his head: his own status as a second son, with no real fortune to speak of. His father might be an earl, but he was not heir to the title. If General Tilney remained as intractable as he recalled from his school days, it was likely he would never approve a match between his daughter and Fitzwilliam. He wondered if he ought to warn his cousin, but then reasoned Theodore was grown and could handle his own private affairs. Besides which, just because he found Eleanor Tilney attractive did not mean she would return his regard or that they would be compatible, so he and Fitzwilliam both might be concerned for nothing.

As the time to ready for the theatre drew near, Theodore's spirits picked up, as did Wickham's. Darcy knew his cousin to be eager to see Miss Tilney again regardless, and Wickham had confessed he'd not seen a play since before his departure from England six years prior. Feeling obliged to do so, since the gentleman was in his home, Darcy went to Mr. Ferrars and invited him to join their party. Ferrars thanked him for the offer but politely refused, stating his intention to spend the evening in quiet reflection, that he might approach his mother after church the next day with a clear head and some idea what to say to her.

It was a merry party that met on the walk outside, with only General Tilney seeming to be at all out of spirits. As Henry Tilney had warned, his father appeared to take particular interest in Darcy, who endeavored to help his cousin along by appearing aloof and gently emphasizing the fact that Fitzwilliam was the son of an earl when introducing him.

That Eleanor Tilney appeared as attracted to Fitzwilliam as he was to her was almost immediately apparent to all the gentlemen, nor was her particular attention to him lost on her father. Darcy mirrored his cousin's dark expression when the general suddenly took her roughly by the arm and marched her over to their carriage. Henry gave a bow, his own expression apologetic, and hurried to follow.

The Tilney carriage pulled ahead of Darcy's as they were climbing in, and they were soon trotting along behind on the way to the theatre. Fitzwilliam immediately launched into a litany of complaints about the general's behavior and his treatment of Miss Tilney, with Wickham trying to soften his ire by pointing out how much Miss Tilney had smiled at him, and how lovely she had looked in her golden embroidered gown. Darcy, as was his habit, remained silent unless spoken to, keeping his thoughts to himself. It had been but moments, but he strongly suspected that General Tilney was not a kind father to either of his children, and he was sure that should Fitzwilliam and Miss Tilney form an attachment, a match between them would be forbidden.

Perhaps it was best he endeavor to put a stop to Theodore's pursuit before it began. He had no desire to see his cousin heart-broken.

That evening after dinner—while Mary was occupied with Mrs. Bennet talking of wedding clothes—Kitty and Lydia occupied themselves with a game of backgammon while Jane and Elizabeth worked on samplers. Mr. Collins and Mr. Bennet were content to read a book and the newspaper, respectively. The family was gathered in the drawing room thus when the noise of an approaching carriage reached their ears. Mr. Bennet stood as Lydia, Kitty, and Mrs. Bennet rushed to the window to peek out.

"Oh, it is a grand chaise-and-four!" cried Mrs. Bennet. "Perhaps your Mr. Darcy comes back from Town in his own carriage, Lizzy!"

"He is not *my* Mr. Darcy, Mamma," Elizabeth admonished with a glance at Mr. Collins. "You really mustn't say such things."

"Oh, but of course he is yours, Lizzy!" said Lydia. "After all, he k—ow!"

Elizabeth was saved from the sure mortification of having to explain the kiss she had received that morning, but was saved from an unlikely source. Kitty, her timing too perfect to be mere coincidence, had reached over and pinched her sister's arm.

"Yes, he came to see her this morning," said Jane quickly. "But that is just what a gentleman ought to do, when he has given his word."

"Indeed, sister," agreed Mary.

"Mr. Darcy gave you his word he would call on you? Why would he do such a thing, Cousin?" queried Mr. Collins.

Elizabeth turned her gaze to him. "Why, because he is a gentleman, of course. He told me at the ball last evening that he would call this afternoon, but he came early this morning instead, as sudden business that could not be ignored called him to London. He said he wished to keep his word in spite of his errand, and so he paid his visit before departing."

Mr. Collins' head bobbed up and down. "Yes, indeed, that is just what I would expect of such a man. Mr. Darcy is the nephew of my esteemed patroness, Lady Catherine de Bourgh, you know."

Elizabeth did not remind him that she was already aware of Darcy's relationship to Lady Catherine, and instead turned her head toward the drawing room door, through which her father had just stepped at the moment the rapidly approaching carriage came to a stop outside—not a minute later, there as an insistent pounding at the door.

Mrs. Hill hardly had time to open the front door when through it swept a thin, elegantly dressed young woman with dark hair under her feathered hat.

"I demand to speak to Miss Elizabeth Bennet at once," the young woman declared.

Mr. Collins jumped to his feet. "Upon my word! That is Miss de Bourgh—quickly, you must go, cousin!"

"I most certainly will not," Elizabeth returned, a frown marring her brow.

"I beg your pardon, madam?" Mr. Bennet was heard to say. "You have no right to come into my home and demand an audience with my daughter, in such as state as you are, without so much as an introduction."

"Collins!" the young woman screeched, making even Mr. Collins jump. "Collins, I know you are here, you stupid man—I demand you attend me at once!"

For the first time since meeting him, Elizabeth felt a twinge of sympathy for her cousin. A pained expression came over his face as he hurried to do as instructed.

"Oh, I cannot like this, not at all," said Mary in a hushed whisper. "How dare she speak to him so! I will endeavor to put a stop to it, you can be sure of that, when Mr. Collins and I are married."

"Introduce us so that we can dispense with the formalities," barked Miss de Bourgh, indicating that Collins had joined them. He quickly made the formal introductions, at which the lady scoffed and said, "So this is the one from whose brood you mean to select a wife? I am inclined to advise you against it, Collins. I have it on good authority that one of the little hoydens means to ensnare my cousin, Mr. Darcy, so that she may throw her worthless sisters at other rich men."

This was too much for Mrs. Bennet. "Worthless!" she cried indignantly as she stood and marched angrily toward the drawing room door. Jane and Mary both made to stop her but it was to no avail; Mrs. Bennet stood in the doorway at her full height, her hands on her hips, and said,

"How dare you, young lady?!" she cried. "My daughters are *not* worthless, not one of them! They are good girls, very pretty and charming—all our acquaintance say so!"

Miss de Bourgh emitted an unladylike snort. "But you have no fortune. No money to give them proper dowries. You have no connections to families of good breeding or nobility, as I have. La, your family is nothing to mine! A solicitor and a tradesman of dubious distinction are all you can boast of, whilst I am the granddaughter of an earl! I shall bring a fortune of fifty thousand pounds to my marriage—what can your wretched daughters bring to theirs, a mere thousand pounds each?"

While it stung that her words were at least in part the truth, Elizabeth decided she had had enough of listening to the harpy. Setting her sampler aside, she rose and made her way calmly over to the door, placed a hand gently on her mother's shoulder and offered her a thankful smile, then stepped past her to stand at her father's side.

"I am Elizabeth Bennet," she said, clasping her hands together in front of her. "You may now say whatever it is you came to say to me, though I must insist you do so with haste and make your departure, that my family may be left in peace."

Miss de Bourgh looked her up and down with a sneer. "She *must* be mistaken," she declared after a moment. "For I cannot fathom any reason why Darcy should find himself attracted to the likes of you."

She? Elizabeth wondered. Who could possibly have had anything to say to Miss de Bourgh regarding her acquaintance with Mr.

Darcy?

Almost as soon as the thought crossed her mind, she had another which made her certain she knew the answer. To Anne de Bourgh she said only, "Mr. Darcy is a gentleman, and I am a gentleman's daughter—so far we are equal."

"He is engaged to *me*," Miss de Bourgh snapped. "Now what have you to say?"

"If that is so, Miss de Bourgh, I wonder at your taking the trouble of coming so far," Elizabeth replied. "Although I have not long been acquainted with Mr. Darcy, I do believe I can say he is a man of honor. Such a man is not likely to pay his addresses to one young lady when he is promised to another."

She would not, could not, think about the possibility that she was wrong. Surely Mr. Darcy would not trifle with her affections if he were engaged to another woman…would he?

Perhaps he would, if he were truly engaged to a shrieking shrew like Anne de Bourgh, she thought. *How unhappy he must be, to seek affection from a lady who is not his betrothed.*

She would put an end to it, of course. Elizabeth knew, no matter how much it would hurt her to do so, that she could not in good conscience allow Mr. Darcy to continue his pursuit when he returned. Already her heart began to burn beneath her breast at the thought of ending their relationship.

"Miss Elizabeth, are you listening to me?" shouted Miss de Bourgh, snapping Elizabeth from her maudlin thoughts.

"Of course, Miss de Bourgh, I can hardly *not* hear you," Elizabeth replied.

"As I was saying, you will cease your pursuit of my cousin at once, is that understood? Our union was planned in infancy, for it was the greatest wish of our mothers that our estates and fortunes be united." She paused and drew a breath. "Now, I demand you tell me at once, Miss Elizabeth—have you an understanding with my cousin?"

"No, I have not," she lied. It was not in her nature to speak untruths, but for this she was sure she would be forgiven.

"And will you give me your word never to enter into any engagement with him?"

Elizabeth fought the urge to frown—why would Miss de Bourgh ask such a question if her marriage to Mr. Darcy was already assured? Had Elizabeth been wrong to doubt him? After all, a union may well have been planned by their mothers when they were children, but that did not signify he had consented to it in maturity.

"I demand your promise!" cried Miss de Bourgh. "Darcy is for me!"

She could feel the eyes of all her family upon her; squaring her shoulders, Elizabeth replied, "I shall never make any promise which does not contribute to my own happiness. As you have insulted me now in every possible manner, I must ask you to leave this house immediately."

Rage colored Anne de Bourgh's face a deep shade of crimson. For a moment she huffed indignantly, before taking an unexpected step forward and striking Elizabeth's cheek very hard. Elizabeth stumbled back into her mother with the force of the blow; Mr. Bennet immediately took hold of the other woman's arm and marched her to the door.

"Unhand me, you cretin!" she screamed.

"Certainly, madam, when you are out of my house," said Mr. Bennet as he opened the door. "I advise you most emphatically to never darken this threshold again."

"How dare you?!" she cried as he walked her out, and then they heard, "He is mine, do you hear me?! Darcy will never be yours, Elizabeth Bennet, I can assure you of that!"

Moments later, they heard the carriage door being shut forcefully, before hooves and wheels moving quickly away sounded on the gravel. Mr. Bennet re-entered and closed the door as Mrs. Bennet was cooing over Elizabeth.

"My dear one, are you all right? I cannot believe that wretched girl had the nerve to strike you. How dare she hit my daughter! I had half a mind to strike her back, you know."

Her cheek stung, Elizabeth mused. It had been some time indeed since she had been struck by another; she and her sisters had ceased fighting in that manner some time ago.

"Elizabeth, answer me truthfully," said Mr. Bennet. Elizabeth turned to him. "Do you have an understanding with Mr. Darcy, yes or no?"

She did not want to lie again, certainly not to her father. Her eyes flicked to Mr. Collins, who looked both anxious and fearful of what she might say. And really, what *could* she say? That she consented to courtship with a man who just might be engaged to another woman?

"Mr. Darcy and I are friends, Papa," Elizabeth replied at last, in as calm a manner as she could. "As I said to Miss de Bourgh, I believe him to be a man of honor, and as such do not think it likely he would pay his addresses to me if he is engaged to her."

Her father studied her with one eyebrow raised, then turned abruptly and headed for his study. Elizabeth knew that to be his way of saying he did not quite believe her, but would accept her answer. For now.

It was not a lie, but not the entire truth, and guilt over what she had held back began immediately to eat away at her. Claiming a headache, Elizabeth excused herself and went up to her room.

Chapter Seventeen

Despite initially having no desire to attend the theatre, Darcy nevertheless enjoyed himself. Mrs. Siddons' performance was as captivating as he remembered, and the other actors in the production were near equally as gifted as she.

Of course, the drama down on the stage was nothing to that which unfolded in the box from which he observed it. When first they had entered, General Tilney had attempted to force Miss Tilney's company on him; though he had his doubts as to the wisdom of allowing Fitzwilliam's obvious infatuation—and hers—to grow stronger, the general's blatant attempt at matchmaking as well as his own dislike of the man's treatment of his daughter, led to Darcy purposely ignoring the girl to focus on the play. This led to much conversation round his back between her and his cousin, and after a time, he gave a performance of his own and sighed dramatically, then said, "If the two of you cannot be silent that the rest of us might enjoy the play, allow me to switch seats with one of you."

Miss Tilney looked almost frightened for a moment, until he chanced to wink at her, and then she smiled. Because Henry Tilney and Wickham were sitting behind them, she stood and moved to the empty seat on Fitzwilliam's left. Darcy moved over to her old seat as though he wished to be as far from them as possible, prepared to bear the brunt of General Tilney's obvious displeasure. But though he cast a scowl in the direction of Fitzwilliam and his daughter, the man said nothing, and with a grunt returned his attention to the performance.

When the intermission came, Henry jovially suggested they all retreat to the lobby for refreshments. All but his father agreed, though he demanded a drink be sent up to him.

Miss Tilney, who had taken the arm Fitzwilliam offered, said to Darcy once they were away from the box, "I really must thank you, Mr. Darcy. Though for a moment I truly believed you cross with us, I appreciate your kindness in enabling Colonel Fitzwilliam and I to speak to one another."

Her cheeks flushed with embarrassment and her gaze dropped to the floor. Darcy, wishing to alleviate her discomfiture, replied, "Think nothing of it, madam. My cousin is often a chatterbox at such outings, and I'd rather he have someone willing to listen to his incessant ramblings to engage with, that I may be left in peace to enjoy the production."

Miss Tilney lifted her head with a soft laugh, while Fitzwilliam raised an eyebrow at him. "Me, a chatterbox? Do not let his dissembling fool you, Miss Tilney. Darcy here has been known to talk as much, if not more, than I during a play or concert."

The five of them made their way to the lobby, with Miss Tilney in the lead of the conversation asking questions of Darcy and Wickham regarding her brother's behavior while at school. Mr. Tilney tried to prevent them answering several of her queries, which made Wickham all the more inclined to do so. Henry had been a bit of a rascal in his youth—had done his share of drinking, smoking, and gambling. He had even broken a few hearts in his time, though he had only ever been proper with the ladies, having been more of a flirt than a serious beau to any of them.

They had each acquired a glass of their drink of choice when suddenly Wickham stiffened and muttered, "Thunder and turf. I think I had better make myself scarce."

Fitzwilliam looked at him. "Whatever for?"

Wickham gestured with his brandy snifter. "Is that not your mother and brother over there?"

Darcy and Fitzwilliam both looked in the direction he indicated. Indeed, his aunt and his cousin, along with the latter's wife, were only about twenty or so feet away from them—they had but to turn their heads and his party would be seen.

He turned back to Wickham and said, "Go. You know I've not had chance to speak to the rest of the family."

Wickham shook his head. "Say no more, Will. I understand. Come, Tilney, let us examine the buffet table together. I always hate to eat alone."

Though clearly confused, Tilney agreed to accompany him. "Certainly, Wickham. I've near forgotten that I was to send my father a drink—I had best do so, that he does not come down and make a scene."

The two walked away quickly, at almost the same moment that Darcy heard his Aunt Frances call out. "Theodore, William! I thought I saw you in a box across the theatre!"

She kissed her son's cheek and then Darcy's when she reached them, with Philip and Marianne behind her. Lady Disley's eyes then widened with pleasure when she turned her attention to the young lady at Fitzwilliam's side.

"Theodore?" she queried.

He nodded his head and turned to introduce them. "Mamma, allow me to introduce Miss Eleanor Tilney. Miss Tilney, may I present my dear mother Frances, the Countess of Disley. With her is my brother Philip, Viscount Rowarth, and his lovely wife Marianne, Viscountess Rowarth."

Miss Tilney dropped into a deep curtsey. "It is an honor to make your acquaintance, Your Ladyship. My lord, my lady."

Philip and Marianne nodded politely, whilst the countess said, "And a great pleasure it is to meet you, my dear. Tell me, how are you acquainted with my son and nephew?"

Darcy cleared his throat softly. "Her family has taken the house next to my own, Aunt, and upon meeting them earlier today, I recollected that I attended Cambridge at the same time as her brother Henry—he is about the place somewhere."

"I confess it was I who impulsively suggested Mr. Darcy and Colonel Fitzwilliam join my family's party," Miss Tilney said. "After Henry introduced us, and I found them to be so very amiable, I figured what better way to begin to know one's neighbors than by sharing a box at the theatre?"

Lady Disley grinned. "Yes, my son can be very charming when he wishes to be. Perhaps I should issue an invitation of my own—say, Darcy, how long will you be in Town?"

"Indeed, we thought you were still in Hertfordshire with Bingley," said Philip.

Darcy exchanged a glance with Fitzwilliam, who replied, "I recollected some business I had with a solicitor here—nothing major, I just required some information. Darcy agreed to join me so I'd not be traveling alone. Unfortunately, the fellow was out of his office on a family matter, and I shan't be able to speak to him until Monday."

A calculating look entered the countess's eyes then, and Darcy could just imagine what she was about. "I know it is short notice, but

I should very much like to have a dinner party this week. Miss Tilney, do you think your family might be interested in attending?"

Miss Tilney's cheeks flushed scarlet again. "I-I am quite honored you would even think of us, my lady. Though I would certainly have to speak to my father on the matter, I feel quite certain that he would accept such an invitation."

"Splendid!" declared Lady Disley with a clap of her hands. "I shall send invitations around on Monday. Do you think Thursday would be too soon?"

"I do not think so—at least, I cannot at present recall any prior engagements fixed for that day," Miss Tilney replied.

"I shall look for your letter of acceptance, my dear. Theodore, William, it was a pleasure to see you tonight. I look forward to seeing you again at dinner on Thursday," said the countess then. "We had best be going; Lady Markham is likely beginning to think we've gotten lost."

"Is Father with you?" Fitzwilliam asked.

Lady Disley waved off his words with a flip of her fan. "No. He says *Macbeth* is his least favorite of Shakespeare's plays, and chose to spend the evening at his club."

After exchanging bows and curtsies, Fitzwilliam's relatives turned to move away. Darcy breathed a sigh of relief when they had gone; thanks to Wickham's quick thinking, a potential disaster had been avoided.

"We're going to have to tell them, Will," Fitzwilliam said.

He nodded. "I know. Perhaps tomorrow after church, you and I can go and speak to them."

Fitzwilliam turned then to Miss Tilney. "Do forgive us, madam, for speaking in riddles about you. There is a very delicate family matter—"

Miss Tilney held up her hand. "Say no more, Colonel. I need no explanation, for I am well acquainted with the need for secrecy in one's family."

As they neared the buffet table, which was laden with a vast array of pastries, cheeses, fruits, and cold meats, Henry Tilney ventured to ask, "Do I even want to know what that was all about?"

Wickham shook his head. "No doubt you are curious, Tilney, but I am not at liberty to speak of it. Suffice it to say, my departure was necessary."

He still looked mightily intrigued, but Tilney gave a nod of agreement. At the buffet, he directed a footman to take a glass of port and a plate of food up to their box, and then the two set about choosing their own repast. "You know, I've been meaning to ask, Wickham... What's with the beard? As you can see from those around you, it is hardly the height of fashion."

Wickham laughed as he reached up and stroked the close-cropped hair on his jaw. "Indeed, I have noticed the curious looks directed my way. I've been in India the last six years, you see, and the men there keep beards, longer ones than my own. Even some of the English who've settled there in the hopes of making a fortune have taken to growing them in an effort to blend in."

"Is that why you did?"

He nodded. "For the most part. And also, frankly, because I liked the way it changed my appearance. I don't really look like myself as much."

"No indeed," Tilney replied. "Remember when I saw you yesterday, I thought you were—"

"Freddy? Is that you?"

Wickham watched Tilney stiffen and roll his eyes at the same time, before he forced a smile to his lips and turned around. After swallowing the bite of scone he'd just taken, Wickham turned as well, and came face to face with a pretty sort of girl with blonde hair, a full figure, and a surprised expression.

"Oh, do forgive me, sir!" she said. "From behind you reminded me quite of someone else I know. Even in the face you resemble him, though you've no scar, and he *never* had a beard. But I see I was not too wrong, for there is at least one Tilney gentleman here. How do you do, Mr. Tilney?"

"Very well, thank you, Miss Thorpe."

The shortness of his tone was not lost on Wickham; clearly something unpleasant had transpired between these two.

"Oh, my dear Mr. Tilney," said Miss Thorpe with a flutter of her fan. "How remarkable that we have met again so soon—such a grand time we all had in Bath this spring! Tell me, sir, where is Captain Tilney? I so long to see your dear, dear brother again."

"Of that I have no doubt," said Tilney in a droll tone. "However, I cannot divulge his whereabouts as I do not even know where he is at present."

Miss Thorpe laughed in such a way that Wickham was sure she

believed to be coquettish, her fan once again twittering in her hand. "No doubt he is on some secret mission for the Army. But pray, sir, if you hear from him, do tell him I miss him so."

"Of course," Tilney replied. Wickham was sure he had absolutely no intention of doing as she requested.

"Really, such a pleasure to see you again, but I must go before John comes searching for me," Miss Thorpe said then. "Before I am gone away, though, I simply must ask: Does your sister hear from Catherine? I know Miss Tilney was near as close with Miss Morland as was I. In fact, I rather thought the two of you might have come to an understanding while she was at Northanger Abbey—you certainly did dote on her in Bath."

Wickham noted the twitching of a muscle in Tilney's jaw, though he remained polite as he answered, "I am afraid I am not privy to the contents of my sister's private correspondence, Miss Thorpe, which is as it should be. Now, if I am not mistaken, that is your brother coming along to collect you. Do excuse us."

Tilney gave a short bow and turned to walk away. Wickham bowed also and followed, asking when he caught up to his friend, "Do I even want to know what that was all about?"

Tilney barked a laugh at having his own words repeated to him. "Isabella Thorpe is the bane of my existence," he said. "Her wretched interference and that of her equally repulsive brother contributed to the ruin of what promised to be a very happy relationship for me."

"This Miss Morland person she spoke of?"

His companion nodded. "No doubt Miss Morland's own innocence and naïveté were the greater contributing factors, for she was young and quite unaware of the ways of the world…"

Tilney paused and sighed. "The Thorpes are not good people. The family has no fortune and no connections—Miss Morland doesn't either, but at least she was not a vain, selfish social-climber. All they seem to care about is finding the biggest fool with the most money, because they have long been tired of being poor."

Wickham chuckled. "Heavens, Tilney, tell me how you truly feel."

Tilney stared for a moment, then gave a mirthless laugh of his own. "In any case, there was a great misunderstanding between Catherine and myself, her thinking on the matter no doubt influenced by stories told to her by Miss Thorpe regarding my family history. I think we might have repaired the damage in time, but John Thorpe's lies to my father regarding Catherine's fortune led to his turning her out of the abbey."

Shock coursed through Wickham. "Your father cast her out? Why, because she wasn't as rich as he'd been led to believe?"

"That is precisely his reason," Tilney confirmed. He sighed again. "It has been now half a year since I have seen her. I do, in fact, know that she and Eleanor write to one another—it was my sister who eventually explained to her the circumstances under which my father acted so cruelly. I wanted to be the one to explain, to beg her parents' forgiveness for her ill-treatment, but..."

"But your pride got in the way?"

Tilney nodded again, then drew a deep breath and squared his shoulders. "What's done is done, as the saying goes. Come, Wickham, let us rejoin our friends, return to the play, and immerse ourselves in someone else's tragedy."

It was, as so happened on a night spent at the theater, quite late when the Darcy and Tilney carriages arrived outside their respective owners' homes. Fitzwilliam was the first to alight, and as Darcy emerged, he saw that his cousin had walked toward the Tilneys who were then climbing down to the sidewalk. He watched as General Tilney handed Eleanor down, as Theodore said a few words and bowed, and as Miss Tilney was taken by the arm and pulled away, leaving her brother to once again apologize for his father's rudeness and wish them good night.

When Fitzwilliam returned to where he and Wickham stood, Darcy found himself compelled to say, "Theo, you know I would not dare to interfere in your personal affairs—"

"Then don't," Fitzwilliam quipped.

"—however, I must tell you that I believe you ought consider giving up any idea of courting Miss Tilney," Darcy continued. "It is obvious that she shares your regard, and normally I would be quite happy for you. But it is also obvious that her father is already opposed."

"He is opposed to my being a second son, yes, but surely his daughter's happiness will out over any such objections," Fitzwilliam argued. "Besides, you helped us in getting to know one another tonight, on purpose I believe."

Darcy nodded. "I did. However, when I see the way he regards you and treats her in your presence, it gives me pause."

"The general agreed to attend my mother's dinner party, even though the notice was short."

Wickham cleared his throat. "I have to say, Fitz, that I think he agreed only because he is to dine in the house of an earl and a countess. 'Tis the influence to his own reputation he cares for, nothing more."

"And do you not think that he must consider how elevated his status would be to have his daughter married to the son of an earl, even the second?"

Darcy sighed. It was far too late and he was far too tired to argue, not to mention the sidewalk was hardly the place to do so. "Let us go inside, for we will attract attention if we remain out here much longer."

His companions nodded and started for the front steps. Darcy gave a nod to his driver and the vehicle pulled away to go around to the mews. He then hurried up the steps and pulled his key from a pocket, turning it in the lock and opening the door at the same moment a most wretched cry was heard coming from the direction of the guest rooms.

"No! Stop, I beg you!" came a desperate male voice, followed by a loud feminine giggle and an equally noisy hiccup.

"Oh, Darcy, I cannot stop now! I am afraid you've left—" The lady hiccupped again. *"—left me with no other choice."*

Dread coursed through him as Darcy thundered up the stairs, Fitzwilliam and Wickham following close behind. He reached the first floor just as a maid—his cousin Anne's personal maid—pushed open one of the guest room doors and gasped, her hands flying up to cover her lips. Darcy took her by the shoulders and moved her out of the way just in time to witness as Anne—clad in a *very* see-through night dress—straddled a thoroughly mortified Edward Ferrars, grabbed both his hands by the wrist, and slapped them to her bare breasts.

"What in God's name is going on here?!"

"Darcy, what the—? Oh, dear God," cried Fitzwilliam at his left shoulder.

"Oh no," said Wickham on his right.

"Mr. Darcy, I swear I didn't—" yelped Ferrars as he snatched his hands away from Anne.

Anne swung her head toward the door, and Darcy was immediately able to discern the cause of her immoral behavior—she was very obviously inebriated. Bleary eyes set into a splotchy countenance blinked at him; her gaze roamed back and forth between the man in the bed and the man at the door for several moments, until clarity finally set in and made her realize just where she was and what she was doing.

"Oh my God!" she cried, then cast up her accounts on the floor and swooned.

Ferrars lurched forward to grab her arm before she could fall and pulled her back onto the bed. He reached for the coverlet and quickly threw it over her, then scrambled out from under Anne's limp body as fast as he could and stood to the side, though it was far too late. The damage had been done.

"Mr. Wickham," said Darcy in a tightly controlled voice.

"Yes, Darcy?" Wickham replied.

"Go to the servants' quarters and fetch my butler and my housekeeper. Bring them to my study."

Thankfully, Wickham did not protest being given an order; he acknowledged and quickly departed.

"Theodore."

"Yes, Will?"

"Take Anne to her room—" He glanced to his right, where the now-frightened, silently crying maid stood. "I am certain her maid knows where to direct you. See to it she is cleaned up and dressed properly."

Fitzwilliam pushed past him and gathered up the unconscious Anne in Ferrars' bedcover without a word. When at last they were alone, Darcy looked to the parson, whose shocked expression was now thoroughly laced with dread.

"Mr. Ferrars, please make yourself decent, then come to see me in my study," he said, his tone a fraction softer than a moment before.

Ferrars bobbed his head. "Y-yes, Mr. Darcy."

Satisfied, for the present, that he had begun to set the chaos to rights, Darcy made for his study on the ground floor. Outside of it he met Wickham and the servants.

"Mr. Wickham, I think it best you retire to your room. There is nothing more for you to do here," said Darcy. "If you would be so kind, do not—"

"Speak of this incident to anyone," Wickham finished for him. "Don't worry, Darcy. I shan't say a word."

Acknowledging with a nod, Darcy turned into his study, trusting the two servants to follow. Thankfully, a low fire already burned; there would be sufficient light for what he needed to do. When he had positioned himself behind his desk, he took a moment to draw a calming breath—never had he spoken in anger to any person that served him, and he was not about to start now. Anger would solve nothing.

"Mr. Tolliver," Darcy began, and the blinking of the butler's eyes showed his surprise at the more formal address. "Pray tell me, what time did Miss de Bourgh arrive at Darcy House?"

Tolliver glanced at the clock on the mantle. "I would say an hour, perhaps an hour and a half ago, sir."

"Mrs. Tolliver, did you show Miss de Bourgh and her maid to a guest room straight away?"

"I did indeed, sir, after Tolliver rang for me," the housekeeper replied nervously. "Well, that is, I showed her to a room in the family wing, as we knowed her to be your cousin."

"And how long after did the two of you retire again?"

The couple looked to each other. "Fifteen, perhaps twenty minutes, Mr. Darcy," his butler replied.

Darcy crossed his arms. He stroked his chin with one hand, trying to think, then said, "Did you notice anything unusual about her condition when she arrived? Was she already intoxicated? Did Miss de Bourgh say anything at all?"

Even in the dim light of the fire he could see that they both colored with embarrassment. Servants might talk to each other about their masters and the guests in homes where they worked, but hardly ever did those servants actually discuss such things with their masters.

"You may speak freely—I do not hold you accountable for any actions of Miss de Bourgh's unless you were a willing party to them."

"Well, Mr. Darcy sir, when I opened the door to her, she made clear who she was and said that though she was arriving late, she was expected," Tolliver said at last. "And the lady *did* smell somewhat of drink."

"She also demanded a bottle of sherry be brought to her room," added Mrs. Tolliver.

"Thank you, you may return to your room," Darcy replied.

After they had gone, he stood staring at the fire, trying to work out the events that must have transpired. Anne had come to London looking for him with the intention of causing a compromise, given what he had walked in on. It was also as likely as not that her mother had put her up to it; he suspected Mr. Collins, the obsequious toad of a parson, had written his patroness a letter containing observations of his behavior toward Elizabeth. Drinking on the way, and the bottle of sherry after arrival, had likely been Anne's way of shoring up her nerves, though she'd consumed so much she must've gotten confused once in the corridor and forgotten where she was, as she had clearly mistaken Ferrars' room for his own.

There came a hesitant knock at the door, and Darcy called for the visitor to enter. Edward Ferrars stepped nervously inside the study, looking very much like a man about to be executed. He could not help but feel sorry for the fellow, who certainly had enough family drama of his own to contend with.

Moving over to the sideboard, where he kept a number of bottles of liquor, Darcy took two of the smaller glasses and poured a couple fingers of whiskey into each. He carried one over to Ferrars and said, "Drink this—trust me, it'll help."

Ferrars didn't hesitate to down the entire thing in one gulp. Darcy raised an eyebrow, then took a drink of his own before saying, "Come and sit. We have much to discuss."

"I-I-I imagine we do, sir," Ferrars agreed.

He took the only visitor's chair positioned directly across from his own. Darcy sat only when Ferrars had, then said, "Given what I witnessed with my own eyes, and the testimony of my butler and housekeeper—as well as my intimate knowledge of the lady—I can assure you that I am well aware you had no willing part in what transpired this evening."

Ferrars had shuddered at his use of the word 'intimate', though his shoulders sagged with relief at the pardon of his own behavior. He lifted his glass for another drink and frowned at finding it already empty.

"Help yourself," Darcy told him, gesturing with his own toward the liquor bottles.

Only when the other man had refilled his glass and had another drink did he continue. "I wish I did not have to say what I am about to," he began, "but there were witnesses other than myself to what happened. Were it only me to have seen my cousin's actions in your room, I would not hesitate to pretend that naught had occurred. But I cannot. Colonel Fitzwilliam, our associate Mr. Wickham, and Anne's own maid unfortunately all bore witness to the shocking scene."

Ferrars sighed. "And I suppose that nary a one of them can be paid to keep silent?"

"Fitzwilliam would not have to be paid, as he is Anne's cousin as well, and a scandal would reflect on him as poorly as any in the family. Mr. Wickham I could possibly keep silent without money since he claims to have his own, but there *is* the matter of Anne's lady's maid, whom I believe to have been a much more willing participant than yourself in the scheme, as she was the first to arrive at your door. Money simply may not be enough to still her tongue."

He did not tell him that he believed Lady Catherine had orchestrated the whole affair.

A deep, aggravated sigh escaped the other man. "There is also the fact that I have not only seen the lady *in flagrante delicto,* but touched her naked person. Whether by my will or no, the deed is done."

Ferrars downed the alcohol in his glass and poured a third. Darcy did not chastise him for it—if he were in the other man's position, he might also find himself wanting to be more than into his cups.

"You do not have to ask it of me, Mr. Darcy. I will do what is right," said Ferrars then, followed by a snort of derision. "It seems I am always to do what is right, and always for a woman that does not love me."

"I will not thank you for agreeing to take Anne to wife, as she does not deserve you," said Darcy, causing Ferrars to turn around in surprise. "I will, however, give you my thanks for your aid to my family in avoiding a scandal."

Fitzwilliam walked in then, without having bothered to knock. "Mr. Ferrars," he greeted the man, offering a nod. The beleaguered parson simply raised his glass of whiskey in salute before taking another drink.

"Is Anne well, Theodore?"

Fitzwilliam nodded. "She came around as I laid her in bed. Her first words were an attempt to set the blame elsewhere, but I let her know in no uncertain terms that lying would not be to her advantage, as we'd all heard her quite clear enough. She then dissolved into tearful begging that we simply allow her to go home."

Darcy sighed. "You know as well as I that we cannot."

His cousin glanced at Ferrars, then back again with a nod. "Aye, as sorry as I am for it," he said.

"As your parents are also in London, I think it best we speak to them as soon as possible," said Darcy. "Only one servant actually saw anything and Wickham has sworn silence, but if we did allow Anne to return home without hearing the earl's advice on the matter, Aunt Catherine is as like to try and force me into marriage to cover it up as she is to try and bury it."

"Agreed." Fitzwilliam then stepped closer to the desk. "Will, you know Lady Catherine probably pushed her to do this. Anne's been near as obsessed as her mother to see the two of you married these last few years, but I cannot believe she contrived such a scheme on her own."

"Can you not?" Darcy countered. "Have you any idea of the number of times she attempted to compromise me when were at Rosings over Christmas?"

Fitzwilliam scoffed. "Clearly not. I had no idea Anne had grown so aggressive in her pursuit."

"So Anne is her name?" spoke up Ferrars then.

"Yes. Miss Anne de Bourgh, daughter of Lady Catherine and the late Sir Lewis de Bourgh, of Rosings Park in Kent," replied Fitzwilliam. "Why do you ask?"

Ferrars snorted. "I should think it obvious, Colonel: A man should know the name of the woman he will soon bind himself to for all eternity."

Chapter Eighteen

Sunday, 25 November 1798

For the second day in a row, despite taking to his bed very late, Darcy found himself waking early.

It was good that he did—in truth, since shouldering the responsibility for his estate he had trained himself to be an early riser—for he heard a not-so-subtle "Shh" out in the hall beyond his door.

The well-oiled hinges aided him in happening upon his cousin and her maid as they were making their way toward the main stair. Leaning against the doorjamb, Darcy crossed his arms and said casually, "Where do you think you're going so early of a Sunday?"

The maid gasped and Anne yelped softly. "Blimey, Darcy! Was it necessary to give me such a fright?"

"Something tells me the answer is yes," he replied. "Now if you would, cousin, pray answer the question."

"I should think it obvious," Anne replied tartly. "I am going home." She looked to her maid then and ordered her to continue to the carriage house with her bags.

"Belay that. You will go nowhere with Miss de Bourgh's things," Darcy countered, standing straight, "except back to her room."

Anne scowled. "Darcy, do be reasonable. No one need know—"

"Reasonable?" he said with a scoff. "You came into *my* home with the intention of compromising *me,* which led to the compromise of a good man of the clergy, and you dare speak of being reasonable?"

"What's this? No, wait, let me guess—Anne's trying to sneak

away on us, isn't she?"

Darcy looked over his shoulder to find Fitzwilliam shaking his head at them. "Really, Annie, did you think you could just get away with it? Pretend it didn't happen—or that we'd forget and forgive why you really came to London?"

"Theodore, please! No one else needs to learn of my folly," Anne begged. "I was intoxicated and not thinking clearly!"

"You were thinking clearly enough to don a night dress that may as well have been nonexistent," said Fitzwilliam. "You were thinking clearly enough to tell Darcy—or rather, the poor man you mistook for Darcy—that you'd been left with no choice."

Anne turned an angry glare in Darcy's direction. "If he had just done his duty years ago, none of this would have been necessary," she seethed.

"My duty?" Darcy snapped, and returned her steely gaze with one of his own until she lowered hers. "My only *duty* is to marry and sire an heir for my estate and fortune."

"You have a duty to honor the wishes of your mother!" Anne cried. "The wishes of *my* mother, which are my wishes also!"

He would not address the preposterousness of his marriage to Anne being one of his mother's wishes. "And what of my wishes, Anne? Did you not think I would have some opinion on the matter? Just because you and Aunt Catherine have wished for a thing to happen does not mean it will. Believe me, had I any desire to marry you, I'd certainly have done so by now."

Fitzwilliam stepped up beside him. "Given what transpired last evening—or rather, very early this morning—I'm afraid you've left *us* with no choice but to involve the earl. Darcy and I are for Bolton Street to discuss the incident with my father, and it will be up to him what is done with you."

"I have passed my majority, Theodore! Your father does not get to make decisions for me!" Anne said.

"On the contrary—as head of this family, he has the authority to make decisions for all of us, whenever necessary," Fitzwilliam replied calmly. He looked to Darcy then. "We'll have to take her with us."

Darcy nodded. "Indeed. She was attempting to escape when I caught her up."

Anne stomped her foot and growled. "This is ridiculous! Uncle Richard does *not* need to know—no one does! I've already agreed to compensate Beatrice in return for her silence. Surely you can do the same with that friend of yours and the parson, Darcy. You have enough money."

Darcy felt his eyes widen in shock. Had she really just suggested he bribe a man of God?

He shook his head with a disappointed sigh. "I am ashamed of you for even suggesting such a thing, Anne. Have you no compassion at all for what Mr. Ferrars has endured and will endure in future because of your actions?"

"No, and frankly I do not care. You said he's a clergyman—if he feels the need to seek absolution for touching me, let him ask it of God."

Anger at her callous disregard and lack of recognition for her guilt quickly replaced shame within Darcy, and it was with tightly controlled fury that he turned to Fitzwilliam and said, "Take charge of her, Theodore. I'll go and see that the carriage is made ready."

Fitzwilliam's countenance matched the tumultuous emotions now coursing through him; his elder cousin nodded and moved to take Anne by the arm as Darcy stepped around them and set off down the stairs. A quarter of an hour later, as the three were putting on their coats—Anne with a scowl on her face—they were joined by Wickham. Darcy moved off to the side to speak with him.

"I am sure I can guess to where you are headed," said Wickham. "Will you be speaking to your uncle about me as well?"

Darcy realized he had not thought of it, but gave a nod. "Now you mention it, I think it best we do. He is, of course, aware of the circumstances under which you were accused. I should like to have the record set straight before anyone of his house that knows should chance to encounter you."

Wickham frowned. "Who else would—? Oh, wait. Of course—your aunt and Philip, I presume?"

Darcy nodded again. "And Philip's wife. She and Aunt Frances were a great comfort to Georgiana."

Wickham's brows drew up. "The viscount is married now, is he? Good God, I shouldn't think any woman able to tolerate his arrogance long enough to marry the man."

A chuckle escaped Darcy unbidden; Philip *had* been rather arrogant and full of his own self-importance in his youth. "You're not the only one to have changed in the last several years, Wickham. Philip is much more like his father now—calmer, more rational. Marianne has done a great deal in humbling him."

"As the Elizabeth you spoke of did for you?"

Darcy smiled. "Indeed, though I imagine there is a great deal more Elizabeth has to teach me. I've only known her a short time."

"Will, we should be going if we're to catch Father and Mother before they away to church," Fitzwilliam reminded him.

"Coming," Darcy replied, then with one last look at Wickham said, "If Mr. Ferrars should wake before we return, keep him company. There is some chance Anne may get her wish and my uncle will decide it best we all pretend nothing happened, which would certainly set Ferrars' mind at ease as well."

"But you doubt it?"

"I do. He may not have done so of his own volition, but he did touch her. I hate to condemn him for it, but if the earl says he must marry her, there's nothing I can do."

Minutes later, he and Fitzwilliam were off to the neighborhood of Mayfair, where many of the nobility had their London homes. He recollected that the Duke of Devonshire was one such man, his great townhome only a block away from that of Theodore's parents. The carriage was rife with angry tension, most of it emanating from the glowering Anne, who sat across from Darcy and Fitzwilliam with her arms crossed, her withering stare alternating from glancing out the glass of the carriage door to her cousins and back again.

Upon drawing up to Disley House, which was near as large as a small country estate, Darcy alighted first. He looked back as Theodore stepped out and turned to reach for Anne, who snatched her arm away and snapped at him that she could very well descend the carriage under her own power. As he watched the colonel nod and abandon her to her own devices, Darcy could not help but wonder whatever happened to the meek, demure Anne he had known throughout his childhood, who had been coddled and fussed over by his Aunt Catherine for being of a "sickly constitution". The one that now marched defiantly up the front steps of her uncle's house was a far cry from that pale-skinned girl who spoke hardly a word and hid behind her governess's skirts whenever the boys came near her.

In the entry hall of Disley House, they were greeted almost immediately by a surprised Lady Disley.

"I did not think to see you boys again so soon, and I am quite surprised indeed to see you, Anne," she said, her eyes moving rapidly between the three.

"Where is Father this morning, Mamma?" asked Fitzwilliam. "We are here on a rather urgent matter."

Lady Disley scoffed. "Where else is your father when he is not entertaining guests? He and Philip are in the study."

"Very well. Will you join us?"

He left her no chance to decline, and once again took Anne by the arm to lead her further into the house. She tried to jerk her arm away but he held firm until they were inside Lord Disley's sanctum; only then did he release her. Anne flounced over to the damask sofa against the wall and sat down with an indignant huff.

To Darcy it looked as though his uncle and eldest cousin were going over account books; on their entrance, the earl flipped the book closed and sat back in his chair.

"I am not at all going to like what I am about to hear, am I?" he asked, his eyes falling on Anne.

Fitzwilliam closed the study door, then approached his father's desk. After offering a terse greeting to him and to his brother, he launched into an explanation as to the purpose of their appearance at Disley House, with Darcy filling in a spot here and there. Richard Fitzwilliam's expression quickly shifted from curious to furious as he regarded his wayward niece.

"Well, Anne, what have you to say for yourself?" he asked when their tale had ended.

She crossed her arms and looked away from him. Lady Disley surprised Darcy by walking over to Anne and giving her shoulder a sharp slap. "Your uncle asked you a question, you insolent, foolish girl! Be polite enough to answer him!"

"It's all Darcy's fault!" Anne shouted. "If he would just marry me like he's supposed to—"

Darcy scoffed. "I've already told you my feelings on that score. It was never going to happen no matter how much you or Aunt Catherine wished it so, and even were I inclined in your favor, I certainly would not be after last night's debacle!"

"Thank you, William," Lord Disley said evenly.

"And I suppose you're of a mind to marry that little country whore of yours, is that it?" snapped Anne with a sneer.

Darcy stepped toward her, his voice furious as he said, *"How dare you?!* You know *nothing* about her!"

"I know that she is as penniless as any strumpet in a brothel, and horridly ugly to boot!" Anne cried.

He took another step in her direction before a hand took firm hold of his arm. "Don't, Will. Come, sit and calm yourself," said Fitzwilliam.

"She will apologize for insulting Elizabeth, or so help me..."

"Indeed she will," declared his uncle. "Anne, apologize to William at once."

Anne huffed and crossed her arms again. "I will not."

Lord Disley stood and moved from behind his desk. "You know, I was of a mind to let your foolish actions remain known only to those here and those who witnessed it. After all, everyone who actually saw you behave like the wanton hussy you surmise your rival for William's affections to be are either related to you or in a position to recognize that silence is a better option than gossip. However, now I think that I shall do as society's rules dictate and order you to marry the man you compromised."

Anne stood, indignant rage written across her countenance. "You can't do that! My mother will never agree to it!"

"I can, I will, and your mother has no say in the matter," Disley replied. "Contrary to my sister's over-inflated opinion of herself, *I* am the head of this family. My only regret is that in punishing you, I must punish poor Mr. Ferrars also."

"Oh, Anne, you stupid girl!" cried Lady Disley. "Have you no idea the ruin you could have brought upon this family had you been caught by one of William's servants?"

"And what of Mr. Ferrars and his family?" pointed out Philip. "Would you really sully their reputation as well with your shameful behavior?"

"Oh, she doesn't care about Mr. Ferrars," Darcy said snidely. "She's already made that quite clear."

"My love," said Lord Disley to his wife, "pray, take our niece to one of the guest rooms and see that she is made comfortable. Dear Anne can hardly stay at Darcy House under the same roof as her betrothed."

"Nor is she welcome there, or at Pemberley, until she can bring herself to issue a genuine apology for her insults towards Miss Bennet," Darcy added.

Anne looked stricken. "Oh, Darcy, you don't really mean that! You'd not turn aside your own family, would you?"

"I meant every word," he told her, then turned away.

She began to cry and protest that they were treating her "most unfairly"; her tone and words reminded Darcy too much of her mother. Lady Disley hushed her sharply as she took Anne by the arm and led her out of the study.

A moment of silence followed, then Disley said quietly, "I am sorry for what has happened in your home, William, and what I must insist Mr. Ferrars do to make things right."

Darcy shook his head as he released a frustrated sigh. "It is all right, Uncle. I did warn Mr. Ferrars that marriage to Anne was likely to be the outcome."

"Had he not touched her, we might have avoided it."

"But he didn't Father—at least, certainly not by his own choice," said Theodore.

"Whether by his choice or no, according to your account, little brother, he *did* touch her," Philip reminded him. "The outcome is regrettable, but I have to agree with Father that it is the right course."

"'Tis not only that, Philip," said the earl. "Though few actually saw anything, Darcy's servants know that *something* happened. They are sure to talk to each other, speculating as to the particulars, and it is as sure as anything that one or another may let slip the story to one of their peers in another household. The story will, eventually, get out. It is best we contain it as much as possible."

Lord Disley frowned then. "What of this other witness? You said there were three of you besides the maid—a friend whose name you never gave. Can his silence on the true circumstances be assured?"

Darcy glanced at Theodore to find him looking back. His cousin gave a nod of encouragement, and so Darcy looked back to his uncle and said, "It was Mr. Wickham."

"Wickham?!" cried Philip. "You were in company with that libertine—by choice?!"

His father drew a breath. "Do keep your voice down, Philip, lest you wish our servants to hear you and start *their* tongues to wagging." The earl's expression was both angry and weary at once, and it was with a sigh of his own that he moved away and returned to his desk chair to sit down.

"I imagine there is a very good explanation for the presence of George Wickham in your house, William," he said.

Darcy nodded. "There is, Uncle. It would seem that Georgiana was mistaken as to the identity of her attacker. Wickham didn't do it."

It seemed quite suddenly that in saying the words, Darcy felt for the first time that he truly believed them. He recalled Wickham's face from the night of the Netherfield ball, the expression of utter horror that had descended when he realized what he had been accused of, and to whom it had been done.

"And I suppose he's the one that told you so?" snapped Philip.

"Of course that liar would deny it, William! How can you be so dense as to believe him?"

Darcy scowled at his cousin. "I believe him, Philip, because there are witnesses that have vouched for his not being the assailant."

"Who?" asked his uncle.

"Lord and Lady Sotheby," Theodore supplied. "Charles Bingley hosted a ball at his estate in Hertfordshire this Friday past, and they were in attendance; my cousins accepted as it would be Lady Sotheby's last public engagement before her confinement. It was Lord Sotheby who first took notice of Wickham when he appeared, and led him away lest Darcy see him and make a scene. But after we both were brought into another room to confront him, Lady Sotheby took a good look at him and realized he was not who they thought him to be. Lord Sotheby, too, regarded him very closely, and agreed she was correct."

"How could they be so sure?" Philip asked.

"Lady Sotheby is certain that the man they met that awful day had a scar through his left eyebrow. Her husband remembered it also, once she pointed out that Wickham lacked the feature," Darcy explained. "They also were in agreement that Wickham is some centimeters taller."

"And they are absolutely certain?"

Darcy inclined his head at his uncle's query. "It is a bitter pill to swallow, to be sure, but as their testimony is unassailable, I am left with no recourse but to accept that Wickham is innocent."

Lord Disley nodded. "Aye. Though I know him little, I can be certain myself that a man such as Sotheby would not proclaim one such as Wickham innocent unless he believed it beyond doubt."

"Now what do we do?" asked Philip. "We had it from Mrs. Younge, Georgiana, *and* the Sothebys that Wickham was the man who hurt her. If he is not the one, then who is, and how the bloody hell did he know enough about Wickham to act in his name?"

"Philip, language," chastised his mother, who entered at that moment and closed the door behind her with a soft click. "So little George is not our Georgie's attacker, I gather?"

Her husband shook his head, at which she gave a soft sigh. "Thank God," she muttered. "For I had a secret hope he could not possibly have done such a thing to his own sister."

The four men looked to her with incredulity. "H-how did you know?" asked Darcy.

"What do you mean, his sister?" asked Philip.

"Who told you, Frances?" Lord Disley asked.

Lady Disley smiled as she moved to sit gracefully in the visitor's chair before the earl's desk. "Your sister told me," she replied. "Just as I imagine her husband told you."

Again he nodded. Darcy's gaze roved back and forth between them. "You mean to say that the two of you have known all this time?"

"Why would you keep such a secret?" Philip queried. "I assume that you mean Uncle George is Wickham's father, for I know Aunt Anne could not possibly be his mother."

Richard Fitzwilliam drew a breath. "The truth about Wickham was kept on a need-to-know basis, Philip," he said, "and you did not need to know. I did not think even Anne was aware—"

His wife scoffed lightly. "Please, Richard. Anne was not ignorant of George's dalliance with that maid. She encouraged him to do it, even, because she could not bring herself to allow him into her bed. You remember how deeply she was affected with melancholy after William was born—it took her nearly a year and a half to recover. By then the girl had been quite nicely and quietly wed to Albert Wickham, the boy had been born, and both the maid's reputation and the family's were saved from scandal."

"Wickham and I only learned of it ourselves when Father was on his deathbed," said Darcy then, his voice soft as he was still reeling from the shock that his aunt and uncle had known all his life that he had a brother. "I… I remember that Mamma was very kind to Mrs. Wickham, and even doted on her son many times…"

His aunt turned to him and took his hand. "Your mother had quite the angelic soul, my nephew. She did not blame Mrs. Wickham or your father for what happened—she blamed herself. It was always her deepest regret that she drove your father to break his marriage vows, for they truly loved each other very much."

Darcy nodded. "I know they did."

"So… We must get little Anne wed to this Mr. Ferrars, and find out who really did attack Georgie," summed up Lady Disley. The men around her nodded. "I have a question of my own now… Why did the three of you come to London in the first place?"

Once again Theodore took the lead, explaining how they questioned the veracity of Wickham's inheritance and had come to speak to the solicitor handling the estate.

"What I want to know myself," said Darcy when the story had finished, "is how Anne found out about my meeting Eli—Miss

Bennet. I've spoken of her to no one save you, Aunt, and Georgiana, and then only in writing."

"Your aunt told me, of course," said his uncle. "But then I'm sure you'd have expected that. I should like to learn more about this Miss Bennet of yours."

Darcy felt his ears grow warm. "Miss Elizabeth Bennet is the second of five daughters. The middle, Miss Mary, may soon be wed to the parson at Hunsford, for he is a relation of theirs, and went into Hertfordshire to find a wife among his cousins at Lady Catherine's behest. He is also the heir of Mr. Bennet, for the estate is entailed."

"Are they a wealthy family, or as penniless as Anne claims?" asked Philip.

"Longbourn brings in about two thousand per annum," Darcy replied. "It could do more, if its master were more diligent. Mrs. Bennet's sister is wed to a solicitor in Meryton, and her brother is Mr. Edward Gardiner, with whom you are already acquainted."

"The Bennets have another relation on their mother's side," added Theodore, "by the name of Jennings, though we know little about the connection."

"Well, if the Jennings connection is perchance Mrs. Gerald Jennings of Berkeley Street, then at least there is one branch of the family that is exceedingly wealthy," mused Lady Disley. "She is an acquaintance of mine whom I remember had thought at one time to marry her eldest daughter to Philip, until the girl caught the eye of a gentleman from Devonshire."

"Which worked out quite well for me, as I'd already had my eye on Marianne," said Philip with a smile.

Darcy, who had been engaged in something of a stare-down with his uncle, grew frustrated with the older man's steely glare and said "What? I'm sure you have something to say, Uncle, so let it be said and done with. I must get back to Darcy House and prepare poor Mr. Ferrars for his doom."

"You like this girl?" his uncle asked. "At two thousand a year, William, her father can hardly offer a decent dowry. She has no favorable connections in society, despite your aunt's opinion of the affability of her uncle."

Darcy stood straight and squared his shoulders. "She is a gentleman's daughter. I am a gentleman. In that we are equal, and her lack of fortune means nothing to me. I have more than enough for the both of us."

Again his uncle stared at him for a long, silent moment, and then he inclined his head. "Very well," he said. "At least you've the fortune of choice in your marriage partner. I think I shall join you in breaking the news to Mr. Ferrars—he *is* willing to do right by Anne, is he not? I shouldn't like having to force him to marry her."

Darcy nodded. "He is, though only because he knows it will be asked of him, considering the circumstances. He certainly does not wish it."

"Ferrars… Why does that name mean something to me?" said Lady Disley then. "Richard, I seem to recall some noise about a family by that name during the Season this year. Do you remember?"

"I'm afraid I do not, dearest. You know I pay no attention to the prattling gossips of the *ton*," Lord Disley replied in a droll tone.

Soon the men were readying themselves to depart. As Lady Disley was going between them to give each one a kiss, Darcy said, "Philip, I think you ought to stay behind to keep an eye on Anne."

His cousin frowned, as he was in the midst of shrugging on his greatcoat. "Whatever for, Darcy?"

"Anne tried to escape on us prior to our coming here," Darcy replied.

Theodore nodded. "Indeed she did, brother—tried to talk us into bribing Wickham and Ferrars to keep quiet about the matter and letting her go on home as though naught had occurred."

Philip's eyes widened a fraction even as he gave a nod and doffed his greatcoat. Darcy, Fitzwilliam, and Lord Disley then quit the house and climbed into Darcy's carriage, which waited at the curb. The earl demanded to hear again the details of Anne's terrible actions as the equipage carried them away, after which Darcy recounted the conversations he'd had with his servants and with Ferrars in his study.

Upon arrival at Darcy House, the three were directed to the drawing room by Tolliver; there they found both Wickham and Ferrars drinking coffee. The latter gentleman looked utterly miserable, and upon sight of the earl Wickham paled.

Both men stood on their entrance and turned to face them. Darcy introduced Ferrars to his uncle, who then said to him, "Mr. Ferrars, would you be so kind as to meet with me in Darcy's study? As you are aware we have a great deal to discuss, sir, but first I must speak with Mr. Wickham on another matter. I will join you momentarily."

Edward Ferrars nodded his head, his expression one of glum resignation. When he had departed, Disley crossed the room and stopped a foot shy of Wickham, whose gaze he caught with a hard one of his own.

"I have heard from my son and my nephew the declaration of your innocence by Lord and Lady Sotheby," he began. "And while I have no reason to doubt the testimony of such honorable persons as they, I would have you look me in the eye, boy, and tell me you did not do this abominable thing to your sister."

That he knew the truth of their relationship did not as much affect Wickham as the gravelly tone of Lord Disley's voice. It was one such as Darcy had, thankfully, rarely heard directed towards himself, as he knew that to displease the Earl of Disley would come with dire consequences.

"I swear to you, sir, on the honored souls of both my fathers, that I did *not* attack Georgiana," replied Wickham, whose own voice was near as grave. "Aside from the fact I was out of the country on that dreadful day, my lord, I could never commit such a reprehensible crime, against her or any woman. I have no need to force myself upon a lady, should I choose to seek such favors as only they can give."

Darcy's uncle scoffed. "No," said he. "You never did—always had you the charm and manners necessary to gain you the attentions of the fairer sex."

He then paced away in obvious frustration. "It pains me that we now know almost nothing about the blackguard who did this to our sweet girl, save that he knows enough about you to assume your character."

"And resembles him, apparently," added Fitzwilliam. "Though I cannot recall having met any such person in the whole of my life."

"Nor I," added Darcy. "But we *will* find him. We must, for I know with certainty that Georgiana will find no true peace until she knows he is caught and can harm no other."

Chapter Nineteen

Sunday, 25 November 1798

Elizabeth was at her dressing table attending to her hair when there came a soft knock at the door. Thinking it was Jane, she bid her sister come in by name. Her looking glass instead showed Kitty stepping around the door.

"Lizzy, can I talk to you for a moment?"

Elizabeth turned toward her. "Of course," she replied, curious as to what might bring Kitty to her for consolation instead of Lydia. She wondered also if this might be a chance for her to broach the subject of her younger sister's decorum, as she'd had no opportunity to do so the day before.

Kitty paced for a moment, twisting her hands before her. She still wore her night dress, her hair was still in a braid over her shoulder. At last she turned to Elizabeth and asked, "Is it true, what you said? What you and Jane told us about how we act affects our chances of a good match?"

With a soft sigh Elizabeth inclined her head. "I am afraid it is, Kitty. What makes you ask?"

"Well, it bothered me the whole of yesterday and I hardly got a moment's sleep. I don't want to ruin my chances of getting married, Lizzy! I want to be a wife and have my own home one day, with a handsome husband and fine gowns and a carriage and everything."

A better opening to the discussion she needed to have with her sister Elizabeth could not have asked for. Rising from her dressing table, she approached the agitated younger girl and took her by the hand to guide her over to her bed. Sitting on the end with her, she patted the back of Kitty's hand as she said, "It pleases me to hear you say you want those things, Kitty. I very much want to see all my sisters happy."

"I do not understand, Lizzy. How is mine or Lydia's behavior so very bad?" Kitty wondered. "We're only having fun with our friends and flirting with the officers. Mamma doesn't seem to mind, and even encourages us."

"And what good has it done you?" Elizabeth countered. "Has any officer singled you out as his particular favorite? Do any of your officer friends speak of getting married? I venture the answer is no, as there is not one of them with enough money. Most men in the militia below the rank of colonel earn barely enough to support themselves—they have not the means to support a wife as well, if she does not have the added incentive of a substantial dowry.

"As to having fun and flirting… It is entirely possible to be amused and enjoy time with your friends without crude remarks, vulgar behavior, and excessively loud laughter. You need not be over-exuberant to be thought engaging. And if you continue to flirt with so very many of the officers, how is any one of them—or perhaps a wealthy gentleman—to think you suitable? A lady who gives her attentions to many cannot be counted on to be faithful to one. At least, that is what society will think of you, and perhaps how any man who has designs on you may think."

"What are you saying? That we should be as dull and boring as Mary? Or as polite and reserved as Jane?"

"Yes, our sisters are rather demure," Elizabeth asked her. "But consider this: Mary is now engaged to be married."

Kitty snorted. "To Mr. Collins."

Here, Elizabeth knew, she would have to speak in their cousin's defense. Drawing a breath, she replied, "It is true that Mr. Collins is…unique in his manner. But his position in society is very respectable, and his income enough to make their lives comfortable. And consider our Mary's inclinations—do you not think that her love of scripture makes her eminently suitable to being a clergyman's wife?"

"Her love of scripture, her annoying moralizing—" said Kitty, her tone derisive.

"That is something else you must cease doing if you truly wish to attract a husband, Kitty. Such cutting and unkind remarks, spoken in such a tone of voice as you have just used, are more likely to cool a gentleman's attachment than encourage it. Gentlemen like Mr. Bingley want their wives to be someone they are not ashamed to be seen with in public or known to be attached to."

Elizabeth turned to face her sister more fully. "If a gentleman does not want one girl from a family because she is loud and uncouth in company, he is not likely to look at her sisters for a wife," said she. "That is what Jane and I were trying to make clear to you and Lydia. How one of us is perceived by society affects how *all* of us are perceived. No gentleman, be he of means or no, will wish to associate himself with a family in which there are those who cannot comport themselves with proper decorum."

Kitty was quiet for a moment, then said, "Well, Mr. Darcy does not seem to mind. He likes you very much, or he would not have kissed you, surely."

Elizabeth smiled, then sobered before saying, "I shall be honest with you, sister—Mr. Darcy near did not consider me at all. Our family's lack of fortune and favorable connections, and the lack of restraint shown by you, by Lydia, and even by our mother, gave him pause for a time. A gentleman of his station must take great care in his choice of bride, as his lady will be much scrutinized, and if she is deemed unsuitable then it will greatly affect the chances of his sister making a good match. He must think of her as well as himself."

Kitty's brow furrowed, and again she seemed to consider what she had heard. "You said if Mr. Darcy were to change his mind, it would not be through any fault of yours," she said thoughtfully. "Do you mean that he really might scorn you because Lydia and I flirt and laugh?"

"Not *just* because you flirt and laugh, but those are certainly factors."

Elizabeth tilted her head and gauged Kitty's readiness to hear the full truth. Perhaps if she were to tell her of Mr. Bingley's regard as well as his reason for declining to pursue her in spite of those feelings, it would open her sister's eyes that last fraction to the reality of how very important it was that she act like a well-bred lady.

"Kitty, what if I were to tell you that I know for certain a gentleman of our acquaintance has taken a fancy to you, but that the unchecked behavior of yourself and our youngest sister is the reason he has thus far hesitated to further any sort of attachment?"

Kitty's eyes widened. "Do you mean Colonel Fitzwilliam? Oh Lizzy, he is so very amiable, and Lydia would be bursting with envy should he like me above her! You know she thinks a man is nothing if he is not in regimentals, and though we've not seen him in uniform, the colonel *is* an officer."

Lydia, Elizabeth mused silently, *would* be envious—to the point of trying to sway the colonel's interest to herself. Though she had been very spoilt by their mother for the whole of her life, and as she had herself declared was given anything she desired by Mrs. Bennet, it was never enough. Kitty was allegedly the very best of all Lydia's friends, but there was little the elder girl had been given that the younger did not covet. Bonnets, gloves, gowns… The affections of a man would be no different.

Elizabeth shook her head. "It is not Colonel Fitzwilliam," she replied.

At this Kitty gasped and drew a hand to her heart. "Surely you do not mean Mr. Bingley! But that is impossible—you know as well as any that he's shown no particular interest in any of the girls in the country. Mamma's been very vexed by him, so hopeful was she that he would take a liking to Jane."

She rose and began to pace again. "It cannot be," she said again. "Mr. Bingley cannot like me."

"And why should he not?" returned Elizabeth. "We may none of us be as beautiful as Jane, as Mamma reminds each of us daily, but you *are* a very pretty girl, Kitty. In fact, Mr. Bingley himself described you thus."

Kitty turned back. "He did?"

Elizabeth offered a nod, and smiled as she said, "He did indeed. He said also that you are very lively and amiable and charming, and he particularly likes the color of your eyes. But you have shown him no particular attention, and your conduct is such that he is unsure courting you would be wise, as not only would your behavior reflect on him, but his sisters also."

When her sister's lip began to tremble, Elizabeth rose immediately and moved to embrace her. "Pray, do not be upset. Mr. Bingley *likes* you, Kitty." She gave her a gentle squeeze and then stood back, capturing her gaze before she added, "Now, you must decide if you like him. Not just for his fortune, as I daresay he does not wish to be pursued only for his wealth anymore than Mr. Darcy. We are to dine at Netherfield after church—be sure to personally thank Mr. Bingley for the invitation. Engage him in conversation, or allow yourself to be engaged by him. And for goodness' sake, try to talk about more than the militia or gowns or ribbons."

"But…" Kitty's lip trembled again, and tears filled her eyes. "But

I don't know what topics gentlemen like to talk about! All I know are gowns and bonnets and officers. What if he decides he does not like me because I am stupid?"

"Tosh, Kitty! You are not stupid. You read books, do you not? You like horses," said Elizabeth. "Ask Mr. Bingley what books he has read, and tell him of those you have. Talk to him about how much you enjoy horseback riding—you never know, perhaps that will inspire him to invite you to go riding one day."

The younger Bennet blinked back her tears. "Very well, that does not sound too dull… And I should very much like to go horseback riding, should he suggest it, as it has been some time since I have gone. But Lizzy, if Mr. Bingley thinks I am lively, and likes that about me, then why should I have to change to be worthy of courtship? It does not seem fair—men do not change for us."

"They do if they believe the change is worth it," Elizabeth pointed out. "My dear sister, I do not mean to suggest that you ought completely reinvent yourself. I should not like to see you do so for any man, and in fact Mr. Bingley did say he would not wish it, either. I only mean to suggest you consider how your behavior impacts your relationships, your chances of making a good match—be it with Mr. Bingley or another—and make adjustments as needed. Consider how lively and amiable Mr. Bingley's conduct is, yet is not considered ungentlemanly. And think of how well liked our Jane is, for all her shyness and modesty."

A smile flittered at the corners of Kitty's lips, and Elizabeth felt relief that she was no longer on the verge of tears. "Indeed, Jane is very much liked by all our acquaintance. And Mamma did try to get Mr. Bingley to like her above anyone."

"And yet it is *you* to whom he has taken a fancy," Elizabeth said with a grin. "You know how much faith Mamma has in Jane's beauty saving us all from the hedgerows."

Kitty laughed, at the same moment that there came another soft knock at the door. This time it was Jane coming to visit. "I beg your pardon, I do not mean to interrupt," she said, and started to back out.

"Oh no, Jane—don't go," said Kitty. She looked to Elizabeth. "May I tell her what you have shared with me? I… I should like her opinion also."

Elizabeth nodded. Jane entered fully and closed the door, and in a rush of breath, Kitty relayed the whole of their conversation. Jane listened with rapt attention, looking to Elizabeth now and then for confirmation or denial, and when her sister had finished, reached for

Kitty's hand.

"Dearest Kitty, I am so happy for you!" said she. "Mr. Bingley is such a charming young man. Lizzy and I like him very much, and I daresay you will also when you come to know him better."

"He does *seem* very agreeable," Kitty conceded. "But what if I don't like him after all?"

"Kitty, I am quite sure that Mr. Bingley will understand if, after some genuine conversation, you find that he is not to your liking," Elizabeth assured her. "But you will never know if you do not afford him, and yourself, the chance of finding out."

Elizabeth's bedchamber door opened for a third time; Mrs. Bennet burst in without bothering to knock, as she was wont to do, crying as she did so, "Oh, you're not half dressed! Girls, what am I to do with you? You must hurry, and put on your best Sunday gowns! We are to dine at Netherfield after church, and I am sure it is a credit to you, my dear Jane. I think Mr. Bingley has only waited for the departure of his friend to make his choice of you known to all. Come girls, make haste! Make haste!"

Taking Jane by the arm, Mrs. Bennet bustled out of the room. Kitty looked to Elizabeth. "Oh Lizzy! How am I ever to be able to talk to Mr. Bingley if Mamma persists in pushing Jane at him?"

Biting her lip as she considered it, Elizabeth suddenly grinned. "I know what to do! I shall speak to Mr. Bingley and tell him to suggest a walk in the garden—the weather will be fine enough for a brief stroll, I think. I will tell him to invite you first and offer his arm, and you know how Mamma feels about taking a gentleman's arm if it's offered."

Kitty giggled. "Oh, indeed! I shan't be able to refuse—how rude that would be!"

Elizabeth grinned again. "Precisely."

The Bennets took their carriage into Meryton for Sunday service, as the church there had been attended by the Netherfield party since their arrival. It was clear that the townspeople were delighted by the attendance of Lord and Lady Sotheby and their relations as well, for it gave them something of a distinction to have such prominent guests in their midst—at least in their eyes.

It was as the families were filing inside to take their seats that Elizabeth was able to speak to Mr. Bingley; in fact, it was he that approached her, to apologize for any unpleasantness her family had endured at the unexpected arrival of Miss de Bourgh on her doorstep.

"It was my sister Caroline who brought it upon you," he confessed, confirming Elizabeth's own suspicion. "She wrote to Darcy's aunt, Lady Catherine—most inappropriately, I might add, for the two have not been introduced. Her daughter intercepted the letter."

Mr. Bingley appeared as though he wished to say more, perhaps something unflattering about his sister or Miss de Bourgh, but held himself in check. To Elizabeth, it was yet another mark in the gentleman's favor, the ability to hold his tongue when he was inclined to scorn.

He sighed then. "As you may have rightly assumed, Miss de Bourgh paid us a brief visit also, demanding to speak to my sister. It was then that I learned of what had been done. Miss de Bourgh, from what I overheard, agreed with my sister that drastic measures were required to prevent so *unsuitable* a match as you and her cousin."

Elizabeth smirked. "I daresay stronger words than that were used, but I thank you for your version, sir."

Bingley was now looking over her shoulder. She did as well, and witnessed Kitty smiling shyly in their direction.

Looking back to her friend, she was certain of glimpsing a smile, and a spark of hope in his eyes. "I spoke to my sister this morning," she said softly. "Kitty was surprised to learn of your regard, and fears you will have little in common. I reminded her of her interests beyond fripperies and the militia—she likes horses, by the by—so it is my hope that conversation between you, when you have chance of it, will not be lacking."

Bingley returned his gaze to Elizabeth. "And we shall have a chance," he said. "I will make sure of it."

Elizabeth's smile grew. "Indeed, sir, and I have conceived of the perfect plan on how to make it happen," she said, then told him what she and Kitty had discussed. Mr. Bingley smiled and agreed to the scheme.

"Lizzy! Come here, child. The vicar will soon be at the pulpit," cried her mother then.

With another smile, Elizabeth bid Mr. Bingley farewell and went to join her family. Mrs. Bennet leaned close to her as they entered the church and chastised her for "taking Mr. Bingley's attention away from Jane." She wanted to retort that Bingley's affections lay in quite another direction, but thought it best to wait until Kitty decided whether or not she liked him.

The vicar's sermon that day—the lesson he imparted was that

one should assist a neighbor in need, whether their burdens were great or small—nearly set Elizabeth to laughing. The soft snort she emitted earned her a harshly whispered "Hush, child!" from her mother and a light pinch of her arm from Jane, though a sidelong glance at her sister showed Jane's lips to be quivering with suppressed mirth.

When the service ended, Elizabeth was approached by Marianne Dashwood. "I understand your family is to break your fast with us," she said with a smile.

"Indeed we are, Marianne," Elizabeth replied.

"Would you care to ride with us in my brother's carriage? I beg forgiveness if my words are impertinent, but your family's modest equipage cannot be very comfortable with so many to carry."

Elizabeth chuckled. "Quarters are certainly close," she admitted, "when the whole of our family is inside. But can Lord Sotheby's carriage really seat three on one side in comfort?" She said this knowing that Lord and Lady Sotheby would sit one side to themselves.

Marianne laughed. "By far!" said she. "His Grace the Duke of Mildenhall, who is my brother's uncle, insisted on their taking the largest of his carriages when he learned of Elinor's condition, that she would always be comfortable when they had need to travel."

"Then I happily accept your invitation—I have never been inside the carriage of a duke before," said Elizabeth, who then grinned widely at a sudden idea, and excused herself to speak to Bingley. With a quick whisper in his ear, she suggested he invite Kitty to ride with him and the Hursts, as Caroline had not accompanied her family to church.

Bingley gave a nod and waited until she had returned to her relations to tell them she would be riding with Miss Dashwood, Lady Amelia, and the Sothebys. He then followed, joining them amidst her mother's squeals of delight—and Lydia's scowls of envy—about what an honor it was to have been asked.

"Excuse me, I could not help but overhear," said Mr. Bingley casually. "Allow my family also to ease your comfort and take one of you along with us. I shall even have my carriage made ready when you take your leave this afternoon."

Mrs. Bennet was already nudging Jane forward as she thanked him for his kindness and generosity, when he astonished both of Elizabeth's parents by turning to Kitty and saying, "Miss Catherine, would you care to join us on the ride to Netherfield? I understand you are fond of horses; Louisa and I both are as well, and though we have been in the country some weeks, we do not know the best riding paths."

Kitty paled slightly at being so suddenly thrust into the spotlight, but when her eyes darted to Elizabeth, who gave her a nod of encouragement, she cleared her throat softly and lifted her chin. "It has been some time since I have taken the riding trails, Mr. Bingley, but I should be delighted to tell you of them."

"Excellent!" cried Mr. Bingley, who then offered his arm. It delighted Elizabeth immensely to see a blush color her sister's cheeks as she accepted, and it occurred to her that Kitty was not as immune to his charm as she had appeared that morning.

"It's not fair!" hissed Lydia as the two walked away. "Why should Lizzy and Kitty be asked and not me? Lizzy will get to ride in the carriage of a nobleman! I am far more interesting than she is!"

Elizabeth chose not to rise to the bait. Ignoring her sister's petulance, she gave Jane's hand a squeeze and her father's cheek a kiss, and nodded politely at her mother when she admonished her to "Please hold your tongue in front of the earl!"

The Northam carriage was indeed very comfortable; Marianne had not exaggerated that there was room enough for three on one side. Conversation was lively and Elizabeth grew to like the family even more than she had at the ball, and knew for certain now that she would endeavor to maintain her burgeoning friendship with the ladies.

Breakfast went much better than Elizabeth thought it would. Caroline joined them and was uncharacteristically polite, though when Bingley drew out the chair to his left for Kitty, quickly hid the scowl that descended. She blatantly avoided speaking to Elizabeth at all; instead, she paid all her attention to the Sothebys, Lady Amelia, and Miss Dashwood—snubbing even her own sister and brother. Elizabeth was certain she was trying to ingratiate herself with the earl and countess so that she could claim a greater acquaintance than actually existed, but they expertly thwarted her at every turn. Certainly they were all polite with their replies to her inquiries, especially Lady Sotheby, but beyond that they spoke little to her.

Much to Caroline's obvious vexation. After the first quarter of an hour produced little result for all her effort, she sulked and picked at her food.

This behavior Elizabeth largely ignored in favor of watching Kitty and Bingley interact, as well as her mother's behavior. Having shared the Hursts' carriage with him seemed to have been just the trick necessary to get things moving between them—Kitty blushed and laughed and, if Elizabeth was not mistaken, flirted openly, although with a surprising amount of restraint. She was not so loud of voice or wild in behavior as she tended to be, which seemed a source of confusion to more than one member of her family. Mary had raised a curious eyebrow more than once; Lydia intermittently scowled, sulked, or spoke loudly in order to draw attention to herself (thankfully Jane was seated by her side and kept her from making too much of a spectacle); and Mrs. Bennet alternated between stunned awe at being in the presence of nobility and vexation—or confusion—that Mr. Bingley found Kitty more engaging than Jane.

Mr. Bennet, Elizabeth noticed with some relief, had given up on his recent favorite activity—poking fun at Mr. Collins—in favor of discussing estate management with Lord Sotheby, whom she knew to have quite successfully managed and improved an estate in Dorsetshire on the same income as her father's. His rapt attention to Lord Sotheby's words gave Elizabeth some small hope that her father might just take a more active interest in Longbourn's management.

As the meal was concluding, Mr. Bingley initiated the original plan of getting Kitty away from everyone by suggesting a walk in the garden and asking if she'd like to join him. He then turned to his guests and casually suggested they all go and enjoy what "might be the last warm weather we have this year"; his invitation was accepted by most everyone save the Hursts, as Louisa was feeling fatigued; Lady Sotheby, who wished to rest and put her feet up; Caroline, who almost immediately retired to her room; Mrs. Bennet, who offered to keep Lady Sotheby company, declaring that Lydia would stay with them also; and Mr. Bennet and Lord Sotheby, who took to the library to talk more about their mutual interests in crop yields and animal husbandry. Although Mr. Collins at first suggested his presence might be desired by the earl and Mr. Bennet, Mary was successful in directing him from the notion by expressing her "great desire" to have him escort her through Netherfield's shrubbery.

During their walk through the garden, Lady Amelia and Miss Dashwood—who walked with Elizabeth and Jane—expressed their delight at the prospect of a romance between Kitty and Mr. Bingley. Marianne admitted that she had thought Lydia the "less manageable" of the two youngest Bennets, based on what she had observed of them at the ball, and the two eldest expressed their agreement. Lady Amelia then observed, from their view of the potential couple walking some feet ahead of them, that in the proper company, with the proper attention, Kitty had every chance of improving herself. She and Marianne hoped, as Elizabeth and Jane did, that she would not waste the chance before her, not only of making a most advantageous match with Mr. Bingley, but also of enlarging her circle of acquaintances with more subdued behavior.

An hour later, when Mr. Bennet emerged from Netherfield announcing he believed it time the family was on their way, Mr. Bingley kept his word of offering his carriage so that the family coach would not be crowded. Mary, of course, rode with Mr. Collins in his curricle, but even without her the confines of Mr. Bennet's carriage were rather stifling and uncomfortable. Elizabeth was more than happy to take advantage of her neighbor's generosity this once, and accepted the hand-in Bingley offered when the carriages came round to the front steps. Riding with her in his vehicle were Jane and Kitty—a most advantageous arrangement, for Elizabeth had found herself rather excited to learn her younger sister's judgment of their neighbor.

The first moments as the carriage pulled away were silent. Elizabeth exchanged a smiling glance with Jane, as across from them Kitty sat glancing out the window, worrying her bottom lip between her teeth. Only when the carriage pulled onto the main road did any of the sisters venture to speak.

"I should not have to change myself for him," Kitty said softly.

Elizabeth stifled a sigh. "No, Kitty, you should not," she agreed.

"But sister, did you not enjoy Mr. Bingley's attentions?" asked Jane.

Kitty's eyes fell to her lap and she began to pick at a thread on her skirt. "I did indeed. And… well, I suppose I have to admit that he has only showed me such attentions because I have altered myself as you suggested."

She lifted her gaze then. "It's not right. I should *not* have to change for him," she said again. "But I find that I *do* like him, and very much so. Mr. Bingley is just what a young man ought to be, sisters! He is sensible, good humored, lively; I never saw such happy manners! So much ease, with such perfect good breeding!"

"He is also handsome," replied Elizabeth with a grin, "which a young man ought likewise to be, if he possibly can. His character is thereby complete. Indeed, Mr. Bingley is very agreeable, and I give you leave to like him. You have liked many a stupider person."

Kitty giggled as Jane admonished her. The former then sighed and dropped her head back against the squab. "I don't want to have to change myself for Mr. Bingley, yet I feel that I must. I know we are not well acquainted, and I own it is only myself I have to blame for it—"

"That is very mature of you, Kitty," said Jane.

"Thank you, Jane. As I was saying, we are not well acquainted, but I should like very much to become more so," Kitty went on. "Mr. Bingley is so very charming and…and they way he looked at me on our walk…"

Here she blushed. "I confess that his gaze made me feel very warm inside. It felt so very good to be gazed upon with such…such adoration, I am sure of it! Such tenderness! He genuinely likes me, Lizzy and Jane—*me*, above every other girl in the country, including my own sisters! I do not wish to lose his affections. I *like* being the particular choice of such a fine gentleman. Mr. Bingley will certainly move in the first circles whenever he goes to Town, or anywhere, and if what you have told me about reputations reflecting on those we are related to is the truth, then I should not like for such a kind and generous person to be tainted by association with someone whose reputation is scorned. I should not like for *my* reputation to be scorned at all!"

Kitty swept her gaze between them. "Tell me honestly… Do you really, truly think that Lydia and I behave so very dreadfully?"

Elizabeth glanced at Jane, then back to Kitty. "I think," she began slowly, "that your conduct until now has been a good deal too forward and uninhibited. That you ask such questions, dearest, is proof enough that you are not entirely beyond amendment. Lydia, if I may be frank, is a bad influence on you for she is far worse than you in her comportment—and if our parents do not take the trouble to check her, she will surely be lost to all hope of being a proper lady."

"Now Lizzy, you cannot mean that," said Jane. "I hardly think even Lydia is beyond reach."

"Perhaps not yet, but I daresay she soon will be," Elizabeth returned. "Kitty, on the other hand, has at last taken the time to listen to our views and is considering that we may have greater knowledge of the ways of the world, if she has not already accepted it. She knows now that even as much as Mr. Bingley may like her, he is *un*likely to make her an offer if she cannot conduct herself in a manner that is acceptable in the eyes of society. Even better, she is considering, at last, that how people think of *her* will reflect on how people will think of the man who is her husband."

The carriage was quiet again for a few minutes, and then Kitty said, "Mr. Bingley and I got on very well, I think, but I still wonder at why, precisely, he even likes me at all. While it is true that I like to read, and ride horses, and have fun and flirt and joke about, what else is there? Who am I, that he should like me above anyone? I have no talents or accomplishments as the two of you and Mary have, or his own sisters."

"Have you ever thought about drawing or playing an instrument, or learning another language?" asked Jane.

Kitty bit her lip as she thought over her sister's words. "I have not the patience to draw, I think, but I confess I have always longed to play an instrument. But not the pianoforte! Mary's dreadful playing certainly turned me off of *that* idea."

"Come now, Kitty," chided Elizabeth. "Even you must admit that Mary's playing is greatly improved of late. Since giving up singing to focus on her instrument, she has become less wooden in her style and form."

"Indeed, our sister is much less determined to be perfect at it," Jane added, "and as such has somehow managed to become even more proficient."

Elizabeth smiled. "It is because she is less focused on the technical aspects of the music and more focused on the emotional. She *feels* it more, and so is better at it."

"Did you know that Lord Sotheby plays the violin?" said Kitty. "Mr. Bingley told me of it when we talked of music briefly. He said that Lady Sotheby lamented her husband had not brought along his violin to accompany Miss Dashwood or Mrs. Hurst when they played at the ball. I think I should like to try learning the violin, as none of the girls I know play it, if I were to take up an instrument. But it is not to be."

Elizabeth frowned. "Whyever not?"

Kitty scoffed. "Who in Longbourn village or Meryton would teach me? The music instructors in this part of the country only teach pianoforte or the harp."

She had, Elizabeth was forced to admit, an unfortunate point. The harp and pianoforte were indeed the instruments of choice in the nearby communities; in order for Kitty to learn the violin, if she were genuine in her desire, a tutor would have to come from Town.

"Or..." she mused aloud, a large smile coming to her lips.

Both her sisters regarded her with confusion. "Or what, Lizzy?" prompted Kitty.

"I have just had the grandest thought, Kitty," Elizabeth replied. "You know that Jane and I are to go to London with our Aunt and Uncle Gardiner after Christmas. What if you were to join us?"

Chapter Twenty

Excited by the prospect of going to London, Kitty readily agreed that Elizabeth should write their Aunt Gardiner straight away and ask if she could be included in the visit.

She then gasped, her hand to her lips, and said, "But what of Mr. Bingley? How will he court me if I away to Town?"

Elizabeth looked to Jane, who seemed as curious as her sister to know the answer. "Quite easily, dear Kitty: Mr. Bingley shall simply have to follow us to London."

Kitty's eyes grew large. "Oh! To be seen at balls and parties with such a man as Mr. Bingley!" she cried. "Lydia will turn every shade of green with envy!"

"Now Kitty," said Jane. "You mustn't crow too loud over your sister. Boasting is neither ladylike nor kind."

Elizabeth nodded her head in agreement. "Indeed, you should say nothing at all about going to London with us until I have received a reply to my letter. We cannot be certain that Aunt and Uncle Gardiner have the means to host all three of us."

These admonitions seemed to do as intended, and Kitty settled back into the squab. Several minutes following were silent save for the sounds of the carriage wheels on the road and the clop-clop steps of the horses that drew it. Then Kitty spoke again, softly, saying, "I think I saw what you meant before."

"What do you mean?" asked Jane.

Kitty looked to her. "What you and Lizzy have said about our conduct being scrutinized. At breakfast Lydia was quite loud, trying to talk over everyone as she was. I noticed that the two of you, and Mary, and more than one of Mr. Bingley's guests cringed at the volume of her voice. It was very ill-mannered of her to act so, was it not?"

Elizabeth nodded. "Verily it was, Kitty; ill-mannered and rude of her to attempt to draw all the attention to herself. But then, that is because Lydia thrives on being the center of attention, and she is quite petulant when she does not get her way."

"It is because she has been taught no better," said Jane, "though you know that Lizzy and I have done what we can to instruct you both."

Where our mother has failed to, Elizabeth added silently. "It was more than a little mortifying," she spoke aloud.

Kitty sighed and looked out the carriage window again. Elizabeth did the same, and noted that they were turning up the drive to Longbourn.

"I do not wish to be an embarrassment," said Kitty. "To myself, our family, or to Mr. Bingley."

She looked back to her sisters, and Elizabeth saw that her countenance was pleading. "Will you help me? I wish to learn to be a young lady that my sisters and my husband, when I have one, can be proud to acknowledge. I do not ever want to see you cringe at my behavior as you did Lydia's."

Elizabeth chose not to say that she already had, many times, or that each time she or Jane had tried to correct their younger sisters, she had huffed and rolled her eyes along with Lydia. But then, Kitty had never had the motivation of being the sole object of a gentleman's affections before—she'd always had to compete with her sisters.

Especially Lydia.

She decided that she could forgive Kitty her selective memory in this instance. After all, the girl had just taken a very momentous step forward by admitting her feelings, as well as asking for their help in improving herself.

"I am proud of you, Kitty," Elizabeth declared. "You have taken great strides already in a *very* short amount of time—'tis not even been a day!"

Jane nodded and smiled her agreement. Kitty lifted a shoulder, then replied, "Perhaps I have just not had the correct motivation—and I do not refer only to Mr. Bingley. For the first time I have judged myself through the eyes of others and… I do not like what I have seen. I do not wish to be judged as still a child when I am almost a woman grown."

"It is good that you have had your eyes and heart opened to the truth before it was too late to correct yourself," said Jane as the carriage began to slow. "Now that you own your mistakes, you shall be able to make adjustments to your conduct which will allow for you to remain the lively creature Mr. Bingley admires but still be seen as a proper lady."

Kitty looked hopeful. "So you will help me, as you have done for Mary?"

Elizabeth reached for her hand. "Of course we will, dearest."

Moments later the carriage had come to a stop, then Bingley's coachman was opening the door and handing them down. Elizabeth bid him express again their thanks to his master for the generous kindness. The young man smiled and nodded before he climbed back onto the vehicle and it started away.

It was then she took note of her mother's voice. Mrs. Bennet was lamenting that she did not understand Mr. Bingley at all. "Why should he give so much attention to Kitty when our Jane was right there? She is far more beautiful than any of her sisters."

Lydia added to the derision by saying, "Nor do I understand, Mamma. Kitty is so dull compared to me—in looks and personality I am far superior!"

Elizabeth saw tears come into Kitty's eyes, and her heart went out to her. This was a day of firsts for her sister—the complaints were nothing she had not heard before, but it seemed Kitty could no longer ignore the sting of their cruelty.

"Mamma, Lydia, you are being unkind," spoke up Jane as the family was going into the house. "Kitty is as pretty a girl as any of us, and given Mr. Bingley's attention to her today, it is clear that he finds her company to his liking."

Mrs. Bennet handed off her hat, gloves, and spencer to Hill, then turned to regard Kitty as though searching for something. After a moment she brightened and moved over to embrace her daughter, saying, "Kitty, my dearest girl! You must do whatever you can to secure him; Mr. Bingley may not have chosen Jane as we all suspected he would, but he has certainly shown great wisdom in choosing one of her sisters and *not* one of Mrs. Long's nieces. Oh, the gowns and carriages you will have! And you could be mistress of that fine house in a very short time, I am sure!"

Lydia huffed and stomped her foot, then whirled and stormed off to her room. Mr. Bennet had already disappeared into his book room, and Mary and Mr. Collins had gone to the pianoforte. They were spending as much time together as could be done, as he was to return to Kent on the morrow. Mrs. Bennet attempted to take Kitty into the drawing room with her, expressing a desire to advise her how she could guarantee an offer from Mr. Bingley, but Kitty claimed fatigue and a desire of going to her room to rest. Jane and Elizabeth followed her up the stairs, the former offering to help Kitty with her dress, reminding her with a smile that "Lizzy has a letter to write."

Monday, 26 November 1798

As the Bennets were sitting to breakfast, a letter came from Netherfield addressed to "Miss Catherine Bennet".

Kitty barely stifled the excited squeal she began to cry, though the shine in her eyes as she broke the seal was not to be contained. Elizabeth grinned as she watched her read, color coming to her cheeks to compliment the smile that would surely split Kitty's face should it grow any larger.

"Come, child! What does it say?" asked Mrs. Bennet.

"Mrs. Hurst writes to invite me, and what sisters of mine are not otherwise engaged, to join her, Mr. Hurst, and Mr. Bingley for an excursion on horseback," Kitty reported. "Their guests Lord and Lady Sotheby, Lady Amelia, and Miss Dashwood are to depart for home after breaking their fast, and Mr. Bingley is eager to be enjoying the country again. Mrs. Hurst says that if we care to join their outing, please send a reply before one o'clock, as that is when they aim to depart."

Elizabeth listened with a small amount of dread as her mother exclaimed that of course they should go. Mrs. Bennet unfortunately did not consider—or perhaps genuinely was not aware, given how flighty she could be—that Elizabeth had refused to ride a horse since the age of nine, when she had been thrown and broken her arm. Only Mr. Darcy's insisting she ride on Diamond that stormy day had led her to do so; it was the first time she had been on horseback in more than ten years, and she had never been more happy to be standing on solid ground than when she had been handed down again. Elizabeth knew she would very much enjoy a picnic with her sisters and neighbors, but already a cold sweat had broken upon her brow at the thought of climbing atop a horse.

Kitty hurried to the drawing room to pen an acceptance; Jane and Elizabeth were to accompany her on the outing. Mary would remain at home working on wedding plans following Mr. Collins' departure for Kent, and to everyone's surprise, Mr. Bennet declared Lydia could not go. His youngest daughter and his wife protested the unfairness of her not being allowed to join her sisters, but he neither explained his decree nor bent his will to their pleas.

Then Lydia cried, "Who wants to go on some stupid horseback ride anyway? I'll just walk into Meryton and visit with the officers. I shall have all the best of them paying their attentions to *me*."

Her sisters knew this was directed at Kitty, who had just then returned from sending off her reply to the invitation. Kitty only smiled and concentrated on her breakfast, her lack of reaction leading to a scowl from Lydia.

"You will do no such thing," said Mr. Bennet to his daughter. "You are but fifteen years old, child, and are not to be out of this house unless accompanied by one of your parents or one of your sisters. And I have no desire or need to go into Meryton today."

"Mamma will go with me then, I am sure," said Lydia. "Won't you, Mamma?"

Mrs. Bennet looked unsure. "I do not know, my dear. All this disagreement is fraying my poor nerves—I have such flutterings and spasms beginning all over me. I daresay could not walk so far, and your sisters will have the carriage."

The youngest Bennet daughter turned then to the middle. "Then Mary can walk with me. Surely there is some…thing…she needs for her wedding to Mr. Collins."

Just as Mr. Collins opened his mouth to speak, Mary glanced at him and gave a shake of her head. The parson's lips snapped immediately shut, thereafter opening only to admit another forkful from his plate. To Lydia, Mary next turned; offering a smile, she shook her head again.

"Thank you, but no. Like our father, I have no need or desire to travel into Meryton. Besides which, I have still yet much to do in preparation for leaving my childhood home. It is, after all, the reason I am not accompanying our sisters to Netherfield, if you'll recall."

Lydia turned a pout to Mr. Bennet. "Papa, it's not fair! Why must I stay at home as though I had been naughty? I've done nothing wrong!"

"And it is my intention that your innocence, such as it is, remains the same. No, do not pout, daughter—I have not the least intention of yielding."

He called for Hill and asked that his breakfast be put on a tray and brought to his book room, then departed the dining parlor. Elizabeth, Jane, Mary and Kitty all looked at each other in wonder at this sudden change in their father. Elizabeth was further surprised by the uncharacteristic silence of Mr. Collins, though surmised that Mary was to thank for his keeping his unwanted opinion to himself.

Lydia sulked through the rest of the meal, intermittently whining and begging her mother and Mary to go to Meryton with her. Mrs. Bennet, instead of commiserating with her as she had been known to do in the past, grew quite agitated and quit the room before her plate was clean.

The rest of the family could only sit in wonder, and when they had finished their own food, Mr. Collins' curricle was called and his trunk loaded. All his future sisters save Lydia walked out with him and Mary to wish him a safe journey. He said a goodbye to his betrothed that was only mildly nauseating to Elizabeth, and then was off. Mary declared she would be taking a walk in the garden, and by her tone the others knew she desired to be alone for a time. Elizabeth, Jane, and Kitty made for their rooms to prepare for the excursion at Netherfield or to spend the next few hours in quiet contemplation of their father's odd behavior.

On arriving at Netherfield at a quarter to one, Elizabeth was relieved to learn that Louisa Hurst planned to drive a curricle and quickly volunteered to ride with her. Mr. Hurst seemed likewise relieved, stating he had been looking forward to going out on horseback. Their destination was "a pond that looked to be good for fishing."

"That explains why Mr. Hurst agreed to join our party," Mrs. Hurst told Elizabeth in a low voice, before her husband moved to hand her up into the curricle. He gave his hand to Elizabeth as well, and Mr. Bingley aided her sisters onto mounts that he promised were perfectly suited for carrying a lady and should give them no trouble.

Bingley rode with Jane to his left and Kitty to his right, and Mr. Hurst rode between the three of them and the curricle. After a few moments of silence, Mrs. Hurst said, "There is a particular reason I am taking the curricle today rather than riding a horse—something I very much enjoy."

Naturally, this made Elizabeth curious. "And what is the reason?"

A smile graced her companion's lips. "My husband insisted, as it was confirmed by Mr. Jones this afternoon that I am increasing. Reginald refused to allow me on a horse."

She had heard that it could be dangerous for a lady with child to ride a horse, though the risk was more in falling should the animal be spooked than in the riding. Elizabeth congratulated her, and Mrs. Hurst accepted with a grin.

"We have been married three years—I admit I was beginning to lose hope of giving my husband an heir. He may be of more fashion than fortune, and he does enjoy his sport and card games and brandy a great deal, but… I believe Reginald does love me. I hope very much that I have a son, and that with a young man in our home that he must teach to be a respectable gentleman, my husband will enjoy his sport and card games and brandy a little less often."

Elizabeth returned her smile. "Well, I am sure that if Mr. Hurst is already acutely aware of your safety when your condition is only just known, then he will do whatever he must to please and protect you and his child."

She drew a breath then. "I confess I have a particular reason for volunteering to ride with you today, Mrs. Hurst."

"Oh, do call me Louisa!" said the lady. "I know that we did not start off on the proper foot, my dear, but I daresay we have since become friends, have we not?"

Elizabeth favored her with a nod. "I should say that we have. And you are welcome to call me Elizabeth."

"So, Elizabeth… Why *did* you volunteer to ride with me?" Louisa asked.

She gave a slight shudder. "I adore horses, truly; they are beautiful creatures. But I was thrown from one at nine years old and broke my arm. I've not been on horseback since, save that day in the rain when Mr. Darcy insisted I take his place in Diamond's saddle. Just the thought of riding makes me shake with fear."

Louisa glanced sidelong at her. "Well, I do hope for your sake that you learn to overcome your fear one day. After all, Mr. Darcy takes great pleasure in a long ride—about as much as you take in your long walks!"

Their laughter caused Mr. Hurst to turn his head and look back; he shook his head and looked forward again. Conversation between the ladies turned next to the subject of Mr. Bingley's apparently sudden interest in Kitty. Louisa admitted she had thought Jane might catch her brother's eye, but when he had shown no particular interest in her—or any other girl in the village—she'd thought he would spend yet another year as a bachelor. Elizabeth then confided what Mr. Bingley had told her of his regard for her sister, as well as that she and Jane had made it clear to Kitty that she *must* amend her ways, as she was already at risk of driving away one potential suitor with her wildness.

"Your argument seems to have been taken quite to heart, Elizabeth," said Louisa. "Why, in only the last day I have seen a marked improvement in her demeanor."

Elizabeth nodded. "Indeed. I do think Kitty has a good deal more to learn, but I am greatly pleased that our advice to her is at last being heeded. And after yesterday's events, where she was able to spend some time relatively alone with your brother, she has found herself quite charmed by him. I am glad they have at least some interests in common, for if they did not I do not know how they could possibly be happy together. I do not know how *any* two persons with nothing in common can live together for the whole of their lives."

"Reginald and I have only our taste in fashion and a desire to be respected in society in common," said Louisa. "Yet somehow it suits us. Though if I may share another secret, Miss Elizabeth, it is my sincerest hope that observing the distinction owning an estate brings to my brother might prompt my husband to purchase one."

"I thought you and Mr. Hurst, and Miss Bingley, preferred Town?"

Louisa laughed. "My sister certainly does and so does my husband," she replied. "However, I have come to appreciate the quiet and the beauty of the country. I should think it infinitely more suitable for child-rearing than London."

Elizabeth said she could not agree more. The party soon reached their destination, which was very picturesque, and as the ladies set up the picnic in the shade of a large oak tree, the two gentlemen gathered together their fishing rods and tackle and headed for the edge of the pond.

Three hours later, it was a merry group—even Mr. Hurst was smiling—that packed up to head back to Netherfield. Mr. Bingley and Mr. Hurst had caught five good-sized fish between them, and they and the ladies had even walked a circuit of the pond, admiring the surrounding nature of the cozy spot.

On their return to the house, Mr. Bingley sent the fish to the kitchen and called for the Bennets' carriage. Jane and Elizabeth had been helped inside and Bingley was just handing Kitty up when another carriage turned up the long drive. Bingley stepped around the horses to have a look at the newcomer, and when he returned he wore a smile.

"I think you ladies should stay to tea—forgive me not asking you to do so already," said he.

Elizabeth glanced from Jane to Kitty before settling her eyes on their host. "Mr. Bingley, you are too kind. We have been in your company each day since Friday—surely you must wish for some time to yourself. Not to mention you've other company coming up the lane now."

His grin grew as he stepped back from the open carriage door and prepared to close it. "Very well then, Miss Elizabeth. I shall just tell Darcy you said you were content to wave as you passed him by."

Darcy's day began with Fitzwilliam rousing him early to go and speak to Wickham's solicitor.

That matter was dealt with swiftly. Mr. Smith acquiesced to Wickham's request to show his benefactor's letter and will to his companions, though he was reluctant to divulge confidential information.

"Do not concern yourself overmuch, sir," Wickham assured him. "The integrity of Mr. Darcy and Colonel Fitzwilliam is unquestionable—believe me, their word is as good as law."

Darcy perused the will, having some familiarity with the language they were written in after having to draw up and approve one of his own, while Fitzwilliam read the letter in which the request to amend said will was contained. Wickham and Smith observed the two as they went over the documents, then carefully laid them on the solicitor's desk.

"Much as I hate to have to admit it, Darce," his cousin began, "the rogue was telling the truth. Old Mr. Franklin spoke very highly of Wickham in that letter, and made reference to his having no other family. Ownership of the plantation in India and the fortune already amassed there—with Wickham's assistance, as also stated—are all to go to him."

Darcy nodded. "The gentleman's will was as straightforward in bequeathing everything to Wickham."

He looked to Mr. Smith, who had already gathered the documents and put them away. "Thank you, sir, for your cooperation. It was an unfortunate necessity given our history with Mr. Wickham, which is not entirely pleasant, I'm afraid. I am relieved there has been such a change in him as to win the affections of one who could grant him relief from the poverty he once suffered."

"Well, Mr. Darcy, I can tell you I've met Mr. Wickham before, on the sojourn to India wherein I brought Franklin's will to be signed," said Mr. Smith. "He was as well-mannered and forthright then as he is now."

"Our dealings with Mr. Wickham go back more than a decade, sir," said Fitzwilliam. "I also thank you for your assistance in settling this rather personal matter. It would seem that he is indeed a changed man."

They departed the solicitor's office soon after. In the carriage, Fitzwilliam declared his intention of staying in Town rather than returning to Hertfordshire. Darcy had expected this would be the case.

"I must avail myself of every opportunity to court Miss Tilney," said Fitzwilliam. "And her father, too—perhaps with our both being soldiers, we can find some common ground."

"For the sake of your happiness and hers, Theo, I wish you every measure of success," Darcy told him with sincerity.

They were all of them silent for a moment, then Wickham said, "Will, when next you visit Georgie in Surrey, I shall join you—yes, I know you've not had chance to write to her and tell her the truth, but I've been thinking that such as this is best said in person, is it not? Besides, I should very much like to see her. Remember, she is my sister also," said Wickham.

Darcy drew a breath. "Upsetting her is not advisable in her condition," he protested.

"There's not likely to be a 'good' time to tell her. Best to have done with it, I say."

"As much as I wish I could say otherwise, Darce, he has got a point," put in Fitzwilliam, who then stretched out a leg to kick Wickham in the shin. "Stop saying things I concur with! It's making me most uncomfortable."

"Would you rather I went back to being a villainous scoundrel?" Wickham countered.

"Certainly not. It's just that I find agreeing with you rather than loathing you to be rather disconcerting."

Wickham raised an eyebrow. "Imagine how I feel, Fitz, to not have either of you scowling in anger every time you look at me."

Fitzwilliam and Wickham then launched into another conversation about their respective service in India. As they chattered on, Darcy drew back into his own thoughts as he gazed out the sideglass. He found it rather fascinating that neither he nor his cousin had been of a mind to seek a partner in life—so focused they had been on finding Georgiana's attacker—yet the both of them had found a lady they desired to court within weeks of each other. His mother's old saying was proving true: *The thing you want most may come to you when you least expect it.*

On their entering Darcy House some minutes later, they found Edward Ferrars preparing to depart it, a servant carrying his small bag down the stairs.

"Mr. Darcy, I do thank you for your hospitality, sir," said Ferrars. "And I apologize for the inconvenience of having to find yourself another parson for the Lambton parish."

Darcy offered a nod. "I wish it weren't necessary, Mr. Ferrars," he replied, knowing that the man would understand his double meaning. "Do you go now to your mother's house?"

Ferrars scoffed. "I do, yes. She insisted that I stay with her while the wedding is planned, as she is overjoyed that I have found a wife with so grand a fortune and connections to the nobility of England and Ireland."

"Be warned, my friend," spoke up Fitzwilliam. "If you think your mother is bad, wait until you meet Anne's."

Ferrars lifted an eyebrow. "Thank you for the warning, Colonel."

He looked wretched, the poor soul, thought Darcy. But then, he supposed anyone would when thrust into a situation over which they had little say or control.

After saying his goodbyes, the parson left them. When he had gone, Fitzwilliam turned to them and said, "Which of you cares to wager that the earl has to get a special license for them? You know that Lady Catherine will try to stop the marriage, I'm sure."

"No doubt she will raise a fuss, but your father has a will of iron, Theo," said Darcy.

He then summoned his valet and ordered his belongings packed. He was determined to return to Hertfordshire—and Elizabeth—before nightfall. Wickham asked if he might join him, to which Darcy agreed, having admitted to himself that he had a curiosity to see how Wickham behaved in society. He wondered if Wickham would find the people in the country as vulgar and rustic as he had at first. Or perhaps the younger man would have a much easier time of getting to know the country folk than he had himself.

Vincent was bringing his bag down when Fitzwilliam came to say his farewells. "Give Miss Elizabeth, Bingley, and the others my warmest regards," he said.

"Theo, I'll see to it your things are sent on from Netherfield. Where should I have them delivered?"

He already knew his cousin's answer before he'd asked the question. "Here, if you please," Fitzwilliam replied. "You know Mamma will only plague me to death with questions—I would much rather have peace and quiet. And there is the added bonus of Miss Tilney living next door."

With a nod, Darcy turned and gave final instructions to his butler. He and Wickham then went out to the waiting carriage, and a moment later they were off. Conversation was stilted without Fitzwilliam as a go-between, and eventually each man fell into a contemplative silence. Wickham even dozed off at one point, though he was as wide awake as Darcy when at last the latter announced they were soon to reach Netherfield.

As they were turning up the drive, he noted a carriage waiting by the steps. *Bingley must be going out*, he thought, then frowned as he noted that the carriage was not his friend's. Bingley greeted him with a wide grin as his own carriage stopped alongside and he was stepping out.

"What convenient timing, Darcy!" said he. "Your arrival at this moment is most convenient, for the ladies shall be staying to tea with us."

"The ladies...?" Darcy said with a frown, until he stepped around the horses tethered to the unfamiliar carriage and saw them—saw her.

Elizabeth.

Chapter Twenty-One

She stood between her sisters Jane and Catherine, and her obvious joy at seeing him stole his breath away.

Darcy was before her in two strides. He held out his hand and she placed hers in it; he lifted it and pressed his lips briefly to the back.

"Bless my soul, it does me good to see you," he said.

Elizabeth smiled. "And I you, sir."

Sensing that eyes were upon them, Darcy reluctantly released her hand and stepped back. Hearing Wickham subtly clear his throat reminded him of his duty, and he introduced him to the Bennet ladies.

"It is a pleasure to make your acquaintance, ladies," Wickham said. "Miss Elizabeth, I have heard a great deal about you these last few days. I must say that Darcy's description of you hardly does you justice."

A soft blush colored her cheeks and she smiled. "You are too kind, Mr. Wickham, as is Mr. Darcy—despite his failure to capture me accurately in words."

Darcy returned her smile. "I shall endeavor to correct the oversight as soon as may be done."

"Shall we go inside?" said Bingley.

"Of course," said Darcy, and he offered his arm to Elizabeth to escort her.

After following Bingley to the drawing room, where his sisters and Hurst already gathered, he saw that the ladies were comfortable before excusing himself to freshen his attire. Wickham and Bingley followed. Darcy took the opportunity to inform his friend that his cousin would not be returning, and asked that he have a footman move Fitzwilliam's things to his own room.

"They should all be packed up, as you know Theo doesn't like to leave things lying around," he said. "We shall stop in London on the way to Surrey, so there will be no need of sending them by post; we'll just take his trunks with us."

"I'll see to it," said Bingley.

They were now outside Darcy's chamber door, and as he reached to open it, Bingley was reaching into the inside pocket of his waistcoat; he pulled out a letter and handed it to him. "This express arrived for you while we were out on a picnic. I knew you would be back today, so I kept it for you rather than sending it on to Town."

Darcy recognized the handwriting immediately and hurried into his room, breaking the seal as he moved. Wickham followed, as did Bingley, who quietly shut the door as he read.

Donwell Abbey
26 November 1798

Mr. Darcy,

Be not alarmed, sir, on receiving this letter. Rest assured that all here in Surrey are in good health.

I write on behalf of your dear sister, though without her consent – and without remorse for doing so. Though she has learned to conceal her emotions well, I daresay Georgiana is very lonely here without you. I am certain, and Roberta is in agreement, that your sister wishes for your presence when her gift to us arrives. She will have need of support from her closest family, especially when it comes time for her to take leave of us.

Send word if you cannot come, for I know if you are able we shall seen you soon enough.

Sincerely,
Fitzroy Leslie
Laird of Glenfairley

Feeling a little shaken, he passed the letter to Wickham, then drew his hands over his face. Would he have to put off his courtship of Elizabeth yet again?

No. Surely he could spend a day or two at Netherfield before making the trip to Surrey. He loved his sister dearly and there was no doubt of his going to see her, but he needed to assure Elizabeth that his intentions had not changed in the few days they had been apart.

While he was of little doubt that Georgiana was somewhat lonely, it was more likely that the reason Fairley had written was because her time of delivery was drawing near. She was probably more frightened by the upcoming event than she was willing to admit even to herself, and it would indeed be difficult for her to part from the child; no matter how indifferent she professed to be, he knew from her letters, and those he'd had from the laird, that she was slowly coming to care for the life that grew inside of her.

"Poor thing," said Wickham as he handed back the letter.

"Is Miss Darcy well?" asked Bingley in a soft tone.

Darcy sighed. "Aye, she is well. But you know her condition, Charles. Her companions believe she is frightened and lonely, and so request I come to comfort her."

Bingley and Wickham nodded their understanding, then quit the room. Darcy folded the letter and put it away, then completed his ablutions and changed his attire. By the time he and Wickham returned to the drawing room the maids were bringing in the tea, along with trays of biscuits and cucumber sandwiches.

"I do not know that I shall be able to eat a thing," said Catherine Bennet. "We already had so many good things on our picnic, Mr. Bingley."

Bingley smiled at her. "I am very pleased you enjoyed it all, Miss Catherine."

"We shall have to have you to Longbourn again soon to repay the kindness," offered Jane.

Her host waved a hand dismissively. "You have no need to repay me, Miss Bennet, though I certainly will not turn down any dinner prepared by your fine cook. Our last meal at Longbourn was most enjoyable."

Jane smiled. "Our cook—and our mother—will be pleased by the compliment, I am sure."

Elizabeth, whom Darcy sat next to, sipped her tea with a smile on her face; she soon turned it toward him. "Sir," she said softly, "I take it your business in London was concluded to your satisfaction?"

Darcy nodded. "It was. In fact, there is much I wish to speak to you about regarding that and another matter," he replied in a low tone, "but I should not like certain of the particulars to be overheard. We shall take a walk in the garden later and I will tell you everything."

She nodded her agreement and they both turned their attention to the conversation going on around them. Darcy soon noticed two things: one, that Caroline spoke little or not at all, and rarely did she look in the direction of himself and Elizabeth. It seemed she was choosing to ignore them, which sat perfectly fine with him—she had, after all, still to apologize for her behavior the night of the ball. Darcy held out little hope that her silence would continue after Elizabeth and her sisters departed, and determined he would do just as he said and ignore her altogether if she did not apologize.

The second thing he noticed was that Bingley was paying an inordinate amount of attention to Miss Catherine. In fact, unless someone else spoke directly to him, his attention was directed solely at the youngest Bennet present.

"When did that happen?"

He did not realize he had spoken aloud until Elizabeth replied with, "If you mean Mr. Bingley and my sister, he has apparently had a *tendre* for Kitty for some time, but found himself unable to reconcile her conduct with what he knew that of a gentleman's wife should be. He confessed this to me on Saturday when he brought your note about having to remain in Town. I offered to speak to her, to tell her if she could not behave in a more ladylike manner, she was at risk of driving away a most advantageous match for herself."

"And she actually listened to you?" Darcy countered, then felt heat rising at the impertinence of the question. "Forgive me—"

She waved her hand. "There is nothing to forgive, Mr. Darcy. Truth be told, I am myself still amazed at the sudden change in her. Kitty has always been something of a follower, doing as Lydia did in order to be noticed herself. But now *she* is the center of attention—at least Mr. Bingley's—and she enjoys it very much. So much that she has asked the aid of Jane and I to help teach her the manners of a lady so she does not lose his interest. The irony of the request, of course, is that we have been trying to teach her those same manners for a number of years already. Well, at least now she knows she has good reason to heed us."

"But does your sister actually like Charles?" Darcy asked. "I should not like to find that she accepts his attentions because her mother wishes her to land a rich husband."

Elizabeth quirked an eyebrow. "Mr. Darcy, you *do* understand that Kitty and I share the same mother? Her desire of securing a wealthy match and raising our circumstances is the same for all her daughters. Is it not possible that I have accepted your suit with the same mercenary motives as my sister may possess?"

"I am sorry," said Darcy, feeling the heat of embarrassment again, "I truly mean no offense. It's just..."

Her features relaxed into a grin and she reached over to pat his hand. "It does *seem* quite sudden on both sides, to that I will own. However, Mr. Bingley himself assured me that his attachment to my sister was true, and Kitty—while hoping for a rich husband as much as any poor girl in the country—has come to realize she likes him very much indeed. They actually have more than one thing in common, which I admit was a great surprise."

It was Darcy's turn to lift an eyebrow in curiosity. "Is that so? Pray, what are these common interests?"

"Horseback riding and a secret love of gothic novels. Lydia made fun of Kitty for liking the latter, so I know she reads them late at night when everyone else has gone to bed, or very early of a morning before our youngest sister has risen for the day."

She looked to Catherine then, who was laughing—at a much more appropriate volume, he observed, than she had done in the past—at something Louisa Hurst had just said. "Something else happened this weekend that prompted Kitty's transformation. Mr. Bingley invited us to dine here after church yesterday, and Lydia was... Well, I shall only say she was not best pleased with how little of the attention she received. Kitty noticed the reactions of more than one person to Lydia's conduct, and for the first time found herself mortified. At last she begins to understand that how she behaves not only affects her, but can affect the rest of us as well."

Elizabeth looked up at him again. "Believe me, sir, I need no one to remind me how ridiculous and uncouth certain of my family can be—they have been embarrassment enough for some years. I know that my having such a family gave you pause at one time, and it did Mr. Bingley as well. But if he does not vex himself about it any longer—if *he* believes Kitty's affections are genuine why should you—question her motives?"

Darcy shook his head and reached for her hand. Briefly he reflected on having told Wickham that there was still more for her to teach him, and he was fully aware that he had just been properly scolded for making an assumption about her sister.

"I feel as though I shall always be asking your forgiveness," he said.

She smiled. "I am sure you will not, Mr. Darcy. You are merely institutionalized by the society in which you have been brought up. And while I am certain there are some of the *ton* with whom it would be delightful to make an acquaintance, I daresay there are far more of them who seek only to mix with the right people and have the right connections. If they are rich, they want to be richer, or for their children to do better than they. It is all about making the most advantageous match and not at all about making connections with people of honor whom you can trust, or perhaps even love."

"I am astonished that you know *so much* about society when you have experienced it so very little."

Caroline Bingley's words startled him—and fairly dripped with disdain. It was an effort for Darcy to contain the scowl that threatened to contort his features.

"Really, Miss Eliza, who does *not* wish to be richer? Who does not wish for the proper connections? Wealth and family and important acquaintances are what will advance you in society, not foolish inclinations like compassion and empathy and love. What have any of those things done for you? What do you gain by them?"

"I gain quite a lot, Miss Bingley," Elizabeth countered calmly. "I gain the society of people I can trust not to deceive me, or rob me, or use me simply for my family name and the connections it offers."

The barb was not lost on Caroline, whose countenance began to turn scarlet. Elizabeth looked around the room at those gathered. "I gain friendship," she went on. "By simply being myself, a person of compassion and kindness with a dash of wit and impertinence, I have in the last month gone by managed to add to my circle of friends your sister, your brother, a countess, an earl, the daughter of a duke, and the countess' own sister. I think even Mr. Hurst is beginning to warm to me."

Hurst snorted softly from his place on Louisa's left, but Darcy noted that the corners of his lips twitched in the barest hint of a smile. Elizabeth then lifted her gaze to Darcy himself, who smiled back at her as she added, "I also gain the affections of one of the most gentlemanly persons I have ever had the privilege to know. I do not admire Mr. Darcy for his vast wealth, nor for his uncle the earl, or the fact that he owns half of Derbyshire. The number of carriages and gowns and jewels I might gain should we marry mean nothing to me. I care only that he is compassionate, amiable, and that he shows true kindness to those less fortunate than himself."

Setting her teacup back on the tray then, Elizabeth stood gracefully. "Now, Mr. Darcy, I believe you said something about taking a walk in the garden."

Having stood as she did, Darcy bowed before offering his arm.

"I did indeed, Miss Elizabeth. If any of you should care to join us, you are more than welcome, as the weather remains unseasonably warm."

The expression of astonishment on Caroline's face was near to comical. Darcy turned away from her with Elizabeth's hand at his elbow and headed for the garden entry. Bingley and Wickham followed, each with a Bennet sister on his arm.

On the garden path, Darcy and Elizabeth soon outdistanced the others. This worked to his advantage, for though Bingley and Wickham were full aware of Georgiana's circumstances, the other Bennet ladies had no need to know of them. Elizabeth, however, he deemed it necessary to tell all to; from her, he wished to hide nothing, and her discretion he was absolutely certain of.

She walked with him in silence for a time, and for that he was grateful, as he knew not how to begin. Darcy then reasoned that it would be best to simply start at the beginning. From the distressing express letters penned by Mrs. Younge and then-Colonel Brandon, to Wickham's appearance at the ball on Friday past and the truth of his parentage coming out, and then to the note Bingley had given him upon his arrival, he told her everything there was to tell.

Elizabeth listened without interruption, gasping softly when he recounted the horror his dear sister had endured. Her grip on his arm tightened and he was fairly certain he saw her blink away tears.

"Oh, the poor child," said she in a voice barely above a whisper. "I cannot begin to tell you how very sorry I am, for you and your sweet sister. I can hardly be selfish at such a time as this—though I want very much to spend time with you, I understand completely your obligation to your family. Of course you must go to Surrey! Miss Darcy has need of your company far more than I, and a greater right to claim it."

He stopped and turned to face her, took her hands in his, and brought them up to brush his lips across her knuckles.

"Dearest, loveliest Elizabeth," he said. "Your generous heart is but one of the many virtues I have come to admire and adore in you. I, too, wish our courtship was not to be delayed yet again. I have missed your company."

Elizabeth smiled. "And I yours." The sparkle in her eyes then turned mischievous. "You know, Mr. Darcy, if I were a superstitious woman, I might imagine these delays were omens designed to tell us we are not meant to be, despite the nobility of your overlooking my unfortunate connections and lack of fortune."

"Pray, do not say such things!" said Darcy as he slipped her hand into the crook of his arm once more and started down the path again. "I have waited quite long enough to meet someone who *doesn't* covet my name, fortune, and connections. Too many society girls seek only a match that makes *them* more important—so few of those I have had chance to meet desire a true connection with their partner in life. My mother and father had such a bond, in spite of the dalliance that led to Mr. Wickham. I desire a similar deep and abiding love, and I think it very possible you and I might have a connection of that kind… at least we would if we could but have the courtship we both long for."

When Elizabeth made no response, Darcy looked down to find her cheeks had colored to a very bewitching shade of pink. He wondered what he'd said that would cause such a reaction and then he realized with the force of a horse's kick: he had just come very close to saying he loved her.

"I share your feelings," she said after a time. "In spite of every obstacle that has been thus far placed before us, despite those who would challenge the propriety of our connection, I believe we have every chance in the world of being happy together. Certainly our chance of happiness with each other is as fair as most people can boast on entering the marriage state."

Darcy favored her with a smile. "I should hope, given how much we both wish for more time in each other's company, that our chance of happiness is more than fair."

"If I could join you in going to Surrey, Mr. Darcy, I would do so," Elizabeth said then. Darcy looked down to find an expression of warm civility in her eyes. "From what you have told me, the way you speak of her, it occurs to me that your sister could use a friend."

He returned her smile. "And I am eager to introduce you, an event that *will* take place at the earliest opportunity, I can assure you."

Darcy then grinned more mischievously. "It occurs to me, my dear Miss Elizabeth, that you *could* accompany Wickham and myself to Surrey—I have only to postpone the journey a few days until I can acquire a license."

Bubbly laughter erupted from her. "Fitzwilliam Darcy, I do believe I have been a bad influence on you—that is perhaps the cheekiest thing you have ever said to me! It is good, however, that I know you do not mean it; if I believed you, I should think you did not want to get to know me at all."

"But would not marriage force me to get to know you?"

She grinned. "True enough, but I firmly believe it the better to know something of the person you mean to spend your life with before you pledge to do so, for once we are married you cannot give me back."

Darcy could only laugh. "Perhaps you are right. But I should tell you, my dear Elizabeth, that giving you up is the last thing I have any desire to do."

The crimson that flushed across Elizabeth's cheeks made Darcy smile with satisfaction. He gave the hand of hers that held his arm a gentle squeeze, and they once again fell into a companionable silence.

The two were turning up the path leading back to the house when he ventured, "By and by, I wish to offer my sincerest apologies for any offense that my cousin Anne may have given. Regrettably, her mother put it into her head that we would marry one day, though I've never encouraged the notion. Of course, she is now paying the price for her folly—after she left Hertfordshire, Anne came to my house in London with the intention of compromising me and forcing a marriage. She succeeded, to an extent, as there will be a marriage, but it was not me she compromised."

"Oh dear, not Colonel Fitzwilliam! Is that why he stayed behind?"

Darcy laughed. "No, indeed. He remained in Town because he chanced to meet a young lady he wishes to know better—you can imagine how thrilled my aunt the countess was by the news. As to Anne, the gentleman she mistook for me in her inebriated state is a good, Christian man. He only recently took up the position of parson at Lambton, my having offered it to him on the recommendation of Lady Sotheby. Now he must give it up that he may learn to manage an estate."

"The poor man—to be forced into a marriage with someone you have only just met over a foolish mistake *they* made… How does your other aunt feel about these circumstances?"

Darcy snorted. "I expect Lady Catherine is haranguing my uncle about it as we speak, as he sent her an express early this morning. It is a shame that Mr. Ferrars must endure the hardship, but I am afraid there is naught else could be done given the particulars."

"Well, I suppose there may be *some* good to come of it. This Mr. Ferrars will be at Rosings with your cousin when they are wed, and my sister Mary will be at Hunsford Parsonage with Mr. Collins. Mr. Ferrars may be of service to my cousin in writing his sermons."

It was then that the couple was rejoined by Bingley, Catherine, Wickham, and Jane, and by mutual decision they went inside the house. Their host called for the Bennets' carriage to be brought around again, and while they waited, Darcy promised Elizabeth he would not go to Surrey until the day after next—he could give her another full day before he had to part from her again. They agreed to an early morning walk to Oakham Mount, after which he would join her family for breakfast. On hearing something of their plans, her sister Catherine asked Bingley to come for breakfast also.

"I am sure our mother would be most delighted to have you join us, Mr. Bingley," she said with a shy smile.

Darcy studied her countenance as she regarded his friend, and though he knew their deeper acquaintance had been but three days, he was forced to admit that there seemed already a great deal of admiration in her eyes. Whether she merely liked the attention he gave her or she truly cared for Charles, he could not yet be certain.

For his friend's sake, he hoped that whatever Catherine's feelings at present, she would truly care for Bingley in due course. Bingley, he noted, was already very much besotted with the girl—a state of mind he had somehow managed to conceal very well from those closest to him.

When at last Darcy reluctantly parted with Elizabeth, he and Bingley both watched the carriage until it turned onto the road before taking themselves inside again. They joined the others in the drawing room, where Darcy dropped somewhat indecorously into one of the armchairs by the fireplace with a sigh.

"Darcy darling, we need to talk."

He opened his eyes slowly to find Caroline Bingley in the chair directly across from him. She spoke again before he could even draw breath to reply.

"I fully understand that a young man likes to sow his wild oats, but *really*, this dalliance of yours is getting out of hand!" she cried. "That little nobody actually thinks she has a future with you! And oh, dear Charles, *why* do you play with that wretched sister of hers? She's such a simpleton—there's not a chance at all of her ever being intelligent enough to manage a household!"

A brief glance at Bingley showed Darcy that his friend was turning red with anger. It was a sentiment he shared.

"Caroline, I believe you have said and done quite enough," Bingley said through clenched teeth.

"Had I done enough, that fool cousin of Darcy's would have

compromised *him* as she said was her intention!"

Darcy sat straight. "You were involved in Anne's scheme? How is that even possible when you have not been introduced?"

"Oh, that one is easy, Will," said Bingley in a cold tone. "After her performance following the ball, my sister decided drastic measures needed be taken to save you from Miss Elizabeth's evil clutches. A letter was dispatched express to your aunt, Lady Catherine, the following morning, which was apparently intercepted by her daughter."

A flash of memory jolted him then: Caroline's maid riding away in a curricle as he and Wickham were returning to the stables. Oh, if only he had known…

Darcy decided then that he had endured quite enough of Caroline Bingley. Her caustic remarks and presumptuous attitude, her ill manners and her interference had swiftly destroyed any feeling of friendship that existed for her. Standing slowly, he straightened his waistcoat and jacket and turned determinedly to her brother.

"Charles, it grieves me to say what I am about to, but it must be done," he began. "Whilst Miss Bingley is in residence in your home, I cannot stay here. I wish her every happiness, but henceforth I must regretfully sever all acquaintance with her."

Miss Bingley gasped and he heard Mrs. Hurst begin to weep as he started for the door. The former stood and grabbed his arm.

"Darcy, please don't do this!" she begged.

He turned to her, his gaze cold and his expression set in stone, and taking her wrist in hand he removed hers from his arm. He said not a word, merely turned away again to make his way out. Wickham quickly followed.

"Charles, *do* something!" Caroline cried.

"I aim to, sister," said he. "Tonight your maid will pack your things. Tomorrow my carriage will take you both into Meryton, where you may rent a carriage to take you into Scarborough to our aunt and uncle. There you will stay until such time as I decide I am of a desire to see you again."

"Oh Charles, don't be so ridiculous! I am your sister—those worthless Bennet girls are nobodies! Don't you see what they have done to us, to Darcy? We must leave this vulgar country at once, to remove you both from their influence before it is too late!"

Bingley scowled. "On second thought, forget waiting until tomorrow—you will go tonight. I will *not* have your foolishness in my house any longer, threatening one of the longest, closest friendships I have ever known. I give you an hour to ready yourself, and I do mean *one hour*. If you are not packed to depart Netherfield at the appointed time, I will send you off without your belongings."

"Charles, do be reasonable! Who will manage the house for you?"

"I'm quite certain Louisa will not mind the duty until I have taken a wife."

Caroline huffed and stomped her foot, then threw up her hands as she shrieked, "This is madness! I refuse to suffer the indignity of being turned out of my own house!"

"Would you prefer the indignity of my installing you at Bedlam?" Bingley retorted angrily. "Your behavior these last few days certainly bears all the markings of a hysterical breakdown. For years you have imagined an attachment to Darcy for which there is no foundation but your own fancy! You have insulted the lady he has chosen and refused apology, written a letter to someone with whom you are not in the least acquainted, and schemed with another to compromise a most distinguished gentleman—who is my friend! For goodness' sake, Caroline, what were you *thinking*—that if you could not have him, at least Elizabeth wouldn't either?!"

He snorted then and threw up a hand when her lips parted to reply. "You know what? I do not wish to know your mind on the matter. I have done with it. You will go to Scarborough or you will go to Bedlam. The choice is yours, Caroline."

Darcy's steps were quiet as he entered Bingley's study. His friend stood at the window, arms crossed as he watched his carriage take his sister away.

"I am sorry, Charles."

His friend snorted. "For what have you to apologize?"

"That I forced you to make a choice between friend and family."

Bingley sighed heavily and turned to face him. "'Twas not you, Will, who forced the choice made. Caroline has brought this exile upon herself."

He emitted a sound of disgust and moved toward the sideboard, where a number of decanters of alcohol were displayed. "She ought to have been taken in hand years ago, rather than my tolerating her fanciful thinking for as long as I have."

"I could also have been more direct in my rejection of her advances," Darcy countered. "We are neither of us without blame for our inaction."

After pouring himself a drink, Bingley tipped back half of it before he turned around and said, "So... you will be going to Surrey."

Darcy nodded. "On Wednesday. I promised Elizabeth tomorrow."

Bingley sipped his drink. "Unfortunate that you and Miss Elizabeth will be parted again so soon after declaring your attachment."

"Aye, but I have explained the circumstances to her, and she was in agreement that I must go." Darcy chuckled. "She even said she wished she could join me that she might also offer comfort to Georgiana, so I offered to acquire a license that she could."

Bingley choked on his drink, and after a short fit of coughing, looked to him with eyes widened by surprise. "Good heavens Darcy, did you really?! That was as good as a proposal!"

Darcy lifted his brow—he'd not considered it that way. "I suppose you could say that. Though I spoke in jest at the time, had she sincerely wished to accept the offer... I daresay I would not regret it."

"So you love her then?"

"I am not yet certain that I can apply that particular word to my feelings, but I *can* say that I care very deeply for her," Darcy answered. "You know I hesitated for a time to pursue her, for all the reasons that society and my family would disapprove, but I have come to realize that rather than rejecting her as a potential wife because of her low circumstances, it is better that I raise her up—and thus her family—with all the power I have as a result of my own. I can now think only of what good our being connected can do for her sisters, rather than what little her family's situation can do for me."

Bingley raised his glass with a grin. "Here, here, Darcy," said he, before he drained the rest of it and set the glass aside. "My thoughts closely mirror yours in regard to my feelings for Catherine."

"Do tell me how in the world you managed to keep those feelings to yourself for two months' time, Charles. Normally you wear your intentions toward a lady like a medal upon your breast."

His friend nodded. "I own that has been my way in the past—I've never cared for concealing my regard for a lady. But this time I knew it would be prudent to do so. After all, your fortune is twice what mine is and then some, and you—whom I have looked to as a guide on many matters for years—hesitated to pursue Elizabeth, whose manner was much more ladylike than her sister's. I realized if one such as you would pause, then certainly I, with far fewer connections and less fortune, should be wise enough to do the same—and for much better reason."

Darcy acknowledged the assessment, then said, "Miss Catherine's conduct has been tempered most appreciatively in a very short amount of time. No doubt it is owing to the knowledge that a gentleman of large fortune thinks her pretty."

"Poke fun if you must, but truly, she's an angel!" Bingley declared. "Catherine has the most expressive eyes I have ever seen. Their color is extraordinary! And despite what Caroline would have you think, she is not without intelligence."

"Indeed she is not, if she has at last taken her sisters' counsel to heart," said Darcy. "You are a fine man, Charles. If Miss Catherine is the mistress of your heart, then you have my every wish that you and she will be happy together. I can think of few who are as deserving of such a reward as are you."

"Thank you, Will. It means a great deal to me to hear you say so." Bingley then grinned. "And consider this: should you and I be of a mind in the near future to marry the sisters, that would make us brothers!"

Chapter Twenty-Two

Elizabeth and Darcy met early as planned on the following morning, his having ridden Diamond to Longbourn; from there they began their leisurely walk to the outlook where they had first met.

Of many things did they speak, from childhood stories to hopes for the future. They spoke of books they'd read, of places they'd been and wished to see. When he learned how utterly terrified she had been on Diamond's back that day, he vowed he would help her learn to consider the prospect with joy and not fear so that they would be able to go riding together, an activity he very much enjoyed. Darcy also spoke very fondly of Pemberley, where he said he hoped to see her in the near future.

Elizabeth secretly wondered if her status there would be as visitor or mistress.

When they returned to Longbourn, Bingley was just arriving by horseback himself, and was immediately greeted by Kitty coming out of the house. Their smiles for each other were bright and cheerful, and Elizabeth was certain that in observing the two together, Darcy could have no further doubt of their mutual affection. After all, Kitty was not Jane or Mary, both of whom were more apt to conceal the true depth of their feelings than show them openly.

Kitty had no such qualms.

Mrs. Bennet, of course, was delighted to have the two gentlemen from Netherfield to breakfast. She thanked them for their kindness in coming, said she would be happy to feed them anytime they wished to visit her table, and lamented the news that Darcy would be departing for Surrey on the morrow when he had only just returned to their company. When he explained that the reason was to aid and comfort his ailing sister, Mrs. Bennet expressed her sympathies and offered her advice on the remedies which "might soon set her to rights, that you may come back again to Longbourn."

Elizabeth had been embarrassed by her mother's unsolicited advice—as if Mr. Darcy did not have the very best midwife he could get attending his sister—but he assured her later that he had not minded at all.

"Indeed, she expressed not only concern for Georgiana's welfare but also yours in a roundabout way. I can find no fault in that," said he as they took another stroll together, this time around the gardens of her home.

Sir William Lucas sent invitations around that afternoon inviting the Bennet family to a dinner party he was having that evening. It was very short notice, but on receiving a note from Netherfield that they hoped to see them there, Elizabeth determined she would enjoy herself—and the extra time with Darcy. He had told her that he and Mr. Wickham planned to leave at dawn the next day and thus he'd not be able to see her before departing Hertfordshire, so she knew she must take advantage of the opportunity to see him again.

Sir William had managed to gather a large party indeed; besides the families from Netherfield and Longbourn, the Longs, Mr. and Mrs. Phillips, Colonel Forster and his wife, as well as several of his officers had seen fit to attend. Card tables were set up following dinner, but this entertainment was not enough for the young people, who rather wished to dance. Mary was applied to for playing jolly tunes on the Lucases' pianoforte, and soon the rug in the music room was rolled up and a few couples took their places. Elizabeth happily danced with Darcy, and Kitty with Bingley; Lydia paired with Captain Denny, and Mr. Wickham asked Charlotte to be his partner. Elizabeth found herself dancing with that gentleman for the second song.

"I am most pleased to have secured you as a partner, Miss Elizabeth," said he in a quiet tone.

Elizabeth raised an eyebrow. "Are you, Mr. Wickham? Might I ask the reason you are so pleased?"

Wickham smiled. "I should like to take advantage of the opportunity of getting to know you a little better. You must be a remarkable young lady indeed to have captured the attention of my studious brother."

"Forgive me, Mr. Wickham, but are you at liberty to speak of that subject?" she asked as they turned together.

Her partner chuckled. "To the world at large, I daresay not. However, I am aware that Will has disclosed the particulars of our relationship to you, and so felt no scruple in referring to him so."

The dancers split apart for a turn, and then came back together. Mr. Wickham sighed softly before saying, "I have grown used to the idea that he is my brother. And despite the animosity that once existed betwixt us, I rather came to like it—being an orphan is not so lonely, you see, when one is not alone in the state."

"But you have not seen Mr. Darcy or Miss Darcy in some six years, I understand," said Elizabeth.

Another turn away from each other, and then when they rejoined, "True enough, Miss Elizabeth, but I contented myself with the knowledge that though we were estranged, at least I was not truly alone in the world. I have family, even if that family does not know of or choose to acknowledge the connection."

Elizabeth considered that she had not heard Darcy refer to Mr. Wickham as his brother at any time other than when he had explained their connection. Perhaps he, even after near eight years of knowing, had yet to fully reconcile himself to it. She recalled suddenly his once having said that his opinion, once lost, was lost forever. It stood to reason he would not admit to himself that he even *had* a brother whilst he still believed the younger man to be as wicked as he remembered. Now that he knew he was changed? In acceptance, it seemed, Mr. Wickham had the advantage.

Then the rest of his words sank in, and she looked to him with some surprise. "Do you mean to say that Miss Darcy does not know of your true connection?"

"No indeed. And given the…difficulty…she endured in the spring, one can only imagine how much more damaging the event would have been had she believed it her own brother to have done so."

Elizabeth's smile was grim. "Indeed, sir. I am so enormously sorry for what Miss Darcy suffered. I hope very much that William—and you, when the truth is explained to her—are able to ease her pain and disappointment."

"So do I, Miss Elizabeth." He then shook his head and offered her a cheerier smile. "As I was saying, madam, Darcy is very studious, and it brings me a great deal of joy to see him besotted! I must admit that I feared his being ensnared by some flibbertigibbet of the *ton*, which would have served no purpose but to make her richer and him miserable."

She laughed softly as they parted for the final split of the dance, and when he had taken her hand again, she said, "It is very gentlemanly of you to have wished for your brother's happiness even when he was thinking ill of you."

"'Tis kind of you to say so, Miss Elizabeth," Mr. Wickham replied.

They then moved apart once more at the dance's end, and curtsied and bowed to one another, and Mr. Wickham offered her his arm and suggested a turn about the room rather than another dance. Elizabeth agreed, as Darcy was engaged in conversation with her father.

"I think," said her companion, "that I like you very much, Miss Elizabeth. You seem perpetually bright and cheerful, and I adore your impertinence—it is just the thing to prevent Will's devolving into a crotchety curmudgeon in his twilight years, and you'll certainly keep him on his toes through all the years before."

"And now *you* are being kind, Mr. Wickham," she replied with a laugh. "I have been witness to Mr. Darcy's reticence, his perceived coldness and pride, and for however long our acquaintance may last, I declare it is my intent that he should not be allowed to become that ill-mannered person again. I intend that he shall always be wondering what I will say next."

"However long your acquaintance?" Wickham queried. "Do not say you mean to give it up while he is gone away."

She shook her head. "Indeed I do not, Mr. Wickham. But though we like each other very much, there is every chance that he may decide we do not suit."

He gazed at her closely, then smiled as he patted the hand on his arm. "I see what you are about. You mean to protect your heart, Miss Elizabeth, despite how much of it is already held in Darcy's hands. By all means, be cautious if you must, but allow me to say that you have no need to be concerned. Though I have seen you together little, it is very clear to me that Will adores you—and I can say with certainty that once he sets his mind to something, there's very little that will sway his course. If he means to have you for a wife someday, I daresay he will. That is, so long as you do not change your mind about him."

They paused in their circuit and Elizabeth turned her head to glance at the object of their conversation. At that moment, Darcy glanced her way also and offered a smile. She returned the expression, feeling her breast swell with emotion that such an adoring gaze was directed at her.

Turning her attention back to Mr. Wickham, she said to him, "I have no intention of changing my mind. But with everything that's happened of late to keep us apart, I cannot help feeling some nervousness, I suppose."

"Part of the blame for that is mine. I am sorry, Miss Elizabeth."

"Do not trouble yourself, Mr. Wickham. William has assured me that once his sister is set to rights, he will bring her to London that we may meet, as that is where I shall be by the time she is well enough to travel. I am to go there and stay with my aunt and uncle, along with my sister Jane, and possibly Kitty as well."

"Which means Bingley will be quitting Netherfield for the winter," said Mr. Wickham, his gaze alighting on the couple as they danced together.

"Indeed, though he does not yet know he will. I have yet to hear from my aunt as to whether Kitty will be able to join us. I expect her reply tomorrow."

"Then I shall pray you receive a favorable one. I do not know your family well, but I think I like you all very much."

Elizabeth snickered. "You do not yet know my mother and youngest sister, Mr. Wickham. I fear making their acquaintance may challenge your resolve to like us *all*."

"Come now, Miss Elizabeth, do not disparage your family so!" chided Wickham. "After all, from what I have heard in the last few days, there has been so remarkable a change in your sisters Mary and Catherine of late that even Darcy has hope of there yet being some chance of amendment for your mother and Miss Lydia."

He paused as a particularly loud peal of laughter sounded from the dance floor, where Lydia was making something of a spectacle of herself with another of the militia, this one named Chamberlayne.

"It is either that," said Mr. Wickham, "or he shall hope you to be very happy living so far away from them at Pemberley when you are married—that is, if he should ask you again and you accept him this time."

Elizabeth laughed. "Ask me again? Mr. Wickham, whatever do you mean?"

Her companion's gaze as he looked down at her then was such as he knew she was being facetious. Still, he said to her, "My dear Miss Elizabeth, pray do not prevaricate. I have it from Bingley that my brother offered to acquire a license before going to Georgiana, and you issued a flat refusal."

"I own that something was said about a license, Mr. Wickham," she replied tartly, "*in jest*. Enticing as the prospect of being Mrs. Darcy so soon was to me, I had to refuse him. I simply do not believe we are either of us quite ready to make so permanent a commitment. Besides, I could not deny my mother the time required to plan the largest wedding breakfast Hertfordshire has ever witnessed."

Mr. Wickham laughed and she along with him. Darcy then moved away from her father and came up to them, at which point Elizabeth immediately released the arm of her companion and took that which Darcy offered.

"What were you speaking of just now? Please tell me, for I must have my share of the conversation."

Wickham snorted. "Darcy, I believe you have just mocked your dear aunt Lady Catherine, unless I am mistaken. I say, Miss Elizabeth, you have been a great influence on him indeed!"

Darcy raised an eyebrow. "I certainly did not. I merely…quoted her."

Elizabeth watched Darcy as he exchanged banter with Wickham, and it occurred to her that he still carried some measure of distrust, in spite of all the assurances he'd been given that his brother was a changed man. Darcy's posture was stiff and he held his chin high, and though he spoke to Mr. Wickham in a friendly way, there was an air of tension about him. She suspected that he was just in need of more time to accept this new version of the man he once knew. Elizabeth hoped that the two could fully reconcile their differences, as she could not imagine being so at odds with any of her sisters—even Lydia—that she could not fully trust one of them.

While her family was preparing to depart Lucas Lodge later that evening, Elizabeth took as long as she dared to hold Darcy's hand and say her goodbyes. Leaving him was much harder than she had imagined it would be, knowing that this was the last time she would see him for two months or longer.

"I promise you, Elizabeth," said he, "that I *will* return. I have decided I shall return at least once a week, or as often as I am able to get away."

"I shall look forward to your visits." A blush rose to her cheeks and she looked at their joined hands for a moment. "I wish you and Mr. Wickham a safe journey to Surrey, ease in speaking to your sister of the truth, and a speedy recovery for her."

Her father cleared his throat then, and announced that the carriage was at the door. It hurt to speak the words, but Elizabeth managed to say "Farewell, Mr. Darcy," before she spun away and joined her mother and sisters in filing out the door.

On their return to Longbourn, Mr. Bennet called her into his book room. Elizabeth went in suspecting she knew already what—or rather, whom—he wished to discuss.

When her father had sat behind his desk, he looked up at her with a steady gaze. "Did you not tell me, when I asked you on Saturday evening, that you and Mr. Darcy were only friends?"

She drew a breath to steady her nerves, and forced herself to hold his gaze. "I own, Papa, that I was not entirely honest, and I ask your forgiveness. Given what had transpired, I was not of a mind to hear you caution me against him, as I feared you would do. He…he has asked if may court me."

"And you like him? I cannot imagine it possible; we all know he is a rather proud and disagreeable fellow."

Elizabeth shook her head. "Oh no, Papa! Mr. Darcy is merely anxious in large, unfamiliar company, and disguises his nerves with aloofness and cold civility," she said. "For him it is easier to appear proud and above his company than to make an effort to converse with strangers in whose concerns he cannot feign knowledge or interest."

Mr. Bennet chuckled. "Never did I imagine hearing such a man as he described so."

She smiled. "When one is able to look past the façade of austere indifference for long enough to engage him in conversation, he can be very amiable."

Her father nodded. "Having put forth the effort a time or two, I am well aware that the young man does know how to partake of a conversation."

Mr. Bennet then drew a breath. "He has asked me if he may write to you while he is away."

Elizabeth thought this an almost redundant request, given he hoped to visit her weekly. Still, she replied, "I should like to correspond with Mr. Darcy. It ought to make the time we must spend apart less difficult to bear."

Mr. Bennet stared at her for a moment, then chuckled again. "You really do like this young man," said he. "There truly must be something worthy in him then, for I know you would not risk your heart for a man that did not deserve you."

Elizabeth grinned. "No indeed, Papa."

"Very well. Off you go now. I did tell your young man I would allow it if you agreed, so you may wish to send him some note and tell him so before the hour grows too late."

Elizabeth came around the desk and bent to kiss her father's cheek. "Thank you, Papa."

Knowing that she had little time to spare before it would be too impolite a time to send a note, she took her father's advice and quickly penned one, then sent it off with a footman. She then sat up with her sisters talking for a short while, and had just finished readying for bed when the footman returned with a reply, brought to her by Mrs. Hill.

My dear Elizabeth,

I am so very pleased to have received your note. Knowing that I may write to you shall sustain me all the days I am forced to be away from your side. I would come see you in the morning before I take my leave of Hertfordshire yet again, but I know it would be unwise, for if I do I will surely not go at all.

Does this make me sound the fool? If it does, I care not. All I care for now is seeing my sister well again and returning to you as soon as I am able. Do take care, and may God bless you.

Yours,
Fitzwilliam Darcy

After reading through the short missive a second time, smiling all the while, Elizabeth tucked it away in the drawer of her nightstand, then slipped under the counterpane and drifted off to a blissful slumber.

The morning post came as the Bennets were finishing their breakfast. Among the few letters was one for Elizabeth from her Aunt Gardiner. Eagerly did she break the wax seal to see what reply she had given to the proposed scheme.

My dearest Elizabeth,

I am delighted whenever you write with news of your family, but never more so, I think, than when reading your last – such surprises you had in store for me!

If your father's cousin is as you describe him, and I do not doubt your word, then you are absolutely correct in your belief that he and Jane would not have suited at all. Had he continued his pursuit of you, I know you would have refused him, as you could never bind yourself to a man who is as ridiculous as you describe Mr. Collins.

Mary, on the other hand, is perfectly suited for him, I think. Could she do better for a husband as you proposed in your letter? I do not doubt it, Lizzy, but you must give allowances for difference of situation and temper. Mary herself has told me in the past that she thought herself the least likely of her mother's children to marry, let alone to marry well. Mr. Collins may not be rich and he may well lack sense, but his position as a clergyman is very respectable, and Mary is one of the most patient creatures of my acquaintance. I believe she will do very well as a parson's wife, and may even find happiness with her husband that you cannot yet imagine.

Now I shall speak of my astonishment regarding your next youngest sister. I am so very happy for Kitty that she has at last been motivated to improve not only her manner but her accomplishments as well. It is funny that she should express an interest in the violin, for my Brandon has recently done the same, and we have been making enquiries as to a music tutor for him. Kitty may absolutely join you and Jane when you come to Town for your visit. We most certainly have room for you all, and if we did not, you know someone in Berkeley Street who would love to have you stay with her.

By and by, Kitty's suitor may not be entirely unknown to us. Your uncle thinks Mr. Bingley to be the son of a textile mill owner with whom he had a business relationship until about two years ago. He is eager to meet the young man to learn if he knows why the relationship was suddenly ended.

And Miss Lizzy... Why was I informed through an acquaintance that you are yourself the object of a young man's attentions?! Lady Disley – the Countess of Disley herself! – came to your uncle's warehouse on Monday as I was meeting him for luncheon. She asked me many pointed questions about you and whether I knew how you became acquainted with her nephew, Mr. Darcy. He declared himself, you see, before both his uncle the earl and the countess. She wished to know all she could of the young lady who had beguiled him so that he did not care that you lacked a fortune and connections. I assure you, my dear niece, that I praised you to the heavens and beyond, and I do believe that Lady Disley is very eager to make your acquaintance. When I mentioned you and your sisters would be coming to London to stay in Gracechurch Street, she seemed rather excited by the news. I imagine Mr. Darcy means a great deal to her.

I should close now, dear Lizzy, for I have gone on much longer than I thought. I have only to say that your uncle says there is a matter he wishes to discuss with you and your sisters when we are all come for Christmas.

All my love and affection,
Madelene Gardiner

"Well?" prompted Kitty. "What does my Aunt Gardiner say, Lizzy?"

Before Elizabeth could reply, Mrs. Bennet exclaimed delightfully, "Oh, my dearest Mary! Your Aunt and Uncle Gardiner send their congratulations on your upcoming marriage to Mr. Collins, and assure me of their being in attendance for the wedding breakfast."

"I have received a note from my Aunt Gardiner as well, Mamma," Mary demurred. "She was most kind in her wishes for my marital felicity."

"And so she should be! You are doing your family such an honor, my girl, by saving us all from the hedgerows when your father is dead."

"I do not marry Mr. Collins to save you and my sisters from the hedgerows. I do so because I admire and respect him and his standing in his community—I have long imagined myself as a clergyman's wife, and soon I shall have that part to play."

"And very admirably so, Mary," spoke up Jane as their mother drew breath to reply.

Elizabeth took advantage of the seconds of silence that followed to turn to Kitty and say, "I have good news. Our aunt says it is fortuitous you should be interested in learning the violin as our cousin Brandon has recently declared the same, and they are making enquiries with the local instructors. In short, you are more than welcome to join Jane and I in Gracechurch Street."

"Absolutely not!"

All the family turned their heads toward Mrs. Bennet at her declaration. "You cannot go to London, Kitty, I forbid it!"

Kitty's expression of joy turned to anguish and her eyes filled with tears. "Whyever not, Mamma?" she asked with a quivering lip.

"Mr. Bingley cannot court you if you are in London, silly girl! No, you will stay here, where you are within three miles of Mr. Bingley and Netherfield."

"Kitty, do not cry, dearest," said Mr. Bennet then. "You may join your sisters when they are gone to Town."

"Mr. Bennet!" cried his wife.

"Mrs. Bennet, you seem to have selectively forgotten that Kitty's suitor has a house in London," Mr. Bennet pointed out then. "If his intentions towards her are true, and all evidence I have seen suggests this to be the case, then he will very likely choose to follow our daughter there, so that he will not be long parted from her as Elizabeth must be from Mr. Darcy."

Mrs. Bennet blinked rapidly. Elizabeth felt her cheeks grow hot and looked down at the letter she still held.

"Oh, do forgive me, I beg you, Elizabeth," added her father. "I did not mean to speak out of turn—I thought you would have spoken to your mother about Mr. Darcy asking permission to court you. You did not say when we spoke last evening that you wished it to remain a private matter."

She could not fault him, she thought, for the slip, as he spoke the truth. Elizabeth cleared her throat delicately, then replied, "It is quite all right, Papa. I did not intend the matter to be a secret; I have simply not had a moment to address it with my mother."

"M-Mr. Darcy… and Elizabeth? Are you quite serious, Mr. Bennet?" asked her mother.

"Indeed," said he. "The young man spoke to me last night of his attachment to our second daughter."

Mrs. Bennet sat back with a huff. "I do not understand it," she said. "I do not understand it at all!"

"You do not understand what, Poppet?"

"These gentlemen from the north are most peculiar! Jane is clearly the most beautiful girl in the county, and yet she has been ignored in favor of…of Lizzy and Kitty! I do not understand it at all!"

Jane laughed softly. "I assure you, Mamma, I do not mind at all that my sisters are chosen and not I. Truly, I am quite content to celebrate their good fortune and cheer their happiness."

"Good fortune indeed! If Lizzy can somehow manage to secure an offer from Mr. Darcy even while he is gone so far away, she will have twice the pin money and carriages and fine jewels that Kitty will have, and *she* will have a great deal as it is!"

Mrs. Bennet's countenance brightened. "Oh, how wonderful for our darling girls, do you not agree, Mr. Bennet? They are not as lovely as Jane or as lively as Lydia, to be sure, but I do think it shows a marked intelligence in Mr. Bingley and Mr. Darcy that they would choose *our* daughters above anyone else's!"

Lydia, strangely quiet through this discourse, suddenly sat straight in her chair, exclaiming, "I think I should go to London as well! Mr. Bingley is sure to take Kitty to all sorts of balls and parties every night, and I just know there will be eligible gentlemen for me to flirt with. Maybe I shall get myself a husband while I am away!"

Mrs. Bennet clapped cheerfully. "Of course you should go, my dearest girl! I am very sure if Mr. Bingley would only introduce you—"

"My dear Mrs. Bennet, before you have all five of your daughters married by Passover, let us come to a right understanding: Under no circumstances will I allow Lydia to go to London."

"Papa, that's not fair!" cried Lydia.

"Mr. Bennet, how can you be so cruel to your daughter?" added her mother. "Do you not understand that accompanying her sisters to Town will throw our Lydia into the paths of many rich men?!"

"It would not matter, Mrs. Bennet, if there should be a rich man on every street corner in London. Lydia has not the sense of her elder sisters, nor has she the maturity. She is still far too much a child to attract a man of any measure of sense for a husband."

"I am not a child!" protested Lydia, who stomped a foot beneath the table as she threw down her silverware.

Mr. Bennet raised an eyebrow in her direction. "And yet you have just proven otherwise. A woman grown, possessed of proper manners and respect for her father, would not show her displeasure in such a fashion as you have just done. And you can put away your tears for another time, for they will not move me."

"Oh, Mr. Bennet!" wailed Mrs. Bennet, her handkerchief in hand and dabbing at her eyes. "I do not understand. I just do not understand *at all* what has been happening in my own house!"

"Revolution, my dear Mrs. Bennet," declared her husband. "The evils of my indolence in regard to the management of this household have very recently been made alarmingly clear to me, as have the all-too-possible outcomes. Oh, I have known my faults for many years, to be sure, but I own that I simply did not care enough to act as I should. Giving in to the whims of my wife and the demands of my children that I might have peace was preferable to arguments and tantrums that would leave me with none.

"But no more—no more will I be an idle participant in the background of my family's lives. I mean to take this house in hand and manage it as I ought to have done from the start."

Once again, in the span of only a day or two, Elizabeth found herself staring in wonder at her father. She could not imagine what had brought on this sudden desire in taking a more active role in their lives, save perhaps something Lord Sotheby or even Mr. Darcy might have said to him. Certainly Georgiana Darcy's misfortune would be such a cautionary tale as would give Mr. Bennet great pause, but would Darcy have divulged so personal an account to a man he knew so little? She did not think it likely, so something must surely have passed between the Earl of Sotheby and Longbourn's master during that hour they spent alone together in the Netherfield library.

"And what of the other girls?" demanded Mrs. Bennet as she sniffled into the white linen square she held. "Why is dear Lydia being so singled out for punishment? She's done no wrong to deserve it!"

"As I said but two days ago, Mrs. Bennet, I fully intend on keeping it that way," Mr. Bennet replied.

Chapter Twenty-Three

Riding alone with Wickham in his carriage from London to Netherfield had been awkward enough for Darcy, given their history.

Spending any time alone with his former nemesis, especially enclosed in so small a space, was one of the more challenging tasks he had ever endured. Reconciling himself with the fact that Wickham had not attacked Georgiana, that he was indeed a changed man—that he was his brother—should not be as difficult as it was proving to be. Wickham certainly seemed to have had no difficulty in accepting their relationship, though certainly the younger man was aware of the tension Darcy still felt being so close to him.

They were just arriving in London for the second time in less than a se'nnight when he felt compelled to at last address his feelings. Being uncomfortable in Wickham's presence did not sit well with him as it was—if there was still tension between them when they reached Donwell, Georgiana was sure to take notice, and he would do whatever was within his power to ensure she remained as comfortable as could be done once he had divulged the truth to her.

"Why did you come back?"

Wickham looked up from the book he was reading. He studied Darcy for a moment before saying, "You mean why did I come back into your life? Why did I not sign the documents that granted me my fortune and return to the plantation in India?"

Darcy nodded. "Something to that effect."

His companion sighed. "I've had a lot of time to think back on my character of old, Will—to reflect and to regret. I wish it were possible to take back all the shameful actions I performed and the bitter, hateful words that I spoke, but I cannot. I can offer no excuse for such reprehensible behavior as clearly still sours your opinion of me. I can't even say that I blame you for still regarding me with some measure of caution and disdain. I recall that your good opinion, once lost, is lost forever."

He turned his gaze to look out the sideglass next to him. "I could have gone back—perhaps I may do so yet. But I stayed because..."

Wickham's eyes found his again, and Darcy was forced to admit to himself that within their depths he could see genuine emotion...

...something akin to hope.

"I stayed because I have, for some time now, hoped that there might yet be a chance of redeeming my character in your eyes. Of achieving at last the goal our father put before us as he lay dying in his bed."

He was as a brother to you once, Fitzwilliam. Be brothers again – be the brothers you always should have been, Darcy recalled.

"In spite of our different situations in life we were close once, when we were children," Wickham continued. "I should like to be close to you and Georgie again—to be close to what family I have left. I should at least like to try, if you are willing, and if not, once I have seen our sister and she is assured I am not the villain she presently thinks me, I will leave you both in peace."

It was Darcy who next turned to gaze at the passing scenery—the townhomes and carriages and citizens going about their business—trying to gather his thoughts. He remembered being close and playing together as boys, and recalled clearly the terrible successive losses of both Wickham's parents, which had opened up in the younger man a great emotional wound that was likely to never fully heal—a feeling he knew all too well.

But *he* had not devolved from a happy, amiable young man to a reprobate scoundrel when both his parents were gone. Wickham had. He'd let his anger and pain at the loss of Mr. and Mrs. Wickham fester and spread through him, seeking to abate it through means that went far beyond "ungentlemanly." He had allowed the snide remarks of their peers at Cambridge who thought it a necessity to remind him of his "place among betters" eat away at him until he had learned to hate the privilege and kindness which had sent him there.

Wickham had, by the time of old Mr. Darcy's final illness, grown to hate him. He had grown to hate the younger Darcy as well, and to deeply despise the class to which he had so long aspired and of which he had been told time and again he would never be a part.

Much more, Darcy understood, had changed besides Wickham's conduct. He'd made his peace, as well as could be done, with the circumstances of his birth and had forgiven those who had brought it about. He had accepted George Darcy as a father, himself and Georgiana as siblings. And not just accepted—at least where their father and Georgiana were concerned—but *loved*. Darcy could read the emotion in Wickham's countenance whenever he spoke of them. Of his affection for Georgiana there had never been much doubt. Save for the time he had believed him guilty of harming her, Darcy could not recall one instance in which Wickham had regarded their sister with anything but kindness.

And while recently acquired, the fact that he had inherited a fortune so grand as to grant him a yearly income of seven thousand pounds was bound to turn more than a few heads among the *ton*.

A chuckle suddenly bubbled up beneath his breast. Darcy tried in vain to contain it, the sound leading to a deep frown on his companion's face.

"Do you mock my sentiments, Darcy?" he asked.

"No," Darcy replied with a shake of his head. Looking back to the other man, he gave a small smile. "Among other things, I was just thinking how your change in fortune was like to gain you a great deal of notice."

Wickham snorted. "No doubt there will be a few mothers among the *ton* who won't mind their daughters being married to new money, as soon as the tenuous connection to the Darcys of Pemberley is made known to them."

"Indeed," said Darcy. A sigh then escaped him, and he looked again into Wickham's gaze. "I've not had the inclination to forgive, as you've already noted. Not before Georgiana was hurt, and certainly not when I thought you responsible. I know it was unchristian of me, but my feelings could no more be helped than yours, I imagine.

"However, since learning of your innocence and being forced into your company by circumstance and need, I have encountered a side of you I thought never to see. You are courteous, kind, compassionate—even gentlemanly! I confess I am overwhelmed, I am confused…and to own the truth, I just do not know how I am supposed to feel about you now. I have despised you for so long that I do not know if I *can* like you again."

Wickham nodded and looked down at his hands. "I understand. As soon as I have seen to Georgiana's welfare, I will take my leave."

"That won't be necessary. I said I did not know if I could, not that I was unwilling to try."

When the words were spoken, the tension that had settled between them since Wickham's appearance at Netherfield the night of the ball began to slowly, finally, dissipate. Both men, it seemed, were able to breathe more freely, and they each settled just a little deeper into the squabs as the carriage rumbled on toward Darcy House. There they would spend the night, with his cousin for company, before making the 16-mile trip into Surrey.

Theodore was not in when they arrived at Darcy House. He and Wickham agreed that, as they were not entertaining guests, they would forego changing for dinner. Each freshened up with minimal ablutions and remained in their traveling clothes, and waited in the library until the simple meal Darcy ordered was ready. Fitzwilliam came in about half through it, surprised to see them there, though when Darcy explained their return he understood. He also offered to join them on the second part of their journey, but when Wickham reminded him of his courtship of Eleanor Tilney by asking how he fared with the lady, Darcy's cousin dropped into a chair, split his face in a silly grin, and regaled them with tales of every moment he had been able to spend in her company. He and Henry Tilney had become fast friends and the latter was always with himself and Miss Tilney as her chaperone.

"Her father the general still seems rather…unyielding, but the dinner at my parents' house is tomorrow, and it is my sincerest hope that in witnessing the earl's treating me no different than he does Philip, I shall yet prevail in winning him over."

"Well, as I said to you Monday, I wish you every success, Theodore," said Darcy. "I've never seen you this determined to court a young lady, so I've no doubt of your regard being genuine."

"Oh, indeed it is, Will! If only you knew her as I do," Fitzwilliam said with animation. "I own that we do not know each other *well* at present, but in the last four days I have taken numerous walks with her and Tilney, have supped at tea houses, strolled through gardens and museums… The lady is intelligent, well-read, is not afraid to challenge me, and has a laugh that sounds like the tinkling of silver bells."

Wickham chuckled. "Did I not already know better, I should think you were Will describing Miss Elizabeth."

Darcy exchanged a look with his cousin, and the both of them smiled. Indeed, by description, the ladies who had somehow managed to capture their hearts were very much alike.

An early start was set for the next day, so both Darcy and Wickham retired early. They were in the carriage and heading south almost before the sun had risen. Books and silence were their companions through much of the morning, though when they had stopped to rest and refresh the horses, over a luncheon of cold meats, soup, and bread, Wickham asked further questions about the couple who would be adopting Georgiana's child as well as the gentleman they were staying with. Darcy described Fitzroy and Roberta Leslie, and the lady's cousin by marriage, George Knightley, as well as he could. He'd only met the couple twice, and Knightley only once.

"Interestingly, however, Mr. Knightley's younger brother John is my solicitor," he added. "Being from an old, moneyed family, many of his clients are wealthy landowners like myself."

All thoughts, even those of Elizabeth, fled from his mind as the carriage turned up the lane that would bring them to Donwell Abbey, the Knightley family's long-held residence. He was now focused solely on Georgiana.

Lord, how do I tell her? he wondered. *How do I tell my sister that not only was she wrong as to the identity of her attacker, but that the man she thought had done so is her brother?*

"It'll be all right, Darcy," spoke up Wickham as the carriage at last began to slow. "It must be, for you are here to guide us."

"Guide us?" Darcy echoed.

"Indeed. You are the eldest of our father's children and therefore the guide to which we the younger will look for direction."

A frown drew his brow lower. "I hardly think this a time for jesting, Wickham."

Wickham shook his head. "I do not jest, Will. I can see that you are nervous about this meeting with Georgiana and what you must tell her, and understandably so. But have you not considered that I might be anxious about it as well? Not only are you to inform her of my innocence, but of our deeper connection. I have thought much on the subject these last days, and it has occurred to me that, even if she accepts I have not wronged her, she may not wish to acknowledge that I am her brother. I admit I should be pained by her rejection of me, as I would have been by yours. Therefore, as my older brother, I have need of you to guide me on what I ought to do in either case."

"That is…" Darcy cleared his throat, unsure how to respond to such a declaration. He had indeed begun to warm to the idea of Wickham being a good, decent man, and though he knew them to be related, calling him "brother" was still something he could not yet bring himself to do.

Yet already Wickham felt comfortable doing so, and he was looking to him for guidance on how to proceed with their sister. It was a little unsettling, though at the same time he felt something akin to pride that the other man should think of him so highly.

He was saved in the end from replying by the carriage stopping before the front of the abbey. Its once-red brick façade was now faded, from more than a hundred years of being subject the sun and rain, to nearly peach. There were several spires round the roof and the front door was nearly enclosed by a square set of stone walls on top of which was a balcony.

The butler opened the door just moments after Darcy pulled the cord for the bell. He greeted them with a nod as he stood aside that they could enter. "May I take your cards?"

"Not necessary, Colborne," said the man then stepping into the entry hall. "I am acquainted with at least one of these gentlemen. Good afternoon, Mr. Darcy."

Darcy inclined his head. "Good afternoon, Mr. Knightley. We are come to see my sister and the Fairleys."

George Knightley snorted softly. "I hardly think you'd come to see me, Darcy," he said, then flashed a grin. "Fairley told me you'd be along this week. Do come in. Colborne, see to it that Mrs. Colborne prepares rooms for the gentlemen."

"Of course, Mr. Knightley," said the butler, who bowed from the shoulders and immediately set off to carry out his master's order.

"So, Darcy… Will you be doing the honors, or should I guess your companion's name?" asked Mr. Knightley with a curious expression on his countenance.

Darcy glanced at Wickham. "Forgive me, of course. Mr. George Knightley, I present Mr. George Wickham."

Knightley's demeanor instantly changed. His expression grew dark as he said, "You can't be serious."

Having been present when the circumstances were explained to Knightley, his reaction was not unexpected. "Sir, all is not as it seems," said Darcy. "Might we go somewhere private to discuss the particulars?"

Knightley turned away without a word and led them to what was obviously his study. He turned around before the desk and braced himself against it, his arms akimbo as he regarded his newest guests.

"How could you bring *him* here? It was my understanding that you or your cousin were like to run him through the moment you set eyes on him," said he.

"I have it on good authority that he is not the villain my sister thinks him to be," Darcy said.

Knightley looked between them. "You are certain, Mr. Darcy?"

"I would not bring him within a hundred miles of Georgiana if I were not," Darcy declared.

"And you are entirely correct, sir," added Wickham. "I would not be alive to say these words to you had I done this evil thing. If not Darcy here, then Fitzwilliam certainly would have had my guts for garters."

Again Knightley was silent, then he suddenly walked over to the door and tugged on the bell-pull beside it. He paced back and forth, still saying nothing, until his summons was answered by a maid. "Go to Laird and Lady Fairley and bring them here at once. They ought to be in the small dining room now sitting down to luncheon."

When the maid had acknowledged and departed, Knightley shut the door again and turned back. "I should think you'd rather not have to tell this story more than necessary."

Darcy glanced at Wickham. "Indeed, Mr. Knightley."

"May I ask, sir, how you are related to the Fairleys?" asked Wickham. "Darcy has told me that the laird is a cousin of his aunt, the Countess of Disley, and that his lady is a cousin of yours."

"By marriage," their host replied. "One of Lady Fairley's aunts wed an uncle of mine."

"And why should they trust you with their secret, and Georgiana's?" Wickham pressed. "Why would they not take her back to Scotland with them?"

"They trust me because I am family, and I daresay Darcy trusts them for the same reason," said Mr. Knightley.

"Georgiana was unwilling to go so far away from the family, and me especially," added Darcy. "My aunt and uncle spoke of being in Town through the end of February, and I was to be in Hertfordshire with Bingley. As I was little more than a day's distance from her should she desire my company, she was content."

"And this distant, not-quite-relative's home is nearer than Pemberley or Disley Court," Wickham observed. "And certainly closer than Scotland."

The study door opened as Darcy nodded to admit Fitzroy Leslie and his wife. The two greeted him warmly, and their expressions were curious as they regarded Wickham. Darcy drew a breath, then explained who his companion was and why he was there. The Laird and Lady of Glenfairley were in turns stunned, confused, and frustrated.

Lady Fairley then looked to Wickham and said, her Scottish brogue slightly thickened with emotion, "I am glad to hear you are not the blackguard who hurt dear Georgiana. She has said she always thought well of you, until this terrible thing happened. Then she knew what it was to hate."

Wickham paled slightly, then he seemed to gather his wits and he stood a little straighter. "I swear to you all, I will kill the bastard myself when we catch him. Georgiana is the kindest, sweetest girl in all the world, and should never have been given reason to know that feeling."

"Bloody bollocks," muttered Fairley. "I do nae know how the lass is gonna take this. Not well, I daresay."

"Has she had a very hard time, Laird Fairley?" Wickham asked softly.

After another moment of staring at him, Fairley relaxed a little. "She speaks to my wife more than myself on the subject, and Roberta honors her confidences, but I have observed her behavior on many occasions and I can tell you that she suffers greatly from melancholy. And nightmares."

Darcy frowned. "I thought you said she'd done with the nightmares?"

"We believed she had, for a time," said Lady Fairley. "But as Roy intimated in his letter, the comin' of the labor, which the midwife says might now be any day, has reawakened her fears. They are kept at bay well enough durin' the daytime, but at night…"

She paused and reached for her husband's hand; he heaved a ragged sigh as he took it. "At night," he said, "she sometimes wakes screamin' in the wee hours, and only my wife sharin' her bed will calm her."

Darcy remembered hearing a similar tale from the Sothebys when they had first brought Georgiana back to Pemberley. His heart squeezed painfully in his chest to hear more of his sister's suffering.

"I ought to have stayed with her," said he, turning away from the others as he ran his hands through his hair. "Fitzwilliam could have tracked the attacker alone—I should not have given in to the desire for revenge and gone on the hunt for that scoundrel. I should have been *here*."

"Forgive me, Mr. Darcy, but I do nae think your bein' here would have made much of a difference," said Fairley quietly. "You know that we have seen to her every possible comfort, as you would have done had she been able to remain at home. And yet she still weeps at nothin', stares silently out the window or into the fire, and rarely is anyone other than Roberta, her maid, or the midwife allowed near her."

"Still she avoids being near men?" Darcy asked.

The laird nodded. "Knightley and I have been very kind and gentle when we've interacted with her, but she has a tendency to start when we get too close for her comfort. She does nae tolerate the footmen comin' near at all."

"Terrible, terrible thing what was done to the poor girl," said Mr. Knightley.

"Why did you take her in?" said Wickham suddenly. "I mean, you're no relation of hers. The Fairleys could have rented a cottage just about anywhere. Why get involved in protecting a girl who had no connection to you?"

"Wickham," cautioned Darcy.

Wickham shook his head. "I mean no disrespect, truly. But like it or not, Georgiana is my sister as well as yours, and I am concerned for her welfare and her reputation. Donwell is a bustling parish and so is nearby Highbury. I'd just like to understand why someone so wholly unconnected to the family would put himself forward this way."

Knightley drew a breath as he regarded him, his expression solemn. Darcy counted five clicks of the clock on the mantle over the fireplace before the older gentleman replied.

"Miss Darcy wished to be near her family," he began slowly. "And knowing not only what she would endure while she carried the child but what pain it would give her to part from it, my family—" He gestured to the Fairleys. "—were only too willing to oblige her rather than spiriting her away to Scotland where she would surely have been full away from prying eyes. Could they have rented a cottage or even an estate elsewhere that would have sufficed? Certainly. But why should they have to do that when they have family of their own willing to host them and her? Mr. Darcy was with them when Roy and Roberta came to me with their need, and it was he who gave the final concession to Miss Darcy coming here. If your brother approved of me, I can see no reason why you should not.

"I am aware of the cruelty not only of what Miss Darcy endured in March but also that which she would suffer should the truth be known to society. While the villages are, as you say, bustling, I can assure you she is quite safe from discovery at Donwell. I rarely have visitors, don't host dinners or balls here, and I've lived alone except for the staff for some years now. This house really is far too large for just me, so I was only too happy to be of service when my cousins and Mr. Darcy surprised me with their request. Miss Darcy has the benefit of the country air for her constitution and the knowledge that family is but a day away for her peace of mind. In short, Mr. Wickham, I have done this because it was asked of me, and it was the right thing to do."

Wickham looked around him, then loosed a sigh. "I beg your pardon," said he. "I just… wished to understand."

Knightley waved off his words. "She is your sister, so your concern is understandable. I hope I have assuaged your fears."

"What of your staff? What do they know?"

"To them she is a young widow who will not be able to care for the child she carries," replied Mr. Knightley. "Considering they are all from the poorer families of Donwell and Highbury, they have none of them even heard of the great Darcys of Pemberley."

"And even had they knowledge of the family, they're not fool enough to turn gossip," said Darcy. He then looked to his host. "Are they?"

"No, Darcy," he replied. "I've made it clear to the staff that they're not to discuss what goes on inside this house outside of it."

Wickham frowned. "You mean Georgie doesn't leave the house?"

"Oh, we go outside very often, Mr. Wickham," said Lady Fairley. "Or at least we did. As the child has grown she has chosen to go out less and less."

"Speaking of Georgiana, she must be wonderin' where we've gone off to," said Fairley. "I should nae like to give her any cause for concern."

Darcy sighed. "Nor would I, but we cannot all of us just walk in there together."

"Indeed not," said Lady Fairley. "But I think, Mr. Darcy, you ought speak to her first before she sees him. As you know, her condition at this point is very delicate—bein' unduly upset might well start the labor."

"Let us go then, that we might get the matter done with," said Darcy then. The others agreed it was best, and so Mr. Knightley led the way out of his study.

"Do wait here, sir," said Lady Fairley to Wickham, pointing to a chair against the wall adjacent to the dining room door. "When it is safe, Fitzroy or meself will come to the door and open it. Then you will know you may enter."

Wickham nodded silently, and moved to the chair to sit as Darcy, Knightley, and the Fairleys stepped through into the room where Georgiana waited.

"William!"

Darcy crossed to Georgiana in but a few long strides. He sat himself beside her and took her hand in his, raising it to kiss the back. "My dearest girl, how are you?" he asked her.

With her free hand she rubbed a circle on her swollen belly, then looked to him with a small smile. "I am well enough, brother, though my spirits are made brighter by your being here—however, I very clearly remember telling Roy he need not write to you and tell you to come."

Darcy glanced over at Fitzroy Leslie, who lifted a shoulder and smiled. "I told you I was nae sorry," the laird said. "Where is Mrs. Annesley?"

Georgiana looked to him. "She said she had a headache, so I told her to go and lie down. Now, as to that letter—"

Looking to his sister, Darcy offered a smile. "Even had he not written, dearest, you know it was my intention to come for a visit at Christmas."

"I know it was your intention, William, but I had rather thought you might choose to stay at Netherfield," countered Georgiana with a grin. "After all, there was the incentive of—oh, how did you describe her? 'She is, truth be told, the most intriguing young lady I have met in all my years.' I must say, I almost wish you could have brought Miss Elizabeth with you, if you were determined to come."

Darcy chuckled, recalling that he had suggested to Elizabeth a way that he might do just that. "When I spoke of Laird Fairley's letter to her, Elizabeth did express a desire to meet you," he said.

"And I long very much to make her acquaintance as well! She must be quite charming indeed to have captured *your* interest, brother."

He smiled again as he gave a nod of agreement. Darcy then glanced again at the Fairleys, at Knightley, his gaze passing the door outside of which Wickham sat waiting. Drawing a breath, he released it slowly, and placed his hand over top of that he held of his sister's.

"Georgiana, there is another reason I am come to Donwell," he began. "I have some news to impart which has great potential to cause you grief."

Her eyes grew slowly wider, and the hand he held squeezed his. "Is it our Aunt and Uncle in Town? Philip? Marianne? Theo? Not little Josephine! Oh, tell me quickly, William!"

It was not lost on Darcy that Georgiana did not inquire after their Aunt Catherine or Anne—she rarely did, as she had been greatly intimidated by their mother's sister in her youth and as such cared little for her, and had met Anne so rarely that she barely knew her.

"No, dearest, they are all well. Theo has even met a lady *he* is interested in courting, should her father allow it," Darcy replied. "What I must tell you concerns you—it concerns what happened to you. You see..."

He glanced toward the door again, wondering if Wickham could hear. Actually speaking the words was proving more difficult than he had anticipated, even though he fully believed in the truth of them.

"William, what is it? Did you catch him? Is he...is he dead?" Georgiana asked.

Sighing, Darcy looked to her again. "No, Mr. Wickham is not dead. In fact, as it turns out, he is not the person who attacked you."

Georgiana began to shake her head as her breathing grew fast and shallow. "Yes he is. Yes he is!" she said as she jerked her hand from his and struggled to her feet. "I saw his face. I saw his face *every day* for two weeks, William! I saw his face as he grabbed me and threw me down on the settee, as he pushed up my skirts and *forced* his flesh into me—no matter how hard I fought him, no matter how much I *begged* for him to stop! You cannot tell me that George Wickham did not violate me in the *worst possible way* and leave me with a child I cannot even raise myself!"

Darcy's heart broke to see her so upset, so near to hysterics. But he had to continue, to tell her all. He'd made a vow he would reveal the whole truth about Wickham, and he meant to keep it. He would have no more secrets in his family.

"Dearest, it pains me to hurt you this way, but I am afraid I have little choice," he told her. "Wickham did not attack you—it was someone who very much resembles him, who knows just enough about him to assume his character. You must know it is possible you were mistaken; just because that man *said* he was George Wickham does not mean he was. Remember that you had not seen him since shortly after Father's death. That was seven years before you were hurt."

"And how do you bloody know it was not George?" his sister retorted angrily. "You weren't the one he raped."

Growing frustrated, Darcy pushed to his feet. "Very well—if you'll not believe your own brother, perhaps you will give credit to the testimony of witnesses. Lord and Lady Sotheby, whom you knew as Colonel and Mrs. Brandon, have vouched for Wickham's innocence."

She looked to him again with wide eyes, her face now pale though her cheeks were flushed red with her anger. "But why? How?"

He moved closer to her. Held out his hands and waited until she placed hers in them. "Do you recall a scar on his face?" Darcy asked.

Georgiana frowned. "In fact, I do," she said after a moment. "It was through his left eyebrow. George told me he'd 'earned' it defending a lady friend of his."

"I would suggest that was another of his lies, dearest," her brother said softly. "The truth, as it so happens, I did not care to hear as much as you do not. But it is the truth. On the night of the ball at Netherfield, Wickham came to call. Lord Sotheby saw him first and removed him from the ballroom, that I would not create a scene if I saw him. He then asked his Lady to call Theo, Bingley, and myself to Bingley's study, where we confronted him… where I tried to kill him."

Georgiana gasped and gripped his hands tighter. "Theo and Bingley and Sotheby stopped me, of course," Darcy continued, "and once Wickham had denied the attack and I had declared him a liar, Lady Sotheby soon noted that he did not have the scar she'd seen on the face of the man who claimed to be your husband. Lord Sotheby studied his countenance also, and he, too, agreed that he was not the same man."

His sister studied him for a long moment, and he was grateful to see that the rapid pace of her breathing began to slow, though the pulse that throbbed at her throat did not. "But I don't understand," said she. "If the man that attacked me was *not* George, then who was it?"

Darcy sighed. "I am afraid we do not know. I am so sorry. I can only say that whoever he is, he's been pretending to be Wickham for some time, both before and after he attacked you."

Georgiana let go his hands and moved back to her chair. After a moment she asked, "Where is George now—the real one? You said he came to Netherfield to see you."

"I shall tell you in a moment," said Darcy. "But first I must reveal a secret that our father told Wickham and me the day he died. Do you think you are ready to hear it?"

His sister frowned and threw her hands up. "Oh for goodness' sake, what secret, William? I should think, after hearing that the man I *thought* to have ruined me is not in fact the man who ruined me, I can handle just about anything. Just have done with it."

If that is your wish, Darcy thought. "Wickham is Father's natural child, Georgiana. Albert Wickham accepted our father's by-blow as his own in order to save his friend and a young maid from ruin."

Again Georgiana began to shake her head. "No. No—*that,* I am certain, is not possible," she said. "Papa loved Mamma with all his heart, I know it!"

"He did, Georgie, and she loved him the same," Darcy told her. "But even a man who loves his wife deeply is capable of making a mistake. Mamma was very ill after she birthed me and it took her more than a twelvemonth to recover. In that time, Father…" He let his voice trail off, as her own condition was proof enough of what he did not say.

Georgiana held his gaze for a long moment. "You are certain?"

"Father told us this on his deathbed, Georgiana," Darcy replied. "He said he could not meet his maker without confessing the greatest of his sins. I tell you now because I see no more reason to keep the truth from you."

"And George? Where is he now?" she asked again.

"He is waiting outside the door," spoke up Laird Fairley.

Chapter Twenty-Four

Georgiana's head snapped toward the dining room door as she gasped in surprise and she began to sway in her seat.

"He... he came with you?"

Darcy nodded, his features contorted into an expression of deep concern. "Yes. He wished to see you, to be certain you were assured of his being innocent of the crime. I know I have just delivered shocking news—if you are not ready to see him, say so at once. I believe he will understand your need for time."

"I will," came Wickham's voice through the door. "Forgive me, I can listen no longer in silence. Georgie, I just... I just wanted to..."

"Come in, George."

Darcy looked to Georgiana. Seeing that she was still greatly agitated, he put an arm around her, and took her free hand in his. Knightley stood by his own chair and the Fairleys moved to stand behind Georgiana as the dark wooden door slowly swung open.

Wickham's first steps into the room were hesitant, and when his gaze fell upon Georgiana's his countenance crumbled. He stepped around the dining table in a few long strides, and fell to his knees beside Georgiana as tears began to fill his eyes.

"Oh, sweet girl, I beg you would believe I could never... I could *never...*"

His voice broke as he tried to get the words out, and he fell silent when Georgiana reached out a shaking hand to cup his cheek. Tears slipped from her eyes as she said in a voice hardly more than a whisper, "Dear God, how could I have been so wrong? These are not the eyes of the monster that haunts my sleep. Those are dark, threatening, and full of anger. These are full only of love and concern and heartbreak—*these* are the eyes I remembered from my girlhood."

Sniffling, she turned to Darcy, who gave what he hoped was a reassuring smile. "I remember telling him that his eyes were different, when first we met. That I could have sworn they were green. He told me I was mistaken, that they had always been brown, though perhaps sometimes they may have appeared green in the sun. How it was an easy mistake to have made when we had not seen each other in so long."

She looked back to Wickham. "The face is different as well. The monster carried himself much the same, but was broader of shoulder, and the face was not quite the same as I remembered. He said that like his eyes, my memory of his face had been altered by time.

"He lied to me," she continued. "He lied to me about so many things he before he hurt me. Yet he could not have imagined I would one day be reunited with the man he claimed to be, that I would know the difference between them. Eyes truly are windows to the soul, and in these I do not see the monster."

Darcy heard another soft cry escape Wickham that was surely a sob of relief; tears fell as he reached for Georgiana's hand and brought it to his lips to kiss the back.

"My dearest, sweetest girl," said he. "I cannot tell you how very much I am relieved to hear you say those words—to know that you do not think me a monster."

"Indeed," said Georgiana. "William tells me I must now think of you as a brother."

"Only if you wish to," Wickham told her. "You were as a sister to me long before I knew of our blood connection, but I will not pressure you in any way to think of me as a brother. It is entirely your choice."

"I must be honest, I do not know at this time what to think," said Georgiana. "I once thought you as much a brother as William, but for too long have I thought you a villain. I see in your eyes the truth of your innocence, yet the feelings I have lived with these last nine months—"

Wickham silenced her with a gentle squeeze of her hand. "You need not explain yourself or your feelings. They are natural and just. I will, however, ask if I may stay here with you and Will that we may begin to know one another again, and hopefully we shall drive away those feelings."

Georgiana smiled timidly. "I should like that very much. But oh, I am quite fatigued now, and have entirely lost my appetite. I think I must go lie down—I do that frequently these days, as the midwife says the little one will come any day now."

Wickham held her gaze for a moment longer, then glanced at Darcy, and finally his eyes flitted between the Fairleys as he rose to stand. "I hope the two of you appreciate what my sister is doing for you."

"I can assure you, Mr. Wickham, that our appreciation for her gift to us is beyond measure," said the laird.

"There are no words to express the depth of our gratitude," said his wife, whose eyes filled with tears as she helped Georgiana to stand. "I know four languages, and not one of them has the words."

When the two ladies had gone, each man in the dining parlor drew and released a ragged breath, and at near the same moment. This, in turn, led them all to chuckle, and then Mr. Knightley invited Darcy and Wickham to a seat at the table if they were hungry. They accepted, and moments after Knightley rang a bell by his place setting a couple of maids entered. One carried a tureen that Darcy surmised held some kind of soup, the other carried a large pitcher. Starting on opposite sides of the table, the two filled the bowls and cups of the gentlemen. While they consumed a hearty beef stew, Laird Fairley asked for more detail on how the truth of Wickham's innocence had been discovered. The night of the Netherfield ball was described to him, after which he said,

"Blimey. I can nae imagine comin' home after years away to find someone's gone and ruined your reputation—and in such a beastly fashion as this!"

"Aye, sir, it was…quite a shock," Wickham replied.

"More difficult for Darcy, I think," put in Mr. Knightley. "I mean no offense, Mr. Wickham, but I can scarcely imagine what it must be like for a man to despise another for years, to believe him guilty of so heinous a crime, and then to have to bring all that hatred up short in finding he's not so much of a black-hearted villain after all."

Darcy felt three pairs of eyes on him, and he sighed as he set his soup spoon down. "As Mr. Wickham knows, it has not been an easy task to reconcile what I *thought* I knew with what I know I must accept. However, I have given him my word I shall endeavor to forgive the past, in the hopes that we may yet regain some part of the good we once thought of each other in our youth."

"And I am very glad of it," replied Wickham. "I only hope that dearest Georgie is able to find it in her heart to make the same effort. I can't bear to live in a world where she is thinking ill of me."

The dining parlor door opened as he spoke with the return of Lady Fairley. Mr. Knightley rang the bell to call the maids while she took a seat beside her husband. "I should nae worry overmuch on that score, Mr. Wickham," said she as soup and wine were brought in for her. "Miss Darcy told me as we walked to her chambers that while she struggles to believe her father capable of breakin' his marriage vows, that you are not truly the monster who attacked her is a great relief. She said that she felt as though a weight had been lifted from her, and now she can breathe easier, knowin' that the person she remembered is not the libertine who forced himself on her."

Darcy caught Wickham's gaze as the younger man's own breath hitched in his chest. The conversation was turned to a different topic when Darcy asked, "Who is Mrs. Annesley?"

"Mrs. Annesley is the lady my wife and I hired to be Georgiana's companion whenever Roberta is away from Donwell," said Laird Fairley. "She is a widowed mother of three from a genteel background—in fact, 'twas Mr. Knightley who recommended her."

"I can assure you, Darcy," began Knightley when he turned a stern glare in his direction, "that Mrs. Annesley is nothing like Miss Darcy's previous companion. She's but a few years older than myself, and I have known her all my life as she was born and raised in the parish as I was. Her family was not gifted with great wealth, but the farm which her nephew Robert now runs does very well. Young Mr. Martin is responsible for his mother and two sisters, and they want for nothing."

"And her husband's family?"

"The Annesley estate is at the other end of Donwell Parish. Brings in about two or three thousand per annum, I believe. Mrs. Annesley's son David is now master; one of her daughters is married to a gentleman in Yorkshire, and the other is presently visiting a cousin in Shropshire."

Darcy considered what he'd heard. "And why would she agree to be a companion, if her family has an estate?" he asked.

Knightley chuckled. "She's a widow whose children are grown. Well, the youngest is only seventeen, so not quite grown—but nearly so. And frankly, Mrs. Annesley does not care for being idle. She's very well educated, and along with Lady Fairley has been working with your sister on how to manage a household."

"We began the lessons," spoke up Lady Fairley, "at first as a means of keepin' her occupied, as when first she came to us here at

Donwell it was understood that she was to keep house for you. She now believes she has no need to be so fastidious, as you have recently met a young lady with whom you have formed an attachment."

Unable to contain the flush that crept up his neck, Darcy only smiled and returned his attention to his stew. Wickham then took it upon himself to describe Elizabeth to their host and his relations, saying that she was a beautiful girl, quick-witted, and "obviously bears some secret gift from the Almighty, if she was able to convince Darcy here that her unfortunate lack of dowry means nothing."

After the meal Darcy and Wickham were shown to the rooms that had been prepared for them, where they refreshed their clothing at last. Upon finishing, the two emerged almost simultaneously from their rooms and together went in search of their host. They were met on the ground floor by Lady Fairley, who suggested a tour of the Abbey. When Wickham inquired as to the whereabouts of her husband and cousin, she explained that Laird Fairley had gone into the village, and Mr. Knightley had been called away to settle a dispute between two of his tenants.

"He told my husband that these two particular disputants have quarreled before and were encouraged by the Donwell steward to settle it between themselves," said Lady Fairley with one corner of her mouth lifted in a lopsided grin. "They were warned it would not be in their best interests to continue squabblin', because if Knightley came to settle it for them, they'd be sure to regret it."

Knowing she had been at the abbey long enough to observe the gentleman's interactions with his tenants, Darcy asked, "Mr. Knightley manages his tenants with a firm hand, then?"

"Knightley is not a tyrant, Mr. Darcy," retorted their hostess. "But nor does he suffer fools. The matter could have been settled peacefully between the two men had either been willin' to compromise, based on what Fraser, his steward, told him. Involvin' their landlord means they both will lose, as Mr. Knightley does not appreciate it when adults behave like bickerin' children."

"What were they fighting over?" asked Wickham.

Here, Lady Fairley chuckled. "Grazin' rights to a plot of land," she said. "One man's daughter is to marry the other's son, but they cannae seem to agree on the marriage settlements; which, as I understand it, was to include grazin' rights to a particularly bountiful area. Both are sheep herders, so naturally, keepin' the stock well fed and growin' is a prime concern for farmers. The matter has escalated, unfortunately, from public bickerin' to an allegation of theft."

Wickham scoffed. "Good heavens. It is a wonder the lovers still wish to marry at all."

Lady Fairley laughed. "I suspect that once an agreement is finally reached, the young couple may well look to moving to Highbury or perhaps another county altogether for their permanent residence."

The tour of Donwell Abbey was brief; Lady Fairley showed the two where the dining, drawing, music and billiard rooms were, as well as the library, and the easiest ways of reaching each. When asked by Wickham, she also explained the connection to Darcy's aunt, which was that a Fitzroy daughter had married a Faulkner son, who was the father of Josephine Faulkner, who was mother to the present Countess of Disley.

"A relation by marriage is still a relation, is it not?" observed Wickham. "Have not both you and Mr. Knightley referred to each other as a cousin?"

"Indeed we have," said the lady with a smile. "Though I was born and raised in Scotland, I am well acquainted with some of my English relatives. Knightley happens to be one of them."

Darcy paused and turned to her, struck by a sudden realization. "If Laird Fairley's connection to my aunt is through the Faulkner line, does that not also make him a relation of the Earl of Sotheby? His paternal grandmother and my aunt's mother were sisters."

Lady Fairley appeared to consider it. "Yes, I suppose it does."

When the tour finished soon after, Darcy and Wickham both opted for the library to pass the time until dinner, though on seeing a writing desk there, Darcy strode to it directly.

Wickham chuckled. "Planning to write to your dear Elizabeth?"

"As a matter of fact, I have two letters to write—but yes, one is to Elizabeth," Darcy replied as he settled in the chair.

"To whom is the other?"

"Theo. I gave him my word I would write as soon as I had seen Georgiana."

"Oh yes, I remember. I imagine your aunt and uncle will be wanting to hear of her, as well," Wickham observed as he perused the volumes along one wall of the library.

"Indeed."

Wickham chose a book, then turned to Darcy as he was putting his pen into the ink bottle. "She…she looked well, all things considered. God, how she has grown since last I saw her—so tall! So fair! Should she ever make a proper debut in society, we will be fighting gentlemen and rogues alike off with sabers drawn."

Darcy looked up, suppressing a grimace. "I daresay Georgiana will have no desire to endure a season in Town after this affair, though I will admit I hope for it. She has need of greater society to help her put this miserable experience behind her."

"For the first time in many years, we are in full agreement," said Wickham with a nod. "And I daresay your lovely Elizabeth will be a great help to you in that regard. She's such a lively creature, and allows nothing to unsettle her."

"Almost nothing," Darcy mused, recalling his foolish jest at the first Meryton assembly. He thought also of her embarrassment the next morning, during the awkward breakfast at Netherfield.

"Elizabeth, like any of us, is subject to being rattled on occasion," said he after a moment. "However, she *is* remarkably able to withstand a great deal of stress before she shakes."

"Which, I say, will serve both you and our sister well when the time comes to break Georgie out of her shell—not this upcoming season, certainly," Wickham replied. "It will be far too soon after what's to happen this week or next. But the first year of a new century? I daresay you ought make every effort to turn it into a new year for Georgiana as well."

Darcy had by now lost count of the number of times Wickham's insightful opinions had startled him, but he nodded his agreement. He then dashed off a quick letter to his cousin, informing him that Georgiana appeared hearty and hale, and had taken the news of Wickham's innocence and his true relation to them about as well as could be expected. Once it was folded and sealed, he pulled another sheet of paper to him and readied his pen.

My dearest Elizabeth,

We are arrived in Surrey. How I wish you had taken me up on my offer to join Wickham and I, for there are some remarkably beautiful sights about that I am sure you would greatly enjoy—though I must say, not one compares to the beauty of your countenance when you smile.

I know, I am being foolishly sentimental again. When it comes to you, I cannot seem to abstain from such besotted ejaculations.

My sister Georgiana does well. She took the news I delivered with equanimity, and agreed to see Mr. Wickham. Her condition should be relieved in a matter of days, and we are like to stay on another four to six weeks to be ensured her recovery is complete – though I mean to keep to my promise to come for a day or two each week if I can. You may be sure I will introduce you to Georgiana when we are come to London; I will have need of your infectious charm, Elizabeth, to aid in reminding her of the beauty there is in life, for I fear being indisposed for so long has robbed her of the ability to bask in its pleasures.

May this letter find you well. I shall pray for continued good health for yourself and your family, and I shall hope to hear from you very soon. Do give my regards to our acquaintances in Meryton and Longbourn.

Yours affectionately,
Fitzwilliam Darcy

When she appeared with Mrs. Annesley for dinner, Georgiana looked to be in better spirits. She greeted the Fairleys, Darcy, Mr. Knightley—who by then had returned to the house—and even Wickham warmly.

Darcy had not imagined Georgiana's companion was a mulatto, but her ethnicity was of no significance to him—there were negroes and mulattos at Pemberley among his staff and tenants. So long as she was not of the same ilk as Mrs. Younge, he would approve her. And though he believed George Knightley a good judge of character—if his younger brother's intelligence was anything to go by—Darcy still asked her a number of pointed questions to determine whether or not she could be trusted to keep the truth behind his sister's stay in Surrey a secret. After all, he reasoned silently, people talked and word traveled.

Mrs. Annesley assured him that Georgiana's business was *her* business, and laid a hand on Georgiana's shoulder as she said, "This sweet young lady has suffered enough. I'd not wish to see her broken altogether by the spread of vicious gossip."

"My brother and I appreciate your dedication to our sister's welfare, madam," spoke up Wickham, who then reminded Darcy that there was further news to be told regarding his cousin Anne.

Darcy frowned. "Wickham, I hardly think it an appropriate topic of conversation for a young lady of her age."

Wickham scoffed. "A young lady of her age, Will? Our sister is a woman grown. She will soon bear a child—I think she can handle a saucy little tale such as Anne has given us to tell."

"Dear heavens, what you possibly have to say about her? She never leaves Rosings," Georgiana observed.

"So thought we all, dearest," said Darcy. "However, she was... convinced, I suppose you might say... to take a carriage into Hertfordshire and then London."

Georgiana frowned. "Whatever for?"

"She'd been informed about Will's interest in Miss Elizabeth, Georgie. And being full of her mother's idea of being married to our brother, sought to put an end to the lady's designs upon him by forcing a compromise," Wickham replied.

"What?!" cried Georgiana before she collected herself, her tone more demure when next she spoke. "Did Anne really attempt a compromise?"

"Unfortunately she did more than attempt it, Georgiana," said Darcy. "Anne had the audacity to think she could compromise me at our house in Town, but in being so far into her cups as to lose her sense of direction, she found herself in the room of another. Our uncle has determined that they are to marry."

"May already be married by now," added Wickham.

Georgiana shook her head. "The poor man. Dare I ask who has the misfortune of having to take Anne for a wife and Aunt Catherine as a mother-in-law?"

Darcy raised an eyebrow at her choice of words, though he still replied, "It was Mr. Ferrars. You may recall I had given him leave to lodge at Darcy House until such time as he had reconciled with his mother."

"Oh yes. That was right before I came away to Surrey," Georgiana said. "Poor Mr. Ferrars—he'd just barely settled at Lambton. And I daresay his heart was still fixed on another."

Darcy could neither confirm nor deny the supposition, and so only lifted a shoulder in response, then tucked into his food. Wickham again took the conversation in hand when he asked Mr. Knightley,

"Sir, I wonder... How frankly may we speak here? There is something I should like to know, but would not have such a delicate subject spoken of where others ought not hear."

Darcy glanced around the room; there were none present but Knightley, the Fairleys, Georgiana, Mrs. Annesley, and themselves.

Knightley set down the goblet of wine he held. "Mr. Wickham, as you are aware, Miss Darcy's companion knows all, though she would not if I did not trust her implicitly. While the staff are out of the room, you may speak freely."

"I am curious as to what the local population knows of

Georgiana's circumstances," said Wickham.

Their host glanced at the Fairleys, but it was Georgiana herself who provided the answer. "They have the same story as the abbey staff—that I'm a widow—but my friends have also let it be known that I am here to take the country air for my sickly constitution. I hardly leave the house nowadays anyhow, except to take a turn about the garden when I have the strength for it. I've not been to the village since before my condition became obvious."

Her lip had begun to tremble by the end and her eyes filled with tears. Darcy's heart went out to her, and a sidelong glance at Wickham told him that he felt her pain also.

"Forgive me, Georgie, for making you uncomfortable with my inquiry," said Wickham softly. "I only wished to ascertain that your reputation had been well-looked after. I should not like it if any rumor were to follow you when you at last depart your gilded cage."

Georgiana sniffled and then replied, "Oh, I am hardly caged here, George. I have the freedom to move about the house as I wish, and as I said I go out into the garden, or walk in the shrubbery, whenever I feel well enough. I'm at the stage now, however, where I simply cannot move about as I once did."

Further conversation centered on other subjects. Georgiana asked a great many questions of Wickham and how he had spent his time the last six years, and Darcy observed that she relaxed incrementally the more she listened. He was glad of it—even if he was still not entirely comfortable with the new and improved George Wickham, he was pleased to see his sister becoming so. Truthfully, he had not expected her to accept Wickham's presence as readily as she seemed to have done, but then his sister did have the gentlest, most forgiving of hearts. Georgiana always had dismissed any slight against her once forgiveness had been begged—perhaps too easily, he mused. But in this case he would not consider chiding her for it even in the silence of his own mind, for anything that brought her peace and gave her cause to smile was welcome.

Toward the end of the meal, Wickham asked if Knightley owned a pianoforte. "I have heard, you see, that Georgiana is perhaps the most accomplished young lady at the instrument, though she was still learning when last I heard her play."

"Oh, I have a beautiful grand in the music room," said Knightley, "which—until these charming ladies came to stay at Donwell—had sat far too long untouched. I never learned to play, and there has not been a mistress or daughter of the house in some years."

"And I am afraid, sir, that you shan't get to hear me play anytime soon," Georgiana added. "Regrettably, I am not quite able to reach the keys properly, I have grown so large. Being indisposed this way has proven to be *such* an inconvenience of late—so many things are more difficult to do, or I cannot do them at all—I cannot even put on my own shoes, for I cannot see my feet anymore! It is exceedingly vexing to have such difficulty doing the simplest of tasks, or not be able at all to do something I enjoy so much as playing!"

"But surely you can sing still," Wickham pressed with a smile. "If memory serves, you were quite the little songbird."

Here, Lady Fairley smiled brightly. "Oh, do please sing for us, Georgiana! I so enjoy listenin' to your voice, dear. I shall play for you, I'm tolerable enough."

Georgiana scoffed softly. "Now Roberta, do not dare dissemble. You are quite as accomplished as I am."

So it was that the party moved to the music room after they had finished dining, the gentlemen and Mrs. Annesley to listen to the other ladies playing and singing. Darcy felt his own tension at last drain away as he listened to his sister's dulcet tones, and he began to hope that all truly would be well in the end.

That is, it certainly would be as soon as he'd caught the blackguard who'd turned Georgiana's life upside down with his cruelty.

His thoughts drifted toward Elizabeth, and he imagined the moment of introduction between his sister and the woman he was growing to care for. Georgiana would be shy at first, he was certain of that, but Elizabeth's pert opinions and quick wit, her warm, welcoming smile—all would surely set his sister at ease within moments. That was Elizabeth's way. She was such a carefree individual, so open and artless, that others were naturally fascinated by her. He certainly had been, almost from the very first moment. How it could be so he was at a loss to understand, but Darcy had given up trying to figure it out. He would simply be thankful for the blessing of having her in his life.

His thoughts were interrupted when Georgiana broke off mid-sentence and cried out sharply. Her hands went to her stomach.

"Oh, my god! I think—I think—!"

Lady Fairley was immediately on her feet. "Come, my dear. We must get you to your chamber. Roy, send a footman for the midwife. Tell him to make haste. Mrs. Annesley, go to her room and make it ready."

The companion nodded silently and ran out, and the laird ran for the bell-pull as Darcy rushed to his sister's side. "Dearest, let me help you to your room."

Georgiana only nodded, for her features were contorted, and she groaned as she stood from the piano bench. "Oh, this *hurts…*"

"How long have you been feeling the pain, Georgie?" asked Lady Fairley.

"Not…long," she replied. "My back has been hurting since last night, but I did not think anything of it, for it has ached so often of late. This is different—it's all around the front now, as well."

They encountered the housekeeper in the hall; the lady was ordered by her master to gather towels and bring water. She hurried off to obey the command immediately, and by the time Darcy and Lady Fairley had gotten Georgiana to her room, Mrs. Annesley, the housekeeper, and a maid were rushing about to get everything in order that the midwife would need.

"All right now, Mr. Darcy. Mr. Wickham," said Lady Fairley, the latter having followed them helplessly through the house. "The two of you can now join my husband and Mr. Knightley in waitin'."

"Is there nothing we can do to aid her?" asked Wickham.

Lady Fairley shook her head. "Beyond prayin' for a quick delivery and speedy recovery, no. Birthin' is not a man's province, sir."

Darcy and Wickham, both reluctant to leave, nonetheless turned away as she began to close the door between them. Fitzroy Leslie appeared at the end of the hall and immediately invited them to join him for a drink in the library.

"You both look as though you might need it."

"As this is her first child, it is like to be a long wait," said Knightley as he entered the room. "The midwife has told us it is common for a first birth to take many hours, even a day or more."

"Good God!" cried Wickham. "Poor Georgie will be exhausted!"

Fairley passed a drink to him, then to Darcy. "Then let us do as my wife suggests. Let us drink to a quick, safe delivery and a speedy recovery for our girl."

"Do you trust this midwife to keep Georgie's secret as much as you do Mrs. Annesley?" Darcy asked Knightley.

Knightley nodded. "I do. She's Mrs. Annesley's sister by marriage."

"Mother of the Martin boy you spoke of?"

"The very same."

"Well then," said Darcy, before tossing back the amber liquid in his glass. "Nothing to be done now but wait."

It was an agonizing wait. All four of the men paced, one at a time or all at once. Each would start and grimace in sympathy each time they heard Georgiana cry out. All but Knightley—who was much calmer than the others, due in part to his being the oldest of all of them—had hair in disarray from running their hands through it many times. Mrs. Annesley was made into a messenger, coming to them in the library and then the small dining parlor every few hours to deliver an update on Georgiana's progress. There had not been much at first, and as the hours stretched on, each man privately despaired that there would be some great difficulty. The wait for a positive report was nigh unbearable.

It was a full six and thirty hours from the time her waters had broken before at last they received the joyful news that Georgiana was safely delivered of a girl.

"We…we have a niece, Darcy," said Wickham with a tired smile.

Darcy nodded, relief flooding through him that his sister's ordeal was at last ended, at least in part, before he turned to Laird Fairley and held out his hand. "Congratulations on the birth of your daughter."

Fairley's expression was a mixture of joy, relief, and solemnity. He took Darcy's hand firmly. "I thank you, sir. And I give you my word of honor that Roberta and I will love her and care for her as if she truly were our own. The child will want for nothin'."

"I shall hold you to that promise," Darcy returned.

Half an hour later, the library door opened to admit Lady Fairley. In her arms she carried a swaddled bundle.

"Gentlemen, may I introduce to you Miss Darciana Joy Leslie, Maid of Glenfairley."

Fitzroy was immediately at her side and smiling down at the little pink face that peeked out of the lilac-colored blanket. "*Tha i brèagha mar a màthraichean,*" he said.

"What did you just say?" asked Wickham.

"You intend to call your daughter Darciana?" said Darcy.

The Fairleys looked to them. To Wickham, the laird replied that he had said the baby was beautiful, like her mothers. To Darcy, his lady answered,

"It has always been our intention to honor the young lady whose sacrifice has given us our hearts' greatest desire, Mr. Darcy. Had the babe been male, we would have called him George."

"Indeed," added her husband. "'Twas my wife who thought to

combine your family name with your sister's Christian name in the manner it is, and call a girl child Darciana. It honors your sister while makin' the name the child's own, though if you strongly object, we will certainly choose another."

"No, not at all," said Darcy then. He offered a smile. "Forgive me, I was only startled by the choice. I do not object to it at all, and am quite certain that my sister will be greatly flattered, if she does not yet know of it."

Lady Fairley looked up at her husband with a wide smile and teary eyes. He returned her smile and leaned to place a soft kiss to her temple. "I think, now, my friends and I shall be able to eat and take some rest."

"Speaking of rest, how does Georgiana get on, Lady Fairley?" asked Darcy.

"As you can imagine, she was well exhausted when at last the babe had come," she replied. "Georgie was fast asleep when I left her, with Mrs. Annesley and Mrs. Martin still in attendance."

"And there were no complications other than the time it took for the child to come?" Darcy pressed.

Lady Fairley smiled. "None at all. Her youth and vitality have served her well, sir."

Wickham placed a hand upon his shoulder. "I think you can relax now, Will. Georgie is well looked after, I am sure."

"I know, but you can imagine my worry after all these months," Darcy replied. "Even young mothers have been known to succumb to blood loss and childbed fever."

"Mrs. Martin will remain for a time to be sure she does not develop a fever, but she believes the chances of it occurrin' to be low, and remarked a number of times that the amount of blood lost was to be expected. Georgiana really did very well, Mr. Darcy," Lady Fairley assured him.

Darcy drew a breath and released it slowly, willing the tension to leave him. Offering a nod to the Fairleys, he then remarked that he would go and refresh himself. Knowing that the new parents would wish to spend the next few hours bonding with Darciana as much as they were able, he requested a tray be sent to his room, saying he would eat his supper there. Wickham said much the same, though neither was awake when the maids came to their doors with the food, each having at last fallen asleep in a chair.

Chapter Twenty-Five

Friday, 14 December 1798

The sudden opening of her chamber door startled Elizabeth enough that she yelped softly.

"Kitty!" she cried on reflex.

Her younger sister giggled and bounced on her feet, much as she had been wont to do before Mr. Bingley's interest had at last led her to curb her behavior. "Sorry, Lizzy, but you won't believe who's come to dinner with Charles."

Elizabeth smiled. Kitty—or Cate, as she now liked to be called, as it was "more mature than Kitty"—had been granted permission to address her suitor by his Christian name, and she enjoyed that honor as much as Elizabeth did with Mr. Darcy. Though, like her, Cate only did so when alone with him, which of course was not more often than appropriate, or when speaking privately with her sisters.

Well, all her sisters except for Lydia, whose behavior had grown more sullen and moody in the days since Mr. Bennet had all but declared her as no longer out. She was still not allowed to leave the house unless with a member of the family, and the first time she had snuck out had found her locked in her room the next day. She defied this restriction by climbing out of her window, and the observation of her escape by a tenant arriving to speak with Mr. Bennet had led to her bedchamber being relocated to the nursery on the second floor. There the window was too small even for her to fit through, and was too high off the ground for the single bed sheet and comforter she was given to reach.

Lydia had thrown her worst tantrum to date upon the discovery that she was to move to the nursery, but Mr. Bennet had escorted her there himself and put her inside with the declaration, "If you choose to act like a child, you shall be treated as one. When you decide to begin behaving as the young lady you claim yourself to be, I will consider amending the arrangements."

When that had happened, Elizabeth's curiosity had won out over decorum, and an hour after he had shewn his youngest daughter her new accommodations, his favorite had visited him in his book room to ask the question that had been plaguing her for the better part of three weeks.

"Papa, forgive me if I am too forward in asking, but I cannot help doing so," she'd begun. "I should like very much to know what has brought on this … this change in you. Toward all of us, but toward Lydia especially."

Her father had sighed, taken a sip of his port, and gazed at her with a weary, almost defeated expression. "As you may have surmised, my dear Lizzy, my discussions with the Earl of Sotheby have borne more fruit than improvements on the estate."

She moved to sit in the chair before his desk. "May I ask what he said to you that convinced you it was time to take a firmer hand with my sister?"

Mr. Bennet had studied her a moment, then said, "What I am about to tell you must not leave this room, as it was told to me in confidence." She nodded her agreement, then he had continued with, "Lord Sotheby, before he was made aware of his lofty connections, had a ward. Still does, I suppose—I daresay such a man as he would not cast her off on being given a title… In any case, this young lady—who was left in his charge little more than a decade past—found herself charmed last summer by a young man who made promises to her he had no intention of keeping. She was a distraction for him, a mere plaything with which he sought to amuse himself. Sometime after he left her, she discovered herself to be in a delicate condition."

Elizabeth had gasped, a hand raising to her lips as she said softly, "Oh the poor girl."

"Girl indeed," replied Mr. Bennet. "She was but fifteen at the time, the age your sister is now. And having observed in our Lydia much the same character as his ward before her ill-usage, when we removed to the library at Netherfield the day we dined there after church, His Lordship took advantage of the opportunity to confide in me and caution me. He recommended I not allow Lydia the freedom which he had so erroneously given to his ward, as their similarities had given rise to the fear that she would fall into the same ruin as the young lady."

Silence had fallen for the space of three or four heartbeats before Mr. Bennet had continued. "I was, at first, incensed that an outsider would dare to presume he could tell me how to govern my own children. But hindsight, as they say, gives the clearest vision. I remember watching her closely, and reflecting on her past behavior. I saw all the markers Lord Sotheby told me he had seen which were indicative of her being too forward, the inappropriateness of your mother encouraging such behavior. And I thought about that unfortunate girl, who had already so few chances of making a decent match before her fall into disgrace, and of my own girls who were in much the same position. I thought of how my being unable to give you anything meant you had only your pretty smiles and your personalities to recommend you. I thought of how one wrong misstep by my wildest child could ruin the lot of you."

He had looked to her then with an expression so heartbreaking that Elizabeth had been hard-pressed not to rise and go to him; she had a feeling, however, that comfort was the last thing her father desired in that moment, so she kept to her chair.

"I am sorry, my dearest Lizzy, that I have not been a better father. Of course, you and Jane have somehow turned out remarkably well in spite of the failures of myself and your mother. And through the two of you, both Mary and Kitty have at last begun to show some improvement. If only you had the power to do so well with Lydia."

"I wish that also, Papa," Elizabeth told him softly. "Regrettably, she is still much too recalcitrant for our advice to be heeded."

"Indeed—which is why I have decided to do with her now what I should have done from the beginning. I only hope my efforts do not result in yet another failure."

"Lizzy?"

Elizabeth blinked, startled out of her reverie by her younger sister. "Forgive me, Cate, I was just thinking about Lydia."

Cate frowned. "Lydia? I come here to tell you that Mr. Bingley has brought someone with him to dinner, and you're thinking of *her*?"

"Now, Cate, do not be unkind," admonished Elizabeth as she stood from her dressing table. "Had it not been for the impetus of Mr.

Bingley's interest in you, you might well be suffering the same restrictions as our sister."

"I suppose you are right. Oh, she was mightily angry that Papa said she could not come to dinner this evening," Cate observed soberly. Then she brightened. "Anyway, Lizzy, do you not want to know who has come with Mr. Bingley?"

Elizabeth scoffed. "I daresay Miss Bingley has not returned to her brother's house, for it would not excite you so and I am sure we would have heard of it by now in any case."

"Quite so, Lizzy, but do be serious. Shall I tell you who it is, or shall you be surprised?"

"Surprised," she declared instantly. "After all, dearest, will you not receive more enjoyment from my setting eyes on this person than your merely telling me his or her name?"

Cate grinned. "You have a point. Come, they are waiting in the drawing room."

With a shake of her head, Elizabeth followed her sister down to the drawing room, where she stopped in the doorway and just prevented a gasp of surprise escaping her lips at the sight that greeted her there.

"Mr. Darcy!" she exclaimed softly as the gentleman and Mr. Bingley stood.

He crossed the room to meet her, reached for her hand, and touched his lips ever so briefly to the back of it. "Miss Elizabeth."

"What are you doing here? I thought you were to remain in Surry with your sister another three weeks, at least?" Elizabeth asked him.

"I'm sure you recall my promising to try and come for a visit," he replied.

Bingley grinned as Darcy tucked her hand into his elbow and led her into the room. "He prevaricates, Miss Elizabeth—'twas Miss Darcy who encouraged him to make the journey. What was it you said she told you, Darcy? 'Go, and stop smothering me with your concern', was it not?"

Elizabeth's family twittered in amusement. She looked to her escort and said, "Smothering her with your concern, were you?"

He raised an eyebrow. "An exaggeration, surely."

"And Mr. Wickham—does he stay with her?"

Darcy nodded. "He does. As I mentioned in my letters, she is pleased to be reconnecting with an old friend."

That was not all that was mentioned in the two letters she had received since his departure a fortnight past. Elizabeth knew that Miss Darcy had born a daughter she feared to love, that the parents who were to raise the child were tempering their joy for her sake, and that both he and Mr. Wickham—seeing her so distressed—were more determined than ever to hunt down the villain who had caused their sister so much pain.

But those were topics not meant to be discussed before her family.

Dinner was announced then, and as soon as the first course was served, Mrs. Bennet asked Darcy how long he was staying.

"I shall return to my sister on Monday," he replied.

"Oh, but you cannot go back so soon! I am sure if your sister is well enough for you to leave her after a fortnight, she can do without you more than two days," said Mrs. Bennet dismissively. "Do say you'll stay longer with us in Hertfordshire. I am sure Lizzy wishes you to stay longer, do you not Lizzy?"

Heat crept up her neck, and Elizabeth was sure her face was turning crimson. "Mamma, please."

"Come, come, now Lizzy," said her mother. "A man can hardly court a young lady if he is not in the same county."

Darcy reached over and gave her hand a reassuring pat; the smile with which he favored Elizabeth at the same moment cooled her embarrassment a degree or two, then he turned to Mrs. Bennet and said, "I agree that proper courtship can hardly be conducted when we are so far apart, ma'am, but Miss Elizabeth and I are in correspondence, with the permission of her good father, and I fully intend to join her and her sisters in Town once my own sister is cleared to travel by her physician. She is much improved, of course, which is why I took this opportunity of paying a visit to Miss Elizabeth in person. But my sister's constitution is still delicate, and it is recommended she remain in the country a while longer."

"I am sure your sister's physician is right, of course," added Elizabeth, "as sure as I am that my mother would agree country air is the finest remedy of all for restoring health."

"Oh, indeed it is, Lizzy! It is unfortunate that Miss Darcy fell ill while visiting with her relations in Surrey—had she been able to come to Netherfield with Mr. Darcy and fallen ill, he could very well tend her here and not have to be away from you for so long."

Cate brought up Mary's impending marriage to Mr. Collins, which took up her mother's attention as she began to talk of wedding clothes and dishes she planned to serve at the breakfast. Elizabeth smiled across the table at her sister and mouthed "Thank you" to her, at which Cate winked and joined in the conversation about the fabrics chosen for Mary's wedding gown.

Turning to Darcy, she then said softly, "I apologize for my mother's insisting you should stay."

"Do not make yourself uneasy, I was not offended," said Darcy. When she lifted her eyebrow he laughed and said, "Truly, I am not. I daresay Mrs. Bennet only fears that my affection for you will fade the more time I spend away from you."

Elizabeth scoffed over top of her wine glass. "If anyone should fear that, I think it should be me." Then she smiled and added, "But as we write to one another in your absence, I do not."

Mr. Darcy smiled then and they spent a few moments concentrating on their food. After a time he leaned close and whispered, "Forgive my impertinence in asking, but I notice Miss Lydia is not in attendance at table this evening."

"My father," Elizabeth returned, "has recently had his eyes opened as to the folly of his ignoring and indulging Lydia's improper conduct. She is no longer allowed to take leave of the house unless one or more of the family is with her at all times. She protested this restriction of her freedom by multiple attempts to escape confinement to her room, and thus has been relegated to the nursery."

His eyes widened in surprise, though he quickly schooled his expression. "Mr. Bennet has gone so far?"

"Indeed, sir. My sister would have been allowed to join us tonight had she done as my father instructed, which was to show true contrition for her behavior and a willingness to follow the new rules he has set down for her. As is evidenced by her absence, she refused to comply."

Darcy shook his head, then said, "I notice also that your mother is less...exuberant, as well. When she spoke earlier about my remaining in the country, her voice was not so high-pitched as I remember."

"Mamma has also been threatened with much the same restrictions as my sister. I am sure you can imagine the humiliation my mother would feel to not only have to explain her daughter's absence from society but also her own, when she was allowed to rejoin it."

"Indeed. I pray your father's renewed sense of purpose bears fruit, and that harmony is restored to Longbourn," Darcy told her.

She looked to him with a smile. "As do I, Mr. Darcy."

As the weather promised to be cool but fair on the morrow, they arranged to walk to Oakham Mount together, and because there was another assembly in Meryton scheduled for the evening, the Netherfield party were invited to meet them there. That evening, the dancing and laughing and conversation left Elizabeth in such high spirits that even knowing her William was to leave early Monday morning did not disturb her as much as his departure for London had a few weeks ago. His letters and personal assurances that his attachment to her only grew had helped to build her faith in their connection. Elizabeth now hoped only for Miss Darcy's continued recovery, and to see them in London as soon as she could be conveyed there by her brothers.

Saturday, 22 December 1798

The arrival of the Gardiners at Longbourn had been greatly anticipated by all their nieces, for various reasons. While the whole of the family looked forward to the company of their relations and that of their four children for the Christmas holiday, the girls each had cause to further celebrate their coming. Jane and Cate were eager to talk of London and all its diversions (and the latter to share her joy at being courted with her aunt), Mary wished to speak of the expectations of a wife with a more sensible woman than her mother, and Lydia hoped to find in her aunt an ally who would advocate for her joining her sisters in Town.

Elizabeth, though like Jane and Cate looked forward to talking of fashions and parties and events to be attended, had long been more intrigued with her aunt's reference to their uncle having a matter he wished to discuss with them. It must be something quite serious for her aunt to not simply tell her in her letter, or for her uncle to not write of it himself.

When at last the Gardiner carriage drew up to the house, she eagerly joined her parents and sisters in welcoming her favorite aunt and uncle, and sharing kisses and hugs with her young cousins. Annabel, the eldest of her aunt's two daughters, had recently begun to wear her hair up, a step towards showing herself to be a young lady instead of just a girl.

"Oh, Aunt Gardiner, I am so desperately in need of your help!" cried Lydia as she pushed her way through the children. "Papa says I shall not be allowed to join my sisters in London, and I know I absolutely *must* go, for surely I will have many beaux there—one of them is bound to make me an offer!"

"You certainly do not waste any time, Lydia," Elizabeth murmured. "Our aunt and uncle have not even had a chance to remove their coats."

"Oh, hush, Lizzy!" Lydia snapped. "You are already going to London!"

"And you are not," said Mr. Bennet. When she stomped her foot and began to pout, he added, "Young lady, we have discussed the matter at length. You will remain here at Longbourn while your sisters go to Town. No amount of pleading on your part will alter my decision, as you well know, so you had best cease importuning your aunt that she may come into the house and refresh herself."

"But Papa, it's not fair! When Mary is gone to Kent with Mr. Collins I shall be all alone in the house!"

"Perhaps, then, you should take the time to learn some useful skill or other. Come Edward, Madelene, children. Come inside and we shall have tea."

Elizabeth fought not to roll her eyes as Lydia growled in a most unladylike fashion, and she was hard pressed not to pinch her sister's arm as she stared daggers at their father's back when he turned and began to lead the way into the house. She had been pleading to go, fruitlessly, from the day Aunt Gardiner's letter had arrived. Much to Elizabeth's surprise—and her pleasure—Mr. Bennet had indeed held his ground and not given in. Mrs. Bennet had at first argued in favor of Lydia's going to London alongside her daughter, but she had seen much sooner that he would not relent and had given up the fight.

Lydia hid away in her room, refusing to come down for tea, and so the afternoon was passed in relative peace, save for the noise generated by the younger children. Their excitability soon set off Mrs. Bennet's nerves, and as soon as could politely be done, she retired to her chambers to wile away the hours until dinner. The little Gardiners were then shuffled off to the nursery, and Elizabeth was sure that whatever news her uncle had waited these last weeks to impart would soon be learnt.

Mr. Bennet rose and stated he would be in his library, but was surprised when Mr. Gardiner asked that he remain for a time. "It is best," said he, "that you should hear of this direct, Thomas. It has been kept from you long enough."

"What has been kept from me, Edward?" Mr. Bennet asked as he took his seat again.

Mr. Gardiner looked to his wife, who gave a nod. "First, I must share with Mary and Catherine the secret of my third sister."

Mary and Cate looked to one another. "Third sister? Whatever do you mean, Uncle?" asked the former.

He quickly explained the circumstances with which Jane and Elizabeth were already familiar: A very wealthy gentleman, eight and twenty years before, had been forced to stay in Meryton for a time after a carriage accident in which he had broken a leg. His having a great fortune was soon passed around town, and every eligible young lady was put forward by her mother in the hope of receiving an offer. Jane Gardiner, as their mother was then known, had quickly become enamored of Gerald Jennings in spite of still being but sixteen, for he was considered a very handsome fellow, but *he* soon revealed an attachment to her sister, Joanna. The two had always been in competition—much as Cate and Lydia, said Mr. Gardiner—and so jealous and resentful had Jane become that her older sister was chosen over her that soon after Joanna's marriage, she declared she had no sister by that name.

"Do you really mean to say that we have another aunt, who is extremely wealthy?" asked a bewildered Cate.

"Indeed," said Elizabeth. "We have also two cousins, named Mary and Charlotte. Their husbands are Sir John Middleton and Thomas Palmer, Esquire, respectively; Sir John and Lady Middleton have four children and Mr. and Mrs. Palmer have recently borne a son. Our new friends Lady Sotheby and Miss Dashwood are intimately acquainted with our Aunt Jennings and her children, for Sir John is a cousin of their mother."

"You know about this aunt of ours, Lizzy?" observed Mary. "How come Cate and I are just now being told?"

"I shall be entirely honest with you, dear Mary," said Mr. Gardiner. "Until recently, neither you nor Cate were considered sensible enough to be informed. I am sorry for it, but I will not dissemble that we did not believe you capable of keeping the information to yourselves."

"You see, my sisters," spoke up Jane, "Mamma flies into *such* a fit of temper if she is even mentioned. If she should discover you know of Aunt Jennings, she will be terribly angry."

The two looked at one another again. "And we have only recently begun to improve ourselves, thereby showing our greater intelligence and reliability," said Mary softly.

Mrs. Gardiner reached for her hand. "My dear, please do not be cross with us. We meant only to keep the peace in the family, and your father was in agreement when we spoke to him of the situation years ago. Had we told you of your aunt sooner, you might have been inclined to share the knowledge with Lydia, who would surely have asked your mother about her, or you might have slipped and spoken of her before your mother yourselves."

"And what of our Aunt and Uncle Philips?" asked Cate then.

"Agnes is the eldest of us all," said Mr. Gardiner. "Joanna was born next, then your mother—there is but fourteen months between them—and myself last. Mrs. Phillips is, strangely enough, more like your mother than Jo ever was, and was pressed upon by her to cut our sister out of her life as well. They have neither of them spoken to Joanna in near thirty years."

There was silence for a moment, and then Mary inquired, "Why do you tell us now? I agree that both Cate and myself are much improved in our manners, for which we know you are all grateful, but what besides that prompts you to speak of this third sister, now in particular?"

"Well, you, for one thing, dearest," said Mrs. Gardiner. "You are soon to be married, and Cate and Elizabeth are being courted by two fine young gentlemen, so we are told. Your uncle and I decided it was time to reveal that your Aunt Jennings and our dear late brother have provided for you."

This must be the reason her uncle wished to speak to them, Elizabeth mused, for it was the first she had heard of it. "Provide for us how, Aunt?"

"Indeed, I should like to know the answer to that myself," said her father.

Mr. Gardiner drew a breath. "Thomas, I beg you would forgive Gerald and Joanna, for they knew it would be a blow to your pride, brother. But my sister grew certain not long after Mary came into the world, knowing Jane as she did and you as well as I was able to educate her, that it was unlikely you would be able to provide for your three girls as well as she and Gerald had provided for their two. She convinced our brother to make an investment intended for your daughters upon the occasion of their marriage. I have had the management of it since Gerald left us ten years ago—that's when I found out about it myself."

Elizabeth looked to her father. His expression was grim, and she suspected he was ashamed of the fault and neglect of his daughters' future that had been laid bare before them.

"Just how much," he started to say, "am I indebted to my late brother for doing what I ought to have done?"

Mr. Gardiner cleared his throat. "At present, each of the girls will have ten thousand pounds."

Cate gasped loudly as Mary's jaw dropped. Elizabeth's eyes widened in shock as Jane leaned on her shoulder.

"Oh my goodness… I feel faint," she said, her hand gripping Elizabeth's tightly.

"Are you quite serious, Uncle?" asked Elizabeth. "How could there possibly be enough money that we should each of us have so much?"

"Your uncle was *very* generous with his investment in the four percents," said Mr. Gardiner. "The interest generated over the last nineteen years has nearly doubled that amount."

Elizabeth frowned. "Sir, if it has only 'nearly' doubled the amount, how then is there ten for each of us?"

Mr. and Mrs. Gardiner shared a smile. "My business has been very profitable over the years, Lizzy—enough that I have been able to contribute occasionally to your account as well as provide for my own daughters. The account is, I admit, a little shy of fifty thousand, but even if we were to pay out forty thousand today, by the time Lydia is of age to marry there is sure to be ten thousand for her as well."

"Therefore, my dear niece, you need not be concerned that any of your sisters will be slighted," added her aunt with a smile.

Cate turned to Elizabeth suddenly and grabbed her hand. "Oh, Lizzy, do you not understand what this means? Mr. Bingley and Mr. Darcy shall not now have reason to think us unworthy of them!"

"Catherine," spoke up Mr. Bennet, drawing the eyes of all. Elizabeth looked to find a solemn expression upon his countenance as he stood and walked over to them. He held out a hand to Cate and waited until she put her free hand in his before he spoke again.

"My dear child, you were *never* unworthy of Mr. Bingley—you had only to see your worth for yourself," he said. "Your sisters have helped you in that regard, where your mother and I failed to. For that I am sorry, as I am that it is your late uncle's doing that you have any dowry at all. Providing you a means of being able to marry well was *my* responsibility, and I ignored it in favor of… Well, it does not matter. A gentleman smarter than myself made me see the error of my ways, and I shall no longer be an idle father. Lydia is feeling the brunt of it, as you have seen, though I do hope the four of you do not resent too much that I did not begin to mend my ways much sooner."

Elizabeth, aware of who and why her father had chosen to amend his ways, stood and took his other hand. "Papa, I feel confident in speaking for all of us when I say that we shall none of us resent your indifference so long as you remain committed to your cause. We are none of us here unaware of the fact that Lydia requires the greatest amount of correction."

Cate gave his hand a squeeze. "I used to follow her everywhere and do everything she did because I thought that was the only way anyone would notice me, what with Jane being the prettiest, Lizzy the witty one, Mary the accomplished one, and Lydia Mamma's own favorite. Deep down I have always desired to be noticed for *myself*, and these last few weeks, with my sisters' assistance, I believe that I have. People noticed me before, but now they notice me not because I am Lydia's sister, but because I am Catherine Bennet, a well-mannered young lady. Which I always ought to have been, I know, but it was only being shown what I stood to lose that finally I was able to see the error of my ways. I think we began to correct our mistakes about the same time, Papa, and in that way, we have worked to better ourselves together."

"Upon my word," said Mr. Bennet as he looked at his daughters. "How remarkably blessed I am, though I've done little to deserve it."

Chapter Twenty-Six

Mr. Darcy came again to Hertfordshire on the evening of Boxing Day.

Elizabeth had been made aware of the intended visit ahead of time by letter, and so was not surprised to find him at Netherfield when her family appeared there for dinner. They welcomed each other as openly and affectionately as did Bingley and Cate, and with such a large party as was there—Colonel and Mrs. Forster, the Phillipses, the Lucases, and a few other families with whom Bingley had made his acquaintance—there were few opportunities for private conversation. She suggested that they take their "traditional" morning walk to Oakham Mount the next morning and he agreed.

"Will you not tire yourself, though, given your sister is to be married tomorrow?" he asked her.

Elizabeth shook her head and smiled, saying that she was not the least concerned she would be fatigued too early. "After all," she said, "we are all to travel into London after the wedding breakfast, so if I am tired then, I can easily get some rest in the carriage."

Darcy laughed and conceded the point, and so it was again agreed that they should meet as planned. Elizabeth rose before dawn and made it to the outlook nearly a quarter of an hour earlier than Darcy arrived. When he did, her smile was wide and her gaze curious, for he carried with him a small package wrapped in brown paper and tied with a ribbon. When they had greeted each other with a brief kiss and a squeeze of each other's hand, he offered it to her.

"Merry Christmas, Elizabeth."

"A Christmas gift? Oh, William, you shouldn't have," she said, fighting the pricking of tears behind her eyes. "Sir, I have nothing to give to you in return—oh, this is terrible! I should have thought to get you something, but this last week has been so full of preparing for Christmas and Boxing Day and Mary's wedding—"

Elizabeth fell silent when he lifted a finger to her lips. "My dear, your pleasure in the receiving of this gift is all the present I need. Now, open it."

"If you insist, sir," she replied cheekily as she untied the blue satin ribbon. Handing that over to him, she unwrapped the paper from around what turned out to be a prettily decorated wooden box; there were trees and wildflowers painted on the top. "Oh, this is lovely."

Darcy chuckled. "The box, while also a gift, is not from me. It is from Georgiana, in gratitude for the kindness of your letters to her. My gift is inside it."

She recalled having suggested writing a letter to his sister when last he had visited. Miss Darcy's first reply had been fairly short, thanking her for her kindness and noting that she continued to improve in health and spirits, and expressed her wish that she might soon be able to meet her in person. Elizabeth had written again on receiving that letter, and spoke of her sister's upcoming marriage, of the gowns she and her sisters had commissioned especially for the day, and mentioned their shared interest in books.

Lifting the lid of the box, she saw a slightly weathered book. "*Evelina*!" she cried softly, then lifted it to find the other two volumes. "You have purchased me my own copy—how very thoughtful of you."

Darcy smiled. "Look at the title page."

Confused as to why he would suggest it she nevertheless complied, and on seeing what was printed there, gasped again and lifted eyes widened by surprise. "You found a first edition copy? However did you manage it?"

"London is crawling with my spies," he replied with a wide grin. "Though in truth, I employed the services of my cousin Marianne and my Aunt Frances. They were quite delighted to undertake so 'romantic' a mission on my behalf."

He rolled his eyes as he said 'romantic', but the smile he wore told her his true feelings. Elizabeth raised on her toes and kissed his cheek. "Thank you so very much, William. I am delighted you were so *romantically* thoughtful."

She then thumbed through the first couple of pages before an idea then came to her, and in truth she could scarcely believe she had not mentioned the matter before. "Oh, I have just realized that I *do* have something of a gift for you—ten thousand of them, in fact."

Darcy's brow furrowed in curiosity. "Indeed? And pray, what could you possibly have ten thousand of that would make a suitable gift for a gentleman?"

Elizabeth laughed. "Pounds. Oh, not on my person, certainly, given how fit I am in body. They are in an account at a bank in London. You no longer need fear too much censure for choosing a young lady of the country, Mr. Darcy, should we ever get serious about that whole marriage business."

Surprise widened his eyes as her own had been a moment ago. "You have a dowry?"

She nodded. "My uncle Mr. Gardiner informed my sisters and I the day his family arrived to celebrate Christmas with us—save Lydia, of course. She is not yet aware we have another aunt, as she is not responsible enough to not speak of the matter within our mother's hearing. There is, apparently, quite enough for each of us to have ten thousand pounds upon the occasion of our marriage. This news brought much relief to my sisters especially, and I daresay no small amount of shame to my father, who learned that it is his late brother-in-law and the sister by marriage he is never allowed to speak of to whom he owes this debt."

Elizabeth cocked her head then. "I do believe I spoke to you of her, my Aunt Jennings?" The shake of his head indicated he recalled no such conversation. "Surely I did…"

Darcy frowned again. "Wait, did you say Jennings?" At her nod, he continued with "I recall now that your sister Jane once mentioned the name to Bingley—she is perhaps the relation that your father spoke of to me as perhaps doing something for you and your sisters, but which he could not count on."

"In any case, sir," said Elizabeth, "it would seem that despite being cut out of my mother's life, my Aunt Jennings took pity on her sister's children when Jane, myself, and Mary were still very young, for she knew my father's inclinations in combination with my mother's would lead to there being little to nothing for us when we were of age to wed. She thus managed to convince her husband to invest a very large sum in the four percents, despite their having two daughters of their own to be concerned for, that there would be some money for the marriages of his nieces. My Uncle Gardiner said he also contributed to the fund when he could."

She paused again and drew a breath. "So, I am not a penniless country chit after all. I am sorry to tell you, but it is so. Pray, do not fear that having a fortune will go to my head, for I was perfectly content being poor. Well, perhaps not perfectly, but as you know I was content."

Darcy laughed softly and drew her to him. "My dear Elizabeth, I am pleased for you and your sisters, though as you well know, madam, I overcame the prejudice of your having no dowry some time ago."

Standing back again, he added, "In fact, as I said to Bingley one day, I came to believe there to be greater reward in the increase of the prospects of your sisters through their association with me than I believed there to be any degradation of my standing in society by my association with you."

Elizabeth lifted an eyebrow. "How magnanimous of you, sir."

"I do not speak in jest, Elizabeth, nor from ego," said Darcy. "I meant only to remark on the good that would come of our connection."

Drawing a breath, she smiled and said, "I know you do. And grateful we would all have been for whatever benefit your standing and connections would have given us. Now, with this most generous gift from my secret aunt and her husband, our connection can only raise us higher than what we might have achieved without it."

She looked out over the valley below them then and sighed. "I only hope my sisters are prepared for the scrutiny."

There had been some amount of fear on the part of the bride and her mother, fueled by Mr. Collins' lamentations that his "esteemed patroness" would forbid the match, that his marriage to Mary would not take place after the unexpected visit of Anne de Bourgh. Mr. Bennet assured everyone that though the lady might be incensed by the relationship between Elizabeth and Mr. Darcy, the only person who could actually forbid the parson and his daughter marrying was himself. And as Mary had assured him it was still her wish to marry her cousin, he bid her prospective bridegroom to gird his loins and stand up to Lady Catherine if she should make any attempt to stop the wedding.

An express was received by Mr. Bennet two days following his cousin's departure, the multiple pages enlightening the family to the circumstances which Miss de Bourgh's actions had wrought. His noble patroness was "overcome with great joy" by her daughter's unexpected engagement to one of his "brother parsons from the north" who had served Mr. Darcy for only a few months. According to Collins, Miss de Bourgh and Mr. Ferrars had met upon his taking up the Lambton living while she visited her cousins at Pemberley and had fallen deeply in love, and her visit to them the Saturday past had been only nerves, "as a young lady soon to wed would be sure to feel."

Elizabeth had heard the truth by then, and in private conversation with her sisters (save Lydia, of course) had explained the whole of the sordid affair. They were each of them shocked by Miss de Bourgh's scandalous conduct, though the three did express they had not believed Mr. Collins' assurances that the union between Miss de Bourgh and Mr. Ferrars was a love match. It was Charlotte Lucas who told Elizabeth, when she had confided the business to her, that Darcy's family was now even more connected to that of their friend Lady Sotheby, whose brother was married to Mr. Ferrars' sister.

Mary Bennet and William Collins were wed the day after Boxing Day. The newly married couple were invited to spend their wedding night in London; as the Gardiners and the bride's sisters were also to depart Longbourn following the wedding breakfast and were to go in the same direction, it seemed a natural choice to offer so that Mary and Mr. Collins would not have to make the long journey to Hunsford all in one day. Officially, they were to lodge with the Gardiners—making for quite a crowded house, according to Mrs. Bennet—but in truth they would be spending their first night as husband and wife in the fashionable townhome of Mary's secret aunt. Mrs. Jennings had made the offer through correspondence with Mr. Gardiner, and wishing to lessen the burden as much as they were able, Mary readily accepted. And though she managed Mr. Collins very well, she had decided to wait until they were underway to tell him so, that he would not accidentally let the information slip in front of Mrs. Bennet.

Mr. Bingley and the Hursts were also to make for London that day. As predicted, when he had been informed that his young paramour would be journeying thither to take part in learning the violin with her cousin, he immediately began to implement plans to spend the winter in Town. Mrs. Bennet fully expected to hear of an engagement shortly after the New Year, and was not ashamed to make it known she believed Cate would return to the neighborhood as Mrs. Bingley. Indeed, she had high hopes that Mr. Bingley would introduce Jane to many rich gentlemen and that she, too, would soon be engaged. As for Elizabeth, though her mother's belief that Mr. Darcy would offer for her on his return from Surrey remained high, she did say that if another wealthy gentleman were to take a fancy to her in the interim, she would not be wholly aggrieved if Elizabeth were to accept him, so long as he had a fortune at least comparable to Bingley's.

Elizabeth had only just refrained from rolling her eyes before replying that she had no intention of accepting any offer but that of Mr. Darcy, when and if he chose to make one.

Though it had been two or three years since either Jane or Elizabeth had seen their Aunt Jennings, they were scarcely less eager to meet her again than Mary and Cate were to do for the first time. It was Jane's belief—and her sisters certainly agreed with her—that they owed the lady every attention they could possibly pay, for it was to her and her late husband they owed their small fortunes. The immeasurable generosity of the uncle they had none of them the pleasure of meeting in his lifetime, for he had passed when Jane and Elizabeth were still young, to their minds could never be repaid.

So it was that in the afternoon of the day of Mary's wedding that two carriages, a curricle, and two men on horseback pulled up along the curb outside a large brick home on Berkeley Street. It was painted white with black shutters, and the small front garden was surrounded by a wrought-iron fence. The mistress of that address—a plump, cheerful woman with graying hair and a wide smile—exclaimed her delight as she stepped out of the door with a waving hand.

"Oh, how wonderful, you have made it!" she cried. "At last, at last! My dear Edward and Madelene—oh, and all your wonderful children—we shall be a very merry party indeed! Jane, Elizabeth, my darlings! I have not seen you for too long!"

When she had embraced and kissed the Gardiners and their children, and then Elizabeth and Jane, Mrs. Jennings at last stood back, her eyes on the nieces she had not yet been introduced to. Elizabeth performed the office immediately, presenting her sisters as well as Mr. Collins, Mr. Bingley, and Mr. Darcy. All had been invited by the lady to attend tea, that they and their horses could all get some rest, through her correspondence with Mr. Gardiner. *Indeed, I am so very fond of good company—and if all is as you say, dear brother, they shall all of them be family to us both very soon!* she had written.

To Mr. and Mrs. Hurst the lady had also extended an invitation, but due to Louisa's condition they had declined tea and gone straight on to their home on Harley Street so that she could rest after the long hours of travel.

Shortly after they were all sat down to an early tea, Mrs. Jennings made two announcements: first, that she very much desired to relieve her brother's burden and have *all* the Bennet sisters under her roof for the duration of their stay in Town. Surely, she reasoned, he and his lady could not comfortably host the three grown girls as well as their four children. Though Mr. and Mrs. Gardiner protested that indeed they could, Mrs. Jennings would not be gainsaid. "'Tis always you, and never I, that is blessed with the company of my sister's children! Allow me this time with them, Edward, for goodness knows when I shall have such an opportunity again!"

On applying for the consent of their nieces, Mr. and Mrs. Gardiner smilingly agreed. Elizabeth secretly believed them to feel some relief, for hosting three of them at once would surely have been a strain on their household finances. She knew that her sisters would share in her pleasure at not burdening them so.

The second of Mrs. Jennings' declarations was that she had reserved a box at Covent Garden that evening, where an opera was to be performed. "I invite you all to share it with me—your brother and sister as well, Mr. Bingley," she said cheerfully. "It will be a fine opportunity to see and be seen, and though it is still early days yet, we will get ourselves an idea of who will be in Town for the Season."

When Cate declared she very much wished to go, as she had never been to an opera, Mr. Bingley immediately declared he would be most pleased to escort her, which caused his young lady to blush furiously. He then said that his brother Hurst was likely to decline the invitation, citing the elder gentleman's dislike of operas, but espoused his belief that Mrs. Hurst would join him, and thanked Mrs. Jennings for her enormously generous invitation to them.

Mr. Collins also noted that he had never seen an opera, to which Mary replied her aunt's invitation was thus an opportunity for him to be exposed to more culture and society. "After all, my dear, there are certain to be some there of high rank and great consequence. What stories you will have to share with Lady Catherine on our arrival in Hunsford."

"Oh, indeed, my dear Mary!" he cried. "Her Ladyship will certainly be eager to know if I have had chance to glimpse anyone of such importance as herself."

With so many of their party, including Mr. and Mrs. Gardiner, agreeing to the scheme, Elizabeth and Jane could hardly decline to attend with them, and Darcy said he looked forward to witnessing her enjoyment of the music. The girls' only concern was that they had no formal gowns to wear; they had a number of evening dresses packed in their trunks, but none which were fit to be worn in a grand theatre. To this announcement, Mrs. Gardiner pointed out that the gowns they had worn for the wedding that very morning, which had been packed in their trunks at the last moment, were quite fine enough to be worn at an opera.

"Oh, indeed, Mrs. Gardiner!" exclaimed Bingley. "Why, that green velvet you were wearing, Miss Elizabeth, was striking even in its simplicity—I noticed more than one young man glancing appreciatively in your direction during the breakfast."

The last earned him a scowl from Darcy, but Bingley only grinned and winked at his friend.

"I agree, Lizzy," said Jane. "Your green velvet with that gray cashmere shawl you brought with you will be lovely together."

So it was that the new gowns purchased for their sister's wedding, each of them sewn by the finest dressmakers in Meryton, were chosen for their first London outing. After tea, the Gardiners, Bingley, and Darcy said their farewells and departed. The sisters and Mr. Collins then settled into their rooms for rest or other relaxation until dinner.

Many exclamations of praise were paid to each niece for their loveliness by Mrs. Jennings when they presented themselves in their wedding finery later that evening, and when Cate mentioned that their mother had helped them choose the fabrics and styles, their aunt lifted a surprised brow.

"Did she now? I am pleased to know she has retained her sense in this matter, if no other," said she with a sniff.

Jane looked to Elizabeth with a pained expression, clearly distressed by the unkind remark, but the latter could only sigh and give a slight shake of her head. It seemed that Mrs. Bennet was not the only one of the sisters whose sensibilities were still wounded by the wide gulf that separated them.

Mr. Darcy, Mr. Bingley, and Mrs. Hurst arrived at the opera house at near the same time as the party from Berkeley Street. Bingley praised Cate's red gown as much as he had that morning, claiming that starlight made her look even more lovely in it. His compliments lead her to blush so deep a shade of scarlet that her cheeks came close to matching her dress.

"I declare, dear Lizzy," whispered Mrs. Jennings as they were ascending the steps into the building, "If those two are not at least engaged by Twelfth Night, I will swallow my own bonnet!"

Elizabeth had laughed heartily, though as she observed Bingley's solicitude of Cate, she could not help but agree that it was increasingly likely that another sister was soon to be engaged.

"You look beautiful, Elizabeth," said Darcy on her other side.

"As if you did not see me in this dress only this morning, sir," she replied.

"Indeed I did, but that does not lessen the veracity of my claim," he rejoined. "In fact, I am inclined to believe as Bingley does—the starlight has somehow enhanced your natural loveliness."

With a blush that no doubt competed with her sister's, Elizabeth only smiled as they made their way into the theatre.

Le nozze di Figaro, the opera they were to see, was a delightful production. Though there was certainly a great deal of people watching—a common occurrence at such public gatherings, where the audience often spent more time socializing than actually watching or listening to what was happening on the stage—Elizabeth nonetheless found herself enjoying the performance. She did not understand the words, not being able to speak Italian, but she could understand the expressions and movements of the singers and so found the story moving. Darcy, however, did know enough of the language to understand what was being said, and quietly interpreted the words of each song for her.

The long intermission between the second and third acts brought a very unexpected surprise to Mrs. Jennings' box. A few minutes after the gentlemen had departed to fetch refreshments for their party, there was a soft knock at the entry. Jane rose to open it, and when the two fashionably dressed ladies, covered in shimmering satin and sparkling jewels, entered with graceful strides, Mrs. Gardiner immediately stood and curtsied.

"Lady Disley, Lady Rowarth! You honor us with your visit!" she said.

Mrs. Jennings, Elizabeth, and the other girls immediately followed her example and curtsied.

The elder of the two visitors smiled. "How delightful! Marianne, I told you it was she. Mrs. Gardiner, how do you do? And Mrs. Jennings, how delightful it is to see you again, as always."

Mrs. Gardiner said she was well, then presented her nieces to the countess and her daughter by marriage. Elizabeth was not remiss to the change in Lady Disley's expression when her name was given, and when they had all been introduced, the countess looked to her with an even more discerning gaze than before.

"So, my dear," she began as she lowered herself into a chair. "You are the young lady who has captured my obstinate nephew Darcy's attention."

Elizabeth sat next to her. "I am, Your Ladyship. Mr. Darcy is here with us also, having traveled with us from Meryton after Mr. and Mrs. Collins' wedding. He is to return to Miss Darcy in Surrey on the morrow."

The countess nodded, then said, "I thought I saw him seated next to you. I have been most eager to meet you, Miss Elizabeth, for you must be very special indeed if William is so willing to forego marriage to a young lady of wealth and rank."

Elizabeth arched an eyebrow. "Whether I am particularly special or not would be the judgment of others, Lady Disley. However, as to fortune my sisters and I are not so very poor as you might have been led to believe. We were recently given to understand that a kind and immeasurably generous relative has left us each ten thousand pounds. You need not be ashamed of me should Mr. Darcy choose to make me an offer."

"Lizzy!" admonished Mrs. Gardiner and Jane at the same time, while Mary and Louisa Hurst gasped. Mrs. Jennings and Cate chuckled softly.

Lady Disley glanced briefly at Lady Rowarth, then looked back to Elizabeth with a lift of her own eyebrow. "You certainly give your opinion very decidedly for so young a person," she said, then her expression relaxed and she smiled. "Truth be told, my dear, I would not be ashamed of finding myself related to you even had you not any dowry, as William did say was your family's situation. I *like* that you speak your mind, though still in such a way as could not be called impolite."

"Impertinent, perhaps," offered Lady Rowarth with a smile at her mother-in-law, "but then I think as you do, ma'am. Our lot could do with more of those who aren't afraid to say exactly what they think."

"You'll certainly get that with Lizzy," muttered Mary.

Elizabeth looked over at her sister and flashed a grin. "Now Mary, you know perfectly well that I *do* know when to hold my tongue," said she. "But not even a countess will frighten me out of defending my character."

"Or suitability to be Darcy's choice," added Lady Rowarth.

"Or that," replied Elizabeth with a grin.

Lady Disley laughed. "I have a very good feeling, young lady, that you and I shall get along quite well indeed. May I ask your plans for tomorrow? I should like you to come to Disley House for tea. Come at one, if you will."

Elizabeth's eyes widened with shock. "I… I did not expect such an honor, my lady. If I may bring my sisters, I should like very much to accept your gracious invitation."

The countess laughed again. "My dear girl, of course your sisters may join you! It would be grievously discourteous of me, would it not, to invite you within their hearing and not include them as well? Mrs. Gardiner, Mrs. Jennings, and you Mrs. Hurst—do say you'll come. We shall be a merry little party of ladies only, and drive my husband to distraction with our giggling and gossiping!"

"You know, I have been in great need of a ladies' day," said Mrs. Jennings. "Ever since my dear friend Marianne's disappointment this past Season, London has not had quite the same charm for me. But we shall make it worthy again, the lot of us!"

"I would say it is unfortunate that Miss Dashwood cannot join us," offered Elizabeth, "had I not a letter from her this morning with such happy news as she told me. La! My dear Aunt Jennings, I cannot believe I forgot until this moment—Lady Sotheby has borne her child. Miss Dashwood's letter said she gave birth to a healthy son late on Christmas Day. The boy is called Nicholas."

"Oh!" cried Mrs. Jennings, clapping her hands together with delight. "I am so happy for Elinor! And the colonel—well, he is an earl now, is he not? I wonder Miss Marianne would write to you and not to me… Well, perhaps I will have a letter on the morrow."

"You are acquainted with my cousin and his wife, Miss Elizabeth?" queried Lady Disley.

Elizabeth nodded. "Indeed, Your Ladyship. My sisters and I had the pleasure of meeting the Earl and Countess of Sotheby in Hertfordshire. Mrs. Hurst's brother, Mr. Bingley, invited them to attend the ball he hosted at his estate there only a month past. I believe he made their acquaintance in March."

Lady Disley and Lady Rowarth shared a look that only Elizabeth could understand. Darcy had told her everything about his sister Georgiana's terrible situation, including Charles Bingley's limited involvement.

The countess then drew a breath. "Well!" said she brightly.

"Though I shall have to wait for official word from my cousin himself, I am absolutely delighted for he and Elinor—she was such a charming young lady when we met her at the Spring Ball in Disley. Did you not think so, Marianne?"

Lady Rowarth nodded. "Indeed, ma'am. So soft spoken and graceful, and such a calming influence on her husband."

"That she was. And oh, I am sure His Grace is there with them, bursting with happiness that the Northam line will continue," added Lady Disley.

"Speaking of husbands," said Mrs. Gardiner with a glance at the box's entryway, "I wonder where mine has got off to? I should have thought he and the other gentlemen would have returned by now with those refreshments."

"And speaking of returning," said Lady Disley as she stood. "Marianne and I better be off if we wish to be back in our box by the time the third act starts. But I just had to come, Mrs. Gardiner, when I saw you across the theatre. I remembered your having mentioned your nieces were to come and stay with you, and had hoped one of these lovely young ladies was the very Miss Elizabeth I had heard so much of."

She held out her hand to Elizabeth, who took it as she rose to her feet. "I really am quite charmed, my dear, and imagine I shall only become more so as we get to know one another."

"You are very kind to say so, my lady," said Elizabeth.

Lady Disley nodded. "Do give my nephew my love, if you will, and if you would not mind terribly giving him a message for me, please tell him I should like him to stop at Disley House before he quits London."

"I should be most happy to convey your message, my lady."

Farewells were then exchanged and Lady Disley gave the address for Disley House before the two visitors departed. Elizabeth could not help staring in wonder after them for a moment before lowing herself back into her seat. Around her there were muted exclamations of surprise from everyone—except her Aunt Jennings, whose excited ejaculations were only an octave or two lower than she imagined her mother's might be.

For sisters who refuse to speak to one another, they share more traits in common than either would ever admit.

"Oh Mary," Jane's voice broke through Elizabeth's reverie. "How I wish you could join us at tea, tomorrow."

"But I can, sister Jane," Mary returned, and the sureness of her tone drew Elizabeth's attention even more. "All that is required is that I inform Mr. Collins we have all of us been invited by the Countess of Disley herself—she is, after all, sister by marriage to his most noble patroness, Lady Catherine de Bourgh."

Elizabeth brightened. "Oh yes, Mary! He is like to *order* you to remain, for you can certainly put off your journey to Hunsford until Saturday."

As Mary nodded her assent, they were all of them drawn to look at Louisa Hurst by her softly uttered, "Thank you, Elizabeth."

A frown creased Elizabeth's brow. "Whatever do you thank me for?" she asked.

Louisa moved to Elizabeth's side and reached for her hand. "For being unapologetically yourself, and for being just the right combination of wit and vivacity to have captured the attention of Mr. Darcy. If you had not, his aunt would not have been curious about you, and I would not be invited to tea with a countess simply by having been here with you."

She turned in her seat and leaned back with a short laugh, a hand raised to her throat. "Oh, upon my word! Caroline will surely burn with envy if she should hear of this!"

"Our wayward sister will burn with envy if she should hear of what, Louisa?" said Mr. Bingley as the four gentlemen of their party at last returned.

Once the refreshments had been passed around—Mr. Gardiner apologized for the long delay, citing "a great many patrons doing just as we were"—Mrs. Gardiner explained that they had missed, by mere minutes, a most illustrious visitor. Darcy glanced across the theatre and lifted a hand in greeting to his aunt and cousin, Elizabeth saw, and she leaned closer to him to convey the lady's message. Mr. Collins's eyes grew wide on hearing the identity of the person who had been there, and when Mary added that all the ladies had been invited to tea on the morrow, his bulging gaze alighted on his new wife in an almost desperate expression.

"My dearest Mary, pray tell me you did not refuse her!" he cried. "The Countess of Disley is the sister of my—of *our*—noble patroness, Lady Catherine de Bourgh! Lady Catherine would be deeply offended by your not attending Her Ladyship, not to mention that Lady Disley herself would be incensed should you decline her extraordinarily kind invitation!"

Mary, clearly feigning a demure attitude, lowered her eyes as she said, "I made no mention of our departing tomorrow, sir. Are you certain we ought not keep to our schedule? Would not Lady Catherine be upset by our arriving later than declared?"

Mr. Collins nearly choked. "My dearest Mary, do be sensible! I have no doubt that Lady Catherine would *insist* you accept the countess's invitation. It was beyond gracious of her to invite any of you, when you are not of her station!"

His wife snatched back the hand he held. "Mr. Collins, how can you be so unjust? We are none of us nobility, to be sure, but neither are we too lowly to be noticed, sir."

He reached for her hand again. "Oh, my dearest Mary, I beg your every pardon! Of course I did not mean anything of the kind. It is just that we are none of us of the first circles, as the Countess of Disley *is*! It is an honor to be singled out by her! I beg you, do not insist we go on to Hunsford tomorrow—to slight Lady Disley by declining her invitation would reflect badly on all your family. You must think of your sisters!"

The theatre then began to darken in preparation for the third act. "My dears," said Mrs. Gardiner then, "perhaps we ought return to this topic at a later time. The opera is about to start again."

Everyone agreed and turned their attention to the stage—everyone, that is, except Mr. Collins, who quietly apologized again to Mary, stating he had no wish to offend his bride on their wedding day … and to continue insisting she accept the invitation to tea.

Elizabeth had been full aware of the eyes on she and Darcy during their entrance to Covent Garden, and was none too surprised that a dizzying number of people came over to speak to him on their way out. Though he introduced her to each, she was pleased that he extricated them from any conversation as soon as could politely be done. At the curb, as they stood by her aunt's carriage, he asked her in a whisper if she cared that he kissed her with so many eyes upon them.

"After all, we part here and I shall not see you again until Georgiana and I are come to Town in a few weeks," he added.

Elizabeth, feeling rather adventurous, flashed an almost wicked grin and replied, "I daresay you *must* kiss me, Mr. Darcy, for I rather believe your friends are expecting such a display."

He scoffed. "I would not put on a play for them when they have just seen an opera. I would kiss you for my benefit, not theirs."

"And for mine as well, I should hope?" she teased.

Darcy smiled. "Indeed," he rejoined, and bent his head to brush his lips across hers, before sighing and handing her into the coach.

"Good evening, Miss Elizabeth. Enjoy your tea tomorrow, and remember that within a month, my sister and I shall join you here."

Elizabeth smiled again. "I will, on both counts, sir. Safe journey to Surrey."

He bowed his head and walked—reluctantly, she was sure—over to join Louisa Hurst at her brother's carriage. Bingley was just lifting his head from giving Cate a kiss on the cheek, and then she was handed in as well.

When they were on their way home again, Cate sat back into the squab with a sigh, likely thinking of having just been kissed in public, then she suddenly sat forward and exclaimed her joy once again at their being invited to tea with a countess.

"But whatever shall we wear?" said Jane. "We none of us have anything fit to be worn in a countess's drawing room!"

Elizabeth glanced at her aunt and the two chuckled. "My dear Jane, since when are you so concerned with fashion?" asked the former.

Jane picked at a fold of her dress. "Since we were invited to tea with a countess, Lizzy."

"My dear Jane," began Mrs. Jennings, "tea is not the opera. Lady Disley may be a countess, but I daresay she will not be offended by your being humbly dressed. Just put on whatever day gown you've brought that's best! We shall all of us go shopping tomorrow and commission each of you some new gowns fit for balls and operas."

The sisters each looked to one another, then Elizabeth said, "Ma'am, whilst I am sure my sisters would agree with me in appreciation for the scheme, we have none of us the funds to commission such a wardrobe."

Mrs. Jennings scoffed and waved a hand dismissively. "Tosh, Elizabeth! It would be my pleasure to purchase a few new gowns for you—yes, for all of you, and the new Mrs. Collins too! No, do *not* argue with me. Consider, my dear, all the years I have been unable to give you any gifts directly."

"But Aunt, our dowries, for which we have you and our departed Uncle Jennings to thank, are surely gift enough," said Jane. "You need not feel you have neglected us in any way."

"Indeed," added Cate. "What you have done for us—giving all of us some chance of a good match—is more than generous when one considers that our mother chooses not to acknowledge you."

"Cate, your mother not wishing to acknowledge me by no

means would excuse my ignoring your existence, and certainly not my doing for you what she and your father either cannot or will not," said Mrs. Jennings. "I have the means, my dear—indeed, your uncle had more than enough to provide amply for his daughters as well as his nieces. Someone had to do something!"

She sighed and glanced out the sideglass. "Do I wish your mother and I were not at odds still? Certainly—it has been near thirty years, after all. So foolish to waste a lifetime in anger! She does not even know she has two nieces, or five great-nieces and -nephews. Jane has missed a great deal of love and laughter, and all because she was incensed that Gerald chose me and not her."

Mrs. Jennings drew another breath, and the lamplight they passed through shewed that she had plastered a smile on her face as she looked back to them. "In any case, my dear nieces, I have more than enough money to spare. I shall not mind at all assisting you dear girls in whatever ways I can to make a good impression, both on the countess and the gentlemen you are sure to meet."

Her usual exuberance soon showed in her countenance, as she added, "Though with Mary now being Mrs. Collins, and you Catherine—and you, Elizabeth—already being courted, we shall only have to introduce our dear Jane to the eligible bachelors we will no doubt be meeting this Season!"

Cate began to giggle and Mrs. Jennings chortled merrily. Elizabeth grinned as well, and Jane—though she could not well see her face—surely blushed at the idea of being introduced to a bevy of eligible bachelors.

Chapter Twenty-Seven

Friday, 28 December 1798

The following morning, after breakfast was done, Mrs. Jennings made good on her word to take all her nieces shopping for new gowns.

Elizabeth, Jane, and Mary delighted in Cate's tempered excitement. She was still exuberant, still chattered almost endlessly of ribbons and fabrics with their aunt, still pored over fashion magazines in the shops, but she did not speak any louder than she ought, did not run about unchecked. The three were not without a little pride beneath their breasts, for Cate's marked improvement in only a month's time and for their own efforts at last bearing some fruit.

Mary, of course—while recognizing the necessity of expanding her wardrobe—did not care to be fussed over. That was one aspect of her personality which had not changed, and likely never would. She preferred gowns of simple cut, and fabrics that were easily cared for, but was at last convinced to have at least two evening gowns made of fine cloth, Elizabeth citing the caveat that should Lady Catherine or her newly married daughter throw a ball, she should have appropriate gowns for the occasion.

Jane's ejaculations regarding the excursion were not so much in words as expressions. Mrs. Jennings more than once directed her eldest niece towards fine fabrics and necklines that would "undoubtedly draw the attention of many an admirer". These words drew a blush to Jane's cheeks and smiles to the lips of all her companions.

Besides the ordering of new gowns, many spools of ribbon and lace, as well as beads, colored thread, and all the things which a lady might need for making over gowns and bonnets were purchased, giving each of the girls plenty of work to occupy their time when they were not entertaining guests or paying calls. Even Mary had a large hatbox full of materials to take with her to Hunsford.

By the time the ladies returned to Berkeley Street, the post had come with Mrs. Jennings' expected letter, though it was in the hand of Lady Sotheby herself. She squealed her joy at reading the short missive as though she were not already aware of the news it carried, and passed it among her nieces with the excitement of a grandmother, though she and the Lady were not directly related. They then had little time to dress for tea, and almost hurried through their preparations with Mr. Collins—who was to spend the afternoon in the company of Mr. Bingley and Mr. Gardiner—urgently pressing them not to be late. Mrs. Jennings' carriage was soon brought around from the mews, and minutes later set off for one of the most fashionable neighborhoods in Town, for Disley House was in the Mayfair district.

Louisa Hurst arrived as the Bennet sisters and their aunts—Mrs. Gardiner having arrived at near the same time as the ladies from Berkeley Street—were being shown into the drawing room. Awaiting them all, besides the lady of the house and her daughter-in-law, was another lady.

"Mrs. Gardiner you know, of course," said the countess as her companion stood; she then introduced the rest of newly arrived party and added, "Ladies, may I present my cousin Lady Diana Markham. Her husband is Sir Phineas Markham, Baronet."

"So you are Miss Elizabeth Bennet," said Lady Markham as Lady Disley and Lady Rowarth began to serve the tea. "My cousin has told me a great deal about you. I hope you have a strong constitution, for you will no doubt be the envy of many a mother and daughter in the *ton*. Mr. Darcy has been considered one of the most eligible bachelors of Society for the whole of his adult life!"

Elizabeth accepted her cup of tea from Lady Rowarth with a smile and took a sip as she thought, *No doubt you have already heard that he kissed me as well*. She then replied, "Which is precisely why, I imagine, his heart sought a companion elsewhere, Lady Markham."

"Oh? Has Darcy made you an offer, then?" Lady Markham queried in an excited tone, her eyes widening as though she had heard the most delicious gossip.

"Not of the matrimonial kind, no," Elizabeth rejoined. "But Mr.

Darcy did ask me before he went to spend Christmas with his sister if I would consent to courtship—and is not courtship the usual precursor to marriage?"

Lady Markham raised an eyebrow. "Most often it is, though there are occasions such relationships fail to take that step."

Elizabeth felt her indignation start to rise, and she unconsciously straightened her posture, lifting her chin as she wondered what the woman was about. "Indeed, Lady Markham, there are some courtships which do not end in marriage. But my affection for Mr. Darcy is strong, and in his letters—our correspondence being blessed with my father's permission—he assures me his only grows whenever he is unable to see me. I am sorry if a young lady of your acquaintance will be disappointed by his having chosen a young woman of the country rather than herself, but I cannot be sorry for having accepted his attentions."

Lady Markham delicately took a sip of her tea, then looked to Lady Disley as she said, "Upon my word, Frances—you did not exaggerate when you said she had a sharp tongue. No need to be girding her back from the daggers of the *ton* mothers and daughters. I daresay Miss Elizabeth is quite capable of standing up to the lot."

She then softened her countenance with a smile. "Do forgive me if I gave you the impression I was affronted—I assure you I am not. I may not be related to Darcy by blood, but he *is* family, and I have been witness to his misery in company on more than one occasion. Too many young women have all but thrown themselves at his feet just for the mere *chance* of one day becoming mistress of Pemberley. I shouldn't wonder that he was attracted to you; besides your wit and pleasing figure, the fact that you *weren't* attracted to his fortune was surely a relief!"

The baronet's wife narrowed her gaze then. "You weren't, were you? Attracted only by his fortune?"

Elizabeth relaxed and laughed. "I cannot say that the possibility of marrying a man of ten thousand per annum is not an attraction, Lady Markham, but I feel there is a great deal more required for any marriage to be successful beyond the production of heirs to the estate. If not love, then at least trust and respect are required to make a lifetime together bearable."

"Very true," replied Lady Markham with a nod. "Love in marriage is God's greatest blessing, I think—and as you say, you and Mr. Darcy already have a strong attachment formed. Let your faith in that attachment give you strength, Miss Elizabeth, for you will endure more difficult trials than my little test once word spreads of your relationship with Darcy."

"Forgive me, ma'am, but how would that happen if Mr. Darcy is not here to make his interest known?" ventured Mary.

"But he has, Mrs. Collins," spoke up Lady Rowarth. "It is already going 'round that my cousin Darcy was seen at Covent Garden last evening with a lovely young brunette whom he introduced to only a few people, and whom he kissed before handing her into the carriage she shared with other ladies of their party."

Well, that certainly did not take long, Elizabeth mused sourly as she sipped her tea.

Mrs. Gardiner began to shake her head. "Oh dear, I cannot like that. Such gossip could be the ruin of my niece's reputation and that of her unmarried sisters, without Mr. Darcy's presence to reinforce the claim. Oh, Lizzy, why did you allow him the liberty?"

Without hesitation, Elizabeth replied, "Because I wished it. Besides, dear Aunt, I do not hear anyone chastising Cate for allowing Mr. Bingley the same."

Lady Disley, who sat adjacent to Mrs. Gardiner, touched a hand to her forearm. "My dear Mrs. Gardiner, pray do not make yourself uneasy. Darcy's reputation in society is impeccable, and while he is away in Surrey with his sister, Miss Elizabeth has myself and my daughter to help enforce the existence of their attachment. As they were seen together last night, people are naturally going to be curious. If she and I are seen together—and I intend that we should be, especially after last night—then any possibly malicious gossip can be contained, if not prevented altogether. I should certainly prefer to reply to such inquiries myself, and with truth rather than fiction."

"And how might you reply to such a question?" asked Mrs. Jennings. "I am of the same mind as my sister, and should not like any of our dear girls to become the subject of parlor talk among the gadabouts of the *ton*—at least, not in a bad way."

The three titled ladies looked to one another for a moment, and then Lady Disley said, "I shall tell the truth: she is a young lady from the country who made the acquaintance my nephew while he stayed with his friend, and that he has asked that I become acquainted with her whilst she and her sisters are in town for the Season. Any questions as to the status of their relationship I will leave to Miss Elizabeth, for it is more her concern than my own at present."

"Very well said, my lady," commended Lady Rowarth. "Though saying nothing further will still set tongues to wagging, I imagine."

Elizabeth, having already endured enough scrutiny for the time being, broke in at that moment to inquire of her hostess as to the whereabouts of Colonel Fitzwilliam. "If he is still in Town, my lady, I should certainly like to meet with him again."

"And I should like it above all things, Miss Elizabeth, for my son to be in our company," said Lady Disley. "But alas, he was only last evening suddenly recalled to his regiment, and he left us this morning. I suppose it was to be expected, for he had taken such a long leave of absence. Oh, how I pray he will be able to soon sell his commission, for I so dislike when he goes away. They are to make for the continent soon and be stationed in France, and I do not know when I shall see him again."

There was then a moment of somber silence, and then it was mentioned by Mrs. Jennings that she had taken the girls shopping that morning to have new gowns commissioned. Discussion then focused on fashion and fabrics, and who among the *ton* liked to wear what styles, and whether the girls were all skilled enough to make over a gown or mend it if need be. This led to a discussion on accomplishments, in which each young lady discussed what she was best at or hoped to learn more of. Mary spoke of being especially glad to have become more proficient at the pianoforte as she could then play it for hymns that would be sung in church each Sunday. Cate talked of her desire to learn the violin, and how she was looking forward to meeting the master her aunt and uncle had enlisted for herself and her cousin on the following Monday.

"I am also nervous, for what if I have no talent for music? I should not like to lower myself in Mr. Bingley's esteem by having no accomplishments at all," said she.

Mrs. Hurst chuckled softly and smiled at her. "My dear Cate, I do not think that is even possible. Charles adores you, and at present you do not play. I daresay he will not be affronted if you are unable to learn an instrument."

"Bingley... That name is familiar to me," said Lady Markham. She turned to Louisa. "You called him by his Christian name—are you intimately acquainted with the gentleman?"

Mrs. Hurst colored a little, though she lifted her chin a fraction as she said, "Forgive me if I was indelicate, but yes, I am. The gentleman of which Miss Catherine and I spoke is my brother."

Lady Markham's eyes widened. "And are you at all acquainted with the Bingley family that owns Bingley Textiles, my dear?"

Elizabeth could not help but feel some sympathy for her friend as she was interrogated. She had just undergone a similar trial, and it was not lost on her that if either of them wished to better their standing in society or be able to hold their own amongst those with whom their husbands were connected, they would have to be able to withstand the censure of the *ton*—Mr. Bingley and his sisters especially so for their fortune coming from trade, which was like to get around no matter how hard the sisters tried to ignore it…or bury it completely.

"I believe, ma'am, that my brother technically still owns the factory, though he has nothing to do with the daily running of it," Louisa replied. "It was my father's wish—and his father before him—that once we had fortune enough, an estate would be built or purchased that our family might become respectable members of society."

The baronet's lady turned to her cousin. "Frances, do you not remember me telling you of that place as well, when I directed you to Gardiner Imports? They make the softest wool there that ever I wore!"

Some measure of pride, Elizabeth suspected, came into Louisa's expression then, for her posture straightened and her lips drew into a small smile. "I am honored you think so well of the wool made at the mill, Lady Markham," she said. "For it is my grandmother's technique for making wool so soft and pliable that makes it so highly sought after."

Elizabeth hid a smile of congratulations behind her teacup as she thought the point well made. She wondered then if Bingley's affability and Louisa's pride might somehow work in their favor; should they own to the origins of their fortune yet present themselves as unaffected by the disdain for "new money," they might perhaps demonstrate to the snobs of the *ton* that there was no shame in having connections to trade.

At least, Lady Disley and Lady Rowarth did not seem to be affronted, and Lady Markham looked almost impressed by Louisa's subtle means of standing up to her. Perhaps, Elizabeth mused, she ought also to consider changing her own mind about the higher circles of society. After all, here before her were three examples of the elite, each lady of wealth and family by birth and by marriage members of the aristocracy … and willingly in the company of young women of lower station.

Finding herself suddenly uncomfortable with her own thoughts, she set aside her teacup and saucer and rose, and strode over to a window. There she wrapped her arms about herself as she looked out into the well-kept street, her mind only peripherally attending the conversation taking place behind her. She stood that way in solitude for the course of a minute or two, before being joined there by the lady of the house.

"Are you unwell, Miss Elizabeth?" she asked softly.

Elizabeth nodded. "Quite well, Lady Disley," she replied. "It is just that…"

Lady Disley seemed to understand she needed a moment to arrange her thoughts into a pattern that would make speech coherent; as such, she took Elizabeth's arm and wrapped it around her own.

"Let me persuade you, my dear, to take a turn about the room," said her hostess as she turned them away from the window. "A walk is refreshing, is it not, after sitting so long in one attitude?"

Though the party had not been sitting together for more than half an hour, Elizabeth nonetheless smiled as she replied, "It is a small kind of accomplishment, I suppose."

"Now come, tell me what is on your mind, if it is not too impertinent of one with whom you are so little acquainted to ask."

Elizabeth drew a breath. "I begin to think, Lady Disley, that until a moment ago, I have never known myself. When first I met your nephew, he made it clear that while he should like to be friends, he could not guarantee he would ever make me an offer, for the objections to a match between us would be numerous."

To her surprise, Lady Disley snorted softly. "I cannot say I am surprised. Fitzwilliam is nothing if not blunt—I do hope you were not too offended by his manner."

"Indeed, I was not. To own the truth, I was rather pleased by his honesty, as we were friendly enough by then that his manner of speaking was not as offensive as it might otherwise have been," said Elizabeth as they trod a slow, languorous path about the room. "And I was thankful he was as forgiving of mine, for I had made it clear soon after our meeting that I knew perfectly well my sisters and I had little but our charms to recommend us, that I had relations which were an embarrassment, no important connections… I assured him that none of the single gentlemen at Netherfield had need to fear *I* should try for them as I was, at the time, completely certain that I was not of a mind to marry anytime soon."

"And now?" her companion pressed softly.

Elizabeth smiled freely now. "Now my feelings are quite the

opposite. At the very least, I am not as opposed to marriage as I was then. I should like more time in Mr. Darcy's company before I would agree to marrying, should he be of a mind to ask it of me, but I will say that if we are allowed the time we both of us wish to become even better acquainted, then I would..."

Here she felt a blush come to her cheeks. "I do not think I would not say nay to his proposal."

"It pleases me to hear you say so, Miss Elizabeth," replied Lady Disley. "First, because I love William almost as a mother does her son, and often did I make my best effort to stand in the stead of his own when she was taken from us. I should very much like to see my nephew happy in his marriage. I should like very much to see life and love fill the halls of that great house of his once more.

"Secondly, because when my niece Anne made it known she had been to see you, William stood for your honor, and defended you more passionately than I have seen him speak of any woman not a relation. He told his uncle that it did not matter to him that you had no fortune, as he had more than enough for the both of you. In his way of speaking I knew that his heart had made its choice; that there would be no dissuading him, even should I wish it, and that if we were of a mind to oppose him, we would lose him. I could not bear that possibility—nor, do I think, could my husband bear the thought of losing one of the last ties he has to his most beloved sister."

Feeling the countess's eyes on her, Elizabeth lifted her gaze to meet them. She found on the other woman's countenance no censure for Mr. Darcy nor the young woman he had chosen. All she saw was a smile and bright, shining eyes that spoke of love for her nephew.

"Now tell me, my dear," said Lady Disley then, as they were just completing their first full circuit of the drawing room. "What you were thinking of just now—how is it you have just come to know yourself?"

"When I first spoke of Mr. Darcy just now, I meant to demonstrate the prejudices between us," Elizabeth began. "He against me for my family's condition in life and our want of connections, me against him for being so proud and conceited because he had what we did not. Yet we could neither of us deny what may well have been between us almost from the first moment, and our tentative friendship has grown into something more that both of us wish to explore further.

"Then he told me one day that he had written of me in two letters, one to his sister and the other to you. When he spoke of your having found my Uncle Gardiner to be 'surprisingly genteel', I admit that I was more than a little incensed on his behalf, as if you were such as I had heard tell of the aristocracy, and looked down upon those who make their fortune by actually working for it as though it were impossible for a tradesman to also be a gentleman. I admit, my lady, that I feared very much meeting only those who would disregard us here, as we moved about more in society."

She glanced over at the group of ladies still gathered around the tea service, talking and drinking and eating amiably. Each of her relations turned their eyes to her briefly—both her aunts showing some small modicum of concern, her sisters curiosity—but she nodded a time or two and smiled at the rest.

Elizabeth's gaze remained on them as she continued. "Just now I was thinking how wrong I have been to allow such prejudice room to take root in my mind," said she. "You and Lady Rowarth, and Lady Markham, have been nothing but kind to us. You have been respectful of my Aunt Gardiner, and have even visited her husband's warehouse more than once, I understand."

She sighed then, and looked once more to her walking partner. "Though I am sure that the shrewd Lady Markham is correct, and we will no doubt be subjected to intense scrutiny—even disdain and censure for our connections and small fortunes—I am humbled and most pleased to find I was not entirely correct. There are some truly good people among the first circles, and those, at least, I should not mind at all becoming much better acquainted with."

For a moment Lady Disley was silent, then she smiled and said, "I will in turn do you the justice of saying that I *was* brought up to think little of those whose station was below my own, as was my husband and all his family. But those teachings, I am thankful to say, did not stay with all of us. Although I do believe each person does have their place in this world, to aspire to be greater—to actually work to achieve that greatness—makes even those of low origin better than those who make no effort at all. If one desires to be a lady or a gentleman, then work for it. Prove yourself deserving of the honorific by the effort to be as kind and amiable as a lady or gentleman ought to be—Mr. and Mrs. Gardiner certainly have done, and that does make them worthy of notice and respect. If only *everyone* could do so, I think the world would be a far better place to live in."

Before Elizabeth could formulate any sort of reply to this speech, they were interrupted by the sudden appearance of a tall, dark-haired gentleman with a regal air, who raised his hand as the ladies stood to greet him.

"As you were, please. Do not let my presence disturb you—I came only to fetch myself a cup of tea and a small plate of Cook's tasty biscuits."

"You might have sent a maid for it," suggested his wife.

The earl shook his head. "And miss the chance of seeing so many lovely faces gathered together in one place? Certainly not."

Lady Disley laughed softly. "Well then, my dear Lord Disley, won't you join us?" said she to her husband in a teasing manner. "I am sure Miss Elizabeth will not object to a third."

Lord Disley raised an eyebrow. "No indeed, my dear—though I thank you for the invitation. You can have only two motives for walking about the room, and I should interfere with either."

"Whatever do you mean, sir? Miss Elizabeth, whatever can he mean?"

Elizabeth grinned. "I think the surest way of disappointing His Lordship would be to ask him nothing about it."

The two were then completing their second circuit and had near come face-to-face with the earl, who—after accepting a cup of tea and a plate of biscuits from his daughter-in-law—had moved to a chair with a side table in the corner to consume them. He smiled at them and sipped his tea as his wife pertly demanded that she must know his meaning.

His eyebrow rose again, and then he said, "My lady, you either choose this manner of passing the afternoon because you are in each other's confidence and have secret affairs to discuss, or you are perfectly conscious that your figures appear to best advantage when walking. If the first, I should certainly be in your way, and if the second, I can much better admire you from my present position."

"La!" cried Mrs. Jennings. "What a shocking reply from one such as he! Should you not punish him, my lady?"

Lady Disley turned to her with a smile. "That I shall do in good time, ma'am, but first let me do my duty."

She then proceeded to introduce her guests to her husband. This time the ladies all did stand and curtsey. He stood and returned their respect with a bow of his own. Elizabeth was not surprised by the scrutinizing gaze with which he favored her as he retook his seat—all of Darcy's family that she had so far become acquainted with had judged her in the same manner.

She was not, however, prepared for the Earl of Disley's first words to her, which were, "I can see why he likes you."

"I beg your pardon, sir?" she asked on reflex.

Lord Disley chuckled softly. "You've an air about you, young lady, which marks you as being nothing like the insipid girls of the *ton*. As often as he is accosted when in Town, I am little surprised that William formed an attachment to a simple country girl."

Were she not now more aware of herself and the character of her hosts, Elizabeth might well have been insulted by his words. Rather than allowing her indignation to rise, however, she merely arched an eyebrow.

"That I am a country girl cannot be argued, sir," said she. "But simple, I assure you, I am not. I daresay even a pretty face and witty repartee would not be attractions enough for a gentleman such as Mr. Darcy if I were so."

"Undoubtedly, Miss Elizabeth. A man may well be willing to accept some degree of deficiency in his partner in this trait or that, but in William's case, intelligence is not one of them. No, my nephew *requires* a woman who can respect him and yet also keep him from hiding away in the shadows, something he is far too apt to do when left to his own accord."

Lord Disley then finished the last of the biscuits on his plate, drained the last dregs of tea from his cup, and stood. "Ladies, though I am loath to take leave of such excellent company, I am afraid I must. Matters of business demand my attention."

He stepped closer to his wife and took her hand with a smile. "My dear, I am for Albermarle Street as soon as the carriage is made ready. Lord Torrington and I have matters to discuss."

"Do tell Lady Torrington I will call on her Monday next regarding the Twelfth Night Ball," Lady Disley said in reply, "and do not forget we're engaged with the Devonshires for dinner."

"My dear wife, I would never forget a dinner engagement with a duke—'tis not worth enduring your wrath," said the earl with a smile. He then encompassed her companions with a gaze about the room and added, "Good afternoon, ladies."

After he had gone away, Elizabeth scoffed softly. "Why do I get the feeling, my lady, that His Lordship came here just to take my measure?"

Lady Disley chuckled, turning back toward the group of their relations as she said, "I do not doubt that was one of his motives, Miss Elizabeth, but I can assure you he liked you very much indeed."

Elizabeth felt herself relax. "I am much relieved to hear it, ma'am. I do admit I was rather concerned that my natural impertinence would make me disagreeable to you all, or perhaps my family's lack of connections."

"I must own that it would be better had you more connections in society other than Mrs. Jennings," Lady Disley conceded. "However, the charm, beauty, and grace of you and your sisters will go a very long way towards winning the admiration of those in the first circle."

"I am sure the ten thousand pounds we each of us have in waiting for our marriages will be of service in that regard, as well," Elizabeth quipped as she and the countess took their seats again.

"Lizzy!" admonished Mrs. Gardiner. "My dear, though Her Ladyship appears to delight in your sharp tongue, I do wish you would utilize more thought in its governance."

A blush crept into her cheeks. "I am sorry, Aunt Gardiner," Elizabeth said. "I will endeavor to be more moderate in my speech, for your sake."

"Do not make yourself uneasy, Mrs. Gardiner," said Lady Rowarth. "My mother and I have heard and seen worse from those that society would consider of higher standing. Miss Elizabeth's remarks are actually rather tame in comparison."

"You are kind to say so, Lady Rowarth," replied Mrs. Gardiner.

"'Tis not only kindness, Mrs. Gardiner," added Lady Disley. "Miss Elizabeth is correct in her supposition. Though my husband and I were in support of Darcy's suit before learning of your nieces' inheritance, I am afraid that had she and her sisters come to Town without the benefit of a dowry, their acceptance in society would have been much more difficult to achieve—in spite of all their beauty, manners, and accomplishments. All that will be said of them now is that better connections and a more substantial dowry would have been beneficial, as there are young ladies among the *ton* who have a great deal more of both to bring to their marriages, making them a more desirable choice."

No doubt our connection to your family will also be of service in our introduction, however tenuous it may be at present, Elizabeth—thinking also of her aunt's admonishment—just stopped herself from saying aloud.

"However, your nieces need have no fear that they will not be desired. Even Miss Elizabeth and Miss Catherine, who are already spoken for, will be sought after as dancing partners at balls and parties," the countess continued.

"But Jane will be the most desired of all, for she is not only available, but is five times as pretty as the rest of us," said Elizabeth with a smile.

"Oh hush, Lizzy," admonished Jane, though she spoke with a blush and a smile of her own.

"I wish now that I were going to be remaining in Town for the Season," spoke up Mary. "I may no longer have need of seeking a husband, but I should very much like to observe my sisters' rise in society. I do not doubt that Jane will have a dozen admirers after her very first ball, and Lizzy and Cate will have several of their own I daresay."

Cate's cheeks colored a pretty pink as she looked down at her hands. "I will admit I should like to be admired, but I have not any desire of being courted by anyone other than Mr. Bingley."

Elizabeth favored her sister with a smile when she looked up again. "I share your sentiments, Cate," said she. "Admirers will be welcome insofar as flattering my vanity, but the only gentleman I have any wish of being courted by is Mr. Darcy."

Chapter Twenty-Eight

Early on Saturday morning—after a hearty breakfast, many long embraces, and more than a few tears—Mr. and Mrs. Collins departed for Kent.

Elizabeth was more than a little sorry to see her sister go away. She had enjoyed watching the growth of her sense and comportment, and in being shown proper attention from her sisters, Mary had even grown in beauty. She smiled more, wore her hair less severely, was more conscious of her wardrobe choices… Not one of the family had been remiss to take notice of the change in her, and only Lydia now made truly unkind remarks. Mrs. Bennet's regular assertions that Jane was the prettiest, that none of them would ever equal her in beauty, had long since ceased to cause the other girls any pain.

It was likely to be some time before any of them would see Mary again, about which even she was more than a little nervous, so the sisters all pledged to write one another as often as they were able. Mrs. Collins demanded full accounts from each of her sisters of their adventures during the Season; she wished to know all about the parties and the balls and the beaux that fought to win their affections.

"I must live vicariously through you all," she said. "For I am married now and have no need of a Season in town."

The remainder of the day was spent in common pursuits of needlework, reading, and practicing on the pianoforte. The only callers they had at Berkeley Street were Mr. Bingley, Mrs. Hurst, and a couple of friends of Mrs. Jennings, all of whom returned later in the evening for dinner and cards. Sunday, following their attendance at services, was much the same, though there was no card party following their meal and Mr. Bingley was their only guest.

Monday brought an unexpected visit by Lady Rowarth, accompanied by her young daughter, Josephine. The viscountess had called to deliver an even more unexpected surprise: Lady Disley had convinced her friend and fellow countess, Lady Torrington, to issue an invitation to all of the Berkeley Street ladies to her Twelfth Night Ball.

"Mr. and Mrs. Gardiner are to be invited, for they are much admired by Lady Disley. Mr. Bingley will receive an invitation as well, I believe," Lady Rowarth added, with a pointed look and smile at Cate. "And if I am not mistaken, his sister, Mrs. Hurst, shall also be asked to attend. Lady Disley was rather impressed with her, as was Lady Markham."

"Upon my word," said Elizabeth to her sisters after Lady Rowarth had taken her leave a quarter hour later. "Caroline Bingley will be envious indeed, should Mrs. Hurst write to her of not only meeting Lady Disley and having tea with her, but impressing her so well that she was included in an invitation to another countess's ball!"

"I shouldn't wonder," said Cate, "if Miss Bingley does not begin to wish she had been kinder to you, Lizzy. After all, had she been, do you not think she would be included in such an engagement as well?"

"She ought have been kinder to *all* of us regardless of the potential benefits to her social calendar," said Elizabeth. "Even if she did not like us, she could have at least been polite and showed us our due respect."

"I am surprised," spoke up Jane, "that we are even invited to such an event! Is it not incredible, sisters, that we have not been in Town a full se'nnight, and yet we have already made the acquaintance of a countess, an earl, a viscountess, and a baronet's lady? I could never have dreamed we would make such connections at all, let alone in so short an amount of time!"

"And now you girls are to meet another countess—her husband, another earl—and perhaps even more grand figures of society!" cried Mrs. Jennings cheerfully as she clapped her hands together. "Oh my dear Lizzy, such a fine thing you have done to elevate your sisters—and without any effort or intention! The dowry my dear Gerald and I have provided for you all is almost nothing in comparison to your having caught the eye of a young gentleman so well connected!"

"Oh, indeed!" agreed Cate. "And despite Aunt Gardiner's warning that you should watch your tongue, Lizzy. Did you not say Mr. Darcy told you it was your wit that first attracted him? Were you as modest as Jane or as wild as I once was, I daresay he would have taken no notice of you."

"Quite so," said Elizabeth. "Though Jane's modesty does her much credit."

Jane smiled. "Thank you, Lizzy."

"I must agree, however, that it *is* remarkable we should make such important acquaintances so soon," Elizabeth went on. "Greater than I ever expected, to be sure, though I certainly would have made the acquaintance of Mr. Darcy's family at some point or other."

"I do not know that I could have wished for better for your first Season, girls," Mrs. Jennings said then. "Due to Lizzy's courtship with Mr. Darcy, you have little else to do but be your charming and beautiful selves! Be assured, my darlings, that Lady Disley and her family move in the first set wherever they are known, and though I have engaged with her rarely in recent years, I can assure you she is an excellent woman, always with good company around her. Your being known to be the acquaintances of the countess will be most advantageous to you all."

Elizabeth scoffed. "Indeed—our acquaintance will be sought merely for the fact that we are on friendly terms with a woman we barely know. This is precisely the reason Mr. Darcy took such a fancy to me, Aunt Jennings. He wished to be liked for *himself*, not for who he knows or is related to, and certainly not for his fortune."

"But it will be very nice to have a fortune, will it not, Lizzy? Should you marry Mr. Darcy, I mean," observed Cate. "I know that I will be very happy indeed to be Mr. Bingley's wife, should he ask me. Five thousand a year, and very likely more! I shall have many fine gowns and jewels, and Mr. Bingley will surely purchase a second carriage for my own use whenever he is away on business."

"Perhaps he will, but I would not have you take advantage of his generosity, Cate," said Jane.

"Nor would I," added Elizabeth. "Our family might not be considered very poor, for Father's income is enough that our lives have always been comfortable, but remember that he regrettably has not arranged for our maintenance after he is gone. Disregard, for a moment, the generosity of our Aunt and Uncle Jennings: Had Mary not married Mr. Collins, we would all become destitute upon the demise of our father, for we would be homeless and virtually penniless. The interest from our mother's dowry will not be nearly enough to support us all."

Cate looked stricken by her words, as though for the very first time being made aware of how truly precarious their situation had been. "What… What would have become of us, do you think?"

Elizabeth shared a glance with Jane, then drew a breath. "If Mr. Collins was not generous enough to allow our staying on at Longbourn, we would have been dependent on our relations for our bread and board. And though I daresay they would none of them complain, our Aunt and Uncle Phillips and Aunt and Uncle Gardiner can none of them afford the expense, long-term, of caring for so many extra persons. One or more of us would have been forced to find employment."

"Oh my," said Cate, drawing a hand to her heart. "I… I do not think I ever gave it any thought before now. Lord, how selfish I have been! I should not like to be a burden on anyone, nor do I wish to take advantage of Mr. Bingley. He is too amiable, too kind … which, now I consider it, makes it easy to see how he *could* be taken advantage of—how any rich gentleman could be, or a young lady with a fortune."

"Precisely, my dear sister. Now, knowing what might have been, I hope you will be more appreciative of what Aunt and Uncle Jennings have done for us—and be wise in your expenditures once you are Mrs. Bingley," said Elizabeth with a grin.

"There is but one error in your narrative, girls," said Mrs. Jennings. When they all looked to her, she said, "I would not have allowed you all to suffer. Even my sister, to whom I have not spoken a word since my marriage—though not for lack of trying, for I did write her some letters she never answered—would have received support from me if I had to feed the money through our brother. I would even have taken in as many of you girls as were willing to live with me, for I adore the company of young people. And you are family! Family connections are *always* worth preserving."

"Is that why you made sure our Uncle Gardiner introduced you to us?" asked Jane.

Mrs. Jennings nodded vigorously. "It most certainly is! Jane might wish to deny my existence and that of my children and their families, but I'll be deuced if she was going to deny me the right to know my own nieces! I only wish I could have seen you all more often, could have done more for you over the years that have already gone by…"

Elizabeth reached for her hand when her eyes began to mist, and gave it a gentle squeeze as she offered the lady a smile. "My dear Aunt Jennings, I beg you would not feel any amount of guilt on our part. As I said before, our lives have been quite comfortable. Although direct influence on our father's part has been… lacking, at least until recently, he *has* made sure we are all well fed and properly clothed. If we desired anything we had only to ask it, and if it was in his means, he made sure we had it."

"Elizabeth is right, Aunt," added Jane. "And consider what you *have* done for us—not only have you managed a few presents over the years, given to us through our Aunt and Uncle Gardiner, you and our late Uncle Jennings have managed to provide for us all most generously! Five girls not your own, the children of a sister who has not spoken to you in years… I hardly think you could have done much better for us if we *had* been your daughters."

"Not to mention all the new gowns and gloves and spencers you have purchased for us!" added Cate.

"Oh!" cried Mrs. Jennings sharply, her hands almost flailing. "Speaking of gowns, girls, I cannot *wait* to see you at the Torringtons' ball on Saturday! You shall be the most splendidly dressed young ladies, I do not doubt it! Fear not regarding your accessories, my darlings, for I have quite enough necklaces and earrings for each of you."

"Speaking of," began Elizabeth with a grin, "how fortuitous, Aunt, that we commissioned ball gowns during our venture to the shops last week. One might almost suspect you had some idea we would be invited to one."

Mrs. Jennings laughed. "Oh, tosh, Lizzy! Yes, I had *some* idea of our attending balls and parties, but I could have none that our first invitation would come so soon. Do not forget, my dear, that the Season has not yet begun—there are dozens of such events that we might well be invited to. I do have many friends with great houses here in Town—and of course I shall certainly host a few dinners here."

When the post came, it brought the first letter from Mary, dated late Saturday afternoon. She wrote that the parsonage was a neat little cottage—smaller than Mr. Collins had boasted of but fitted out with pleasing furniture, wall paper, and paint. The ground floor afforded not only a fair-sized dining room and kitchen, but also a book room for Mr. Collins and two parlors. Mary said she planned to convince her husband that the smaller of these ought to be for her private use and the larger for receiving important guests and formal entertaining. On the first floor were four medium-sized bedrooms. Three had shelves in the closets—a recommendation of Lady

Catherine's, as Mr. Collins had informed her—and the fourth had for some reason been given a closet so large that, with the space managed well, it could be used as a dressing room. Mary had been relieved that Mr. Collins had already installed himself in one of the other bedrooms and so had taken that room for her own, and said that the small size of her new dressing room did not bother her—she could only wish that it had its own window so she would not always need a candle.

The second floor of the parsonage was a large attic to which had been added dividing walls so that it could house both male and female servants as well as be used for storage. They had two of the former, the elder of whom was butler, valet, and curricle driver when Mr. Collins did not wish to drive himself. Their younger man performed the duties of footman, groom, and farmer, helping to keep the Collins's few animals well tended. Both men saw to household repairs and fetched parcels from the village that Mr. Collins couldn't be bothered to pick up himself.

Female servants at Hunsford Parsonage consisted of a cook who doubled as housekeeper and two maids-of-all-work that saw to the laundry, cleaning, and busy work in the stillroom. The younger of the maids had been directed by the housekeeper to help Mary with dressing, though she intended to care for her hair on her own as best she could.

All told I am quite pleased with the house and the staff, whom I do not think it unpardonable to say are pleased to have someone of my sense to manage them. Indeed, though I have only just met them and have not lived here a full day as yet, I am certain I shall take much pleasure in running my own home. Mamma did teach us all that much, at least, and in what subjects her instruction was lacking, I know I can count on my Aunt Gardiner or Aunt Jennings to advise me. Yes, my dear Lizzy, I am sure I shall bear my life here very cheerfully.

As to my new esteemed patroness, I have yet to meet her. Mr. Collins has gone to Rosings almost from the moment of our arrival to inform her of our return, and no doubt to speak of my having met Lady Disley. He has told me I am sure to receive the condescension of her notice after church tomorrow. We may even be invited for tea, perhaps tomorrow or Monday, says he, no doubt so that Lady Catherine may take her measure of me. I find that I do not fear meeting her, though I am somewhat apprehensive of meeting Miss de Bourgh again – rather, Mrs. Ferrars, I should say. Not that I am in fear of her, either, only her disposition. You know how I dislike acrimonious persons.

I conclude here, my sisters, with further wishes for your health and happiness, and for experiencing much pleasure during your first full se'nnight in Town. Remember to tell me every detail, and yes, Jane, I shall write next to Mamma and Papa.

Yours affectionately,
Mary Collins

"Well, I am happy that she is pleased with the house," said Cate after Elizabeth had finished reading the letter aloud, "but what I really can't wait to hear of is what she thinks of the illustrious Lady Catherine de Bourgh!"

"I am sure we shall hear of that in the next day or two," said Elizabeth as she folded the letter again. "Surely she has met her by now."

"You, on the other hand, ought to be getting ready for your music lesson," said Jane then. "You are to be meeting your teacher at Gracechurch Street in less than an hour."

Cate sprung up from her seat with a gasp and hurried from the room. By the time she returned in a fresh day gown, Mr. Bingley had come to call. On hearing that Cate had an appointment to get to, he offered to convey her there himself.

"Would it be proper for us to ride alone together, sir?" she asked him. "Did not a maid accompany you when you drove Lizzy from Netherfield that one day?"

Bingley looked around at her sisters and her aunt and said, "Indeed—but then, I was not courting your sister. I am, however, courting you."

The last he said with a smile that caused Cate to blush prettily. Bingley's smile grew wider at the change in her features, then he continued. "I cannot foresee any impropriety in my merely conveying you from one location to another. Besides which, this will regrettably be my only chance to see you today. I've my own appointment this afternoon with my solicitor and man of business here in town, and a dinner engagement with some friends I chanced to meet at a shop."

"Oh, that is unfortunate!" cried Cate. "Not that you met with friends, of course, but that we shall see so little of one another."

She then glanced sidelong at Elizabeth, who slowly arched one eyebrow. Cate stifled most of a sigh, then added, "However, I cannot be a selfish creature. I know you have friends beyond my family, and

I must own that you owe them some duty of being in their company when they ask it of you."

Bingley reached for her hand and lifted it to his lips. "My dearest Catherine, you are an angel. Do not despair—I shall make several calls tomorrow morning to fulfill some of that duty, and in the afternoon I shall call upon you. For a whole hour, if Mrs. Jennings does not mind."

"Indeed I do not, sir!" said Mrs. Jennings. "We shall have a nuncheon around one o'clock, does that suit you?"

His grin widened. "That suits me very well, Mrs. Jennings. I should be delighted!"

The elderly lady clapped her hands together. "Then it is settled! Now, Cate, off you go for your bonnet and pelisse, for you do not want to be late to your first music lesson."

Cate hurried away to do as she was instructed, and her sisters chatted with Mr. Bingley as he waited for her. Soon they were off and those that remained moved to other pursuits. Mrs. Jennings set about planning a large dinner party, Jane to re-trimming a bonnet, and Elizabeth to writing letters. The first was to her parents, informing them of the honor of being invited to Lady Torrington's ball, though she left the letter unsealed should Cate wish to add anything regarding her music lesson. She next read Mary's letter again before penning a response, and then started a letter to Charlotte.

Though the day had already brought them two delightful surprises, Elizabeth counted neither Lady Rowarth's visit nor the invitation to the Twelfth Night Ball (which was to include dinner beforehand at Disley House) above seeing Charlotte Lucas follow her sister Cate into the drawing room on the latter's return that afternoon, along with Maria and Lady Lucas.

Elizabeth embraced her friend heartily after the family was introduced to Mrs. Jennings. "Charlotte, what do you do here?" she asked. "I thought you said that you weren't to take up your post until the first week of February?"

"Aye, and that is still true," said Charlotte. "However, Mamma insisted that I must have some new clothes, as befitting the daughter of a knight, and insists that no place will do but London for having them made."

"Charlotte, my dear, the best dressmakers and linen drapers in the entire country are here in Town!" said Lady Lucas. "You may have chosen to become a governess, but I will not have it said that you are not the daughter of a knight of the realm!"

"But how came you to come to us here?" spoke up Jane.

"That would be my doing," said Cate. "Their carriage was just coming to a stop at my uncle's house in Gracechurch Street, as Aunt Gardiner was walking me down to hers and uncle's own carriage to come home."

Charlotte took up the narrative then. "I had asked Mamma if we might stop at Gracechurch Street that I could leave my card and let you know we'd be in Town for a few days. When we saw Cate and Mrs. Gardiner, Cate told us you had decided to stay with another aunt, and so we offered to convey her home ourselves, that we could visit a while."

"Well, I am enormously pleased that you have come," said Elizabeth. "I shall be able to tell you of everything that has happened in just the last few days rather than finishing the letter I started."

Charlotte laughed. "Oh, Cate has already told us you've had tea with Darcy's aunt the countess, *and* that she has managed an invitation for all of you to a ball on Twelfth Night."

"If only my Charlotte could join you all," said Lady Lucas wistfully. "She might make herself a match at the ball and have no need of becoming a governess."

"Mamma," said Charlotte, her tone one of tempered exasperation. "Even were I to go, it is not likely that a gentleman would take a fancy to me. Not with the likes of Jane Bennet in the room."

The last she said with a kind smile, though Elizabeth was sure Jane knew she was not bitter.

"Tosh, I say!" her mother retorted. "You may not have the beauty of a Bennet, my dear, but you can be quite pretty when you make an effort. With the right gown, and perhaps some cosmetics to enhance your eyes and lips, I daresay it entirely possible you might catch the eye of a gentleman here in London—goodness knows you've no chance of securing a husband in Meryton."

"On that score, at least, we can agree," Charlotte rejoined. "However, Mamma, while I am aggrieved at having disappointed you and Father by reaching seven and twenty without having found myself a husband, I am not ashamed to be single. I am not ashamed of becoming a governess, either. I will be doing some good in the world by educating a child and preparing him for life as an adult."

It was an argument, Elizabeth knew, that Charlotte had already given to her parents. Sir William, however—affable gentleman as he was—was less inclined to complain of his daughter's choice than Lady Lucas.

"I'm surprised, I must say, that these Dashwoods accepted you," said the lady. "After all, it has always been my understanding that boys were educated by men and girls educated by women."

At this, Charlotte closed her eyes and drew a long breath. "No doubt, Mamma, young Mr. Dashwood will go on to a school for young men of standing for greater education at some point, but at present he is not yet eight years. I am well qualified to instruct him in those subjects that will prepare him for such an education."

"Maria!" cried Cate suddenly, grabbing her friend's hand and pulling her to her feet. "I have some fashion magazines in my room with pictures of the gowns we commissioned the other day. Let me show you!"

Maria, to Elizabeth's discerning eye, appeared quite eager to be out of the room and happily went along. Taking advantage of the opening, Mrs. Jennings engaged Lady Lucas in a discussion about hosting dinner parties, and so Elizabeth gestured to Jane and Charlotte that they might move across the room for a little more privacy.

"Remind me to tell Cate and Mrs. Jennings thank you," said Charlotte softly. "And please, accept my apologies for what you were forced to bear witness—as you know, Lizzy, my mother has been the least accepting of my choice, even though I *am* qualified and shall be well paid for my work."

"So you have heard, then, what they will pay you?" Elizabeth asked.

Charlotte nodded. "I received a letter from Mrs. Dashwood on Saturday—they are being most generous, though I own it is likely only because they wish to remain in favor of Lady Sotheby."

"If it is not too indelicate to ask," said Jane, "what will your salary be?"

"I shall be paid five pounds a month."

Elizabeth did the math in her head. "Good gracious! That is sixty pounds a year!"

Her friend nodded. "Indeed, and twice the amount teachers receive in some schools, if not even more. But if they are going to be so foolish, I shan't say nay, and will put it to much good use."

Elizabeth scoffed. "Oh, I do not doubt it in the least! Far be it for me to advise taking advantage, as we have recently spoken to Cate on the subject regarding Mr. Bingley's fortune, but if the Dashwoods are willing to pay you that much just to impress the gentleman's sister, I certainly would not recommend reminding them that the average pay for a governess is half or less."

The Lucases took their leave soon after, and with the lady's family on her mind, Elizabeth determined to write again to Miss Dashwood. In her letter, she expressed her surprise that the brother she had so disparaged could be convinced to offer Charlotte so generous a salary, asked after her sister and little Lord Nicholas, and expressed a wish that they might meet again soon. She also relayed the news about tea with Lady Disley and the invitation to the Torringtons' ball on Twelfth Night. Marianne, she was sure, would be delighted to hear about what the ladies were wearing, and promised to give as accurate an account as she was able of every dress she set eyes on, including her own.

After writing to all the family and friends she could think to pen a note to, Elizabeth wrote to Mr. Darcy. As she had already written to him about the tea engagement where she had met his uncle and Lady Markham, she now wrote of being invited to the Torringtons' ball, the visit from Charlotte (though she glossed over the argument between mother and daughter), and how she looked forward to seeing him again in the coming weeks.

I have already started Evelina *though I read it those days I stayed at Nertherfield in October. I felt I could not accept such a gift as a novel and not begin to read it directly. Thank you again for so thoughtful a gesture as purchasing the first book I read in your presence, and for the effort of finding a first edition when you know I would have been content with the latest printing.*

An official invitation to the ball on Saturday arrived as the Bennet sisters were dressing for dinner. Mrs. Jennings was impressed by the obvious expensiveness of the card stock and embossing.

"First grand ball of the Season," said she excitedly, "and you girls will be there! Oh, how happy I am for you!"

As there was no company expected, the small family party was relaxed. Cate told them all of her first music lesson, which she believed had gone well though she said she had "learnt little more than how to hold the instrument and its bow, and where to place my fingers." The music master also had instructed her and their cousin Brandon on the different musical notes as they appeared on paper, and warned that he would quiz them at the next lesson on Thursday.

"Do you think you will like your lessons, then?" Jane asked.

"I cannot say just yet, but I am sure in another week or two, I shall know if the violin is the right instrument for me," Cate replied. "I should like to be good at it—should like to be good at *something* other than knowing how to sew a ribbon to a bonnet."

A memory surfaced in Elizabeth's mind at those words. "Whether the violin is for you or no, dear sister, I rather think you are good at something. Do you not remember how well you planned the celebration for Papa's fiftieth birthday?"

Jane brightened. "Indeed! And last year how you helped Charlotte plan Maria's sixteenth birthday party?"

Cate nodded, though she still appeared somewhat disheartened as she said, "Planning birthday parties is hardly an accomplishment worthy of notice."

"Think that now, you may," spoke up Mrs. Jennings, "but when you are Mrs. Bingley—and I do not doubt you soon will be—you will be in charge of planning all the entertainment in your home. Dinner parties, card parties, birthday celebrations… From the food to the decorations, it is all *your* responsibility! You simply *must* be good at it, for with each successful engagement you hostess, people will talk of it the next day. Word will soon get 'round at how splendid the evening was, and soon even people of whom you know nothing at all will wish they had been invited."

"Think of the fact we are to attend dinner at Disley House and a ball after on Saturday," added Elizabeth. "Remember that Lady Rowarth told us how grand the ball usually is, and that we ought prepare ourselves for quite the crush. That means—"

"That Lord and Lady Torrington invite too many people to their parties?" Cate suggested.

Her remark generated laughter, then Elizabeth said, "Well, besides there being too many in attendance, that so many would *wish* to be invited speaks very highly of Lady Torrington's ability to plan for and provide desirable food and entertainment. Such parties are always the talk of the town after, and as Aunt Jennings said just now, people who hear of so lively a party will lament that they could not be there themselves."

"Do you mean people like Caroline Bingley?"

Elizabeth exchanged a glance with Jane, then nodded. "Yes. For someone who is so very desperate to cast off her connections to trade and raise her standing in society, a party such as this is exactly the kind of event Miss Bingley would wish to attend. Not only do people talk of how grand or entertaining such an event is, but they talk of who was there. Anyone wanting to be noticed or make an advantageous match hopes to be invited to such an evening as we shall be at on Saturday."

"So what you mean to say is that being an excellent hostess really is an accomplishment?" Cate asked with a frown.

Mrs. Jennings nodded vigorously. "Indeed so, my dear girl, indeed so! And just as people will talk of how excellent the duck or how many candles were on the table or who sat around it, they will also talk of how dry the venison, how crumbly the cake, and how terrible the music. No lady in society wants a poor report of her evening party to get about, you can be sure."

"And a wife who cannot even plan a simple dinner party would be an embarrassment to her husband," Cate observed. "If it turns out I cannot take to the violin, then I shall focus on what I *am* good at, and plan the best parties in Town!"

Happy to see her sister's spirits rising again, Elizabeth agreed, and a relaxed evening was had when the four sat down to cards after dinner. They competed good-naturedly between them at whist and vingt-et-un before supper was served, after which they were all of them contentedly fatigued and gone off to bed.

Chapter Twenty-Nine

Saturday, 5 January 1799

The last curl was pinned in place by the maid her aunt had sent to help her dress, and Elizabeth found herself smiling at her reflection in the mirror over her dressing table.

She looked remarkably well.

There was a braided and curled knot at her crown with sparkling seed pearl and diamond pins placed throughout, and delicate, wispy curls framed her face. At her lobes were diamond and sapphire stud earrings that complimented both the pins in her hair and the diamond and sapphire pendant that sat just above the hint of décolletage at her gown's square neckline. The borrowed jewelry set off her ensemble perfectly.

The gown she had chosen for this first grand event in Town was white satin with a blue sarsnet sash; small, sky blue flowers had been embroidered around the cuffs of her sleeves and around the hem of her skirt. It was a modest gown compared to those her sisters were wearing: Cate's peach colored taffeta frock was adorned with lace and pearls, and Jane—the only one of them that actually wished for male attention that night—had been coerced into commissioning a pale yellow gown made not only of silk and lace, but which also bore embroidery sewn with shimmery golden thread and small yellow crystals that sparkled brilliantly each time they caught the light.

Jane was sure to draw attention anytime she entered a room. Tonight, she would *shine*.

As though her thoughts had caught her sister's attention, a soft knock sounded at Elizabeth's door, and the maid opened it to Jane. "Oh, Jane, you look marvelous! You shall be the envy of every unmarried woman at the ball."

"Do not speak such nonsense, Lizzy," said her sister with a blushing smile. "I surely cannot outshine them all."

Elizabeth stood and crossed to her, and taking up her hands, said, "You will in my eyes, dearest Jane. And I am certain that more than one man shall end the night half in love with you."

"I only need one man to fall in love with me, Lizzy," Jane admonished.

Elizabeth gave her hands a gentle squeeze. "I maintain that you shall be spoiled for choice."

Cate poked her head around the door just then. "Oh, don't the two of you look stunning!" she said. "Come on, sisters, our Aunt Jennings is near to bouncing out of her slippers waiting for us."

Jane smiled and Elizabeth laughed; she gathered up her shawl, reticule, and fan and went out with her sisters to meet their aunt down below. Mrs. Jennings was in raptures over her nieces' ensembles, saying they were absolutely in their best looks.

"You will all of you have many admirers this night, I am certain of it," said she.

"Well, *I* am certain that Mr. Bingley's attentions will deter most of the gentlemen from pursuing our Cate," said Elizabeth, "and that talk of my courtship with Mr. Darcy will deter most of them from soliciting my affections. At least, I do hope so."

"Indeed, Lizzy," agreed Cate as they were heading out to the waiting carriage. "We shall just have to make sure that we divert all the extra attention to our dearest Jane."

"I should appreciate any genuine interest," said Jane as the carriage door was closed behind the last of them and Mrs. Jennings knocked on the roof to get them going. "But I would not have either of you be rude to any gentleman who asks for a dance."

"I cannot refuse anyone if I wish to dance at all, and it will be on Mr. Bingley if he wishes to share Cate with other gentlemen or if he wishes to declare himself—and therefore our sister—to be off limits."

"Oh, Lizzy, do stop saying such things," said Cate, though Elizabeth could tell her sister blushed by her tone. "I should not like to get my hopes up that he will make me an offer. I know that we have all of us speculated about it, and I… I have dreamed of it. But though Mr. Bingley has been enormously attentive during our courtship, he has as yet given no indication he will ask for my hand."

As her younger sister sat beside her, Elizabeth reached for one of those hands. "My dearest Cate, I would not worry yourself so. It is clear to any who sees you together that Mr. Bingley adores you. He has displayed his affection for you in public, and has given you leave to address him by his Christian name. And are those not the earrings he presented to you the other day?"

Cate smiled as she withdrew her hand and reached up to touch the flower earring at her lobe. The petals were heart-shaped pieces of coral set in gold, and at the center of each was a small diamond. She had cried when Bingley presented her with the gift—purchased, he said, solely because "They immediately brought your lovely countenance to mind"—before spontaneously throwing her arms about his neck and kissing him soundly. Mrs. Jennings had been highly amused, and even Elizabeth had smiled alongside Jane, though it was the latter who politely cleared her throat to put an end to the display.

"I concur with Lizzy, Cate," said Jane then. "I have no doubt that Mr. Bingley will soon make you an offer."

"Well, I wish he would hurry up! All this anticipation is most vexing!" cried Cate, leading her sisters and her aunt to laugh.

Conversation was then turned to the dinner they were soon to sit down to with the Earl and Countess of Disley, as well as the ball at the Torringtons' after, for the remainder of the ride to Bolton Street. When they at last pulled up outside the grand home of Darcy's uncle and aunt, Elizabeth was reminded of just how wealthy the family was, and it occurred to her that, should he eventually follow in the stead of his friend and offer for her, she might well be a frequent visitor here.

They were shown in and announced by the butler in moments. Lady Disley was quick to greet them and welcome them into her home again, and after parting from his conversation with a gentleman Elizabeth suspected was Sir Phineas Markham, for Lady Markham was at his side, Lord Disley also stepped over to pay his respects. Moments after they were introduced to the gentleman, who indeed was Sir Phineas, and as that was being concluded, Mr. Bingley and the Hursts arrived. After bowing respectfully to their host and hostess, Bingley made straight for Cate with a wide smile on his face.

And she worries he does not wish to marry her, thought Elizabeth wryly.

Louisa Hurst, she noticed then, was trying to hide her slightly rounded middle—the way she held her fan and reticule were evidence of it. Elizabeth shook her head, as there was no shame in being an increasing woman, though she smiled at the way Mr. Hurst seemed so much more aware of his wife, standing at her side rather than joining the men across the room.

Mr. and Mrs. Gardiner arrived next, much to their nieces' delight, and soon after a family called Tilney were announced. Elizabeth recalled then that name had been brought up at tea by Lady Disley, and on sight of the young Miss Tilney, she could see why Colonel Fitzwilliam had become smitten with her—she was absolutely lovely. The Reverend Mr. Tilney was a fine-looking young man with an easy smile, though Captain Tilney looked as cheerless as their father the general.

"Lizzy," whispered Jane into her ear as the Disley's were greeting their guests, "am I mistaken in thinking that the captain looks familiar?"

Elizabeth studied the elder of General Tilney's sons as surreptitiously as she was able. He wore a patch over his left eye, but seemed otherwise hale and hearty. His head was crowned in dark blond curls, and he carried himself in a fashion similar to that of Colonel Fitzwilliam.

"I do see something of Colonel Fitzwilliam's military bearing," she observed.

Jane shook her head. "It is not the colonel of whom I think. He reminds me of someone else."

Just then Lady Disley was walking over with Mr. Tilney and Miss Tilney. Mr. Tilney smiled and greeted Bingley warmly, showing that they were already acquainted, and he grinned even wider as he was presented to Elizabeth and her sisters.

"At last I meet the lovely sisters Bennet," said he. "I have heard talk of you exceedingly from Colonel Fitzwilliam, and I am most pleased to say that he did not exaggerate your shared beauty."

"You flatter us, Mr. Tilney," said Elizabeth as her sister blushed at the compliment.

"That is part of my brother's charm, Miss Elizabeth," said Miss Tilney wish a smile. "He knows how to flatter and does it very well."

"I know the ball at the Torringtons' is not for a couple of hours," said Mr. Tilney then, "but I do hope I shall have the pleasure of dancing with each of you at some point in the evening."

"I should be honored, sir," said Jane.

"And I," said Elizabeth, "though you shall have to ask Mr. Bingley whether he is willing to part with our sister as a partner."

The Tilneys glanced at Bingley and Cate, who were talking then with Lady Disley, Mr. and Mrs. Gardiner, and Mrs. Jennings.

"You know, I do not think I have ever seen so besotted a chap," Mr. Tilney observed. "Except for Theo, of course."

Beside him his sister blushed and cast her eyes down—and if Elizabeth was not mistaken, was doing her best to stifle a sniffle.

"Oh Elle, I am sorry," he said in a hushed tone. "I know how painful has been your parting."

Elizabeth recalled then that Darcy had told her the girl's father did not approve of his cousin. Why would have been beyond her understanding if she did not know already how such things worked—though he was the son of an earl, Colonel Fitzwilliam was but the second. He was not his father's heir and had no fortune of his own, therefore he was not good enough for Miss Tilney in her father's eyes.

Poppycock, thought Elizabeth, as she looked to the general with some disdain. *He should care more for his daughter's happiness than the wealth of her prospective suitor.*

Dinner was announced then, and the party headed for the dining room. Much to her surprise and delight, Elizabeth found herself seated between the younger Tilney siblings, though she felt very sorry for Jane to have been seated next to Captain Tilney. The soldier seemed to speak amiably enough, and Jane attended to him as she should, but Elizabeth could tell that his manner made her sister uncomfortable. She would be sure to ask her about it.

With Mr. Tilney and Miss Tilney she had very pleasant conversation. Mr. Tilney's jovial spirit soon rallied his sister's, and they had a very lively chat that included the gentleman relating some humorous stories from his years at university involving Darcy and Mr. Wickham. Miss Tilney also shared some of her brother's own foibles, and in a moment when he was engaged by Mr. Bingley, who sat to his left, she shared with Elizabeth her pain at the loss of Colonel Fitzwilliam's company.

"He is so very amiable, Miss Elizabeth," said Eleanor Tilney with a sad smile. "So kind, so gentlemanlike..."

"Not to mention handsome and charming," Elizabeth added.

Miss Tilney nodded. "Oh, very much so! I like him exceedingly, and it pains me so very deeply that Papa will not consent to courtship. Theodore and I had to..."

Her eyes flicked to her father for a moment, before she leaned closer and said, "Theodore and I—that is, Colonel Fitzwilliam and I—

we had to enlist Henry's aid in spending time together. They would arrange between them where and when Henry and I might go that he could 'chance' to join us. I so disliked deceiving our father, but what else could I do? I can't believe he is so set against the son of an earl just because Theodore was born second and not first."

"Yes," mused Elizabeth. "One would think a connection to the nobility would be most desirable even if to a second son."

"Unfortunately, my father is not of such a mind," Miss Tilney replied, her voice once again laden with sadness. "I must marry the heir to a rich estate, or a titled man of great wealth, and no other will do."

Elizabeth offered her a sympathetic smile, and said, "Perhaps you and I should be wallflowers together, Miss Tilney, for my desired partner this evening is also absent."

Here, her new friend brightened a little, saying, "Oh my, we are two of a kind, are we not? But at least you have the comfort of knowing your suit with Mr. Darcy is approved by your parents. And you shall see him again soon enough. Not only does my father not approve of Colonel Fitzwilliam, I do not know when next I shall see him, for he is gone off to his regiment again and they are for France within a fortnight."

Placing what she hoped was a comforting hand on Miss Tilney's shoulder, Elizabeth said, "Oh, Miss Tilney, I am sorry. I so wish I could think of something to cheer you."

"You are very kind, Miss Elizabeth," replied Miss Tilney. "That the colonel's family and friends approve of me and wish us happiness is a comfort, I can assure you. I shall do my best to enjoy this evening regardless of the colonel's absence, though I shall dread having to dance with all the 'more appropriate' suitors my father is sure to force upon me."

As the dinner continued, Elizabeth reflected on the vast differences between her father and Eleanor Tilney's. Mr. Bennet had not always been the most attentive parent, it was true, but at least he cared about his daughters' happiness. She knew he had been concerned for Mary's felicity in marrying Mr. Collins, knew he would never have forced herself to marry him had their cousin's attention not been redirected toward her sister. But General Tilney seemed an uncaring tyrant, more interested in increasing his family's wealth and standing in society than in the happiness of his children.

When at last the dinner was ended, the large party began to make their way out to carriages that they could start for Torrington

House. Upon their arrival, Elizabeth and her sisters and Mrs. Jennings marveled in great delight at the splendor of the decorations. They were soon presented to Lord and Lady Torrington, the latter of whom eyed Elizabeth with open curiosity, before making their way further into the grand house.

Some minutes later, Mr. and Miss Tilney approached with Captain Tilney in tow. Mr. Tilney made further introductions between his brother and those he had not formally met, and then Captain Tilney said, "Miss Elizabeth, I have engaged your delightfully charming sister Miss Bennet for the first two dances, but I would be honored if I might claim you for the second two."

Mr. Tilney himself had engaged Elizabeth for the first two dances, and as yet no other name was on her card. She could think of no reason to refuse, and so acquiesced to his request. When the three had stepped away, she turned to Jane and in a quiet voice said, "I see what you meant, sister. Now I have seen him up close, there is indeed something familiar about him, though I cannot think what."

"And his manner—what did you make of it, Lizzy?" Jane whispered back. "You know I dislike speaking ill of anyone, but Captain Tilney seems very cold. Very calculating. I find I cannot like him at all."

Elizabeth looked to her sister with some surprise. "This is a moment indeed, for you to speak so. If you did not like him, Jane, why did you agree to dance with him?"

"For the very same reason as you, I imagine—I could conceive of no reason to refuse, and knew that in so doing I would be forced to sit for the whole of the evening. I mean to enjoy myself tonight."

"And so you should, dearest Jane," Elizabeth said firmly. "After all, we are here tonight in order that you may make as many conquests as you like."

Jane laughed softly. "Oh, you are ridiculous, Lizzy! As I said before, I need only make one."

"And as I said before, I am certain that nearly every man in the room shall end the night half in love with you!" Elizabeth returned. "Just look around, Jane. Take note of all the eyes that are upon you."

As they gazed around the room, Jane blushed, for there were indeed several gentlemen who openly admired her. Still, generous heart that was hers, Jane said, "I daresay I am not the only one they stare at, Elizabeth. Your gown may be simply adorned, but it is no less beautiful than my own."

Before she could demure a reply, the two were claimed by their dance partners for the first set. Mr. Tilney's charm made her forget, for a time, that he was not the man she truly wished to be dancing with. When the set was ended, she turned to Captain Tilney and accepted the hand he held out to her.

The first of their two dances was a slower pace than either of the first two, and he held her just a little closer than was necessary. This instantly made Elizabeth uncomfortable.

"I understand from my brother, Miss Elizabeth," said the captain, "that you are engaged in a courtship with our neighbor, Mr. Darcy."

Confusion marred her brow. "Your neighbor, sir?" she countered.

"Indeed. Our house here in Town is right next to Darcy's." He smiled then, and to her it was a cold smile. A chill ran down her spine, but Elizabeth dismissed the sensation as nonsense.

"My father the general was most vexed when he was made aware that Darcy had formed an attachment to a girl from the country," Captain Tilney continued. "He was hoping, you see, that Darcy and my sister might make a match."

"I would say I am sorry to disappoint the general, but I am not," Elizabeth rejoined. "I happen to be very fond of Mr. Darcy and am honored by his attentions."

"As well you should be—his is a very old, very moneyed family, and your dowry much smaller than my sister's," the captain said. For a time they were silent through the moves of the dance, and then he asked, "By chance, have you met Miss Darcy?"

Elizabeth studied his face. It seemed placid enough, but in his tone she heard a note of the calculation Jane had spoken of. There was a reason behind his query, some secret she could not fathom the meaning of.

"I regret to say I have not," she replied. "Miss Darcy has unfortunately been ill for some months, though she is well on the mend now as her brother has been taking prodigious good care of her."

"And yet he has found the time to court you," said Tilney then.

"Looking after his sister does not mean he has no time to himself, Captain."

Tilting her head to the side, she studied him again. He definitely looked familiar—like someone she had met before but could not recall where. Her gaze then fell to the black patch over his eye.

"If it is not too indelicate of me to ask, Captain, what happened to your eye?" Elizabeth queried. "Were you wounded in battle?"

He chuckled. "If only I could answer in the affirmative—it would make for a much better story. No, the truth is I've a mild infection, and our family physician recommended the patch in order to keep dust and other particles from getting in my eye whilst the medicine does its work to clear the infection away."

"I am sorry to hear of your trouble, sir, and pray you will be recovered soon," she replied politely.

She was not, however, sorry when their set together ended. Elizabeth found herself in agreement with Jane—Captain Tilney seemed very cold and calculating. His inquiries were not unreasonable given their mutual acquaintance with Darcy and Colonel Fitzwilliam, but she could not shake the feeling that there was some greater reason behind them than neighborly curiosity.

On returning to her Aunt Jennings and Jane, Elizabeth found them in the company of a pair of finely dressed ladies and three gentlemen who were surely related, given their shared features—brothers, perhaps, or cousins at the very least. Two of the gentlemen, she surmised, were married to the two women who held their arms.

"Elizabeth, my dear girl, come meet some friends of mine!" said her aunt cheerfully. "Mr. and Mrs. Arthur Knightley, Mr. and Mrs. John Knightley, Mr. George Knightley, I present my niece, Miss Elizabeth Bennet."

The six of them exchanged greetings, and then Mrs. Jennings said, "Mrs. Arthur Knightley, my dear Lizzy, is the sister of our mutual acquaintance Lord Sotheby!"

Elizabeth brightened as Mrs. Arthur Knightley smiled. "You have met my brother and his wife?" the lady asked.

"I have, Mrs. Knightley," she replied. "My family was introduced to Lord and Lady Sotheby, as well as Miss Dashwood and Lady Amelia Northam, at Netherfield in Hertfordshire by Mr. Darcy and his friend Mr. Bingley, when they attended the latter's ball there November last."

"Fitzwilliam Darcy?" queried John Knightley, and at Elizabeth's nod, he said, "Why, he is one of my clients. I am a solicitor here in London, Miss Elizabeth. You could not know a better man than Darcy, to be sure, except perhaps my brother here."

Elizabeth looked to George Knightley, whom John Knightley had indicated, and noted that he was staring at Jane…and she at him. Elizabeth fought a smile as the pair of them became suddenly aware of their surroundings again; Jane looked down at the floor with a blush and Mr. Knightley cleared his throat.

"John, you only say so because you are my brother," said he.

"Oh, come now, George!" said John Knightley. "You *are* a good man. You pay such attention not only to the family estate and the whole of Donwell Parish, but to the Woodhouses as well."

"And why should he not, dearest?" said his wife. "My father and sister are as much his family as they are yours."

She moved from his side then and tugged at his hand. "Now come, John. We must dance again."

"Isabella, darling, you have only just come out of confinement—should you not be taking it easy?"

"John, I am perfectly well enough to dance another set, or even two. You were there when the doctor declared me remarkably recovered for having borne my fifth child," countered Isabella Knightley. "Please let us enjoy the evening—it's out first out together since little Emma was born."

John Knightley shook his head at her, though he smiled as he did so. He then turned to his brother and said, "Will you join us then, George? Which of these two lovely young ladies will you dance with?"

Elizabeth, seeing her sister color again, demurred, saying, "Oh, it must be Jane, Mr. Knightley! I have already danced two sets, and must take a rest if I am to dance again later this evening."

"Well, George?" prompted John Knightley.

With so many eyes turned his way—between his family and her own—Elizabeth knew George Knightley could hardly refuse to ask Jane to dance. Indeed, from the way he had been looking at her, she was sure he did not wish to.

Stepping past Mrs. Jennings then, he held out his hand to Jane, "Will you dance with me, Miss Bennet?"

Jane looked up at him and smiled radiantly, and instantly her sister knew she had been hoping he would ask. "I should be delighted, Mr. Knightley."

Elizabeth watched as he led her out onto the dance floor, followed by John and Isabella Knightley, and then Mr. and Mrs. Arthur Knightley.

"Oh, my dear Lizzy!" cried Mrs. Jennings with muted excitement. "I do believe our Jane has made a conquest!"

"They do seem to admire one another, do they not?" Elizabeth replied. "What do you know of him? How do you know the family?"

"Well, as I said, Mrs. Arthur is sister to Lord Sotheby. I've known him for many years, long before he discovered his noble lineage, as he is a good friend of my son-in-law Sir John Middleton—your cousin Mary's husband," her aunt replied. "Lord Sotheby and Mrs. Arthur were raised together, you see, when he believed himself a Brandon by birth. Mr. Arthur Knightley is master of a large estate in Devonshire called Whitwell, and he is a cousin of Mr. George Knightley and Mr. John Knightley. Mr. George, I understand, is master of a parish estate in Surrey called Donwell Abbey, and—"

"Wait, did you say Donwell Abbey?" Elizabeth interrupted her.

Mrs. Jennings nodded. "Why, yes—why do you ask?"

"Because that is where Mr. Darcy is now, with his sister!" Elizabeth looked out at the dancers, easily finding Jane and her partner, who seemed to have eyes only for each other. "I am rather surprised that the master of the house would be absent when he has guests in residence."

"Well, dearest, Mr. and Mrs. John Knightley *have* just had a child recently," Mrs. Jennings pointed out. "I would surmise that the elder Mr. Knightley is in Town to meet his newest niece. And Donwell is, I understand, only about sixteen miles from London. He has likely not been here but a day or so and will return again soon."

Elizabeth nodded. "Of course, you are right. Where are Cate and Mr. Bingley, and my Aunt and Uncle Gardiner?"

"Lady Disley wished to further acquaint my sister Gardiner with Lady Torrington, I believe—I see them over there," said Mrs. Jennings. Elizabeth looked to where she pointed, and was delighted to find her aunt engaged in what appeared to be a lively conversation with both countesses.

"Your uncle, I believe, is in the card room with several other gentlemen, and Cate was whisked away by Mr. Bingley to be introduced to some of his other acquaintances."

They watched the scene before them in silence for a moment, then Elizabeth said, "It is interesting to me that Lord Sotheby was raised in a family called Brandon. Aunt Gardiner's maiden name was Brandon, if I recall."

"It was indeed. How funny that is—I did not think of it myself until just now. Would it not be delightful if Madelene and Mrs. Arthur were somehow related?" said her aunt.

"It would indeed—Mrs. Arthur Knightley seemed a charming woman," Elizabeth replied.

As she looked about the room again, hoping to spy Miss Tilney or the younger of her two brothers, Elizabeth's eyes fell on Captain Tilney. He was watching her, and when their gazes met, he flashed a knowing smile and inclined his head toward her.

I find I cannot like him at all, Jane had said, the words causing a tremble to flitter through her. Elizabeth found herself in full agreement—she could not like him, either.

Although they had been warned that the Torringtons' Twelfth Night Ball typically did not end before dawn, the ladies of Berkeley Street, and the Gardiners, took their leave around two in the morning. Mrs. Gardiner had grown quite fatigued, and even the excessively exuberant Mrs. Jennings had declared herself near to being worn out. Cate was mildly disappointed to be taken away from Mr. Bingley so soon, but he had assured her that his family would not be long in following, given Louisa's condition, and that he would be sure to call on her later in the day.

Jane, though she had danced only once with George Knightley, was to Elizabeth's mind also disappointed that she had not more time to spend with him. He was some fifteen or so years Jane's senior, but she had declared him serious and intelligent, and said their short conversation had not been lacking. She was happy that her sister had met someone she admired, but a part of Elizabeth wished to advise caution. Though Mr. Knightley had clearly admired her sister in return, further observation of the man had shewed him to be almost as uncomfortable in company as Darcy had once been. He did not ask Jane to dance a second time, and spoke with her little after the one time they had.

When Elizabeth shared this with her Aunt Jennings after their return to Berkeley Street, the elder lady had laughed softly and said, "My dear, do not distress yourself. I daresay Mr. George Knightley was just as smitten with our Jane as she was with him—and was likely so surprised to be so taken with her on first sight that he knew not what to do with himself. Men who wait until they are older to marry are often reluctant to act, as they believe beautiful young women will want nothing to do with old men like themselves. They need only a little careful prodding. I will speak with Cassandra—Mrs. Arthur Knightley, that is—and we will see what we can do to help them along."

Her aunt had then kissed her cheek and bid her good night. After seeing to Jane, who declared she was quite tired indeed and wished to go directly to bed, Elizabeth said goodnight to her and went last to Cate's room. Her younger sister, though clearly tired, was still awake enough to chatter excitedly about the grandeur of the ballroom, the excellence of the supper feast, and the attention she had received from Mr. Bingley.

"His friends from Cambridge were all very kind," she said. "One of the gentlemen he introduced me to was recently married, and his wife said she would call on me sometime this week—I should like that very much. And he danced three sets with me, Lizzy, did you see? And when I danced with other gentlemen, I do think he was quite jealous. Perhaps you and Jane are right, and I shall hear that most blessed of questions from him very soon indeed. Then he will not have to share me at all!"

When she was unable to stifle a great yawn, Cate declared she was for bed. Elizabeth smiled and bid her pleasant dreams, before at last retiring to her own room. There, as a tired maid helped take down her hair and undo the laces of her gown, she reviewed her own experience at the ball, and found little disappointment in it save for the fact she had not been able to share it with Darcy. His presence would have made her enjoyment complete.

As she was later settling under the counterpane, Elizabeth wondered at having met his host at Donwell. She had managed an enquiry as to Mr. Darcy and his sister at one point, and George Knightley had informed her that when he had left his home a few days prior, Mr. Darcy, Miss Darcy, and Mr. Wickham were doing well and looking forward to being in London in another week or two.

Elizabeth then sat bolt upright in bed—Wickham! *That* was who Captain Tilney had reminded her of! How she had not made the connection before she was unsure, though perhaps it was due to his face being partly covered by the eye patch.

Icy dread suddenly trickled down her spine as she recalled that Darcy had told her his sister's attacker had pretended to be George Wickham. That the libertine had known enough about him to assume his character, to convince his sister that he was her old childhood friend. He'd told her that the scoundrel who'd harmed his sister looked enough like Wickham that the latter had been mistaken for the former by Lord Sotheby.

Mr. Tilney had attended Cambridge at the same time as both Darcy and Wickham. He would have heard all of Darcy's complaints about Wickham, who was then in the height of his former disreputable behavior. Would Mr. Tilney have shared those stories with his brother? Could Captain Tilney have been acting a part in Bath last year, using another's name in order to protect his family's?

Was she making wild assumptions? Elizabeth acknowledged she

had not liked Captain Tilney, and he did resemble Mr. Wickham to some small degree, but that certainly did not mean he was Georgiana Darcy's attacker.

Lying down again, Elizabeth willed herself to put the matter out of mind until she had rested. When she had had a full night's sleep, she could then consider the matter with a clear head, then decide if she ought write to Darcy and tell him of her suspicions.

Besides, it was going on three o'clock. There was naught that could be done at that hour of the morning.

Chapter Thirty

Elizabeth was surprised by the hour at which she woke—she had not slept until noon in years.

Hurrying to dress, she found her sisters already below, partaking of the small feast of items on the sideboard in the breakfast room. Her Aunt Jennings was not present, however, and she wondered if the lady was still abed.

"My my, Lizzy, you have slept very late," observed Cate as she was filling her plate with buns and bacon and sausage.

"I am as astonished as you are that I was abed so long," Elizabeth replied. "I must have been far more worn out by last night's event than I realized."

"Oh Jane, Lizzy, wasn't it magical? And only the first of many balls—the Season has only just begun!"

Elizabeth grinned at Jane as she carried her plate and a cup of tea over to the table. "It was a splendid evening indeed," she agreed.

"We must each of us send a note of thanks to Lady Torrington for our last-minute inclusion on her guest list," Jane said then, "and perhaps to Lady Disley also for asking her to do so."

Of course Jane would be the first to consider the proprieties, Elizabeth thought, and she smiled again at her sister. "You are absolutely right, my dear Jane—I shall take care of my own after I have eaten."

"Oh, Jane—how can you think of such things when there were so many splendid beaux at the ball last night?" Cate challenged her. "I may no longer have need of suitors as I already have a very fine one in Mr. Bingley, but you! Oh, did you not see how you were admired?"

"Now Cate," put in Elizabeth as Jane began to blush, "you know that such compliments as a gentleman's attention take our Jane by surprise and us never—though I admit to a great deal of curiosity as to which of her admirers she liked best."

At this, Jane's rosy cheeks deepened to scarlet, but before she could formulate any reply, their aunt bustled into the room at last.

"Forgive me, my dears, for the horrible tardiness of my arrival," she said as she went to the sideboard. "These old bones of mine were worn out more than I realized."

Cate giggled. "That is almost the same as Lizzy said to us."

Mrs. Jennings winked at Elizabeth as she joined her nieces at the table. Talk was, of course, centered around the ball and all its splendor—and, of course, the bevy of admirers Jane had danced with. Her card had been full almost from the moment they entered the ballroom, and she had hardly sat down the whole of the evening, save for when they had all gone to supper.

"Now Jane, do be serious," said Cate at one point. "Which of the gentlemen did you like best? There must be one of them you liked the best."

By now, Jane's face and neck were almost crimson with embarrassment. "Well," she began at last, "there was one whom I did admire more than the rest. But I do not know that I should speak of him, as I cannot be sure he admired me in return."

"Mr. George Knightley," said Mrs. Jennings. When Jane covered her face with her napkin, her sisters and her aunt laughed.

"'Tis nothing to be embarrassed about, my dear," said their hostess. "It's true he is some years older than you—about Edward's age, I believe—but he is a handsome man with a fine figure, a prosperous estate, and a fortune to match Mr. Bingley's. He's soft spoken and serious, much like yourself, and I daresay he would make a splendid husband for you."

"Oh, but Aunt, we danced only once and spoke so little to one another," Jane said then. "I can't think why my mind has singled him out over the others with whom I conversed more."

"The heart knows reason which reason does not know, dearest," replied her aunt kindly.

"Just look at our Lizzy, Jane," offered Cate. "She said for so long that she had no intentions of marrying anytime soon, yet she has accepted the suit of Mr. Darcy."

A realization came to Elizabeth then, and she smiled widely at her sister. "I've just recollected something, Jane, and I think Aunt

Jennings is right—he was so taken with you that he knew not what to do with himself."

"Whatever do you mean, Lizzy?"

"You were the only woman he danced with," Elizabeth pointed out.

"Good gracious, Lizzy, I do believe you are right!" cried Mrs. Jennings. "I do not recall Mr. Knightley dancing with any other lady, not even his sister or his cousin's wife."

"I… I am sure that means nothing," protested Jane weakly, though once again she blushed prettily. "Mr. Knightley only asked me to dance because his brother forced his hand, I am sure."

"I agree that may be so, Jane," Elizabeth conceded, "but I saw the way Mr. George Knightley was looking at you beforehand. He could not take his eyes off you, and only did so when spoken to. When you danced together, he gazed at you as though you were the only woman in the room."

"But then why would he not talk to me, Lizzy?"

"Men, my dear Jane, are as like as women to get flustered and not know what to talk of," offered Mrs. Jennings.

As it was Sunday, the ladies reasoned there were like to be few callers, so were content to be mostly idle through the afternoon. Of course, even while performing such easy tasks as reading or sewing, Elizabeth could not help being reminded what she had realized—and begun to suspect—before falling asleep that morning. Now that she recalled those dark thoughts, she could think of little else.

Comparing the two men in her mind, Mr. Wickham was slightly taller and not quite so broad of shoulder as Captain Tilney, and his skin was rather tan from all his years in India. Captain Tilney was also not so handsome as Darcy's half brother, his features sharper and less striking. Where Wickham's smile was warm and inviting, Captain Tilney's was cold and sinister.

Oh, do be sensible, Lizzy! she admonished herself. *You know perfectly well you may be suspecting him merely because you did not like the man.*

Still, she could not help mentioning at least the resemblance between the two, nor did she leave out her instant dislike and Jane's, when she wrote of the ball to Darcy.

That evening at dinner, Mr. Bingley and the Hursts were their guests. As the second course was being served, Bingley stood unexpectedly and turned to Cate, and to the utter delight of all the ladies, asked the very question his lady had been hoping to hear.

"My dearest Catherine," he began as he took her hand in his. "These last few months have seen you grow into such a charming and amiable young woman, and throughout my admiration for you has grown alongside. Your sparkling eyes were the first feature to capture my special attention, and your radiant smile never fails to make my heart swell beneath my breast. Last night you were in your best looks ever, and seeing you dance with other men made me realize that I do not want to have to share you with anyone else."

He then lowered himself to one knee, to the gasps of his sister and Jane and a squeak of delight from Mrs. Jennings—even Mr. Hurst was smiling as he watched him—and Cate's eyes filled with tears that fell in heavy drops as Bingley said, "In fact, I do believe I am very much in love with you, Catherine Bennet. Will you do me the extraordinary honor of becoming my wife?"

A moment of silence passed, and then Cate threw her arms around him as she cried, "Oh, Mr. Bingley!" He returned her embrace, lifting a brow as she sat back and took his face in her hands. "Oh, my wonderful Charles—of course I will marry you! I do believe I have quite fallen in love with you as well, and have only been waiting so very anxiously for you to ask!"

Laughter sounded around the table as Bingley rose and returned to his seat, taking Cate's hand again and pressing his lips to the back of it. He then informed them that he had been to Longbourn already and secured Mr. Bennet's permission to ask for her hand.

"And what of our mamma?" Elizabeth asked with a knowing smile. "Did she shatter the windowpanes with her delight?"

"Lizzy!" Jane admonished softly, though she smiled as she did.

"I cannot tell you, Miss Elizabeth, for I stayed only long enough to speak to your good father," Bingley replied. "Though Mr. Bennet did warn me his lady had long been expecting Catherine and I would return to Netherfield as husband and wife."

"Husband and wife," Cate said. "Oh, I can hardly believe I shall soon be a married woman!"

"Just how soon should you like to be wed, my dear?" Bingley asked. "I can acquire a common license and we can marry in two weeks, or we can wait for the reading of the banns, which would be a total of four weeks from today."

Cate's eyes widened. "You want to marry me right away?"

He smiled and kissed the back of her hand again. "My darling, I would marry you tomorrow if I could."

"Oh, Charles, really!" cried his sister. "A lady needs time to *plan* for her marriage—you can't expect Catherine to be ready to marry as soon as you ask her!"

Laughter once again went round, then Mrs. Jennings said. "Tomorrow after your music lesson, Cate, your sisters and I will join you at Gracechurch Street to begin planning your trousseau. You are most welcome to join us, Mrs. Hurst."

Louisa smiled at the invitation. "I should like that very much. After all, Catherine and I are to be sisters! And I know some habits of my brother, my dear, that you are unaware of. It is best you are prepared."

Bingley protested that Cate knew everything there was to know about him, but his sister maintained there were secrets still to tell.

Elizabeth was thankfully distracted from her maudlin thoughts about Captain Tilney through the rest of the evening as talk of the upcoming wedding prevailed, though when they were all gone to bed that night, her suspicions crept back into her thoughts. She found herself wishing that either her letter to Darcy would bring him to London sooner, or that the captain would take his leave.

The Gardiners were, naturally, overjoyed to hear of Cate's engagement the following morning. Mrs. Gardiner declared that as soon as the music lesson was over, they would make for her husband's warehouse. Mr. Gardiner said he would be only too delighted to supply his niece with all the fabrics and trinkets she could want for her wedding clothes.

"However shall I pay for all the things I will need?" Cate asked that afternoon. "I have not near enough money, and I know I shall have to purchase many fine things. Mr. Bingley is a wealthy man, and I must prove with my dress and decorum that I am worthy to be married to one such as he."

"Oh, my sweet Cate," said Mrs. Gardiner, "you need not concern yourself as to the money. Mr. Bingley sent word to your uncle while you were in your lesson that you are to use as much of your dowry as necessary, as he considers those funds to be yours. Now, we *will* be keeping the purchases within reason, mind you, but as you say, becoming the wife of a wealthy gentleman means you must look and act the part, and we will certainly get you started today."

"Mr. Wilson says I will also need an instrument of my own," Cate added. "Today he brought with him another called a dulcimer, and I think I like it better than the violin."

When at last their party reached the Gardiner warehouse, they were welcomed heartily by Mr. Gardiner, and he personally showed the ladies to the section where textiles were on display. No doubt with ballgowns and evening gowns in mind, Cate was shown several rich fabrics, as well as finely made cotton and muslin for morning and walking gowns. Riding habits were also considered, as were night dresses, spencers, gloves, and pelisses. Cate marveled at all the bolts of cloth her aunts and sisters helped her to select, speculating that she was like to have a whole new wardrobe by the time she was married.

"Oh, I can just imagine Lydia's reaction when she heard the news," she said as their party exited Gardiner Imports more than an hour later. "She is surely jealous already that Mr. Bingley liked me above her, and that Mr. Darcy decided he liked Lizzy."

"I do not doubt that your sister is envious of you and Elizabeth, Cate," said Mrs. Gardiner as they approached the two carriages that awaited them. "But you ought not be pleased she is unhappy."

"Oh, but I am not!" Cate assured her. "To be sure, I really feel quite sorry for Lydia—if only she had started to listen to Jane and Lizzy as Mary and I finally did, if she had only followed Papa's new rules for her, she might well have joined us and been having all the same enjoyment of Town as we have had so far."

When the ladies had loaded into the two carriages, Jane opting to ride with Mrs. Gardiner and Mrs. Hurst, and were on their way to Bond Street, Cate said, "You know, Lizzy, you really ought have been selecting your own fabrics while we were in Uncle's warehouse."

"Pray, why should that be, Cate?" Elizabeth asked.

"Well, because you and Mr. Darcy are sure to marry not long after Charles and I. You might as well be prepared."

Mrs. Jennings laughed, and Elizabeth could not help but join her. "My dearest Cate, you are surely blinded by wedding fever. You know perfectly well that Mr. Darcy and I desire more time in each other's company before we consider marriage, and we've had too few opportunities to spend any time together since his sister has been ill. I am truly content to wait until the time is right."

This declaration did not dissuade her aunt and sister from teasing Elizabeth as the carriage rambled on. When they had arrived outside the *modiste* shop Mrs. Hurst had recommended, Cate was the first to alight and had shared her idea with the others in their party before Elizabeth could set one foot on the pavement. Mrs. Gardiner, Louisa, and even Jane agreed that it certainly could not hurt to be ready for when Mr. Darcy *did* make his offer. She would then, her aunt said, have a great deal less to concern herself with in preparing for the wedding, and could thus enjoy the day more.

Following the long stop at the *modiste*—and much to Elizabeth's delight—the party encountered Mr. and Miss Tilney at the milliners, where the brother was paying a debt to his sister and purchasing a new bonnet for her.

"'Tis my own fault," said he, "that I must replace the hat, as I am the one who knocked it off her head and into the river."

"Well, whatever the occasion, we are so pleased to meet you again, are we not, Jane?" said Elizabeth.

Jane smiled. "Indeed. I am most delighted to meet you both again so soon."

As Jane then moved off with Miss Tilney to look over some ribbons, Mr. Tilney stepped closer to Elizabeth and said, "Forgive me if I seem impertinent, Miss Elizabeth, but my brother expressed an interest in knowing the degree of acquaintance between yourself and Mr. Darcy."

Elizabeth suppressed the urge to scowl. "I should have thought our degree of acquaintance was made clear to the captain already by you, Mr. Tilney. After all, he did say it was from you that he learned of our courtship."

"Indeed, I *did* tell him that we would be meeting the young lady who had foiled our father's hopes of a match between Eleanor and Darcy," Mr. Tilney replied. "But I figure Frederick thinks he a chance with you."

It was all she could do not to snort aloud. "Are you certain of that, sir? After all, my fortune is not even equal to that of your own sister—I should think it hardly enough to attract the attention of one such as your brother, or your father. Please, do me the courtesy of asserting to Captain Tilney that he would do well to set his sights on another—but *not* my sister Jane. Sweet and amiable creature that she is, apt to like everyone in general, I am afraid that she did not find his manner to her liking. Frankly, neither did I."

Tilney's eyes widened a fraction at her blunt declaration, then he smiled. "I am truly sorry if Frederick upset either yourself or Miss Bennet," he said. "I beg you would not allow his ill manner to offend you—that is how he is, I'm afraid. According to our mother, God rest her, he was even ill-mannered as a baby."

"Your mother no longer lives?"

He shook his head. "No, sadly she does not."

Elizabeth offered what she hoped was a sympathetic smile. "I am sorry to hear of your loss. Makes me feel guilty, now, for so often being vexed with my own mother," she said.

"Our parents do drive us to distraction sometimes, do they not?" said Mr. Tilney.

Elizabeth suspected his remark was meant more toward his father than his late mother. "I imagine there is no one relation in our lives that does not at some point or other."

She then thought once more of the suspicions she felt regarding his brother and ventured to say, "By and by, Mr. Tilney, it occurred to me on observing Captain Tilney's person that he reminded me a great deal of Mr. Wickham, in both look and comportment. Has anyone ever mistaken your brother for Mr. Wickham?"

"Not to my knowledge, though I and one other recently mistook Wickham for Frederick, when we observed him from behind," Mr. Tilney replied.

"Do you think, then," Elizabeth pressed, "that someone who had not seen Mr. Wickham for some years might mistake your brother for him? Or perhaps someone who saw Mr. Wickham from afar might think they were one and the same?"

Her companion's brow furrowed briefly as he considered it. "Well, Wickham's a might taller, but yes, I suppose such a mistake could be made."

Such a mistake *had* been made, Elizabeth thought. Though she had no proof other than her instant dislike of the man and his resemblance to Mr. Wickham to go on, she was certain all the way to her bones that Captain Tilney was guilty of attacking Georgiana Darcy.

Oh, why hadn't she sent her letter to Darcy by express?!

Tuesday, 8 January 1799

Time passed quickly in Surrey. Georgiana recovered at a steady pace, and little Darciana grew. The babe became the apple of her adoptive parents' eyes, and though it was clear—to Darcy, at least—that his sister wished to hold her, each time the infant was offered she politely refused.

He asked her why one night as he was escorting her to her chambers for bed. "I do not think it wise, brother," she began, "that I should take the child into my arms. If I do, I fear I should never be willing to release her, and I know that I must."

She sniffled as they reached her door, and he could tell it was an effort for her to meet his eyes with hers. "Roy and Roberta are the kindest of people, and I am most pleased to call them family. I know that they will love Darciana as their own, and I am happy for my… for the little one that she will be so adored by them. I wish this new family every possible happiness. Knowing that I must leave her behind when we depart is difficult enough; to hold my daughter—no, *their* daughter—in my arms would be agony. I would never be able to put my heart back together again."

She had stifled a sob then and swept into her room as though desperate to get away from him. From the sounds he heard on the other side of the door, it seemed her tender heart was already broken. Darcy had placed his hand to the aged wood, closed his eyes, and prayed that she would not be made to suffer the loss of her first child for long.

The only consolation Darcy received in those days were letters from others he cared for. He received a letter from Fitzwilliam regarding the marriage of their cousin to Edward Ferrars in the first week of his stay. Lady Catherine—Anne's mother—had indeed stormed into Disley House that Monday afternoon after receiving Lord Disley's express, full of righteous anger as she declared her brother had "ingested tainted opium" if he truly believed he had any right whatsoever to force her daughter into marriage. His uncle had, according to Theo:

…calmly and succinctly, his tone brooking no argument, reminded her who the head of the family was. I declare, Will, it was a sight to see—our banshee aunt rendered speechless! After Aunt Catherine fell silent, Father informed her that her daughter had inescapably rendered his actions necessary by the 'abhorrent, unladylike behavior' displayed in her choice to compromise you that led to her compromising poor Ferrars instead, and that a marriage between them was the only chance we had of avoiding a scandal. Our aunt then attempted to refute his claim, declaring Ferrars 'a liar out to score a rich wife far above his station'.

Mother then spoke up and informed her just which family Anne was to marry into—she was not idle, my mother, during those hours before Aunt Catherine arrived. She paid a call to Mr. Ferrars at his mother's house, spoke to both, and quite expertly—according to Mamma—led Mrs. Ferrars to reveal a great deal of the family's history. Apparently, your former parson's dear mamma came from the prestigious Barrows family, and old Mr. Ferrars' lineage and wealth goes back at least half as far as yours. That Ferrars comes from old money seemed to settle Aunt Catherine, and Mother is determined that the minor scandal from the spring involving Ferrars' unfortunate alliance with his brother's now-wife will be forgotten. She's spreading news of Anne's match even now, and the story is that Anne and Ferrars met when he took the parsonage at Lambton, falling irrevocably in love at first sight. They are to be married on 20 December – Aunt Catherine insisted on an even-numbered day.

Elizabeth and Bingley had also written, both of them more than once. Bingley spoke briefly in one letter about learning that his father had once done business with Elizabeth's uncle, Mr. Gardiner, and though he did not know for what reason the relationship had been severed, after meeting with the man during a day trip to London he was eager to re-establish it. Though he and his sisters lived mainly off the profits of the textile mill their grandfather had built and which their father had enabled to greatly prosper, Bingley was not ashamed of the fact that the family still owned it, that it still did well, and that his fortune grew steadily because of it.

Bingley and Elizabeth both reported that the romance between the former and Catherine Bennet was proceeding apace; Elizabeth was most pleased by her sister's continued improvement in conduct, and Bingley was over the moon that the "loveliest, liveliest creature" of his acquaintance had grown to adore him as much as he did her.

I am sure of it, Darcy old boy, his friend had written. *I believe she is growing to love me as I do her, and so soon I shall tell her the true depth of my feelings. I am in love, my friend, truly in love, and I do not doubt that soon I shall have even grander news to share with you.*

The declaration was a strong indicator that Bingley was thinking of marriage. Darcy did not doubt that Bingley was certain, of both his feelings and Catherine's, as he had never even hinted at marriage before.

I so wish you were here to witness the change in them both, Elizabeth wrote in one of her letters. *It is truly remarkable to see how the love growing between them continues to effect change, especially in my sister. Cate no longer despairs of having to change in order to gain Mr. Bingley's affections, for she has seen a glimpse of what advantages proper behavior can give her. She is looking forward to our time in Town even more, for Mr. Bingley and Mrs. Hurst have promised to introduce her to a few of your sophisticated friends whilst we are there.*

In another letter, after he'd informed her that the Fairleys now had a daughter, she wrote: *I am so very pleased for them, and even more so that Miss Darcy shall soon be recovered enough to join you in London when you come. I look forward to making her acquaintance, and shall certainly do as you ask and use all my questionable charms to help her recover her spirits. We shall shop, make music, visit parks and museums, and see every play and opera you can afford to take us to. I declare that Miss Darcy will have little time to think of her regrets if we are attentive enough.*

Write again soon, preferably with the news that we will have the pleasure of your company in London ere long.

Yours affectionately,
Elizabeth Bennet

P.S. Though the news is not likely to bring much pleasure to Miss Darcy at present, I have heard from Miss Dashwood that Lady Sotheby bore a healthy son in the evening on Christmas Day. Mother and child are doing very well, and Lord Sotheby, I am told, is quite in raptures.

Darcy smiled as he moved on to the next letter—he enjoyed re-reading Elizabeth's words, and often passed idle time doing so. He expected to receive another any day, as the Bennet sisters had attended Lady Torrington's Twelfth Night ball on Saturday. He wondered how often Elizabeth had danced, and whether she had wished him there with her. Even a dowry of a mere ten thousand pounds, as each sister now had, would garner attention among the *ton*—especially among the second- and third-born sons desperate for any measure of independent wealth. Jane Bennet, who really was a great beauty, was sure to be admired and pursued.

He considered that her sisters would be also, though Cate would soon be marked as spoken for by the attention of Bingley at the soirées and dinners they were sure to attend. That Elizabeth, with her pert opinions and fine eyes, would be pursued by the rakes and rogues of the *ton* was also certain—and aggravating. She belonged to *him*, or she would as soon as could reasonably be arranged. At the very least, he intended to make sure it was known that her smiles and charms had been claimed by him as soon as he could get himself to Town, and that would happen when he had been assured that Georgiana could travel.

Darcy's thoughts were interrupted by the appearance of Wickham and Fairley; Knightley was again out of the house, this time in London himself as his brother's wife had recently ended her confinement with their fifth child.

Wickham stepped over to him with a letter in hand and held it out. "Your dear Elizabeth writes again."

Darcy took the letter without comment, and setting the lady's previous letters aside, broke the wax seal and began to read her now-familiar scrawl. She wrote of the dinner at Disley House and the Torringtons' ball, as expected—and to his delight, expressed her belief that she'd have enjoyed the evening much more had he been able to share it with her.

I pray, dear William, that you will be able to join us here very soon, for I am sure your presence would put my mind at ease on another matter. Perhaps I am being foolish, but I feel compelled tell you about my meeting a gentleman whose manner unsettled not only myself, but even my unflappable sister Jane! Captain Tilney, brother of your friend Mr. Henry Tilney, was a guest also at both your aunt's dinner and the ball – Mr. Tilney and Miss Tilney were both very delightful, but I am afraid their brother was not. There was something in his manner, which I cannot quite put my finger on, that just did not sit well with me. It is unfortunate he should so much resemble Mr. Wickham. I say, Captain Tilney looks enough alike Mr. Wickham that I am sure if I did not already know the latter was with you in Surrey, I should have thought them the same person on first sight.

Darcy did not realize he had frozen in place until Wickham put a hand to his shoulder and gave him a light shake. "Is all well, Darcy? Miss Elizabeth has not written to end your courtship, has she?"

He stood suddenly, forcing Wickham to take a step back. "What color eyes does Frederick Tilney have?"

Wickham frowned. "How the devil should I know? I don't recall ever meeting Tilney's brother. Why do you ask?"

Fitzroy Leslie stepped across to them. "Darcy, what's happened? You really don't look well, mate."

"Elizabeth has met him," Darcy replied to Wickham's query. "She took an instant dislike to now-Captain Tilney. And she says he looks a great deal like you."

Wickham paled instantly as realization dawned. "Oh my God… He's the one—he *has* to be!"

Pacing away, he raked a hand through his hair. "Henry thought I was his brother November last when we met in Bond Street, at least until I'd turned around to face him. And an acquaintance of his from Bath thought the same that night we went to the theater—thunder and turf, Will, the Tilneys were in Bath last spring, at the same time as Georgiana!"

"I recall your tellin' me early on durin' your stay here that whoever the attacker is, he had to not only know the history between you," put in Fairley, "but resemble Mr. Wickham enough that, from a distance at least, he bore a passin' resemblance."

"Enough for Wickham to have been mistaken for him by Lord Sotheby, yes," Darcy agreed.

"And you now think that this Captain Tilney is that man?" Fairley pressed.

He held up the letter he'd been reading. "Elizabeth's exact words are: 'I say, Captain Tilney looks enough alike Mr. Wickham that I am sure if I did not already know the latter was with you in Surrey, I should have thought them the same person on first sight.'"

Horror and anger both began to twitter along Darcy's spine. "And Henry Tilney, trusting fool that he has been at times, spoke of your…misadventures…to his brother. Of our deteriorated relationship since the death of your parents. How else could Frederick Tilney have learned anything about you? How could he have passed himself off as you more than once over the last six years?"

A crinkling sound soon made Darcy realize that he was crumpling Elizabeth's letter. Drawing a breath, he smoothed the paper out as determination filled him, and he turned resolutely to the other men.

"I must depart for London at once," said he. "Frederick Tilney is there at this very moment, and Henry Tilney, his sister, or his father are sure to know where he may be found."

"I'm coming with you," said Wickham at once.

"You do not wish your sister to travel with you?" asked Fairley.

Darcy shook his head. "No, not until the brigand has been caught. I will not put her at risk."

The laird gave a nod. "Georgiana is welcome to remain with us for as long as necessary," he said. "Though given her reticence to be near Darciana, I believe she will wish to take her leave as soon as may be done. Her confinement will be ended within the next fortnight."

After folding the letter he held and gathering up the others he had been reading, Darcy tucked them into the inside breast pocket of his jacket and started for the library door. It was time to bring this nightmare to an end.

Chapter Thirty-One

It was near to six in the evening when Darcy's carriage arrived before Darcy House—he'd made his driver push the horses as fast as they would go, and they had stopped only once, long enough to change them out for a fresh set at an inn.

He did not go directly to his townhome when he alighted from the carriage, however; instead, he went straight to the one next to it, banging on the black wood of its entry door with his fist rather than ringing the bell.

An aged, sour-faced butler opened it a minute later. "May I help you, sir?"

"I must see Captain Tilney at once," Darcy demanded.

The butler raised an eyebrow. "Captain Tilney is not in, sir. Shall I take your card?"

"Have you any idea where the good captain might be?" asked Wickham in a placating tone. "It is rather urgent that we speak with him."

The butler's eyebrow climbed ever closer to his receding hairline. "General Tilney, Captain Tilney, Mr. Tilney, and Miss Tilney are out to dinner, sir. I believe their hostess for the evening resides in Berkeley Street."

Berkeley Street… where Elizabeth resided with her sisters and her Aunt Jennings.

Darcy turned immediately away and hurried back down the stoop. Wickham issued a hasty 'thank you' before he followed him back to the carriage.

"Berkeley Street's not far, Will," said the younger man as the carriage moved off a moment later. "And they're in company.

Elizabeth will be well."

"She'd better be," Darcy muttered.

"How do you want to do this? I should not like to give Tilney the chance to run away," Wickham said then. "Should I wait outside with the carriage, do you think?"

"Nay, I want us to confront him together, before witnesses," Darcy said immediately. "Your being in the same room is like to throw him off balance; he'll make a mistake, and we'll have him."

"Let us hope that the scoundrel is not near any women when we go in," said Wickham. "I should not like to give him the opportunity to take a hostage if he is frightened into running."

Darcy nodded his agreement and silently urged the horses to go faster. The Jennings house in Berkeley Street was but three or four blocks from his own; he could walk the distance and not be fatigued under ordinary circumstances. But these were not ordinary, and the carriage horses—though not the four he'd started out with—were tired from being pushed hard; they were plodding along at barely a trot. Now that he was here, now that his sister's nightmare was so soon to be ended, he could only desire haste. He wanted to confront Frederick Tilney, he wanted him to face justice.

To that end, knowing that General Tilney was likely to vehemently dispute any charge brought against his son, Darcy had charged Laird Fairley with sending an express he'd written to Sotheby Hall. They would need the witness testimony of Lord Sotheby if they hoped to see that Captain Tilney got his due. The word of both he *and* his wife would be even better, but Lady Sotheby was still in her confinement, and would certainly not be willing to leave their infant son without both his parents even for so short a time as Darcy would need them. Nor could he bring himself to ask it of them.

No, just the earl's account of meeting Tilney would have to do, because Darcy certainly would *not* make Georgiana face the libertine if he could help it, and he hadn't a clue where to find Mrs. Younge at this point. Darcy prayed it would be enough, and he hoped fervently that the older man's arrival in Town would not be too long after theirs.

"Tell me again why we are forced to endure the company of two men that no one in this house cares for?"

Jane frowned at Elizabeth in the mirror over her dressing table.

"Now Lizzy," said she, "you know very well why. The first invitation to the family must include the head of their house since he is in Town with them—it would have been an affront to the general had Aunt Jennings invited only Mr. and Miss Tilney."

Elizabeth mirrored her sister's expression. "Our aunt was foolish to include them based on that silly old notion—had she not, we would neither of us have to put up with the captain, and she not the general."

At the Torringtons' ball, Mrs. Jennings had been so amused by Henry Tilney's jovial manner and captivated by Miss Tilney's sweet nature that she had instantly invited the two to join their dinner party at Berkeley Street the following Tuesday evening. Unfortunately—in Elizabeth's mind, at least—General Tilney and his elder son had been invited as well. Mrs. Jennings had included the pair merely as a courtesy, though on later hearing that both Elizabeth *and* Jane had not cared for Captain Tilney, and after Elizabeth had shared how the general was set against Lady Disley's son courting his daughter, she declared that she wished wholeheartedly she could have left them out.

A small part of Elizabeth had wished to share her suspicions about the captain, but she dared not until she'd had chance to speak to Darcy, and it would be at least another week before he came to Town, unless her letter urged him to make the journey sooner. There was also the matter of Miss Darcy's reputation—Mr. Darcy had told her of his sister's circumstances in great confidence, and she couldn't very well speak as to her fears regarding Captain Tilney without breaking that confidence. No, she would simply have to bear a few hours in the man's company no matter how uncomfortable her belief in his guilt made her feel.

"Lizzy, do not be unkind," Jane was saying.

"You are right, our Aunt Jennings is blameless," Elizabeth said as she stood. "She did not know we thought poorly of the captain until well after she had issued her invitation. Though I must say I *am* curious as to why the general agreed to attend—we could none of us be of any real interest to the man, given our fortunes are less than his daughter's."

"Whatever his reason, Lizzy, it is only one evening, and I am determined not to allow Captain Tilney's presence to spoil my enjoyment of it," Jane declared as the sisters were departing Elizabeth's bedroom.

Elizabeth nodded. "Yes, it is only one evening. If you can bear up, dear Jane, I can do no less. Besides, there are to be fifteen of us at dinner—thus, there is every chance we shall be required to converse with Captain Tilney very little, if at all."

Jane slipped her arm around Elizabeth's as the two reached the ground floor. "Now that's the spirit, sister—always look for the good in every situation," she said with a laugh.

The gathering tonight had been planned some days in advance; their cousin Mary and her husband were to come to London themselves a few days after the lady's mother, and of course Mrs. Jennings wanted to welcome them with a fine dinner. Sir John and Lady Middleton's journey had been delayed, however, when one of their four children had fallen ill, so it was through letters that the evening was arranged. Joining them would be the Gardiners and Bingley and the Hursts, with the Tilney family rather a last minute addition.

Soon after their arrival in the drawing room came the arrival of the Gardiners, followed in minutes by the Middletons. Elizabeth and Jane greeted the cousin they had met only twice as warmly as they could, and then she and Sir John were introduced to Cate. Bingley arrived at near the same moment as the Tilneys a few minutes later; he conveyed the regrets of the Hursts, who were unable to join them as planned due Mr. Hurst's mother taking ill, and they were to attend her. Elizabeth had not even been aware the lady still lived, as Mr. Hurst wasn't much of a conversationalist unless the topic was sport, and Louisa Hurst had never mentioned her husband's family. By the time further introductions had been made and all the party were at least acquainted with one another's name, the butler announced dinner.

Elizabeth found herself pleased with the seating arrangement as the group filed into the dining room. Mrs. Jennings' dinners to date had been rather informal affairs, with the lady allowing her guests to sit where they wished—a very convenient arrangement for Mr. Bingley to make his proposal to Cate on Sunday, the two of them having naturally chosen to sit next to one another. Tonight, she adhered to etiquette and directed the ladies into the dining room in order of rank; the gentlemen, therefore, followed suit. Elizabeth found herself seated on the same side of the table as Captain Tilney, but between them were Mr. Henry Tilney and Miss Tilney—she could therefore avoid speaking to the man if she wished.

As soon as each person had taken a spoonful or two of their soup, conversation began. Elizabeth was happy to engage with Miss

Tilney, who sat on her right, as well as Jane and Cate, who sat across the table from them; Mrs. Gardiner, on Elizabeth's left, was engaged in talk of children with Lady Middleton, who was across from her. The gentlemen, it seemed, were all of them taken up with the latest politics, and given her seat at the head of the table, Mrs. Jennings was uncharacteristically quiet, having no lady near her to drown out the talk of the men.

The second course was just being served when the dining parlor door opened to admit the butler; he was just announcing Mr. Darcy and Mr. Wickham when the two of them appeared.

He's here! Elizabeth's heart sang.

"Why, Mr. Darcy, what a pleasure it is to see you again, sir!" cried Mrs. Jennings heartily. "Won't you join us? We are two short this evening, as Mr. and Mrs. Hurst were unable to come."

Darcy, his countenance flushed and set in what Elizabeth knew instantly to be a controlled scowl, inclined his head, then said gruffly, "I am afraid I must decline, ma'am. I am here on urgent business and demand that Captain Tilney come away with me at once."

General Tilney stood, and Elizabeth glanced at him as he barked, "On what authority do you *demand* the attendance of my son?"

Captain Tilney's uncovered eye focused on Wickham, Elizabeth saw—and not without some degree of alarm in its expression, if she were not mistaken. Why should he not be? she mused. He'd probably never expected to actually meet the man whom he had been impersonating for some years.

"General, in deference to the sensitivity of the ladies present, I should not like to discuss the matter before them," replied Darcy. His hard, angry gaze then fell to Captain Tilney. "If you have even a shred of honor left, Captain, you will come away without incident."

Captain Tilney smirked. "I'm afraid I must decline, sir," he said, mimicking Darcy's own words of a moment ago. "I cannot imagine what sort of 'urgent business' you might have with me, as you and I have not even been formally introduced."

"Balderdash!" snapped Mr. Wickham as he stepped further into the room. "You know perfectly well why we are come, you wretch! Impersonating me and running up debts in my name are the least of your crimes."

"Upon my word," said Miss Tilney, her gaze swinging from Wickham to her brother and back again. "Frederick, there *is* a resemblance…"

"Captain Tilney, do the gentlemanly thing and come away," said

Darcy. "Let us not make a scene."

"My son will not be going anywhere with you, sir, until I hear an explanation!" General Tilney all but shouted.

Captain Tilney stood slowly…and laughed as he did so. "Why should I go anywhere with you? You've interrupted a perfectly pleasant dinner party—uninvited, wildly disheveled—and you are making demands of a man whom you have never met for which you refuse to give explanation. Any reasonable gentleman would be disinclined to acquiesce to your…request."

As he spoke, the captain had, in fact, been walking slowly toward Darcy and Wickham. When he came abreast of Elizabeth, he moved so suddenly to grab her and drag her out of her chair that she had not even time to cry out, nor had any of the other gentlemen time to react. Lady Middleton immediately swooned as Tilney pressed Elizabeth to his chest, the carving knife no one had seen him take from the table held at her throat.

"Frederick, what in God's name are you doing?!" cried Henry Tilney.

"Tilney, if you harm her, I swear I will kill you," Darcy said with a growl.

Captain Tilney laughed again, this time the sound bearing a sinister note. "Come now, Darcy, let us prevaricate no longer—you already want to kill me. I'm merely giving you further incentive."

"You are a monster!" Elizabeth snapped.

He leaned his head down and spoke into her ear. "I am a Captain in His Majesty's Army—and since I am holding a very sharp knife, you should be more polite."

"So what now, Tilney?" Wickham asked then.

"What happens now is the two of you get out of my way," Tilney replied. "I'm going to take sweet Elizabeth here for a little ride—I assume your carriage waits at the curb, Darcy—and when I have had sufficient head start, I shall leave her at the side of the road for you to find. Your cooperation in allowing me to leave here unimpeded will determine if she is left there alive or dead."

Jane and Cate, who by now had begun to weep, both gasped with alarm; Cate clung to Mr. Bingley as Jane was forced to attend the unconscious Lady Middleton.

"You won't get away with this, Tilney, anymore than you will what you have already done," Darcy said even as he and Wickham moved away from the door. "I promise you, you'll not grow an hour older."

Captain Tilney laughed again as he forced Elizabeth to walk with him away from the table. "We shall see about that, won't we?"

Strangely, Elizabeth felt more pain at the anguished expression on Darcy's face as they passed him than she was frightened of the knife at her throat. But she said nothing as Captain Tilney walked her out of the dining parlor and through the hall. They startled more than one of the servants going about their duties as they made for the door, which her captor ordered her to open.

Outside, he hurried her down the stoop so fast her slippers barely made contact with the cement. Captain Tilney yelled at Darcy's coachmen to abandon the vehicle even as he shoved her toward the box. Climbing up to it was difficult to do in her evening gown, and her awkwardness in so doing led to Tilney planting a hand on her bottom and shoving her upward to hasten her ascent.

Elizabeth yelped indignantly, and glared at him in the low light of the street's oil lamps as he climbed up beside her. Tilney quickly took up the reins, keeping the knife in his right hand, and gave the leather straps a sharp crack. The horses started immediately into a trot, and Elizabeth was forced to grab onto her seat as the carriage jerked away from the sidewalk.

They were near the end of the block when the captain reached up and pulled the eye patch from his head, then cast it into the street. "I suppose there's no point in wearing that anymore."

"I *knew* your story about an infection was false!" Elizabeth declared.

"Ah, so you'd met that bounder Wickham before me, eh? I ought to have known—you and that sister of yours were rather cold little fish at the Torringtons' ball," Tilney replied.

"I *had* met him before you, in fact, though my sister knows nothing of what a despicable fiend you truly are!"

After giving the reins another sharp crack to urge the horses to a faster pace, Tilney lifted his left hand and took her neck in a painful grasp. "Elizabeth, darling, what did I tell you about being polite? If I should throw you from this carriage seat, I daresay you would find the result very unpleasant."

"I already find my company more unpleasant than the possibility of death," she seethed through clenched teeth.

Tilney squeezed harder. "I could also simply snap your delicate little neck—your precious Mr. Darcy is not likely to marry a corpse," he said coldly. "Now, if you value your life, you'll keep that sharp tongue of yours still."

Releasing her then, he snapped the reins a third time. Elizabeth did remain silent, though mostly due to the need to focus on remaining in her seat as they careened around a corner—if memory served they were now on Manchester Street. Every lamp they passed shewed Elizabeth that the horses were drenched in sweat—Darcy and Wickham must have made great haste from Surrey for the team to be in such a state. He must have received her letter that morning; only her note of the resemblance between his half brother and the crazed man beside her could have brought them here so quickly.

"How could you do it?" she felt suddenly compelled to ask. "How could you pretend to be a friend, to love that poor girl, and then force yourself on her in so vile a manner?"

"Georgiana Darcy was but a means to an end," Captain Tilney replied. "Like Wickham in days of old, I've a large number of debts to pay—"

"In his name as well as your own," Elizabeth muttered.

"—and I need money to pay them," he said, ignoring her remark. "I cannot go to my father for the funds as he'd never consent, given how great a sum I require. When I saw Darcy's advertisement for a companion in a newspaper, I thought it a perfect opportunity to get myself in cash again. I'd given Wickham's name before, not wanting any stories left behind of my activities to besmirch my family's honor. My father would not have liked that, and really, who is George Wickham? A nobody son of a steward."

The last he said with a sneer, then directed the horses to turn again onto Oxford Street, and from there onto New Bond Street. The horses were slowing, and it was then that Elizabeth took note of the sound of a carriage coming up fast behind them. Tilney noticed as well and urged them on, cracking the reins again and again.

"And what of… of the rape? What kind man who claims to be a gentleman commits so horrid an act?"

Tilney snorted. "That silly little girl had the audacity to tell me no. Women never tell me no, dear Elizabeth—no woman has the right to deny a man anything. If the chit had just done as she was told, I wouldn't have had to take it from her, now would I?"

Tears stung her eyes as she thought of how terribly frightened Miss Darcy must have been. "You really are a monster, Captain Tilney. You had no right whatsoever to harm Miss Darcy as you did—what you took was meant to be given freely to her husband!"

"I would have been her husband if she'd only cooperated! I was assured by my dear Diana that the girl was submissive and compliant," Tilney cried angrily.

"Except you hadn't counted on Miss Darcy having a mind of her own, had you? She wasn't as submissive and compliant as you'd been led to believe—she's a young woman who knows her own mind, Captain Tilney, and she didn't want you!"

"Foolish girl," said Tilney, then he growled. "Why won't these wretched beasts go any faster?"

"Because they're tired! Mr. Darcy probably wore the poor things out to get here—and another team, no doubt—once he'd read my letter."

"Your letter? You wrote to that fool about me?!" Tilney raged.

"Yes, I did!" Elizabeth cried proudly. "I did not tell him I suspected you of being the blackguard who hurt his dear sister, but I certainly made sure to tell him how I took an instant dislike to you and thought you looked remarkably like Mr. Wickham—clearly that was all it took to bring him here!"

"You blasted strumpet!" Tilney yelled as he raised his hand.

Elizabeth feared for an instant that he was about to plunge the carving knife into her chest; instead, he swung at her backhanded, so hard that she lost her tight grip on the box seat and went over the side.

Darcy wasted no time in demanding a carriage be brought from the news the moment the front door closed behind Tilney and Elizabeth.

The villain had to know she meant something to him—it was not as though he'd made secret his regard the night they'd attended the opera, and he knew his aunt had been promoting the match among their circle. Tilney could have taken his own sister or even Mrs. Gardiner, who were also on his side of the table and convenient for a hostage, but he chose Elizabeth.

Mr. Gardiner hurried out to follow Darcy's instruction as General Tilney marched up to him. "Now I demand you tell me at once what the devil is going on!"

Wickham beat Darcy to the explanation; stepping around him, he got in the general's face and said, "That worthless lump of flesh you call a son impersonated me and raped my sister! He has used our passing resemblance to his advantage for years and ruined my good name all across England, while I was conveniently out of the bloody country!"

Darcy, for a moment, rather wished that Wickham had not claimed the victim was his sister, but reasoned it could not possibly come back on him or Georgiana as no one still in the room knew of their deeper connection.

"Preposterous! Frederick doesn't need to force himself on a woman, he has more than enough natural charm to get any—"

Now Darcy stepped between Wickham and the general. "They why did he run, hmm? Why did he take a hostage if he's done nothing wrong? Your son was witnessed in the presence of the young lady who was assaulted. He schemed with her former companion to elope with the girl that he might steal her fortune, and when she proved unmalleable he forced himself on her. He has ruined virtues and rung up debts in Mr. Wickham's name for no less than six years."

General Tilney drew a breath, no doubt to bluster on about how wrong they were, when Mr. Gardiner returned to the dining parlor.

"My carriage is at the door, Mr. Darcy," he said.

Darcy turned away from Tilney and strode toward the older man. "Then let us be off," he ground out, knowing that there was little chance of the man staying behind when his niece was in danger.

His own coachmen were ambling about with Gardiner's when they made it outside. His driver hurriedly told Darcy what had happened and in which direction Tilney and Elizabeth had gone.

"Thank you, Peter. Stay here and keep watch over the ladies of the house," Darcy told him as he hurried into the carriage behind Wickham. Mr. Gardiner had climbed up on the box beside the driver, who had the reins already in hand; as soon as the door was shut, he gave them a sharp crack and they were off.

"I think I can see them!" Mr. Gardiner shouted a moment later. "We're not far behind!"

Darcy jerked the sideglass down and stuck his head out. "Go as fast as you can—we must catch them before Elizabeth is harmed!"

He knew well that her uncle was aware of that fact, but he could not help but say it. He *needed* to save her—it would destroy him if anything happened to Elizabeth. And even as he had that thought, a more powerful realization occurred to him:

He loved her. In spite of the time apart being so much greater than the time they had actually been in each other's company, Fitzwilliam Darcy knew without a doubt that he had fallen in love with Elizabeth Bennet.

The horses' hooves and the wheels of the carriage roared down the cobblestones—nearly tipping the vehicle at one point as they charged around a corner—but neither sound drowned out this heart beating in his ears. Darcy began to silently beg Gardiner's horses to run like the wind, so desperate was he to see Elizabeth safe again.

They'd been following behind his stolen carriage for several minutes when a shout from the box had his head snapping forward in alarm. "Stop!" Mr. Gardiner cried, moments before the carriage lurched and threw Darcy into Wickham's lap.

"What the—" Wickham muttered, even as Darcy righted himself and turned to throw open the carriage door.

"Gardiner, what the devil—?" he began as he stepped around the panting horses, then cut himself off. The heart he'd just admitted to himself was hers plummeted to his stomach as he looked to see Elizabeth crumpled on the ground at the side of the road.

Chapter Thirty-Two

"Go—go after him!" Mr. Gardiner cried. "I'll see to Elizabeth. Just go!"

Torn between wanting to stay and wanting to catch Frederick Tilney—to wring his neck for daring to harm the two persons most dear to him—Darcy hesitated for the length of a heartbeat, before giving a sharp nod and hurrying back to the carriage. There, he climbed hastily up onto the box, and the driver immediately set the horses to running again. He saw Tilney now turning his carriage 'round the corner onto Piccadilly Street.

Moments later, as the Gardiner carriage was nearing the same corner, the sharp cries of frightened horses and the unmistakable sound of a carriage overturning reached his ears. Thankfully, Gardiner's driver was intelligent enough to slow their pace before they approached the turn, going around it at a steady clip that kept all four of their wheels on the ground.

A few blocks ahead, Darcy saw the wreck of his carriage. The overtaxed horses—still attached to the broken hitching post—were in the middle of the road, one of the four lying partly on the ground. The poor beast's head hung in the air due to still being tied to the post. The carriage itself had rolled off the street and into the grass around the Chelsea Reservoir—it was actually partway over the water itself, propped up on the stone surround.

He didn't see Tilney anywhere.

Before Gardiner's carriage had come to a complete stop, before Darcy could even climb down from the box, Wickham threw open one of the doors and hit the ground running. He sped toward the wrecked vehicle and climbed over the surround, and as Darcy came near he heard a guttural cry and the sound of splashing water. By the time he reached the surround, he could see Wickham and a surprisingly still alive Captain Tilney fighting one another. In his right hand, held aloft by Wickham, was the carving knife from Mrs. Jennings' dinner table. Tilney seemed to be trying to bring it down on his opponent, and Wickham trying to keep him from succeeding.

A solid punch to Tilney's jaw threw him backward; as he went under the water he dragged Wickham with him. Darcy now strained to see what was happening, as the nearest streetlamp was almost a block away. The two men fought under the surface now, their motion setting the water to churning noisily around them.

"Wickham!" Darcy cried out when the battle fell suddenly silent. "Wickham!"

Alarm seized him then, and he cried out a name he'd not used but once or twice in the whole of the last ten years.

"George! Do you hear me? George!"

Movement at last where he'd seen the two men go under soon revealed Wickham, who broke the surface gasping for air. Darcy climbed over the stone surround and dropped into the water to aid him.

"Come, George, let me help you," he said as he swam over.

"Take this piece of filth, won't you, Will?" Wickham said tiredly, lifting up the unmoving Captain Tilney by the collar of his jacket. "Wouldn't want it to spoil the city's drinking water."

Darcy took charge of the body and dragged it along behind him as he headed back toward the surround. Mr. Gardiner's driver stood ready to help haul Tilney out of the water; once he'd been dropped unceremoniously to the ground, he reached a hand down to help Darcy climb out. The moment his feet were on the ground, Darcy turned to give his hand to Wickham.

"Darcy, do me a favor, won't you?" he asked as he threw his legs over the top of the surround and sat with his back to the rocks.

"Of course," Darcy replied. "What do you ask of me?"

Wickham was pressing a hand to his abdomen; lifting it away, he stared at the blood now visible to Darcy, before looking up at him to say, "Tell our sister she's safe now. Tell her I love her."

His eyes then rolled back before falling closed; his head lolled to the side and he went still. Darcy laid him to the ground to check for a pulse; Wickham's heart still beat, but its rhythm was weak and growing slower.

"You there!" he called out to the driver. "Apply pressure here."

The man did as instructed, pressing his hands together over the bleeding wound as Darcy tried to rouse Wickham. He spoke to him, lightly slapped at his cheeks, tried whatever came to mind to bring him back around. He was almost unaware when more men came on the scene, some of them nearby residents, others uniformed constables. Much to Darcy's relief, one of the former informed them he was a physician and knelt immediately to tend to Wickham after the driver informed him that the other man on the ground was dead. Before Darcy knew it, they were surrounded and questions were being asked one on top of the other, each uttered by one man before the one beside him had even finished speaking.

Darcy, though still deeply concerned for Elizabeth and Wickham, knew that—for a time, at least—he must suppress his emotions and take control of the situation. He had been trained almost from the moment he was off his leading strings to manage a crisis, and this unfortunate episode most certainly qualified as such.

Seeking among the growing crowd the senior-most man of authority, Darcy introduced himself and explained precisely what had happened, starting with the "vile assault of a young lady of my acquaintance" to the carriage chase through the London streets. He made sure to inform the man that he could produce witnesses should they need be called, including among them the Earl of Sotheby.

It was then he suddenly recalled that Sotheby ought to have arrived in Town by then, or would soon, and would make for Darcy House as requested. Some few hours passed, however, before Darcy was able to make his way home, and he was not idle in that time. He'd had to not only answer to the inquiry of the constabulary, but also to arrange having his carriage hauled away for repairs and the horses taken to the nearest coaching inn. He had personally seen to having a hospital wagon come to take Wickham away for treatment and another to carry the body of Frederick Tilney to the city morgue; a constable had been dispatched to the Tilney residence to inform them what had happened to the captain.

As he had determined early on by way of another young constable that Mr. Gardiner and Elizabeth were safely back at Berkeley Street, when all was said and done he found himself torn once more—this time between wanting to see how fared the woman he loved to wanting to see how fared his brother. Because he could not do both at once, Darcy chose to do neither, and thus bid Mr. Gardiner's driver to convey him to Grosvenor Square before returning at last to his master's service.

Tolliver greeted him upon his stepping through the door with an anxious expression, holding out a note as he was taking his coat off.

"This was delivered about half an hour ago by a boy who said his mistress's name was Jennings. And a gentleman who says he is the Earl of Sotheby awaits you in the drawing room, sir—he arrived not ten minutes ago."

Darcy snatched the noted in one hand as the other passed over his coat. Breaking the seal, he scanned the quick missive from Edward Gardiner stating that Elizabeth was well on the mend for her ordeal: She had been seen by a physician and declared "extraordinarily fortunate," in that her fall from the carriage had resulted in only a few minutes' unconsciousness, a concussion, some scrapes, and some bruising. Jane and Cate had both declared they would sit with her through the night to ensure no other trauma presented itself.

Relief that she was safe and well coursed through him as he refolded the note, then looked to his butler and told him, "Should any message come from Barts Hospital, it is to be brought to me at once—no matter the hour."

Tolliver nodded. "I'll see to it, sir."

Darcy thanked him and turned tiredly to his left toward the drawing room. Sotheby stood immediately upon his entrance.

"Did you catch the scoundrel, Darcy?" the earl asked.

He nodded. "Frederick Tilney is dead. I pray Georgiana will finally be able to rest peacefully when I am able to give her the news."

Darcy then went on to recount the day's events, ending the recitation with the words, "Never in my life have I been so terrified as when he held that knife to Elizabeth, nor have I been so grateful for the notoriety of my family name and connections. Once I'd presented myself to the chief constable, much was done and quickly so."

Sotheby snorted softly as he moved to the sideboard, where he poured two snifters of brandy. Bringing one over to where Darcy stood, he handed it over as he said, "Forgive my taking the liberty, but you look like you could use it."

"I'm of a mood to consume an entire bottle," Darcy replied before taking a drink.

"One of the few great advantages of rank that I've noticed since my unexpected elevation," Sotheby went on, "is that when people know you are someone of importance, they tend to do exactly what they're told without argument."

The two moved in silent accord to the armchairs before the fire.

"Was Mr. Wickham conscious when they took him away?" Sotheby asked after a time.

"No. The doctor said he'd lost a great deal of blood, and would likely require surgery to repair the wound. I requested he be kept under guard in hospital for his protection, as I suspect that even with all he witnessed, General Tilney will make some noise about the loss of his son."

"Ansel Tilney is definitely the sort of chap who would," Sotheby agreed.

Darcy's brow rose. "Do you know General Tilney?"

The former army colonel shook his head. "Only by reputation. Word in the army is that he was a cruel taskmaster who demanded absolute perfection, and woe betide any soldier that did not perform to his standards. Other whispers hint of his also being a coldhearted father."

"That I can attest to myself," Darcy said. "I have personally observed his unkindness toward his younger children, his daughter especially. He even refused to sanction a courtship between our mutual relation Colonel Fitzwilliam and the lady, merely because he is a second son."

"Even though Fitzwilliam's father is an earl?"

Darcy inclined his head. "Even so. Theo could support a wife even had she no dowry, as he receives a generous allowance from his father as well as his military pay," he said. "But of course, being an earl's son he is used to the finer things in life when he is at home, and so—given he desires independence from my uncle's assistance—requires a match with a lady of at least some fortune so as to maintain it."

He sighed heavily then, and threw back the last of the brandy; it burned going down but he ignored the sting as his gaze moved to the fire. How long he stared at the flickering of the flames he knew not, as he started when his companion said,

"I am sure they will be well, Mr. Darcy."

Blinking, Darcy looked to him. "A note awaited me on my arrival, from Elizabeth's uncle," he said. "I was assured she was not grievously injured and is on the mend, with her sisters Jane and Catherine watching over her. I have no recourse but to trust her to the care of her relations, though I intend to call on her tomorrow as soon as propriety allows."

He sighed. "It is Wickham I think of now. For so many years did I despise him, for too long did I believe him guilty of Frederick

Tilney's crime. Yet when I thought him drowned—when I saw how horrific his injury—I could think only that I was about to lose my brother when just I'd found him."

"Or rather, had just found room for him in your heart," Sotheby observed.

Darcy inclined his head wearily. "Indeed," he replied, adding a silent prayer that now he was of a mind to accept Wickham as his brother...Heaven might see fit to spare him.

About an hour after his return to the townhouse, a message came from Barts Hospital that Wickham had survived his surgery, but due to the amount of blood he'd lost his condition was still considered critical. The surgeon was still hopeful of a full recovery, barring any complications such as infection. He had then taken himself to bed and tried to sleep, though he had been disturbed by dreams of the deaths of Elizabeth and Wickham, so managed only a few hours before rising just after dawn.

Lord Sotheby was also rising then, and the two took coffee and pastries together in Darcy's study. They spoke of the possibility of an official investigation and how they would handle it if General Tilney insisted on one, and with that possibility in mind made up a list of possible witnesses, including the earl's former coachmen—who were now in the service of his wife's family—and Mrs. Younge.

"I'll have to have a man search for her," Darcy mused, "as I've no idea what became of her after Philip delivered her severance package in my stead. I simply did not have it in me to care, given her complicity in the scheme to elope with and then compromise my sister to purloin her fortune."

Afterward, Sotheby stated he had some issues of business he wouldn't mind seeing to since he was in Town, and Darcy announced his intention to visit Wickham in hospital before paying a call on Elizabeth.

Sotheby had nodded and said, "Do give my regards and those of my family to Miss Elizabeth; my wife, her sister, and my cousin were most concerned for her welfare after I'd received your express."

"I should be happy to convey your sentiments," Darcy had replied, then he departed.

At Barts Hospital, he was glad to meet there the same physician who had treated Wickham on scene the night before, Dr. John

Bamber. Bamber told him that Wickham had survived the night and had improved in color, but was still very weak.

"How soon can he be moved?" Darcy asked as he looked down at his brother's still pale features.

The surgeon beside him sputtered softly. "Moved, sir? I say, 'tis far too soon to think of that!"

Looking to him, Darcy said, "Be that as it may, I should like for my brother to be in the best of comfort as he recuperates. I am of a mind to have him at Darcy House, where I will have a qualified nurse attend him."

The other man frowned. "Your brother, Mr. Darcy? I thought the gentleman's name was Wickham?"

"It is. Regardless, he is my brother. Do you think he may be well enough in a few days?"

Dr. Bamber rubbed his chin in thought as he looked down at Wickham. "Well, Mr. Darcy, if his vitals continue to remain strong and the wound clear of infection, I will not object to releasing him to your charge on Saturday."

Darcy nodded. "Thank you. Has he woken at all?"

The physician shook his head. "Nay, sir. The laudanum I gave him to do the surgery will keep him under for a few more hours yet. I should like for him to sleep, truth be told, for the rest can only do him good."

Suppressing a sigh of resignation, Darcy inclined his head again. "Very well. I should like to be notified if his condition changes, for better or worse—as before, have the messaged conveyed to Darcy House, whatever the time of day."

"As you wish, Mr. Darcy," Bamber replied, then Darcy immediately took his leave, making a mental note to send word to his personal physician asking him to recommend a skilled nurse.

After quitting the building, Darcy directed his horse toward Berkeley Street. He needed to see Elizabeth.

On his arrival, he was greeted heartily by Mrs. Jennings, who drew him with her to the drawing room, saying, "I know you're here to see my niece Elizabeth, Mr. Darcy, but Mr. Bingley is also here—to call on Cate, of course, but I suspect you will want his account of the evening after you were gone, and he is sure to give you a more rational narration than I. Oh, what a to-do!"

He believed the recitation could wait, but as soon as the parlor door was thrown open, Bingley stood and greeted him warmly.

"How is Mr. Wickham?" he then asked.

"He does well, though he remains in hospital for observation. The doctor is concerned about infection, so he will remain there until Saturday, when he will be conveyed to Darcy House for further recuperation. I intend to hire a nurse to care for him."

Bingley nodded, then quickly gave him a run-down of all that had transpired after he, Wickham, and Mr. Gardiner had gone after Captain Tilney. As Mrs. Jennings had ushered Elizabeth's sisters and Miss Tilney from the room, with Mrs. Gardiner assisting Jane with the still-light-headed Lady Middleton, General Tilney had thundered about in his certainty that there had been some mistake. He was reminded by Sir John Middleton that his son *had* just kidnapped a young woman at knifepoint and stolen a carriage belonging to Darcy; if nothing else, he was guilty of those crimes, though he'd reiterated Darcy's point of there being no reason for the action if he wasn't guilty of *something* of which they had accused him.

Henry Tilney had then recited, in a wretched tone of voice, a litany of crimes both great and small—both legal and moral—that he could attest were greatly to his brother's charge. "I have no doubt, though it pains me to admit so," said he, "that Frederick is also guilty of this ghastly crime, Father."

He'd stood then, and said, "Let us go and collect my sister. We should take our leave and await word at our own residence. I believe Mrs. Jennings and her guests have been grieved by our family quite enough for an evening."

General Tilney, his countenance a deep shade of puce with his rage, had growled and quit the room at once, though he barked for Eleanor to attend him the moment he was in the hall. Bingley said that Henry Tilney had then offered his most sincere apologies for the trouble caused, expressed his hope for a satisfying resolution, and then followed after his father. The gentlemen had then joined the ladies in the drawing room, Sir John going immediately to his wife. Bingley had gone to a weeping Cate and embraced her as Jane was comforted by Mrs. Gardiner, and Mrs. Jennings had offered everyone a brandy. Some minutes later, the butler stepped into the room to quietly inform them that the Tilneys had gone away.

"Half an hour or so later, Mr. Gardiner returned with Miss Elizabeth and a doctor was sent for at once. I remained as long as propriety allowed," he concluded.

"Oh, Mr. Darcy, it was such a horrid affair!" cried Cate. "Did that terrible Captain Tilney really…did he really…?"

Darcy nodded solemnly. "I regret to say that he did, and though

I should have liked him to face justice in a court of law, he has already paid the ultimate price for his wickedness. You need not fear him, Miss Cate."

Bingley returned to her side and she leaned into him. Something about the intimacy of the way he held her and kissed her temple made Darcy narrow his gaze. "Charles… is there something you wish to tell me?"

His friend started, then smacked a hand to his forehead. "Blimey, I can't believe I forgot—I meant to write to you straight away, but I've been so overcome with planning, and then last night happened… Darcy, Cate and I are to be married!"

"That is excellent news, Charles! Congratulations to you both," said Darcy with a smile.

Cate returned his smile. "Thank you so much for the kindness, Mr. Darcy. As you can imagine, Mamma is in raptures. I've had two letters from her about wedding clothes already, and have only been engaged since Sunday!"

Speaking of marriage led to Darcy thinking of Elizabeth—not that she had ever truly left his thoughts—so he said to them, "We shall certainly speak further, Bingley, but right now I really must go and see Elizabeth. I have had word from this house, of course, but I should like to see with my own eyes that she is well."

"Oh, of course you would, you dear boy!" cried Mrs. Jennings. "Come, I'll take you to her."

She bustled past him at a quick pace, leaving Darcy to follow. As he walked out behind the lady, he heard Cate giggle in much the same manner as she once did, and say to Bingley, "My dear Charles, did you notice? He did not call her *Miss* Elizabeth!"

Bingley's reply was lost as he and Mrs. Jennings ascended the main stair and moved down the left hall. His guide stopped before the third door on the right and gave a light knock before opening it. "Lizzy, my dear, you have a visitor."

Mrs. Jennings moved aside, and Darcy's breath caught in his throat as he stepped across the threshold. Elizabeth was sitting up in her bed much as she had been that morning at Netherfield after the assembly: wrapped in a dressing gown with the coverlet pulled up beneath her arms. This time a bandage about her head accompanied the ensemble, from under which peeked a bruise. There was another bruise on her right cheek.

"William!" said she the moment she saw him. Elizabeth smiled beautifully as she spoke and held out her hand. "I thought I heard your voice."

Darcy felt as though he'd never heard anything sweeter than his name spoken in the sound of hers. "Good morning, Elizabeth," he replied as he stepped into the room and took her delicate fingers in his, lifting her hand to press his lips to the back.

He then looked across the bed to where her sister Jane sat with a book in hand. "Good morning, Miss Bennet."

She inclined her head. "Good morning, Mr. Darcy."

Standing then, she held the book out to Elizabeth. "Aunt and I will leave you to your guest."

"Oh Jane, you do not have to go!" Elizabeth said.

"I shan't be away long; I'm just going to see about arranging some refreshments for you both," Jane replied with a smile. Darcy looked to note a nearly identical sly grin on the lips of Mrs. Jennings, who took her leave without saying a word.

He was not remiss to the point of the door being left wide open as Jane herself passed through it.

Returning his gaze to Elizabeth, he smiled again. "Bless my soul, it does me good to see you," he said.

Elizabeth's eyes twinkled. "I seem to recall you saying that once before," said she.

"And it is as true now as it was then," he countered.

She then gestured to the chair her sister had occupied. "Come, won't you sit and be comfortable?"

"But that seat is too far from your side," Darcy said.

"Well, the last time you visited me in my bedroom, sir, you moved a chair closer in order to be near me," Elizabeth reminded him with a saucy smile. "Mightn't you do so again?"

Darcy laughed. "Perhaps I will," said he, moving around the bed to take up the chair—which appeared to belong to the dressing table on one wall—and bringing it back around to sit on the side of the bed she occupied.

Seating himself, he took up her hand again and repeated his earlier gesture. "I am so very relieved, my love, to see you so little worse for wear for all your exertions."

Elizabeth reached up to touch the bandage lightly. "'Tis but a small cut, and so close to my hair one would hardly notice. Dr. Cheney said it certainly bled worse than it looks, as head wounds tend to do. Though I am otherwise relatively unharmed, I have been ordered to remain in bed for at least a day to rest."

It was then that she seemed to realize what he had said, her eyes widening for a moment as their gazes held, and then a smile formed that made Darcy's heart soar.

She loved him too, he was sure of it.

"Have you heard the blessed news?" she asked as she gave the hand that still held hers a light squeeze.

"Do you mean that of Charles and your sister? Indeed, they informed me only moments ago," he said.

"I think it a splendid match," Elizabeth observed. "Knowing he likes her has done such wonders for Cate, and I daresay that finding a young woman that admires him for who he is rather than for his fortune has made Mr. Bingley even happier than he could have imagined."

Darcy nodded. "As you have observed them together far more than I, I shall take you at your word. Though I will say, what I have seen of Bingley since their courtship began is much as you describe. Loving her has done as much for him as loving you has done for me."

"And loving you has shown me that I should never put a challenge to God."

With a grin he asked her, "You dared challenge God?"

"Oh, yes. Remember, sir, that when we first met I swore that I was not of a mind to marry anytime soon—indeed, that I was content to see all my sisters made brides before me," Elizabeth replied. "And then I walked one late autumn morning to Oakham Mount…and there you were. I begin to think that God put you before me on purpose. 'Ha!' said He to the angels. 'That will teach her. Miss Impertinence shall be bound in marriage 'ere long, you wait and see.'"

Another grin then set upon Darcy's lips. "May I presume, then, that you are ready to get serious about that whole marriage business?"

Elizabeth laughed at hearing her words of nearly a month ago. "Indeed I am, but I am afraid I still cannot get married just yet."

Darcy frowned. "Whyever not?"

Again the saucy grin flashed. "Why, because you have not asked me, sir."

Mirroring her expression with his own sly smile, Darcy then lifted her hand once more and held it tenderly between both of his. "In vain did I struggle, and it would not do; my feelings would not be repressed. Now I must tell you how ardently I admire and love you."

Elizabeth leaned forward. "Then by all means, my dear William, please do."

"My darling, please! I am endeavoring to be serious," he cried.

With a sigh, she sat back against the pillows. "I am sorry, it's just that I enjoy so much seeing you flustered when I tease you."

Elizabeth then laid her other hand on top of their joined ones. "I ardently admire and love you as well. In fact, I think I have almost from that first moment. Shall I tell you when I knew my heart?"

"By all means, Elizabeth, please do," Darcy said.

She smiled once more and lifted her eyes to his. "The very moment you stepped into the dining room last night. I did not even need to pen the dreadful suspicions I had begun to entertain about Captain Tilney for you to come, only that I had likened his appearance to Mr. Wickham's. I know, of course, that you were motivated more by the need to see justice served for your sister's torment than your regard for me, but—"

Here he took one of his hands and reached to silence her by holding a finger to her lips. "I was motivated as much for your sake as hers," Darcy told her. "On realizing that Frederick Tilney was the man I had been hunting for nigh on a year, and knowing him to be in the same city as you were, I was afraid for you. I could not bear to think that the blackguard was so near to you—especially when the Tilneys' butler informed us they were dining here."

"I imagine now that they will not keep the house next to yours," Elizabeth mused. "And I feel so sorry for Colonel Fitzwilliam and Miss Tilney."

"As do I, for a match between them is rather more hopeless now," he agreed. "As much as my aunt and uncle may have admired her, knowing her brother to be responsible for what happened to Georgiana is unlikely to garner more support for their cause. Such a shame, for Miss Tilney really is the first woman Theodore's ever been serious about."

Darcy drew a breath then, and once more capturing Elizabeth's gaze asked, "Shall I procure a common license, that we might possibly be wed on the same day as Bingley and your sister? That is, if you will do me the honor, dearest, loveliest Elizabeth, and consent to become my wife."

Chapter Thirty-Three

Elizabeth's eyes misted as she smiled the brightest smile Darcy had yet seen.

"Yes, dear William, I will marry you."

He felt as though his heart would burst with happiness as she said the words. Rising from the chair, he leaned down and touched his lips to hers, lingering in the position as long as he dared.

A moment later, Mrs. Jennings came bouncing through the open door, clapping and crying out her joy. Jane entered behind her with a wide smile, followed by a maid who carried a silver tray laden with a tea service.

"Oh, my dearest Lizzy, I am so happy for you!" Mrs. Jennings cried as she bent to kiss her niece. "I am sure you will be so splendidly happy."

The lady then turned to Darcy and, to his utter surprise, embraced him and kissed his cheek. "My dear sir, you could not have found yourself a better wife, I am sure! Our Lizzy is such a remarkable young lady, and you need not worry she will be unable to run so grand an estate as yours, for she is a very smart girl!"

Darcy, though somewhat uncomfortable with the familiarity of her affections, was nevertheless able to smile at her exuberance. "I am in complete agreement with you, ma'am, and I have no doubt that Elizabeth is well up to the task of being mistress of Pemberley."

As the tea was poured and passed around, Mrs. Jennings chattered happily, saying that she would be taking Elizabeth out the very next day to go shopping for her trousseau. Knowing how cold the winters in the north could be, Darcy politely inserted a suggestion of having several gowns and petticoats made of wool.

"I do hope, though, that you'll not tax our dear Elizabeth too much, Mrs. Jennings," he added. "Given her recent trauma, I should not like it if excessive walking about were to set back her recovery."

"Do not trouble yourself, Mr. Darcy," said Jane. "I promise you I will endeavor to check the excitement of this second grand shopping venture in a week."

Darcy nodded his thanks, and though he'd have liked to remain with Elizabeth all day, he stayed only an hour. He was invited by Mrs. Jennings to return for dinner that evening; though he wished very much to accept, his having a guest of his own led him to decline.

"I regret that I cannot in good conscience leave Lord Sotheby to his own devices in my house. It would be an unkindness, when it was I who requested his presence."

"Lord Sotheby! He is here?!" cried Mrs. Jennings.

"You are acquainted with the earl, Mrs. Jennings?" Darcy asked.

Mrs. Jennings emitted a merry scoff. "Acquainted with him? Why, it was I and my son Sir John Middleton who introduced the recently minted earl to his darling wife!"

Elizabeth scrutinized him then. "Lady Sotheby mentioned she had met you and Mr. Bingley in March, before their elevation to the nobility—did she not speak of her family at all?"

Darcy's brow furrowed for a moment as he thought back to that first meeting with the Sothebys, when they were merely Colonel and Mrs. Brandon. "Now you mention it, I do vaguely recall something said of a Sir John Middleton and his mother-by-marriage, but I don't recollect if either of them gave the lady's name."

He looked to Mrs. Jennings then. "If he is agreeable, Mrs. Jennings, I shall bring him along to dinner."

"You must tell him that I insist you both should come! I would like so much to hear how dear Elinor and little Nicholas get on."

Soon after, when the announcement of his engagement to Elizabeth was made known to her younger sister and Charles, Darcy took his leave and Bingley went out with him. His friend offered to take him wherever he needed to go next, and because he wished to speak with him about a few things, Darcy agreed and they set Bingley's footman the task of riding his horse back to Darcy House.

When they were set off toward the carriage maker's where his equipage had been taken the night before, Darcy asked Bingley, "Charles, what say you to our sharing a wedding day?"

Bingley's countenance brightened immediately. "I say it's a capital idea! And I'm sure I can speak for Catherine and say she'll feel the same. You and I shall be brothers after all, and become so at the very same moment!"

The two agreed that they would discuss not only having a double wedding with Elizabeth and Cate at dinner that evening, but also how soon they might hold it. Now that they'd decided to marry, the two friends were eager to become husbands at the earliest opportunity, and would both of them have liked to procure a license that very day—but neither wanted to rush the sisters if they needed more time to prepare themselves.

Darcy found that the damage to his carriage was not as extensive as he'd first feared, and he was informed it should be ready the following day. Next they went to the inn where the three surviving horses were being stabled (for the fallen one had died), and much to Darcy's relief they were well on the mend. The inn's stablemaster did advise him that they ought not be made to work for at least another day, which suited him as he had no carriage for them to pull at present. The timing was such that he would take the opportunity of going to Longbourn to speak to Mr. Bennet, that he might have official permission to marry the man's second daughter.

On his return to Darcy House, he could not help but glance next door and wonder if the stillness of the house meant the Tilneys were merely keeping to themselves or if they'd already abandoned it. His curiosity was such that he made a mental note to ask Tolliver if he had heard anything.

Darcy found a second, unknown gentleman in conference with Lord Sotheby in his drawing room when he stepped inside his home. Sotheby introduced the man as being with the Bow Street Runners; he, in turn, said he was there on behest of the present magistrate in charge of the organization.

"He has received a complaint regarding the death of one Captain Frederick Tilney, lodged by the gentleman's father, General Ansel Tilney."

Stifling a groan, Darcy glanced at Sotheby. He then suggested they move into the study to discuss the matter. There, Darcy produced from his desk drawer the list of witnesses he and the earl had put together as well as his own lengthy written statement, the latter suggested by Sotheby as perhaps being helpful. Sotheby then handed over his own statement.

"I should say, I am really only here as a formality," the Runner admitted. "We've already read the report from the constabulary and I've personally spoken to Mr. Henry Tilney and Miss Eleanor Tilney, as well as their father. I've also spoken to Sir John Middleton and Mr. Edward Gardiner. Seems to me a rather straightforward business—even if the captain weren't guilty of the crimes you accuse him of, Mr. Darcy, he'd not be able to escape charges of kidnapping and horse theft. With there being so many witnesses, the general could hardly deny his son's guilt on those counts. I plan to recommend the case be closed."

The man took his leave then, and when he had gone Darcy heaved a great sigh. "At last," he said. "This horrid nightmare is over."

Dinner that evening was a splendid affair, though their party was intimately small. Only Bingley, Darcy, and Lord Sotheby were their guests; Mrs. Jennings had invited the Gardiners to come and celebrate the engagement of another niece, but Mr. Gardiner had written saying his wife was feeling unwell and they were sorry to decline. The felicity of both was conveyed, however, for Elizabeth's happiness, and Mrs. Gardiner had included in her own hand a promise to call the next day if she was feeling better.

Elizabeth was delighted by the account of Lord Sotheby as he spoke of the continued recovery of his lady wife and the health of their son. "His aunts and his grandmamma, his cousin Amelia and his great uncle the duke, are all of them absolutely delighted with the boy."

Elizabeth smiled. "As is his father, I do believe."

Sotheby smiled. "Indeed I am, Miss Elizabeth. You know… the poet Milton wrote that a wife was 'Heaven's last, best gift', but since the moment my son came into the world I have thought him not entirely correct. It is our children who are God's greatest gifts to us—my dear Elinor agreed with me when I voiced the thought."

"You are right—you are absolutely right, my dear Colonel! Er, my lord," said Mrs. Jennings, who blushed a little at the slip. "As a mother myself, I can attest to that sentiment being absolutely true, sir. Mary and Charlotte have been the greatest joys of my life, and I daresay our friends here will know the truth of it 'ere long."

"Aunt Jennings, please!" said Cate with a deep blush, even as Bingley smiled beside her. "Let Lizzy and I at least marry before you would have us become mothers!"

"Thank you, Cate," said Elizabeth. "I shall be quite content to be

Mrs. Darcy for a year or more before the little Darcys start coming."

On her left, Darcy echoed her smile. Taking her hand in his, he gave it a soft press as he said, "I am in full agreement, my dear Elizabeth, though I am compelled to admit that I do very much like the idea of there being little Darcys in our future."

She grinned and leaned closer. "Truth be told, so do I."

The next morning, after saying his farewells to Lord Sotheby—who was understandably eager to get back to Kent and his family—Darcy went to retrieve his carriage and horses. When his accounts were settled, he next paid a call to Wickham at Barts Hospital. The younger man was still weak, though thankfully well on the mend; he was awake and flirting with the nurse who was just delivering his breakfast.

"Some things never change, I see," Darcy quipped as the lady left the room.

Wickham grinned before slipping a spoonful of what looked to be porridge into his mouth. His expression immediately soured, though he forced himself to swallow. "Ugh, how ghastly! Could they not have at least put some sugar in it?"

Darcy chuckled. "You're in hospital, George. The food is meant to be nutritious; I suspect little regard is given to palatability."

Wickham ate another mouthful. "Apparently," he groused. After he'd taken a third spoonful, he asked, "So, when am I to be sprung from this fine institution of healing?"

"Has Dr. Bamber not spoken to you?"

"I've not seen him today, and saw him only briefly yesterday. I believe I was still under the influence of whatever medications they have been giving me, as I felt rather out of sorts, and didn't think to ask him," Wickham replied.

"I have arranged for you to be removed to Darcy House the day after tomorrow so long as you do not develop an infection," Darcy said then. "I have also contracted a skilled nurse to tend you through the remainder of your convalescence, though I daresay you will not consider Mrs. Whitman handsome enough to flirt with. She's older than my Aunt Frances."

Wickham's answering smile was wicked. "Will, not even elderly ladies are immune to my charms. I'll have the woman wrapped around my little finger by Sunday morning."

Darcy, who knew well the lady his physician had recommended —his own wife—merely shook his head. He then changed the subject by saying, "I have other news to share, George."

"Oh? Such as?"

He smiled wide as he relayed the news of his engagement. "When I take my leave, I am for Disley House to inform my uncle, and then I shall make for Hertfordshire to beg her father's permission."

Wickham smiled. "Congratulations, Will! I had a feeling the two of you would marry—Miss Elizabeth is just the type of lady to keep you from withdrawing into yourself as I am sure you still do sometimes."

As he could not deny it, Darcy did not bother to try. After a few more minutes' conversation, he turned to go but stopped and turned back as Wickham called out to him again. "Yes?" he queried.

"I, uh… I noticed you called me George. A few times, in fact."

Darcy lifted an eyebrow. "It is your name, is it not?"

"Aye, but you've not addressed me by my Christian name since we were boys. It… It's rather nice to hear you say it again," Wickham replied.

A look of understanding passed between them, then Darcy bowed his head and went out of the room.

Elizabeth was delighted to receive a call from Lady Disley on Thursday afternoon, conveying her happiness that she and Darcy were to be married. "My husband also sends his warmest regards and wishes for your happiness," said the lady.

"You and Lord Disley are very kind, ma'am," Elizabeth replied. "I hope very much to make your further acquaintance in future."

"Oh, you certainly shall, my dear!" said Lady Disley. "Did I not say I would take you about Town this Season?"

A glance at both her sisters, with whom she had been sitting when the countess arrived, showed her surprise. "I do recall, my lady, that we talked of it at tea, but that was when William and I were only courting. It is hardly necessary to promote the match now we're engaged…is it?"

Lady Disley smiled. "It will not so much be promotion, my dear Miss Elizabeth, as it will be getting to know one another. And I shall be more than happy to show off my soon-to-be niece to all my acquaintance, as well as the more ridiculous and vulgar of our circle who made fools of themselves and their poor daughters, thinking they had a chance with William."

Elizabeth managed to stifle most of the giggle that bubbled up. The ladies then spoke for a time of the places they would go to and wished to see, and of course they discussed the wedding clothes she and Cate had both been obliged to commission that week. Lady Disley also shared that she intended to host a number of dinner parties over the next weeks, to which the Bennet sisters would certainly be invited.

"And those dinners, my dears, will lead to your being invited to other dinner parties, and to balls—you shall make a number of important acquaintances, and the more ladies of wealth and rank that you delight with your charms and accomplishments, the more important your soon-to-be husbands will become," Lady Disley continued. "And as Miss Elizabeth and Miss Catherine no longer have need to find themselves a husband, we shall have to combine our efforts to assist Miss Bennet in being so fortunate as her sisters."

Though she blushed deeply, Jane said in reply to her, "My lady, you really are too kind to take so much interest in not only furthering Elizabeth's position in society but mine and Cate's as well, when we are all of us essentially unknown to you. Though truly, I would not have you put yourself to any trouble on my account. I feel somewhat confident in being able to secure a husband on my own efforts—I do have some dowry now, after all, and though I am near three and twenty, I need not succeed this Season. There is always next year."

Lady Disley laughed. "Oh my, you are a humble one, are you not, Miss Bennet? Such humility will serve you well, and that you are so willing to demure in favor of your sisters is a very attractive thing in a well-bred young lady. If only more of the young women of the *ton* had such manners as you do."

"She is humble indeed, Lady Disley," said Elizabeth. "Jane truly is the best of us in that regard. But sister, Her Ladyship is right—we must show you off in all the best places, that you will have more than one gentleman to choose from."

Elizabeth said the last as a reminder to Jane that she had been admired by more than one man at the Torringtons' ball; Mr. Knightley, whom *she* had so admired, had not called even once. Mrs. Jennings had issued an invitation to the fateful dinner on Tuesday, but he had sent a polite reply stating he was already engaged elsewhere. Jane had been greatly disappointed, but had borne it well and given every appearance of being cheerful.

That is, until the whole evening had fallen apart because of Frederick Tilney.

Shaking off her maudlin thoughts, her attention returned to the conversation in time to hear Lady Disley asking if she believed her father would give Darcy any difficulty in consenting to the match.

"Oh, I should think not, my lady," she replied. "My father is quite well aware of Mr. Darcy's interest, as he had already asked him for permission to write to me while he was tending his sister in Surrey."

"Oh, that reminds me, Lizzy!" Cate cried softly. "Mr. Bingley said he would be returning to Hertfordshire with Mr. Darcy that he might reach an agreement with Papa on the settlements. Do you think my father will make any difficulty about that?"

"I do not see why he should," Elizabeth replied. "Papa is already exceedingly fond of Mr. Bingley, and though he does not know Mr. Darcy quite as well, he knows that my betrothed is more than capable of providing me a comfortable home."

"Indeed, Lizzy, but recall that you are Papa's favorite," put in Jane. "And Cate will not be living so far away from Longbourn as you will. I daresay he will demand yearly visits be a part of your marriage contract."

Elizabeth grinned. "And if Papa does not, dearest Jane, you can be sure I certainly will. I know that Pemberley will soon be my home, but Longbourn will always have a special place in my heart. I shall miss Hertfordshire when I am living so far to the north."

"You are a dear girl, Miss Elizabeth, to be a little sorry to leave the home of your youth," said Lady Disley then. "But I daresay you shall not long be melancholy once you have seen Pemberley for yourself. And do not be intimidated by the size of the house, nor old Mrs. Reynolds who has had management of it since William was but four years. You are a strong-willed and intelligent young woman, and if you are brave enough to stand up to that ruffian whilst he was running away with you, then you are strong enough to be mistress of so great a house as Pemberley."

That the countess had been told of her ordeal and what she'd shared of that wild carriage ride during Darcy's visit Wednesday morning did not surprise Elizabeth. She could understand he would want to give his relations a full account of the end of their niece's tormenter. Telling of her own abuse at the hands of Frederick Tilney and how she had stood up to him—had needled the reason for his nefarious scheme out of him—would certainly have given them further insight into her character.

Still, heat suffused her cheeks as she listened to Darcy's aunt praise her. "My lady, you are most generous to speak so highly of me when, as my sister Jane pointed out, you know me so little."

Lady Disley took up her hand. "My dear Elizabeth—I do hope I may call you Elizabeth?"

Elizabeth nodded. "I should be honored, ma'am."

Another warm smile answered her concession. "Elizabeth, you are correct in that I do not know you well, but what I do know of you—from my nephew and from your own lips—tells me a great deal. And I like what I know so exceedingly well that I feel sure we shall become great friends in future. And if I am so sure we are to be friends, then why should I not bestow kindness upon you?"

"Too right you are, ma'am," declared Mrs. Jennings as she stepped then into the drawing room. "Forgive me, I overheard as I came through the door. My dear Lizzy, I wonder at how little you seem to think of yourself! For all your pert opinions, you are quick to shy away from praise."

"Dearest Aunt, I think it is just that such kindness from a near stranger overwhelms me," Elizabeth said.

"Near strangers we may be now, my dear, but very soon we shall be family," Lady Disley reminded her. "And I, for one, am quite relieved that I *do* like you so very well. I confess I dreaded my nephew settling for some insipid little girl with very little intelligence in her head—or none at all!"

This set the ladies to laughing. "Upon my word," said Elizabeth as she settled herself. "I cannot imagine my dear William marrying an empty-headed girl just to sire an heir. I should think he would rather pass Pemberley into the hands of his sister's children or even to his cousin the colonel than do that!"

Lady Disley laughed merrily. "Indeed, dear Elizabeth, I daresay he would."

When Darcy returned to London and had let Bingley off at his house following their mutually successful journey to Longbourn, at his own home Tolliver informed him that his sister had arrived around dinner time with her companion. She'd waited up for him as long as she was able, though the butler had overheard Mrs. Annesley advising her—and after some minutes' gentle persuasion, successfully—to go to bed.

Due to the lateness of the hour, Darcy determined he would not disturb her. Declining any sort of repast, he elected to retire for the evening himself.

In the morning, Georgiana came into the breakfast room with Mrs. Annesley as Darcy was opening the newspaper. He stood and welcomed her warmly, said a polite greeting to Mrs. Annesley, then directed them to the sideboard. When the two had filled their plates and taken a seat at the table, he turned a curious gaze to his sister.

"Georgiana, whatever are you doing here?" he asked, though not unkindly.

She set down the teacup she'd just been drinking from. "I could no longer stay away, not after receiving your letter."

He had posted a letter Wednesday that let her know her nightmare was at an end. Though he had not gone into explicit detail, Darcy had also told her that both Elizabeth and Wickham were injured in the ordeal.

"You know I am glad to have you, but are you certain the rigors of travel were not undertaken too soon?"

Georgiana shook her head. "I am perfectly well, William. Given my condition was alleviated going on three weeks past, I did not see any further reason to remain in Surrey."

Her spirit was clearly not yet recovered, neither from the attack nor the giving up of her child—Darcy was aware she needed a good deal more time for both. But, as his sister did seem otherwise hale, he decided not to argue.

"Very well. I *am* greatly pleased to have you here, Georgie. This is your home as much as it is mine, after all."

"Thank you, brother," Georgiana replied, then asked after Wickham.

"He recovers apace," Darcy replied. "And he is eager to be out of hospital, so he will be transported here on the morrow. A nurse will come daily to tend to his injury and see to his recuperation."

"I am glad to hear it," his sister replied. "I have just been getting used to thinking of him as a brother again."

Darcy snorted softly. "I have just begun thinking of him as a brother for the first time. Coming so close to losing him opened my eyes to the truth that I should not waste the opportunity of knowing him better, nor negate the possibility that maybe one day we *can* be family to one another."

Georgiana smiled. "I am rather proud of you, William, for your willingness to forgive the past."

"And I am proud of you, sister, for the courage and resilience you have shown this last year," Darcy told her. "You really are becoming such a remarkable young woman."

A soft blush colored her cheeks, and for a moment she looked down at her plate. "Speaking of remarkable women," Georgiana said when she lifted her eyes again, "when might I be meeting Miss Elizabeth?"

The mention of Elizabeth brought her countenance to mind, and Darcy smiled. "This afternoon, I should think. I will send a note after breakfast to inform her of our intention to call."

"Wonderful. I shall look forward to it very much."

Darcy realized suddenly that he had yet to tell his sister he and Elizabeth were engaged. He informed her immediately, adding that he hoped she would, on meeting Elizabeth, welcome her as a future sister.

Georgiana's expression lit with joy, the first such genuine happiness she had shown since March. "Indeed I will, though I am glad we shall be introduced before your wedding—I have always hoped to meet my sister before she *is* my sister."

It was time for the two women Darcy loved most in the world to meet.

The carriage ride to Berkeley Street was not long, and almost before he knew it, he and Georgiana were alighting onto the sidewalk before Mrs. Jennings' house.

After a maid had taken their coats, the butler showed them to the drawing room. Elizabeth stood immediately and came toward them.

"Welcome," said she. "I am so happy you are come."

"Georgie, may I introduce Miss Elizabeth Bennet, my fiancée. Elizabeth, my sister Miss Georgiana Darcy."

The two curtsied, and when she straightened, Elizabeth wore a smile. "It is a great pleasure to meet you at last, Miss Darcy. William has told me so much about you."

"He has spoken a great deal about you as well," Georgiana replied. "'Tis nice to at last be able to put a face to the name."

"I feel the very same. Come, do make yourselves comfortable."

She led them over to the seating arrangement, taking a chair for herself while Darcy sat with his sister on an adjacent sofa. "Might I inquire as to your sisters and your aunt?" he asked.

"Aunt Jennings thought it would be better that I meet Miss Darcy alone for the first time, giving us more of a chance to become acquainted without the interference of others," Elizabeth explained. "She is calling on her daughter Charlotte, who arrived in Town last evening, and Jane and Cate are spending the afternoon with our Gardiner cousins."

"I understand from my brother that you have four sisters, Miss Elizabeth," Georgiana ventured.

"Indeed I do," Elizabeth replied. "Jane is the eldest, then myself. Next is our sister Mary, then Catherine and Lydia."

"It was Miss Mary who recently wed our aunt's parson in Hunsford, correct? And Miss Catherine is the one who is now engaged to Mr. Bingley?"

Elizabeth nodded. "I see you *are* well informed," she said with a smile.

Darcy was relieved to see an answering smile form on his sister's lips, though it was not of equal brightness. "I must say, I do so look forward to meeting your sisters, especially Miss Catherine," said Georgiana. "I've always been fond of Mr. Bingley, and should like very much to see him happy."

Elizabeth grinned. "I understand from his sister Mrs. Hurst that his other sister, Miss Bingley, had hoped the two of you would form an attachment."

Georgiana's eyes widened in shock. "Me? And Mr. Bingley? I cannot imagine why such a notion ever came into her head! Mr. Bingley is very kind and amiable, and I enjoy his company, but I hardly know him."

"I think, dearest, that Miss Bingley had in mind that many marriages are made between a man and woman who know little of each other," Darcy suggested.

"Or she hoped that one marriage between your families would lead to another," said Elizabeth.

"If that is so, then she set herself up for disappointment," said Georgiana. At his surprised expression, she added, "Come, brother, do not look at me so. I may not be as close with the Bingleys as are you, but I've been in their company enough to observe the designs Miss Bingley has had on you almost from your introduction. And though she is not entirely without intelligence, Miss Bingley was a foolish creature indeed for ever thinking she could capture your interest. She was more concerned with elevating her position in society than she cared for you—she sought the prestige being your wife would bring her, not your love and devotion. Such a woman would not do for you at all, as you'd quickly grow to resent her."

She took his hand then. "And I know you are like me in that you hope for a strong, loving bond with your partner in life. One such as Mamma and Papa had together."

Darcy gave her hand a soft squeeze and offered a smile, then turned his gaze to Elizabeth to find her smiling at him.

"And I will have it," he said. "Of that I have no doubt."

Epilogue

On the first day of February, Longbourn's village church held the first double wedding it had seen in many years.

Mrs. Bennet had adamantly insisted that her second and fourth daughters follow in the stead of her third, and marry at Longbourn Church where all their friends could see. Indeed, it *was* a rather large crowd that awaited the new Mr. and Mrs. Darcy and Mr. and Mrs. Bingley upon their exiting the church at the head of their families following the ceremony. Many cheers and well-wishes rang in their ears as the brides were handed into a waiting carriage by their husbands. From there, they lead a long processional to Netherfield, where a hearty wedding breakfast was enjoyed by all.

Mrs. Jennings, in much the same manner as Elizabeth and Cate's mother, adamantly insisted she would attend the nuptials—whether her sisters Agnes and Jane wanted her there or not. Thus, Mr. Gardiner and Mr. Bennet decided that a reunion before the happy day was necessary, that the ladies could get any hysterical nonsense done and over with and the two couples could enjoy the day in peace. Mrs. Phillips gasped loudly and Mrs. Bennet emitted a high-pitched shriek at seeing the sister they'd not spoken to in near three decades step into Longbourn's drawing room; the latter immediately voiced her anger by issuing complaints of ill usage and betrayal. Mr. Bennet ended her tirade with a booming "Be silent, madam!" before informing her of the generosity that her sister and late brother-in-law had shown toward their daughters.

His lady blinked rapidly for several seconds before straightening her posture, lifting an eyebrow, and saying in a supercilious tone, "Well, why should they not do for our girls what we could not?

Gerald had money enough for two or even three families when first I knew him, and earned a great deal more before he died, I daresay."

Mrs. Jennings had smirked and replied that indeed he had. She followed this admission with a recital of all she had done for her nieces during their stay with her, as well as what she hoped to do for Jane still and Lydia when she was of age. Such promises of gowns and gifts, of Seasons in Town, of balls and parties uncounted served to soften Mrs. Bennet's ire, and she tolerated Mrs. Jennings' presence if not with pleasure, then at least with equanimity. Mrs. Philips, in turn, followed her sister's lead.

It helped that Mrs. Jennings had been invited to stay at Netherfield until the wedding by Mr. Bingley, thus negating the need for either sister to host her at their own home.

The wedding breakfast was perhaps the grandest feast Mrs. Bennet had ever planned. The duck and venison were roasted to perfection, the jellies and puddings set just right, the pastries and cake baked with exquisite fluffiness—not a single person left without a full stomach. The newly married couples were given countless congratulations, along with wishes for many happy years together and houses full of children. Many effusions were heard of how fine were the gowns of the brides and how fine a figure the grooms cut in their wedding finery. The wedding bands that Mr. Darcy and Mr. Bingley placed on the fingers of their wives were heirlooms of the gentlemen's families; Elizabeth had been presented with a large round cat's eye moonstone encircled by a ring of diamonds set in silver, and Cate received a yellow topaz stone surrounded by tiny pearls set in gold.

After the breakfast, the two couples set off together for a grand wedding tour. Darcy and Bingley took Elizabeth and Cate all around the best coastal towns, including Ramsgate, Sanditon, Brighton, and Weymouth. They spent so many days taking in all the delights of each new place they visited that they were in the first week of March before the party of newlyweds returned to Hertfordshire. There, Darcy and Elizabeth stayed a fortnight with the Bingleys, having already collected Georgiana from Disley House in London, before heading at last into Derbyshire.

Elizabeth found herself quite in raptures as the carriage reached the edge of Pemberley Park—there were woods and groves enough to satisfy her, indeed! Oh, the many long walks she could take, and carriage rides… She hoped that William would teach her to drive a curricle, and she was even giving serious consideration to learning to ride a horse again. Many a pleasurable hour could be spent with her new husband circumventing the ten miles of the park.

She could not help the soft gasp of surprise that escaped her as she took in the façade of the house for the first time. Darcy and Georgiana smiled at her obvious pleasure in seeing the place of which she would be mistress.

"Oh, William... It's lovely!" she cried softly as she looked out of the lowered sideglass. "And so perfectly situated! I do believe I have never in my life seen a place where nature has done more or where natural beauty has been so little counteracted by awkward taste."

She looked to him then with a brilliant smile on her lips. "Your house really is magnificent."

"*Our* house, my darling," he reminded her, before lifting the back of her hand to his lips.

Some minutes later the carriage was drawing to a stop before the front. Awaiting their arrival were the servants, lined up according to position to greet their master and new mistress. Elizabeth was even more impressed with the handsome stone building as she examined it before taking Darcy's hand and stepping out, after which she was quickly introduced to Ralston, the butler; Mrs. Reynolds, the housekeeper; and about twenty different maids and footmen. She offered a cheerful smile to each and promised her best efforts at remembering all their names as soon as possible.

Life at Pemberley soon settled into a routine, though for Elizabeth it took some getting used to. Simply living on an estate, as she had done the whole of her life, was a far cry from being mistress of one. There was a great deal more responsibility, for one thing, as she had to learn to plan meals, manage the household accounts, see to the procurement of anything the house required, and of course hostess dinners and parties.

One of her favorite new duties was getting to know the people in the local communities over which Darcy was patron. Elizabeth rather enjoyed giving her assistance in acquiring supplies for the schools and poor houses, meeting Darcy's tenants and seeing to their needs, and making herself known to the local shop keepers.

So busy were they in the first weeks of their arrival that the times which she and Darcy were alone together, just enjoying each other's company, quickly became most precious to her. Not just late hours of night in which they made love and held each other close, but also those stolen moments in the daytime going on an impromptu picnic or curricle ride, or just reading quietly together in the vast, multi-level Pemberley library.

It was one such day, when she found her husband in his study after having returned from business in the village, that Elizabeth stood quietly in the doorway and simply watched Darcy as he was writing. After a moment, he looked up to find her there and his expression lit up with delight. Though Elizabeth had once feared loneliness in living so far from Longbourn and her family, on seeing her husband's loving smile, she knew she was home.

About the Author

Christine, like many a JAFF author before her, is a long-time admirer of Jane Austen's work, and she hopes that her alternate versions are as enjoyable as the originals. She has plans to one day visit England and take a tour of all the grand country estates which have featured in film adaptations, and often dreams of owning one. Christine lives in Ohio and is already at work on the next book in the series.

Want to let Christine know what you think? Then be awesome and go post a review on the purchase page at the retailer where you bought your book! Reviews don't have to be long—just a few words will do—and they can totally make an author's day. You can also contact her on Facebook, visit her website, or send her an email. She would love to hear from you!

https://www.facebook.com/AuthorChristineCombe

http://allthattheydesire.blogspot.com

authorchristinecombe@gmail.com

Austenesque Must-Reads

Karin Aminadra
Charlotte
Christmas at Longbourn

Jann Rowland
Murder at Netherfield

Leenie Brown
Confounding Caroline

Jayne Bamber
Outmatched
NorthFanger

Alexa Adams
Being Mrs. Bennet

Printed in Great Britain
by Amazon

78368785R00258